ALSO AVAILABLE FROM VINTAGE

At Play in the Fields of the Lord
Far Tortuga
Partisans
Men's Lives
Raditzer

RACE
ROCK

PETER MATTHIESSEN

RACE
ROCK

VINTAGE BOOKS

A DIVISION OF RANDOM HOUSE NEW YORK

First Vintage Books Edition, January 1988

Library of Congress Cataloging-in-Publication Data
Matthiessen, Peter.
Race Rock.
I. Title.
PS3563.A8584R28   1988   813'.54   87-40096
ISBN 0-394-74538-8 (pbk.)

Manufactured in the United States of America
10   9   8   7   6   5   4   3   2   1

*To
My Wife*

O Trees of life, what are your signs of winter?
We're not at one. We've no instinctive knowledge,
like migratory birds. Outstript and late,
we force ourselves on winds and find no welcome
from ponds where we alight. We comprehend
flowering and fading simultaneously.
And somewhere lions still roam, all unaware,
while yet their splendor lasts, of any weakness.

RAINER MARIA RILKE, *Duino Elegies*

RACE
ROCK

CHAPTER 1

ABRAHAM'S PATH, WHICH RAN EAST FROM THE OLD COMMON Pasture and through the woods, then doubled north around the inner reaches of the salt marsh and made its way eastward again out of the trees and onto the open headland of Shipman's Point, is nearly forgotten in the village. The great flat rock at its foot, sunk like a fallen gravestone at land's end, has become one corner of the McConville terrace, and the cowpath which crossed at the head of the trail like the top of a T lies now beneath the highway. The Common Pasture itself has been cut to its poorest corner, four acres of milkweed and bramble behind a listless sign reading VALUABLE SHORE PROPERTY. The black tin letters of the sign are long since distorted by birds and small-caliber bullets, and the sub-lettering, APPLY TO CYRUS F. MCCONVILLE, is only decipherable or meaningful to the villagers of Shipman's Crossing, because the property is worthless and Cyrus F. McConville is dead.

The path is named for the first in the village to travel it, an innocent, Abraham Shipman, who followed it into the ocean. His body was never returned. Like an invalid, he had lived out his days at the place of his death, finally to withdraw entirely into the background of existence as over the years a stray face in a photograph of others withdraws its identity. Some swore he had perished on purpose, some saw the hand of God, and some had to struggle to remember him at all.

1

Who among them knew on what lonely walk he found it, this path from the world to freedom, by what instinct he traced its ancient shadowed course through the mile of wilderness, north past the salt marsh, and out upon the headland where once he was seen, a dark silhouette like a fallen cypress on the rock, by a fisherman beaching his dory below the Point?

Who knew how he felt, this man remembered for one aspect and one age, that of middle years, attained too early and worn like some shabby suit of decent origin until the crabs and snails and sand fleas at the sea bottom relieved him of age and flesh and brain, returning him to eternity as presentable as any drowned man before or after him—or who cares? To the world he was known for a happy creature, as children and dogs and simpletons are known, and surely he died without fright or further derangement, at the end of a last long walk through the whisper of leaves, moving down by the marsh and over the old gaunt trees lying fallen in the shallows and up again through the laurel bank, tuning his ear to the clarion jays and the faraway strife of crows and the patter of rodent feet on last year's leaves like wind-falling September seeds, and stepping out upon the sea field where the long wind bends the grass and the gulls balloon like white distress signals from the rocks below the headland, he nearing now and peering over the grassy crest to see the old black cormorant plunge headlong from its snowcapped stone and flick the water with its tail and beat away across the gathering ocean like some mute herald of his coming.

Perhaps he stretches on the sunny rock and thinks a while, it is the summer of 1924, the world is at peace, and perhaps he smiles a little. Beneath him the tide climbs the rounding rocks, resounding in slow rhythms and sighing back among the sea stones. The prevailing wind of afternoon August is ruffling the sleeve of his shirt, sends shivers up and down his side. He scratches his leg, leaving white streaks in the sun and dirt of his bare ankle, then rises, undresses. On the stone beside his shirt and pants he lays his lucky piece, a rabbit tail salvaged from the leavings of an owl, and makes his pale way down beneath the banner of gulls to the sea, Abraham, heir in name and property to the village of Shipman's Crossing.

HERE LIES ABRAHAM, CHILD OF SORROW,
HIS GRAVE IS WIDE AS HIS PATH WAS NARROW
1879–1924

George McConville stared at the set of rainworn ciphers marking the barren grave. They were inscribed in the year of his birth, the same year the Shipman Piece had passed into his father's hands and the house had been constructed by the rock. As a little boy, this coincidence of dates had astonished him, he had sprawled for hours on the terrace imagining the point as Abraham had seen it, uninhabited New England coast, maybe redskins and bears, he had exulted, peering down in terror at the secret ocean life for a sign of the innocent's bones.

And because it contributed to the romance of death, he later accepted the tale of Abraham's reappearance in the Race, that jagged meeting ground of current and broken tide where the Sound emptied into the ocean and where a fisherman in the week of the drowning had come upon a body and lost it again when his boat yawed in the heavy chop. Naked, he reported, the body was naked, and George, bluefishing there in later summers, could imagine the white desolate shape and its soft descent to the channel floor.

The Race was forever in a state of change, and its faces were gray and blue and black, and red with torn menhaden when the

bluefish ran, and scarred with white. Its force gave him the feeling
that nothing lost there was recoverable but would fade into some
deep oblivion of anonymous salt tatters and marine rust. Once he
himself had clutched at a green glass ball only to see this unsink-
able thing drift down from the light into the shadows of water
rushing hard upon Race Rock, and had wondered if the glass
would shatter on the Rock or lie quiet in a crevice until the current
swept it up again. More particularly, and refusing beforehand to
recognize such a possibility, he asked himself if he, who had seen it
sink, would be there when it reappeared. George could not account
for this idea nor for the uneasiness it gave him, any more than he
could account for his conviction that the glass float would remain
forever in the Race. And although Race Rock had been surfaced
with granite blocks and a lighthouse glowered upon it, the struc-
ture was man-made and seemed in this place somehow less permanent, less to be reckoned with, than the transparent clean green
glass which had escaped him.

Today, however, the epitaph meant nothing to him, his eyes
saw past it out across the rocks where the sea flew high on the
heels of the storm. It was Monday morning of late October, 1952,
and through uneasy clouds wild desolate sunlight stalked back and
forth stiff-legged across the ocean reaches. South of the headland,
where the beach rolled a rough gray back to the autumn, dark
foam and kelp and sea wrack scarred the sand.

Monday morning, he thought, when one faced facts again, like
some animal started from its earth and made to run. The beginning of the climb from the bottom of the week toward some thin
disappointing pinnacle from which one fell again at Sunday twilight—it had been this way since the earliest days at school. But
today was the beginning of nothing, no end lay in sight, he felt

exhausted, powerless to act. And he asked himself if he had ever acted, if he had not been pushed and chivvied through his youth toward this particular Monday morning. He knew without thinking that a change had taken place in him, a victory of reason the cost of which, to himself and to the others, had made it seem meaningless, even grotesque.

On the headstone the wind laid a hand of rampant grass whose pettish fingers, scraping across the dates, pointed up the peculiarity of this moment, the feeling he had that now, in this very hour, he was leaving youth in favor of maturity.

There exists, perhaps, such a moment for every man, but too often it is passed unwittingly, or simply felt, as pain is felt and not remembered. One learns much later that time has passed and taken with it the ideal and the dream, leaving acceptance, resignation in their stead. And it is the sign of change that one does not greatly care.

For a few, however, the transition is much harder. They are the fortunate and the unfortunate ones, the imaginative and the irresponsible, who sense what they are losing when they lose it. George McConville, who found at last the courage of the loss, was one of these.

The sun withdrew again, he felt the sea wind beneath his jacket and turned the collar up. When the sun reappeared, stealthily and at a distance, he turned on cold legs and stared through the naked window of the house built on the rock. She had not moved. He could just make out the small white oval of her face against the back of the chair. Grief and anger started in his lungs, and he turned away again. At least I *feel*, he shouted inwardly, how can she sit there cold as stone?

He thought again of the Easter weekend, so like this one for having been spent among the very people, adolescents then, who had borne witness in the last few days to what had happened, two distant weekends, years apart, two Fridays, Saturdays, Sundays.

Friday, Saturday, Sunday. But perhaps things had started Thursday night, and perhaps they had never started at all, like lovers' arguments, but simply ended

He had feared for months the night she would ask him, and did ask him, watching him in the dark,

"George? George, what would you do if I were to have a baby?"

And the hush of silence, as once when he and Cady Shipman stood at the edge of the wood and a Cooper's hawk had flicked across the leafy sun, flick, flick, flick, its wings had rasped, a dry harsh survival sound like the mouths of feeding fish on a river surface, and in its wake the bated forest breath.

"What do you mean?" he said.

"Darling, it's very simple," she whispered. "What would you do?"

"I'd wrap it up and roll it down the stairs," he said.

"No, darling, seriously, what would you do?"

"I don't know, Eve," he mumbled. "Maybe we'd get married, maybe . . ."

"You're not ready to marry, my darling." She laughed quietly. "I just wanted to hear you say it."

"Damn, Eve, don't scare me like that." He stalled without hope. She didn't seem to have heard him.

"I'm glad, George, I'm so glad."

George knew then that she was pregnant, that he must say something, something good, something worthy of this crisis, anything. He could not speak, his voice would not function at all. And it occurred to him to pretend he hadn't understood, to pretend, to pretend.

He thought of Life before Eve and Life after Eve, Life with and Life without Eve. Then came Mother Eve, Father George and ex-husband Samuel Rubicam standing between them, grinning. He thought of what would be said if they were married, what would be said if they were not. And he thought of Eve with a child and no husband.

"God!" George said, at last.

She watched from out of the warmth beside him.

"Hey," she said.

She was heavy against him, undesirable. But she always felt that way afterward, he remembered irrelevantly. He listened to the late cars slicking down Park Avenue through the rain, and the idea of flight had crossed his mind, like the Cooper's hawk through the childhood trees, like a dirty thought passed over into a shadow world.

Or an operation.

"George."

She pressed her lips to his neck.

"Never mind, George, it was my fault, not yours, and it's quite simple, really. Doctor What-sis-name will arrange something, he's sure to know of someone, don't you think?"

"No! Anyway, it's wrong, a crime. I'll do anything you say, but abortion . . ."

He stopped.

"Dear George, what will you do?" she whispered, finally.

He glared at her, overcome.

"No, George, you're making it much harder for me. It's taken a week to make up my mind to it, to this 'crime,' as you say. And you're right, it is a crime, a terrible crime. I know it as well as you."

She paused, then said to him carefully, coldly, "I don't ask you to marry me, George. Just to be a man."

Both were startled and lay still.

I am twenty-eight, he thought, educated, intelligent, a veteran of one war and several women, and still I am a boy. She wants me to be a man—what in the name of God do I do to become a man? Do I suffer? Just decide to go someplace and suffer? Do I take responsibilities? She won't let me take this one. Do I affect a dignity, a wisdom, and try to live up to it? What do I do, then? What does one ever do?

He lay beside her, angry and hurt, and within him turmoil. And then, knowing but refusing to know, he rejected manhood once again by stepping suddenly, melodramatically, from her bed and quitting the apartment, the glory of the gesture like a brief flame on a mounting pile of ashes.

That had been Thursday night, in New York.

He had awakened Friday before light. The city was quiet now, austere, and he lay in the anguish of bad conscience peculiar to the hour. Before he could slip back into sleep, Sam Rubicam appeared. He was broke, he said, calling in to George over the running water in the bathroom, where he was shaving with George's razor. He needed a job, he shouted, how about a position with McConville, Incorporated, Wall Street?

At breakfast they talked about getting Sam a job. George was embarrassed to admit that he himself was thinking of quitting. When Sam asked him why, he didn't know. Eve hadn't asked for reasons, he thought, and there weren't any, he simply felt useless and wanted to quit, do something else. At this, Sam Rubicam was overjoyed. George had come to his senses at last, he said, they would make a tour of the world. "Travel, Change, Adventure!" Sam cried, waving a bun. "Like Toad, in the *Wind in the Willows*, 'We'll see the world!' "

"I thought you needed a job."

"I do, as a matter of fact. Let's go down to Wall Street and beard old Pickens in his lair."

"All right," George said.

In the afternoon they went down to see Mr. Pickens, who said sure, any friend of George was a friend of his, and laughed to show them he knew a cliché when he saw one. George sat back in a leather chair and listened to his friend. Sam was trying too hard, President Pickens was not impressed, and there were awkward pauses. George thought about what Eve had said to him the night before and was still thinking about it after Sam had gone, nodding his head in absent-minded agreement with the circumlocutions of Mr. Pickens. Not until he was out in the street again, and the harsh air struck him in the face, did he fully realize he had not got Sam the promised job. He entered a bar immediately, and a little later made his way uptown to Eve's apartment. She had expected his call that morning, and in excusing himself he wandered somehow into an argument. He had hardly got there, he thought, when she asked him to leave, without so much as a word about her pregnancy.

He hurried down the block and around the corner to Michael's Bar where, in a very short time, he got drunk. Then he telephoned Sam.

"Hey Sam," he said to the telephone. "Downa Michael's. C'mon over."

"Celebrating my new job, I take it."

"C'mon over," George said.

He had hardly stepped from the booth, he thought, when Sam was there. In the mirror behind the bar, George watched him greet the hatcheck girl in a manner suggesting past intimacy.

"Cut it out, Sam," George said. "C'mon."

"All right," Sam said. He seated himself fastidiously on a stool.

"You've been guzzling my Scotch," George said.

"Scotch-type. Terrible stuff. A very badly appointed household."

"Listen," George said. "Guess what?"

"No job."

"Right," George said. "Have a drink on me."

"You knuckled under, did you?"

"I didn't say that. Apparently . . ."

"Look, George, I saw Pickens, remember? Going out, I said to myself, even money on George versus Pickens, basing my hopes on a new stouthearted George versus an old chickenhearted Pickens. And you, Cyrus McConville's son and heir, you failed me."

"I guess I did. I know I did, in fact. I cast aspersions on your dependability."

"You screwed me, in other words."

"Dead right. I screwed you to the wall, you might say."

"And kissed his butt into the bargain, right?"

"Right again. And they offered me a raise for my good work."

"They did, eh?"

"Yes, they did. Said McConville and Company depended on me."

"And you're proud of yourself."

"Proud as a peacock."

Then suddenly it wasn't a joke any more. They ordered another round, and halfway through it Sam said, "I don't understand how you have the courage to admit all this, and not enough to stand up to Pickens."

"No courage at all. Just a little in my cups."

"Don't take it so hard," Sam said. "I'd have done the same for you, Old Pal."

"It's not you I'm drinking about, Old Pal." George shook his head back and forth several times for emphasis. "It's bloody Eve."

"Screwed her to the wall, too, did you?"

George resented Sam when he talked like this, there was a sort of soured vulgarity about him, he decided, but he only said, "In a manner of speaking," and returned to his glass.

"How *is* old Eve?" Sam said. He averted his eyes and stirred nervously at the ice in his whiskey.

"Funny. She asked the same thing about you. How's Sam? she said. Those were her very words." George shook his head. "Listen, I've got a great idea—"

"I'd better rush right over," Sam said. "So she's kicked you out, has she?"

"On my princely behind. Listen, why don't we go down to Shipman's Crossing and—"

"Good for her. We'll be married tomorrow, Eve and I."

"Remarried," George corrected him. "You've been married to her before."

"Right you are, remarried. I think I'll phone her this very minute."

"Do, by all means," George said, but Sam was already entering the booth. A curious thing, George thought, to watch Sam telephone to Eve on the other side of a plate of glass, as if, nursing his drink, he had always been a spectator to Sam and Eve, Eve and Sam, a tawdry melodrama. As if his life was slipping past him while he sat and blinked at it—he sat forward on his bar stool and glared at the mirror. "You pitiful son-of-a-bitch," he said. The bartender turned and glared at him suspiciously, holding a white napkin away from a glass. George could not focus on the man's eyes, and his smile wasn't working at all. "Me," he mumbled. "Talking to the guy in the mirror." As if to turn his back on the image, he shifted on his stool and immediately became so dizzy that he slumped back onto the bar. Before his eyes swam a melted

still life of ashtrays, fallen ice cubes, puddles, whiskey labels, at his
temples a cacophony of hostile voices screeching above the rant of
the television, which glared down upon him from a shelf like the
eye of a god gone mad. I'm blacking out, he decided, and then—
he remembered this later—there was an odd high silver singing
and, simultaneously, a deep sense of permanent loss, he heard his
own voice mutter, "Stop exaggerating, drunken jackass," and felt
his hand grope through the shadows for the ice cubes. Then it
cleared again, the dark hot fume, he saw Sam wave from the telephone booth, and it was over. Drinking too much, Eve had said,
and Sister Celia said it, too, half-drunk herself but very sisterly
was Sister Celia, and neither she nor Eve Rubicam was aware that
he could stop at will. That they thought differently, however, was
rather exciting. Often, as now, he would imagine himself in the
corner of some cocktail party, empty glass in hand, just faintly
aware of the voices which whisper (as he turns a tragic gaze upon
the dying day beyond the window), "Really a shame, and when
you *think* what he might have been," as, drawn by the harrowed
sadness in his eyes, a lovely girl moves to him and takes in hers his
shaking hand and murmurs mistily, "O George, my George, poor
George," and leads him (he, alone in the room, is tearless) past
old, unrecognized friends and helps him into his threadbare topcoat while he listens to the echo on each trembling lip, George,
George, poor George, and smiles a smile of infinite compassion
(he is Christlike now, and sober as a judge) as darkness descends
on the world's misunderstanding. . . .

"Eve wants me over right away, with my toothbrush," Sam said.

"Cut it out," George said. "I've got an idea."

"What do you think of that? My own ex-wife. Back from my
travels and everything, and she wouldn't see me."

"Was she rude? Listen, that doesn't matter, I've got a great idea."

"There is no greater idea than the one I had. I'm in love with my ex-wife. You forget." Sam focused, wrinkling his forehead. "No, she wasn't rude. Very sweet, in fact. She said she was a little mixed up and wanted to be alone for a day or two. We're lunching Tuesday, today's Friday."

"I'm in love, too. I'm also mixed up."

"What's your goddamned idea?" Sam was restless and impatient. "Going to Shipman's Crossing? I told Eve that if she wanted to remarry, she could probably reach me there, as a matter of fact."

"We'll go down to Shipman's Crossing and see things in the light of the past."

"On you? Because I'm penniless, as you may have guessed."

"On me. And we'll do some duck shooting."

"All right," Sam said. "Why not? Shoot our fool heads off." He signaled for the check. "Let's go celebrate something somewhere."

"Celebrate what? Your homecoming, or something?"

"Now you've gone and hurt my feelings," Sam said.

"Never mind me. Just brooding."

"What about?" Sam was balancing his highball glass on his finger tip, to the morose delight of the bartender.

"A way of life for myself," George said.

"Oh *that* old thing! That's easy. Every man for himself and the devil take the hindermost," Sam said.

"You said it, Buddy," the bartender said. "Only watch that glass, I'm short."

"I'm very serious," George said. "Very serious," he repeated, when the bartender glanced at him.

"You're very drunk. He drinks too much," Sam said, and George said to the bartender, "You got any comment to make on that?"

"I ain't paid to make comments, wise guy." The bartender wandered wiping down the bar, and George, waving his finger at Sam, missed with his elbow when he set his arm down on the rail. Sam said, "Something's the matter, isn't it?"

"Nothing in particular. Just indecision."

"About what? Eve?"

"Indecision," George repeated. He gritted down a surging impatience with himself, with Sam, with the voices which swarmed from the misty bedlam about him like a black smoke of gnats from a swamp. He knew he would hurt something, hurt Sam, he had to in order to breathe—"Why are you always poking around about Eve?" he said.

"Oh for God's sake," Sam said. "Don't take your crappy little troubles out on me."

"I'm sorry," George muttered, and after a moment added, "But you think about her quite a lot, don't you, Sam?"

Sam was silent for a moment, exhaling heavily and peering through the smoke at the cyclops eye of the cigarette reversed between his thumb and forefinger. Then he grinned, too suddenly, at George.

"You bet I do," he said. "And she thinks about me."

"When do you plan to forget her?"

"I don't. At least I have no plan, about her or anything else. When do you?"

"Why should I forget her?"

"You're a pompous bastard, George, did she ever tell you that? I mean just because you're sleeping with her doesn't mean she's an asset of McConville and Company."

"What makes you think I'm sleeping with her?"

"You boast of it sometimes," Sam said, "between the lines, as you did just then. Besides, she wrote me."

"The hell she did." George tried to smile.

"She wrote me," Sam repeated. "She writes me about everything. I happen to know you don't satisfy her, for example. You're inhibited, I think she said." Pointedly, Sam stared at the ceiling and hummed.

"I happen to know you're lying," George said. He felt his small smile waver, slip away from him entirely, as Sam turned once more to him and slowly shook his head.

"You're lying, aren't you?" George accused him, embarrassed by his own concern.

"Yes." Sam's face was humorless now, and George, uncomfortable, blurted, "You shouldn't speak of her that way," and Sam said, "You shouldn't have brought it up. It's none of your business what I think about her."

"The hell it isn't."

"Listen, I think maybe I won't come down with you to Shipman's Point, after all, George, I think maybe you . . ."

The Point. That was it. They were going to go down to the country and there he would think things over, get a perspective again.

". . . I think you'd do better by yourself. And besides, you give me a pain."

"All right, all right," George said. "I'm only kidding, Sambo, you ought to know me better than to think . . . Look, you've got to come with me, I can't go duck shooting alone, can I?"

I can't go alone.

But later, much later, it was long past midnight, he said, "I'm going now." They stood by George's car in the hollow street.

"Going now? What do you mean, going now? You're too plastered to walk across the street, much less drive."

"I'm going now. You coming or not?"

"How about clothes? You have to pack."

"Stuff down there. You coming?"

"Hell, no. I'll come by train in the morning. I have to pack, and even if I didn't . . ."

"All right, see you in the morning, on the eleven-ten, right?"

". . . head through the windshield in some weedpatch. Listen, you've got to sober up. . . ."

"Right you are, Sambo. So long, Sambo, ol' kid."

It was wonderful taking leave of the world, the decision to go had been so clean, so forthright, so bloody goddamn-well decisive, he thought, that was the only word for it, decisive. He flew exultant through the city night, the lights, across one hundred bridges, rivers, hills, and when the light came he was far down the long gray silence of the coast and singing at the top of his voice a song called "Lover." The crows passed back and forth across the highway like laggard scraps of darkness, and from the ocean to the east the sun rose raw and seared the purple dawnland mist, there was a glint of frost, and curling colored leaves flew up before his tires like panicked sparrows: he was omnipotent, and godlike spared an early rabbit. Then the earth awoke, a lonesome hound bound nowhere, a flock of doves, two white-breathed hunters, and old black country cars which bumped from side roads into the growing morning, he hurtling onward, singing the same song over and over, over and over again.

At the last long bend in the road before Shipman's Crossing, a saddled horse veered white-eyed heavy-running from his path and crashed across a stone wall into an inland field. The falling granite and echo of hoofs on the highway startled him out of the ecstasy of flight as he slowed to stare after the animal. It mounted the high field to the broken sky and disappeared over the hilltop with a last dark flick of its tail and crazy buttocks.

He drove on dampened, but saw no sign of an early rider, no sign of anything. Run to earth by fatigue, he drew into the diner across from Abraham's Path for coffee.

Entering, he was struck in the face by the redolence of ham and eggs. There were hunters there in black patched hip boots, carpenters, mechanics, fishermen from the Crossing, and they knew George, some of them, grunting to him full-mouthed over their jacket collars.

"Young McConville, ain't you? Come down duckin'?"

"Put such ducks as we seen in your hat."

"Ought to do pretty fair out'n that marsh o' yourn, though."

"Well I gis. Well I gis the feller knows that, Henry."

Laughter, quiet, sly, exclusive, from the row of turning heads.

He did not belong and, lacking confidence, sat in a booth instead of squashing in among them, a canary among crows in his flannels and Paisley tie. Separately, one by one, the men turned and gazed at him, punctuating their suspicion in the manner of cattle, with sounds of eating. If I had sat with them, he thought, they wouldn't even talk to one another, much less to me, as if there were some sort of unspoken tribal law. Even the two his own age whom he knew by name, Cady Shipman's cousin Bart, and Joe Ferrari, would not acknowledge him with their elders there, not until he shared something with them, a meal, a duck hunt, a glass of beer. He never had shared anything.

Outside again, he found them idling by the door.

"How's it goin' there, George?"

"How are ya, Joe, fine thanks. Cady been around, Bart?" George caught himself affecting their taciturn, clipped speech, and wondered if he'd always done it.

"Ain't seen him. They say he's workin' over to Mister Murray's there, up the river, gamekeepin'."

"Joshua Murray's?"

"Don't know what he calls himself. The one that was friends of your folks, had that nice little Eve for a daughter."

Bart Shipman's face had the bland, half-smiling look which marks all country slyness. He scratched himself suggestively, and Joe Ferrari laughed.

"So Cady's workin' there, is he?" George said.

"I gis so," Joe Ferrari said. "Ain't no more sociable than in the old days."

They moved away without saying good-by.

In the old days

The cat was a large yellow tom belonging to Percy Shipman. Cady came one morning early and called out George and Sam Rubicam, who was spending his Easter vacation with George, they were sixteen then and Cady Shipman seventeen, and they followed him to the toolhouse where he had the cat in a gunnysack and nine rats in a barrel, asking him questions which passed unanswered in the wind of a bright April morning.

In the damp winter shadow of the toolhouse, Cady rapped the barrel with his knuckle, saying, "Pa says his yeller tom is the best ratter on the coast, and we're gonna try him out."

George knew that Cady was angry with his father for taking their guns away from them the day before, they had been shooting at signs down by the highway, and although he knew little about the fighting capacities of rats and cats, he sensed what the outcome would be from Cady's manner. He said, "Wait a minute, listen, Cady, it wasn't his fault, it was my old man who told him to take the guns away."

"George's old man is very pious," Sam Rubicam said, and belched. Sam had his hands in his pockets, staring apathetically at the new daffodils which bordered the wet place by the woods. "His old man has never been to church in his life."

"This cat'll show us whose fault it was," Cady said. He removed a big stone from the lid of the barrel, and George said, "Maybe we'd better give him the rats one at a time, nine is a lot of rats." "All or nothing," Cady said. "A real fair test."

He seized out the kicking yellow cat by the scruff of the neck and shoved it into the dark maw under the barrel lid. One terrible noise, high tortured for an endless second, was replaced by the harsh wet squeaking of the rats.

Then Cady whispered, "If that was the best ratter on the coast, it's not any more," and grinned uneasily, licking his lips. His eyes dared George to lift the lid, but George stood sick, and Sam, his face evolving belly white, blinked tearfully at Cady. "You knew that would happen," he choked. "You knew it. It never had a chance."

"From the sound of it," Cady nodded, leaning back defiant against the barrel, "the best ratter on the coast gave a pretty poor account of himself." Sam Rubicam punched him then in the mouth, a clumsy swing less a blow than a spasm of rejection, and the barrel spun backward and fell in a very slow rolling arc, the rat feet snicksnicking up the inside as the barrel fell slowly, so slowly that Cady Shipman was on his feet again when the nine rats spewed out among the red brick flower pots and crusted spades and rushed in jerking turns and pauses into the crannies and corners of the shed. Inside the barrel rim, the twisted cat lay damp and amorphous, as solitary as a run-over stray.

From outside the broken window, the sunlit head of Daniel Barleyfield bobbed down out of view like a target in a fairgrounds gallery, and Cady was whispering,

"You want to scrap, Sammy? Because if you do, I'm gonna hurt you bad."

He moved with the stiff tight steps of a stalking dog, and Sam retreated, his face a flux of fear and anger and nausea, Cady coming in his thin sure way, his arms bent hard as wire. George reacted now to save the cat, save Sam, save something, pinning Cady's arms from behind as both fell forward into the litter, Cady's cheek, unprotected, opening wide on a twisted trowel. Sam kicked Cady in the ribs, and then Cady was standing over both of them. His cheek was white behind the crimson smear, and he panted, waiting. Neither rose.

"Let's go, boys," Cady said.

George and Sam said nothing. Sam was crying.

"You shouldn't have done that, George," Cady said. "It was between me and Sammy Sissypants there," and when George did not answer, Cady added softly, "Your little pal kicked me just now when I was down. I'm not going to take that. I'm going to hurt him a little."

"Cut it out," George said, his voice dry as dust. "It was because you did that to the cat."

"I know it. I'm still going to hurt him unless he drags his tail over here and licks my boots and tells me how sorry he is."

"You know where you can go," Sam blurted. "You sound like somebody on the radio or something. You're nothing but a goddamned sadist or something, a lousy goddamned animal."

"I don't know what 'sadist' is," Cady said, speaking to George as if Sam had no place in the conversation. "He better explain it." Cady settled on his heels and lobbed a clod of dirt at Sam's chest. "Explain it," he said.

"You know where you can go," Sam repeated, but he did not stir to remove the dirt from his sweater. His face was very thin around the large straining eyes, and to George, who sat beside him feeling hot and foolish, his hair seemed suddenly much too long, wispy black and ridiculous around the ears. Sam's hair had always been too long, George thought, he *looked* like a sissy sometimes, he—

"Explain it." Cady lobbed a second clod.

"You're too goddamned ignorant to understand it," Sam told him.

"That's right," Cady said. Picking in the litter, he found a fossil dog turd, crumbling and white, which he dropped down Sam's open collar. "Explain it," he said. Cady's eyes were fixed on George, flickering sideways only long enough to direct the lumps. He was small and slight, less gangly than George and Sam, and his head, cocked and tense as a bird on a briar, carried wan hard hair draping straight downward to eyes neither warm nor cold, nor ever two moments the same.

"Cut it out, Cady, be a good guy," George said. On impulse, he rose, using both hands to brush off the seat of his corduroy pants as Cady rose with him. George knew he himself was safe, had been safe all along for reasons he only sensed and which had little to do with the roles of their fathers and even less with friendship, knowing, too, that Sam would not be safe until Cady had satisfied himself and that the hurting of Sam would be Cady's demonstration of Sam's inferiority to both of them, whether George liked it or not. He turned away when Sam got up.

Cady seized Sam's wrist and twisted him back to his knees so swiftly that Sam cried out. "Let's go, Sammy, let's lick them boots," Cady grunted, his eyes still following George. Sam gasped, "Get him, George," but George stood still in the doorway, and when Cady moved the arm, Sam's head bent moaning to the boots. He licked them, spitting, one then the other, crying softly, "All right, All right," and when Cady released him, he remained on his knees, staring, blinking at the ground as he ran his hand up and down one arm.

George said, "You satisfied now?" longing to strike his shame to

the floor with Cady and kick all memory of the scene into dirty
oblivion, as once he had done in horror to a foraging centipede.
Yet he was afraid, less of pain than of being reduced to Sam's level
of sobbing foolishness, and adopted an expression of adult impatience with both of them.

And Cady said, "I guess so, yes." Absently, smiling a little, he
righted the barrel. When the cat carcass slumped to the bottom,
he reached and hauled it up by the vestige of its tail and skittered
it across George's knees out into the yard. It skipped with a wet
rock-slapping sound and came to rest in the green spring weeds.

George glimpsed once more the face of Daniel Barleyfield, which
slid out of view like a dark turning bottle on the sea. The empty
window stared out broken wide-eyed on the reality of the day.

"You going to tell, George?"

"I guess I know better than that."

"I guess you do," Cady said. He put his hand up to his cheek,
then glared at the bloody finger tips. Redhanded, George thought;
he remembered him that way ever afterward. George did not
tell Cady that Daniel had seen, in secret hopes that Cady would
be punished, but said instead, "I'm sorry about cutting your face."

"To hell with it," Cady muttered, as Sam, his white face twisted
up at them, a scowling possum, mimicked George's apology and
spat, and George, fortifying himself with the memory of Sam's
humiliation, turned slowly to face this other Sam who had had
the courage to defy Cady Shipman when he had not. Through one
long moment of disaffection, each faced the other two, the corners
of a stilted triangle, and childhood escaped them like a breath,
and with it, innocence

Although it was very early, a little after eight, old Barlow Shipman was sitting in his usual place in the hardware store. He
shifted uneasily as the young man bounded over from the counter
and grasped his hand. "How are you, Cap'n?"

"Not bad," Barlow said. "Goin' duckin'?"

"Just over the weekend," George said. "They been gettin' any?"

"My boy Bart was out this morning. Don't know how he did, though."

"I saw him just now, out at the diner. He tells me Cady's working over at Murray's." The young man moved backward toward the counter.

"That's what they say." Cady, the old man thought, Cady. Hadn't seen him in years, and didn't want to. A bad one, all right, nephew or no nephew, there'd only be trouble, wait and see. . . .

". . . the blind is in the corner of the marsh, where Abraham's Path turns east out over the Point to our house. . . ."

The young man was talking to him from the counter. To our house, he'd said. And young McConville probably never knew that we were going to build poor Abraham a house there on the Shipman Piece—and it's still called that, McConvilles be damned —build him a little house there on the Point. . . .

". . . there's a big dead tree right behind there. . . ."

Barlow Shipman creaked restively on the nail keg, clearing his throat in the tearing juiceless manner of ancient men, and peered out the window of the hardware store. "I know the place you mean, boy." The early sun of autumn Saturday was heatless on old hands, lumped and clumsy on his thighs like rusted tools. And he thought, my time is coming, all right, and he thought of how at Abraham's death so long ago the village heads were shaken over him for the last time, a thousand odd of them bobbing and turning and swaying back and forth like so many glass balls strung on a gill net in the sea, heads that today were underground, most of them, in pieces like old white clam shells.

". . . these ought to do me, with the ducks thinned out the way they are."

Young George McConville had five boxes of shotgun shells in

his hands, a tall thin boyish man with a small face and an eager smile, like a hound going hunting, Barlow thought. "What you usin' for load, boy?" He scratched his wrist and waited, feeling his breakfast stir in him. Yes, it was to this boy's father, damned feller Cyrus his name was, dead now, that they had sold the property, the whole Shipman Piece sold and shot to hell to city people. And what did the Shipmans have to show for it? Money, and not too much of it, at that. Every fool had money these days, but nobody had a coast piece like that except the McConvilles. Land was like everything else, like a wife or a trawler, "A man don't work to get it won't work to keep it," as the feller said.

"Number .4 shot," George McConville told him. "I need the heaviest I can get, the way I shoot."

"Too heavy. Blow your bird from here to Sunday. Better turn 'em in again for .5's."

"Maybe that's a good idea." The young man hesitated, but when Barlow said nothing, only coughed and pushed his thumbs together, he went unwillingly to the counter.

"Don't matter to me, of course," the old man addressed his back, "but you ain't shootin' geese or shag."

The young man said nothing. When the shells were exchanged, he looked at the old man a moment, then turned to go.

"Listen," Barlow said, "I bet you never knew how Abraham's Path got its name?"

"Sure I do, your brother, wasn't it?" George McConville paused impatiently by the door, shoving the shell boxes into a Gladstone bag, and when the old man cleared his throat, he said, "I have to go, Cap'n, I haven't been out to the Point yet. Might see you later on."

The old man grasped the outstretched hand, it was soft as dough in his own. "Whereabouts?" he said, confused, but the screen door slammed on the word, the damned screen door that they should have taken down two months ago, it was near November now, the end of another year. "Ought to take that screen down before she gets all clogged with snow," he muttered, but nobody heard him and he shifted wearily again, his old man's feet banging loose against the nail keg. Today was Saturday, there was never anybody to talk to, Saturdays, they all listened to the football and went to the pictures in the evening. He drew unconsciously from his watch pocket Abraham's tattered lucky rabbit tail, yellow now and choked with tobacco crumbs, and pressed it in his fist.

Outside, George thought about the old man rising still at fishing hours every morning, to breakfast and wait an hour and a half before going to his nail keg when the store was opened at eight o'clock. In the summer Barlow Shipman could be found at the fish wharf, perched on a coil of hawser against the background of masts and netted trawler booms, his baitless handline dangled in the marbled shadowed green of the pier water where the minnows and bony cunner darted for oddments under the hairy pilings, his eye cocked in the weatherbeaten sun as he answered questions about fish and tide for nautical summer people in sun visors and Bermuda shorts. And yet he belonged, his life had meaning for himself and for others, George thought, he could even be sure of that ultimate consideration usually reserved for old boats, landmarks, and friendly dogs, that he would be missed when he was gone.

The car moved down the early street and out upon the highway. He drove too fast, fatigue against his shoulders, racing the swarm of motley doubts and rages which had ruled these recent days, and swerved off at last onto the road through the sandy woods at a point a half mile north of Abraham's Path, which paralleled it seaward in wandering permanent impermanence.

CHAPTER 2

ON FRIDAY MORNING SHE HAD WAITED FOR GEORGE UNTIL eleven o'clock, clutching to her constricted chest the certainty that his presence, or even his voice over the telephone, would be a solution in itself. Please come, she prayed, please come. And when he did not, she tried a second course, the family doctor. He was a pink-and-white old gentleman who could remember unattractive aspects of her childhood, and often did.

"Oh my," he sighed, a little pinker, when she had told him. "You've always been in mischief, you were a crazy little thing. Why, I remember—"

"Doctor, if you will just give me the name of someone . . ."

"I'm afraid I can't. Does your father know of this?"

"You can't or you won't?"

"I won't, if you prefer. I'm sorry, my child, but I won't be a party to such a thing."

"But you don't mind being a party to the scandal."

"Evelyn, do be reasonable. It's a little late to decide that you don't want this man's child, I cannot be held responsible."

"But I do want the child. I simply can't have it, under the circumstances."

"You haven't told me the circumstances," the doctor said, a trifle bitterly. "Do you love him?"

"Is that a professional question, Doctor?" Eve was startled by her remark, yet felt somehow suffocated and angry under the weight of the old man's principles. And besides, she thought, isn't his question insulting?

"Yes," he snapped. "You're being very rude, young woman."

"I'm sorry. I love him, yes."

"You know that you put me in a very dangerous position? The law says—"

"All right," Eve said.

"However, if you can establish the problem more clearly in my mind . . ."

"That's all right." She rose and went to the door. "I knew I was putting you in a dangerous position. I was hoping you wouldn't say it."

"But do be reasonable!"

"Forgive me, Doctor, but I haven't time to be reasonable."

From the doctor's office she wandered to a drugstore and had a cup of coffee. It was there, anonymous among the joyless creatures at the counter, that she felt the first panic of loneliness. She thought about calling George, decided against it. He'll be waiting for me at home, she told herself, he'll have found a solution to everything by now. But she didn't dare go back. Supposing he wasn't there, supposing . . .

"Kinda chilly today," the soda jerk observed. He was trying very hard to look down her dress.

"Yes," she said. She went into the telephone booth and rang up George's sister.

"Celia? This is Eve Rubicam. I've got a great favor to ask of you."

"Do be quick, Lambie, I'm just on my way out," Celia McConville said.

"Well, a friend of mine is in trouble, and you mentioned once
a little doctor you knew of."

"Oh my God, you don't mean it! You, Evelyn? And where's
George?"

"George has nothing to do with it. It's for a friend, Celia."

"It always is. Will you be in this afternoon, with your friend,
that is?"

"Yes, I'll be there."

"I'll see what I can do. Poor darling! You'll call me later if you
need me?"

"Yes," Eve said, giving up all pretense. "I'll see you this afternoon, then?"

But Celia had hung up. Eve sat and stared a moment at the
phone, as if it might suddenly reassure her in a hollow voice about
her call, then left the booth. "You said you lived around here?"
the soda jerk queried. She paid for her coffee and hurried home.
When she arrived she was running, but George was not there.
He's come and gone, she thought, I've missed him.

In the afternoon there appeared at the door not Celia but a
small dark man in a bright tweed topcoat. His lapels were loose
and very wide, they seemed to extend beyond his shoulders as if
the coat, made for a much larger man, had been lopped off just
below its bottom button. Outside the topmost button, which sat
like an ornament in the area of his navel, an orange tie wafted
suggestively in the draft from the elevator shaft, suspended from
two sharp collar points. One of these, erect, was aimed straight at
her like an accusing finger.

"You were expecting me?" he whispered.

"No," Eve said. "That is, I don't know. You're . . .?"

"Doc-tor Living-stone," he said, and smiled a quick gold smile
like a nervous tic. He bowed, moving past her into the apartment,

where he placed a nondescript brief case, suitable for any profession, on the hall table and rested upon it eight square pale fingers with rings and hair on them. Turning his head ever so slightly, he smiled again. "My little joke," he said. "Doc-tor Living-stone. Sometimes people are asking me, where is Doc-tor Stan-ley," he added encouragingly. When Eve did not smile, he shrugged his shoulders, almost imperceptible under the clumsy coat, and said, "Some people like to joke a little bit, some people don't. We go in there?"

She led him into the living room, feeling suddenly tired, incapable of any reaction, and they sat down. The white fingers with the rings and hair drummed upon his knees, which were directly opposite her own. He seemed to be waiting for her.

"I didn't introduce myself, Doctor. I'm—"

"Excuse me," he stopped her. "It does not matter, the address is sufficient for the moment. In these things, names are so often like the fathers, they are better to be forgotten. If you tell me your name, then later you will think, maybe this terrible little man will blackmail me." He smiled apologetically. "So how long is it?"

"Two weeks, approximately." She paused. The doctor's hands, bristling clean as his heavy face, gave her a little start of confidence, yet she felt compelled to say, "But you could find out my name so easily."

"Of course. But my ladies know I will try nothing like that, it would be worse for me. This is the only way I work. I use the office of a friend if is necessary the operation. This way is safer for everybody, especially me. I look like anybody, you see, I could always be selling neck-tails." He held up his tie and stared at it with pleasure.

"Neckties," Eve said, smiling.

"Neck-ties," he repeated. "So. Now two weeks is not very long, I think."

"No. I feel it, though." And she added quickly, "I'm very sure."

He nodded, smiling again, looking around the room. "A funny thing," he said. "Some ladies feel it, some ladies don't. Very funny. But I think all the same maybe you should have the laboratory examination. It is not I don't believe you, but sometimes the emotions, the heart, gets mixed up in these businesses."

"I've already had the test," she lied, and wondered why. Because there isn't time, she thought, if I do it now I can be sure and perhaps avoid the operation. Then George will know what I will suffer for him—she felt herself blushing, you bitch, she thought, you crafty bitch.

The doctor was watching her carefully. "They could not be sure in two weeks." His doubt was kind. "In two weeks is nothing happened." His eyes lifted humorously, but he did not smile.

"Will you help me then, Doctor Livingstone?"

"Yes, if you want me. You have no objections to the i-dea?"

"It seems a little unnatural, that's all."

"Un-natural?" He shook his head. "No, excuse me, I do not think so. It is more natural to have an unwanted little child? One must think first about the child." The doctor raised his square white hands and slapped them down again upon his thighs. "Yes, of course, these things should be controlled, but they should be legal. They will be done no matter how many laws are made. I ask you," and he whirled on Eve so suddenly that she sat back into the sofa, "is it better the young girls kill themselves with knitting needles? This I have seen myself, so many times. And they make the streetwalkers against the law, all the prostitutes, and what do they get? Morality? No. People are just people. They get venereal disease, excuse me."

The doctor smiled self-consciously and sighed. "For many years I helped ladies in trouble like this"—he waved at Eve as if he were addressing somebody else. "Now I should suddenly look at myself and say, 'Rudolf, you are a criminal'?"

"No," Eve said. "But supposing you are caught?"

"I see you are a practical lady. All ladies are so very practical. No," he said, excited. "Who made this law? Society. Who made my law?" He tapped his heart. "The people. And who made the people? God. I am not a criminal because I do this, but because I take too much money for doing it and because I am frightened what will happen to me for doing what God wants I should do!" He gasped with rage. "I should not get so upset, it is bad for my digestion, and besides I am perhaps mistaken."

"*How* much money?" Eve said. She sensed that he had brought up the subject himself, as tactfully as he knew how, and that he had excused his bargain with God many times before.

"Two hundred dollars, no operation," he apologized. "Five hundred, operation included."

"That's much too much."

"Excuse me, I know it is, but my clients do not think so."

"No," Eve said. "I suppose they don't."

"Besides, for less I could not do it, I am too timid." He gazed benignly across the room, fingers tapping on his knees.

"All right," Eve said. "When do we start?"

"You have the two hundred dollars?"

"I'll have it tomorrow."

"We start tomorrow." He rose from his chair and bowed. "Saturday. Of course. Somebody is here, you will say, I do not need any neck-tails today. I will go away, come back on Monday."

They went outside into the hall. While the doctor was putting on his coat, the elevator door clanged open, shut again. There were footsteps, a key in the lock, and George appeared.

"Hello," he said, startled.

"Hello, George," Eve said. She turned, a little frightened, toward the doctor.

"Okay, lady," the doctor said. "I will see about this plumbing tomorrow."

"That will be fine." But when he had gone, Eve called to George, who had entered the living room, "Just a minute, darling, I'll be right there," and went out into the corridor. "I wanted to thank you," she whispered to the doctor. "You've been very kind, Doctor Livingstone, I feel much more at ease."

"I must tell you," he said, "that by mistake I have seen your name on a letter in there. For this reason, so we will be even, I will tell you that my name is not Doctor Livingstone. Perhaps you know this already," he smiled. "I do not have a British accent. Living-stone is what you call a corruption of my real name, which is Lichen-stein. Herr Dok-tor Rudolf Lichen-stein." He laughed outright, and bowed. "Excuse me, my little joke, you understand. As to being kind—" he paused and looked at her seriously—"that is my business. And I will also tell you that if you did not have two hundred dollars I would do it for twenty, and if you did not have twenty, I would do it for nothing. I might ask you for something else, but you would not have to do that, either."

Again his eyes were humorous and a little wistful, but he did not smile.

"I believe you," she said.

"Of course you do, excuse me, my dear lady, you have no reasons not to."

The elevator opened and the little man stepped into it, turned around, and bowed. The face above the bright tweed topcoat, as

it disappeared from view down toward the evening streets, was
smiling.

She returned to the living room, where George had sprawled
himself face down upon her sofa. He did not see her, and regarding
the conscious helplessness of his pose, she knew that he had not
come in the morning, had not even called. How could he be so—
look at him, he'd been drinking again, it was too much to bear.
"George," she said, she didn't want to be angry, but otherwise she
would cry. "George, I thought you'd call this morning."

He rolled onto his side and blinked at her. "Meant to," he
muttered, and wandered off on a tangent about Sam being home
from Europe, scratching his head and refusing to look at her as he
spoke. Sam. So Sam was back. But what did Sam have to do with
it, she wondered, was Sam more important than she? Perhaps she
should tell George about the doctor, that would sober him up a
little. But her instinct forbade this, the disclosure would be more
useful later on. She thought of Herr Doktor Rudolf Lichenstein
hurrying along the city streets, perhaps he was laughing at her,
horrid little man. She shuddered, knowing as she did so that the
shudder was artificial, self-pitying—he wasn't horrid and he was,
in his way, a man, kind and probably honest and, right or wrong or
rationalizing, sincere in his desire to help "the ladies," that was his
term, "the ladies," with those scrubbed little hairy hands of his.
And the way he had said, I might ask you for something else, but
you would not have to do that, either. So sad that had been and
gentle, and curiously courteous because he had known of the im-
possibility before he had said it and was recognizing his own
frailty, not probing for hers. Herr Doktor Rudolf Lichenstein,
where was he now, and where was he going, a little man like so

many others in the subway, hanging and swaying by a strap to the rhythms of clanging transit?

". . . sadness is like blood, it's part of people. . . ."

And now George was philosophizing again, rather heavily into the pillow. What did he know of sadness, what could he know? The small things were sad, the soda jerk trying to see down her dress, the orange neck-tail of an alien abortionist, not the generalities offered up from the grab bag of introversion, like sticky gumdrops from the pockets of a child.

George seemed to sense her displeasure, for he paused and watched her in mute irascibility, his green eyes deep drawn into his head and his mouth pushed forward. She knew his anger was less with her than with himself, he was awaiting forgiveness for the night before, when she had told him about her pregnancy. But how could he fail to understand that, by the simple fact of her love for him, she had forgiven him irrevocably and long ago for being George? To expect forgiveness for being himself was silly. He must have known that, how had she failed to show him? Straightening the flowers, she was conscious of his eyes on her face, on the small breasts and the hips a little heavy for her slender waist, self-conscious still although he had persuaded her of his love for her figure, "It just suits me," he had laughed, caressing her, and this so recently. But now he brooded, he was trying to lose himself in some vague vast universal sadness for which, by deft rationalization, he implied her responsibility—"You don't understand it, do you, Eve, our pathos?" he demanded, sitting up. "It's blurred for me, but for you, for all women, it hardly exists."

"Poor thing," Eve said. She came to him, kneeling artlessly on the floor and pressing her face against him, her long fingers drawing down tight from the small of his back onto his rump and thighs. "Poor thing," she whispered, and staring straight up at him, laughed.

He made himself laugh, too, placing his hands on her hair.

"And then I saw something else, just now, on my way uptown," he said. "This man . . ."

"Georgikins, listen to me," she said.

"You should have seen the expression on the face of the man," George went on. . . .

"George, listen, darling . . ."

George paused and looked at her. She kept her face noncommittal, then blurted, "You're drunk. You drink too much."

She stood up and turned her back to him, leaning to the sofa table for a cigarette. He stared at her in silence.

"How's Sam?" she said, shortly. She refused to be the terms of his self-pity, self-pity worn always in terms of other people, like a negligee or a stylish coffin.

"You won't let me forget about Sam, will you, Eve?"

"No," she said. "It's you who won't forget, my poor man. And even Sam doesn't matter today. It's last night that bothers you." As she spoke, she caught in his eyes the sharp false hatred of her understanding.

"Poor George," she stalled. "You'll be a malcontent as long as you live."

"You know me very well, don't you, Eve? You can read me like a book."

"Not terribly well," she said to him, pointedly disregarding his tone. "But better than the rest of your friends, I think, except Sam. And possibly Cady Shipman."

"To hell with Sam!" George said. "And you hardly know Cady Shipman."

"You speak of him so often that I've learned a little," she prated, and when George turned in surprise, she added, "Isn't he the other person you wish you were, the craggy, outdoor type, the breath of the woods, the hard-bitten, laconic sage of the swamp-land, that you wish . . ."

"I have never seen you so bitchy," George said.

"Live and learn," Eve said.

"God. And you can't imagine how sick I am of your psycho-analyzing."

"I'm a little fed up with it myself." She yawned, tapping her mouth with two fingers, and lay back onto the sofa, adding, "You've always insisted on it, though, because . . . ho, hum."

"Because what?"

"Because if I speak your conscience for you, you only have me to face up to, instead of yourself. How's that?"

"That's great. A drugstore analysis at its best."

"I thought you'd like it. You're always such a stickler for the truth about yourself."

"It seems to me that you and I have just about had it," he told her, and that moment the rage forsook his face, as if he had wakened, amazed, from an angry dream. He took a step forward, frightened.

"Pretty," Eve said. "Prettily said. A very pretty speech, under the circumstances." She rose quickly and went for his overcoat, her heart tightening.

"You don't believe me, do you?" he blurted. "I'm a little drunk. . . ."

"Yes," she whispered, holding the coat out between them. "Even if I didn't, you will believe me."

"Listen, Eve, I'm not trying to get out of anything, believe me. I . . ."

"George, George, George, I'm tired. I didn't ask you to come, and I'm not asking you to stay."

Then he was gone, and she was confronted with the blank face

of finality, a metal door on a corridor down which she had sent
George McConville before he could flee her by his own devices.
She heard his footsteps pause at the elevator, then ring through
the door to the fire stairs and disappear, he would go and drink
and be sorry for himself, but afterward—perhaps he had left her
willingly, although he would never admit this, perhaps he would
not come back. And staring at the door, she felt the breath go
out of her. But he loved her, as much as a man, a boy could love
who took everything, gave nothing, and good God, she was having
his baby, he had to come back. Her hand lay on the doorknob,
she would run to the stairs and call him back, but she could not
stir. And I, she thought, do I love him still, how can I love him
after this? A foolish question, she could love him as she had
before, his behavior had not changed things because it had not
surprised her. And yet there was rejection of him, she could feel
it waxing in her chest and seeking exit, but her throat was tight
and dry and the anger swelled unlanced, like grief.

She felt unbearably alone, she had to do something. She ran
from room to room turning on lights, as if to beat away the
suffusion of cold city lights now searching through the windows.
She went to the window and closed it, then drew the curtains.
Behind her the apartment waited, startled but unchanged.

She lay down on the sofa and cried, giving way to final despair
so completely that the sharp clarity of the day was shrouded over,
lost in gray unthinking, like a clean black woodland pool submerged in fog. Then suddenly, as in a dream, there was confusion,
her mind kited wildly on a dark storm of fancy, there was a fierce
tugging, a sense of falling, and she thought, it has gotten dark
and George has gone. Then she knew it was the telephone. It
was George, George was calling her. She sat up. "Hello," she
whispered. "Hello, George."

"No," the voice said. "This is Sam."

And later, hanging up, she felt herself smiling at the mouthpiece and winced. She replaced the receiver and lay back again. George was going to Shipman's Crossing, Sam had said, George was deserting her. She thought of George at the bar, he drank too much, how weak he was, how childish, was he even thinking of her?—George, George, please think about me, think of me now in this instant, George. She called to him, anguished. If she thought hard enough, concentrated, surely he would think of her, share with her the senselessness, as so often they had shared each other's everything, even when apart, it had been uncanny, sometimes, whispering of it afterward.

Hadn't it? Oh God, hadn't it?

Not knowing what she wanted nor where she was going, but with some vague idea of washing the tear streaks from her face, Eve Rubicam wandered through her bedroom and into the bathroom and confronted herself in the mirror. She was a tall girl but not large, with a soft round hood of bamboo hair worn very short, and the expression of a Correggio angel, deceptively childlike and bizarre. The face had downcurved elliptical eyes and a high full mouth, in harmony with a nondescript nose and chin. The eyes were the cohesive feature, alive and suggestive of emotional depths as yet unexplored, an expression somehow indomitable which inspired men to dominate it, as if she were holding in reserve until a moment not yet arrived the very essence of herself. Sam first, then George, had sensed that, although the part of her being known to them was purely Eve, there remained much more of her to be known. Eve herself had felt this without knowing it, there was a touchstone to an inner richness of feeling which no one had ever discovered, and which made itself known to her through a vague desire to be raped. Not raped, precisely, it was not the criminality which intrigued her, but truly possessed, by a man who wanted her so badly that she wanted him for that very reason, and she had imagined many times the scene of the act, it was always near the sea, in the wind and sand, and the possessor bore always—she had not realized this at first—an unmistakable likeness to Cady Shipman.

The mirror face had streaks and a speckle of white toothpaste dots, and she thought, look at the ghastly creature, what's to become of her, and laughter started in her chest but never came.

She wandered back to the living room, the apathy coming again like heavy wool, it made her ache. She went to the sofa and lay without stirring, hands fisted against her chest, elbows pinned to her stomach by her knees, the oval of her thighs and back curved around the twisted heart of her like some fleshed ineffectual carapace, and sleepless, listened to the cadence of her mind which stumbled forward, beset by odd impressions, queries, details. She asked herself, shall I call George, and tell him . . . tell him what? Tell him he owes me a little consideration, it's not as if I were demanding, or given to fussy vanity. Up jumped the king, crying, I am not a fussy man, but I *do* like a little bit of butter with my bread. Daddy had been so like the king, jumping up out of his chair as he read to her, the little red book in his hand, *When We Were Very Young* the book was called,

When we were very young

She did not see him at first, nor was she ever sure that he had come after her, walking with his curious tight yet careless gait down across the lawn toward the beach. She only knew that what she had so often planned was coming true, and this without any admission to herself that she had planned it, that she and Cady Shipman would find themselves alone. Her heart raced so furiously at the thought that she quickened her pace to give herself time to breathe, terrified at the same time of the speechless confusion in her which would surely undo everything.

It was a Saturday morning before Easter Sunday, and under the spring sun the ocean evolved from its winter drab to changing greens and grays. To Eve Murray, with her parents a guest of the McConvilles on the first country weekend of the year, the longing to see Cady alone, though nurtured from the previous summer through an endless autumn and winter in boarding school, was inadmissable. She thought nothing, weighed nothing, felt only a violent flowering within her.

"Hi," he said. He had a cigarette in his hand, and his voice was very deep, and she realized for the thousandth time how old he was, nearly seventeen, and she a miserable three years younger. She heard her silly voice which said, "Hello," and he came nearer, walking much more slowly, reluctantly almost, it seemed to her. And then she knew he had not come after her, for he blushed and looked disagreeable. "What are you up to, down here?" he said. He had dark heavy eyebrows in striking contrast to his lank fair hair, and on his cheek a crimson cut.

"Nothing," she said. She could not take her eyes from the cut. "I don't know *what* I'm doing, I mean, nothing in particular." I'll kill myself for this, she agonized, right in the bathroom with a razor, before lunch.

"I thought you might be going down to see the fishing." Cady Shipman took a last elaborate drag upon his cigarette and spun it away into the white lace of the surf.

"No, I wasn't."

"That's where I'm going," Cady said. He had stopped right next to her, no more than ten feet away, but now he started walking again, looking angrier than ever.

"I didn't know there was any fishing," she pleaded.

"Well, now you know," he said, over his shoulder.

"Cady?" She followed him, tentative, praying.

"What?"

"Do you mind if I come? I won't get in the way or anything, I'll just sort of look."

He kept on walking. "Why should I mind? I was going to ask you, but I thought you said you didn't want to go."

"No, I said I didn't know where I was going, I didn't say I didn't . . ."

"Well, come on, then. They'll be going home for lunch." Heroically, he shoved his hand out behind him and Eve took it, stumbling in her haste. Struck dumb by the presence of her hand in his, she could not for several moments think of anything to say. Cady, too, was silent and would not look at her. When she could bear it no longer, she said, "What happened to your cheek, did you cut yourself?" and was embarrassed immediately by this intimate reference to his person.

"No," he said. "I was born with it."

"I don't mean to be stupid," Eve stammered. "I don't know what's wrong with me."

"You're all right," he said, looking uncomfortable. "No, it got cut this morning down in the toolshed. We were just horsing around, me and George and Sam, and there was this trowel."

"Boy, you really cut yourself."

"I didn't cut myself. It was on account of Sammy Sissypants, and that dumb George—" He stopped. "Never mind," he said.

"You mean it was their fault?" She tried to imagine what she would do to them for hurting Cady.

"I said never mind," Cady said. He wrenched his hand away and went on faster. She hurried behind him confused again, it

was as if she had come too close to him and caused him to flee
her, like some wild animal. But still she followed, not knowing
what else to do, sensing that even under the best of circumstances
his female would always follow Cady, never accompany him. He
was moving very rapidly, shoulders high and tight, head carried at
a slight characteristic angle, and every few moments she was
forced to trot in order to keep up. She wanted to reach and touch
him, implore him to turn to her, but he was always too far away.
The spring sand was dark and heavy and dragged at her shoes, she
was losing her breath. Then he paused and kicked at a stranded
lobster buoy, and said, "Let's wade at the edge of the beach,"
slipping off his sneakers before she had even caught up with him
and tying them by the laces and circling them like a bolo high up
into the dune grass. "Will you find them?" she said. He took her
own from her and hurled them after. "Yes," he said. He was
rolling up his blue jeans. She wore bright tartan shorts and a
boy's white shirt, which freshened her open untouched face, and
a red scarf which held her hair and hid a slight shameful rash of
adolescence at her temples. He straightened up and looked at her,
and his face softened, saddened. They went down to the water.
"Be careful," he said. "Your mother'd throw a fit." "I know," she
said, delighted, but the wind plucked her words and cast them
into the roar of the surf, they were walking rapidly again, the
water swirled white against their ankles and pulled them seaward.
How cold the April ocean was, she wished she had a sweater like
Cady, his was black and had a damp salt smell and something
which was part of him. Did caretakers' sons smell differently, or
was it his cottage, his existence that she scented? She called to
him, "Cady, what's it like to live here all year round, in the
winter and all?" and he turned one brief moment, watching her,
and said, "All right," as the spent wave slapped against his calf

and soaked his pants. "Christ," he said, "look what you made me do." He moved up onto the beach again, skirting the undulating water tongues, the foam, and left her sloshing through the water, her apology unheard.

Cady stopped at a distance from the fishermen. There were six of them, and they stood by an open truck with a winch on its platform and huge soft tires. Attached to the truck, on rollers, was a green surf dory, highsided and angular, over the stern of which could be seen the thick brown folds of netting. The fishermen were smoking, watching the sea.

"What are they waiting for?" Eve said. She stood at his shoulder, just behind him; when she came abreast, he stepped a little forward.

"Just waiting."

Cady was watching the fishermen, she saw that he was anxious to join them and said, "Can't we go any closer?" He shook his head, "We'd only get in their way." He would not look at her, and she guessed that he was ashamed of having a girl with him, especially a fourteen-year-old, because they were at least a hundred yards away.

As if in apology, Cady explained the operation to her, digging and kicking his toes at the sand, his hands in his tight hip pockets. He spoke in a low monotone, his eyes squinted forward away from her, away from the casual glances of the fishermen, away from the world. He told her about the striped bass, how they ran the coast in the spring and fall, the heavy silver schools of them, they were large in the fall and April was too early, the frontrunners would be small and few. In another month, perhaps—but the fishermen started before he had finished. They watched the men flip away their cigarettes, moving slowly at first in their rubber suits, thick-legged and unearthly at a distance, as the truck backed around and down the hard round slope and the dory slid forward supported to the sea fringe by a dozen short-stepping backleaning legs, like a huge balky insect. On the wash of the first long wave the dory moved into the sea a little and was held there, nervous and buffeted on its flanks by the ocean set on its windward side, the fishermen to leeward, as two figures clambered into it and took two oars. Now they waited again, watching the sea, the men in the dory were shouting something, and in a lull Eve could not distinguish, "Now!" Cady said to the wind, the dory sprang forward, accompanied a way into white oblivion by two dark figures at its gunwales and a third at its stern who, as it reared and stood on end against the water wall, clung to and scrambled into it over the netting. And she was astonished to see that the two figures had regained the beach before the sea. They had a heavy line which they ran up the sand slope to the truck. The plunging dory was wallowing in the trough with another wave impending, the oarsmen rowing furiously, they were standing, and the man in the stern with his weight crouched forward at their knees. Then they were clear and headed straight to sea, all three still shouting.

Cady was grinning, and Eve gloried in his excitement.

She had gravitated forward until her shoulder touched his arm, and he turned but did not move away. She felt a peace in the nearness and an excitement, as if together, watching this struggle with the sea and wind, they were nature, a part of life, caught up in its melancholy force, as if in this sharing of their physical mortality they, and their love, became immortal. Strengthened, she lifted up her head, half-conscious, dreaming, faintly ridiculous.

The oarsmen were seated now, but still they rowed a violent stroke, sitting up a little from their bench at each pull in order to hurl their backs into the effort. In the stern, the third man unheaped the netting, which fell in brown heavy slaps onto the gray plateau beyond the surf and sank, leaving a thin indefinite wake of corded cork floats to trail back through the combers to the beach. There the net line was already secured to the winch on the platform of the truck. The driver, an old man with a bright white head, stood one foot on the running board of the cab and watched the dory as he scratched himself. The dory had swung and was paralleling the beach, moving downwind in a series of resonant oarlock sounds which rang now and then between the surges of the sea. After a short run it headed inshore again, still urgent in its pace although Cady muttered, "Too slow, too slow," until entering the surf area, it slowed, coasted, backwatered too late, for it was seized from underneath and shot forward on a pouring crest and down, for a moment stable and then, on the verge of the sand, capsized in a maelstrom of dark masses and angles and cries against the triumphant foam. The men on the beach were already in the water groping for the net line, the oars, four staying hands on the turtled sliding dory as its crew reappeared, shouting still in cold anguish, and sloshed up out of the sea like primeval bathers.

Cady was laughing, a long silent laugh which barely altered his expression, "All that for an empty purse," he said, and she laughed, too, and shivered.

On the truck the winch had started, grinding hard on the wind, and the net line shimmied, bounced on the hard sand, then palpitating rose into the air, and at the other end, down the beach, two fishermen hauled leaning halfway to the ground and called to the wet boatmen. These walked in a circle shedding their rubber suits and cursing and only moved to help against the sea strength when the white head shot from the cab of the truck and added its voice to the din, a bellow so huge that for a moment even the wind and water drew back startled before closing down on the scene again. Cady laughed, a snicker like rolling sea shells on the tide line, "Old Barlow," he shook his head self-consciously, "Old Barlow Shipman."

She followed his gaze to the old man. He was out of the truck now, planted on the sand in dungarees faded silver, like some thick sea-smoothed tree he stood, his roots in the sand, clean, windburned, waiting, as below his men heaved hard on the line, outdistanced by the chewing winch at the other end, and the cork floats bobbed peacefully in a slow half circle as if detached from the wall of cord drawn painfully shoreward across the current. When the floats fringed the outer breakers, the old man Barlow Shipman speeded up the winch and the men down the beach hauled harder, digging their heels in the sand as they leaned backward up the slope. In the center, unnoticed, the dory had slid from the sand again, a black beach whale before the oncoming sea.

"Wait and see," Cady said. "A few bunkers, maybe a sea robin or two." His face wore an I-told-you-so expression. He lit a cigarette, and she thought how complimented she would have been at the chance to refuse one. Around them the morning widened, it was nearly noon, and the white gulls settled at vantage points down the beach like rays of the breaking sun against the sand. And still the sea came pounding, the net was in full surf now, caught and twisted by the set, the men were shouting again, stumbling hurrying hauling, and then Barlow Shipman stopped the winch and shambled swiftly forward to help them. Several men were in the water, out toward the middle of the closing circle. They were braced on something. Eve tugged at Cady's sleeve and he muttered, "They don't want to dump the bunt. The fish are in the bunt, it's called a haul seine, it's a kind of a bag in the middle of the net. Look out." He shook her off, moving forward a little. Now all the men were in the water, hurling useless excited orders at one another, and in a moment the bunt was washing loose in the shallows, they were staring into it, and one man whooped. "That's Joe Ferrari," Cady said. "He's only a kid, he's younger'n I am." He glanced at Eve as if to warn her not to shame him, then walked rapidly forward. The men did not look up when he came, and, spindly among their heavy suits, he helped them drag the net onto the beach.

Here and there in the netting fish flopped and turned, a tail, a gleam of silver, and the fishermen wrenched them out, some were caught by the gills, and tossed them aside. The live ones struggled until gray with sand and then lay still. A score of fish in all, perhaps, all but four of them menhaden—the men called them "bunkers," or "alewives," and left them where they lay—a flat silver-white case of bone and oil, valuable only in huge quantity, popeyed, anonymous, inert. Of the other four, two were thrown in with the alewives, spiny swollen-headed red-finned sea robins, and two were handed to Barlow Shipman—the first striped bass of the year, and probably the smallest. "Three and maybe four pounds," he muttered. The men stood hands on hips and stared at Eve, who had come forward to poke the trash fish with her toe, and Cady stood dark-browed in front of her, his gaze self-consciously on Barlow Shipman and the two hard handsome fish which hung by their crimson gills from his middle fingers.

"How you doin', Cady?" one of the men said. He was a thin good-looking boy with thick curly hair and a leer, and he kept his eyes on Eve. She turned and looked at Barlow Shipman, who was pondering the fish.

"I'm doing fine, Bart," Cady said. "Why?" His face was angry, uncomfortable, and he touched his hand to the scar on his cheek.

"We was just wonderin'," another boy said. "Ain't seen you around in a couple days now." This was Joe Ferrari. The other men, all older, had turned and were spreading out the net before folding it, and Joe Ferrari turned to help them.

"He's given up fishin'," Bart Shipman said loudly to Joe. "More money in baby sittin'." Both of them laughed, and old Barlow Shipman said, without looking up, "Maybe if you weren't so busy being fresh, Bart, you'd be a better fisherman."

Cady, who had started forward, stopped.

"I was only kiddin'," Bart complained. "Least he could do is introduce her to his friends."

"Her name is Evelyn Murray," Cady muttered. "That's Bart Shipman and Joe, Joe Ferrari, and of course, this here's Captain Barlow Shipman."

The two boys leered, and several of the fishermen paused to stare at her.

"Well, of course she is," Barlow Shipman said. "I know your dad there, Miss Murray, known him a long time, Mister Joshua Murray, a very fine man."

Eve and Cady flushed for separate reasons as Barlow Shipman stumped forward and put a hand on the shoulder of each. "Now Cady here is my oldest nephew, that's right, ain't it, Cady?" Cady muttered, "That's right." He was watching Bart, who nudged Joe Ferrari. Barlow said to Eve, "I guess you didn't know that, young lady?" Eve smiled. Oh say something, she told herself, please say something, don't be so stupid! But she was conscious of Cady's eyes upon her, there was no love in them, only judgment for having caused him embarrassment and shame. "Well, listen," the old man said, looking from one to the other. "Is your daddy down here?" She nodded, and Cady said, "He's staying with the McConvilles. She wanted to see the fishing." His words were directed at Bart and Joe Ferrari. "Well I want you to do something for me, take him one of these little stripers, tell him

Old Barlow sent it, tell him—" "No," Cady said. He stepped apart, and would not look at them. "No?" "The catch belongs to the men," Cady blurted, glaring at Eve. "C'mon," he said to her. "Yes," Eve said, "I couldn't do it, thanks an awful lot, Captain Shipman, I just couldn't do it, but I'll tell Daddy you—" "C'mon, will you?" Cady said. He was walking backward down the beach, and she followed him, waving back blindly over her shoulder at the old man's deep laughter, hearing the imitative bray of Cady's friends who did not understand why they were laughing, her eyes held in Cady's by a sort of hypnosis, he was walking backward still, as if he were leading her somewhere distant and forever. She was afraid of him, the fear slid between them like a shadow on the sun before he turned and went on.

Cady walked along the sea and Eve walked behind him. She wanted to call to him but could not, there was nothing to say, nothing to be sorry for but a set of intangibles spun in a web of anger. And though fourteen, she was wise enough to sense that he was struggling, too, in the web, but struggling to find a purchase from which to attack her. He could not say simply, "Why did you have to come and look at the fish!" That was the fact of the anger, and the fact was ridiculous. Once, nearing home, he turned and glanced at her, and so certain was she now that he had found a weapon that she stopped and said, "Cady," but he did not turn again. He sidetracked up the beach in search of their sneakers, and then he was waiting for her at the foot of the dune path to the lawn. She stopped a few yards from him. After a moment he said, "What's the matter? Aren't you coming?"

"Nothing," Eve said. She came forward a few steps and stopped again.

"You ought to know better than to take that fish," Cady started.

"It's not as if you needed it like those guys." He tossed her sneakers at her, and she caught them clumsily.

"I didn't take it. Captain Shipman wanted to *give* it to me. And anyway," she added, resenting him, "what can they do with two little fish like that?"

"You shouldn't take one, that's all."

"Well I *didn't* take it, did I? You act as if—"

"Never mind," Cady said, grinning suddenly. He seemed to have lost interest in the fish, in her, in everything, and went on up the slope. At the top he turned and waved to her. "I'll see you later," he called, still somehow angrily. "Good-by."

"Good-by," she said. He could not have heard her against the breeze, and by the time she waved, he had turned and gone

Good-by, good-by. That was her first important parting. How long ago, ten years? No, twelve, the year before the war, in 1940. Easter, 1940. There had been so many since, more important ones, perhaps, but one hardly remembered good-bys, only the circumstances of them, the rest was imagination. Things interceded like pushing people in a terminal, the errands, supplications, nostalgia, the rush itself. The moment of leavetaking, like the moment of love, was frenetic and so very rarely serene. There were two partings with Sam, one when she was unsure of him, during the war, the other when she was sorry for him, in 1948. The last time she had seen him he was standing alone in the rain, a lost little boy. Of both partings, only the confusion was left to her. And now this afternoon with George—how had it been? She could not recall the look in his eyes, nor what her own expression had shown of her disillusionment.

Good-by. Good-by.

CHAPTER 3

AT TWENTY-FOUR, THE INDIAN DANIEL BARLEYFIELD WAS small-eyed, olive-red, serene, and he stood planted on the lawn, squat not fat in his gray jersey, khaki shirt, and dungarees, his long-beaked Montauk cap worn backward, clown and catcher fashion. His hands leaped upward in mute embroidery of his words, curling like thick sea flowers, closing again and falling away to his sides, and his smile was constant, enigmatic as a scar. He was saying that he would get a girl in to clean, just for the weekend, although the girl was there already, watching her lover from an upstairs casement. George McConville nodded abstracted, and Daniel expanded upon his subterfuge as if to justify the night of plotting behind it, for he knew it was passing unheard. He smiled, constantly and broadly, with the humor of his private world, remembering at the crux of his account the love made the evening before in the master bathroom, the soapy warmth of his Rosa and how she laughed as they played animals, and remembering, stirred uneasily at the swift heat in his loins.

George McConville did not listen to his caretaker. He stared over Daniel's shoulder toward the woods, shifting his muddied cordovans impatiently while the Grinning Jackanapes, Sam called him that, played the fool in the corner of his eye. George knew about the girl, had guessed the truth of most lies proffered him by Daniel, and Daniel knew George knew, yet on he went, fantastic

51

and incorrigible, a bucolic bland buffoon who smelled of fish. The
fish would be striped bass, George thought, and Daniel was seining
with the Shipmans on George's time again, the least he might
have done was change his jersey, but no, he couldn't even . . .
Never mind, George told himself, the hell with it.

"Listen," he said, "listen, Daniel," and Daniel laughed in
baffling triumph, slapping George on the shoulder, before shifting
his ground with the grace of a runner and hurtling onward into
exposition of his caretaking feats on the Point.

Damn, George thought, do I have to listen to this? In the metal
glare of the sun, he was conscious of his forehead's numbness, a
certain whiskey queasiness, and the weight of the shotgun shells in
his Gladstone bag, which he did not want to put down for fear
of encouraging Daniel. Daniel's eyes were twitching now in heavy
cunning toward an upper window of the house.

"Listen, Daniel, when you go to meet Sam on the eleven-ten, I
want you to stop by the hardware store and change these Number
.5 shells for Number .4's. I made a mistake."

"Hokay, George." Daniel Barleyfield turned his cap around to
the front, took the Gladstone bag from George's hand and put it
on the ground, then turned the cap back to the rear again, and
winked. "So like I was sayin', the marsh was too full, floodin' up
onto the lawn and all, so I told 'em to bring a bulldozer out here
and open a new gut across the beach. You can bring a skiff right
through there now when the ocean's calm, there, you can just see
it," and George followed the pointed finger to the beach gut,
opened every year whether Daniel Barleyfield ordered it or not.

He didn't want to think of Eve, not now, not until he could
think more clearly, decide. His mind recoiled once more into
memory, ricocheting from subject to unpleasant subject like a
trapped thing fled backward into an impasse: that Easter with

Cady and the cat, it had come up again in the bar with Sam the night before, momentarily, like the shade of an old sin shared by both and by both forgotten. Forgotten. George would never forget it. The memory clung to him, symbolic of all shame, as in childhood his nightmares had clung to his waking terror like remoras dragged from the depths by some doomed frightened fish. The good dreams, so rare, had been self-consuming, leaving only wistful remembrance of happiness and mystery, like colored twilight in a chapel. . . .

"So I said, keep your goddamned horseshit, and I went over there to the fish factory, they're gonna send over eight barrels of trash fish for fertilizer instead, there'll be some fine stink around here for a week, maybe two, but hell, you don't have to smell it if you ain't here, ain't that right?"

Mystery, George thought. And horseshit. Sam would have an epigram for that.

"Something the matter there, George? You look kind of under the weather."

"Look," George said. He put his hand up and loosened his tie, twisting it down in a hard vicious knot, then jammed his hands into his pockets. "Look," he said, "maybe it would be better if you called me Mister, Mister George or something, Daniel. If you want to, that is. Then if people are here—you know what I mean." George wrenched a hand from his pocket and waved it vaguely in the air, frowning thinking, hell, what am I doing, I'm useless this morning, telling this poor guy I've known all my life. . .

"Hokay George. Mister George." Daniel Barleyfield's eyes were farther open than George had ever seen them. They squinted again when Daniel laughed.

"What's so funny? You don't like the idea?"

"It ain't that. It just seems kinda queer to me, you know what I mean? Like I've known you all my life here, called you George and all, and I'm still callin' you George when I ought to say Mister George, only I can't, it sounds so funny. Makes me feel like I don't belong here or somethin'."

"Forget it. Forget I ever said it."

"Hokay. Mister George! If that don't beat . . ." Daniel emitted a ululating whoop, like a loon, the heavy clay of his cheeks pushed back in wrinkles.

"Forget it, I said," George snapped, and when Daniel stared at him, the smile askew on his face like the tail pinned on the donkey, he added more gently, "I'm going in to change. Don't forget about Sam."

"Do I call him Mister Sam?"

"Call him whatever you please," George said.

"How about 'Sammy Sissypants,' like in the old days?"

Daniel laughed loudly for a moment, coughing.

"You've got a memory like an elephant," George said. He went away across the lawn to where the path descended to the dunes and, watching the sea, picked up a handful of white sand. The sand seemed more permanent than the sea, which was always changing and thus strange, and he wondered if it had shifted in the storms of fall and winter or if it was the same sand they had played upon as children. What had they played, that night at Easter long ago, and who were the players

Cady and Sam and himself and Daniel and Celia and Eve were playing nigger-baby, and Cady had picked on Sam.

"Get Sam again," Cady had whispered in his ear. "Let's get Sammy Sissypants," and he hurled the ball high into the gathering darkness, "Sam! Sam!" Cady shouted, and Sam running around with that funny tight expression as if he had hurt himself and his hands stuck out as if he were trying to explain something, and all of them laughing at him but Daniel and George. Watching Daniel, George thought, is it because he saw the cat killed this morning, does he know that Cady is out to humiliate Sam, or is it simply that he is too young to know what to laugh at—he hadn't time to decide, his own name was being screeched, "Georgie-Porgie!" by stupid Celia, right in front of Eve she called him that, and he threw himself across the sand in a dramatic try, missing the ball by several feet. "George is showing off, as usual," his sister said, and he heard Eve laugh.

When he threw it up again, furious, he called Sam's name by mistake, he had meant to say Celia, and even before he knew where it would land, he was ashamed. Sam would be nigger-baby for the second straight time, he heard Cady's gleeful whoop, and Eve say, "Oh honestly, George—" as the ball dropped in the shallow surf and Sam, running wildly, desperately, eyes staring into the air, fell in after it. There was silence then, as Sam waded out, and Cady had broken it with sarcasm, "Nice going, George, that was a beauty."

"I guess that makes me nigger-baby," Sam said. His voice was strained, and he was shivering.

"I think George ought to be nigger-baby instead," Celia said.

"I'm sorry, Sambo," he said. "That was really dumb."

A strand of hair was plastered black across Sam's forehead. Beneath it, the dark eyes stared out at George, unbelieving.

"You better go up and change," George said. "I'm really sorry."

Sam turned away. "You look it," he said, over his shoulder. He stood for a moment, the ball in his hand, then repeated, a little dazedly, "I guess that makes me nigger-baby."

"To heck with it," Cady said. "Go on up to the house."

"You better go up to the house, Sam," Daniel said. Daniel's voice was changing, and he spoke very rarely.

Sam looked at George again, a queer expression on his face, and in the instant before he handed George the ball and crouched down over his knees to await his penalty, George sensed that Sam had run into the water on purpose, that he was going to let himself be pelted unnecessarily for the same reason—because Sam had been humiliated once that day, in the toolshed, and some last-ditch hysterical pride in him would not let it happen again, however much he was made to suffer. And George was stunned by the hatred toward himself expressed by Sam's mute genuflected form, hunched dark and amorphous and painful against the sand. He wanted to run forward and say, it was all a mistake, Sam, I meant to say Celia. Then Cady came and took the ball from him. "He asked for it," Cady said. He seemed to sense what George had sensed, winding up elaborately like a major league pitcher, as if to make Sam pay dearly for his gesture.

"Listen, don't burn it in, come on," George said.

"Oh don't, Cady," Eve said.

"Stand back," Cady said. He grinned at Eve, holding the ball as his arm stroked through the air and letting it pop from his fingers at the last moment and float in a foolish little arc onto Sam's behind, from which it bounced and rolled away down the hard sand into the water. Eve and Celia and Daniel laughed in relief, and George did too, halfheartedly, knowing there was nothing funny because Eve had forbidden hurting Sam, not Cady's conscience. Nor did he like to see Eve laugh with Cady, he wanted to say something to amuse her himself but could only think of "What happened, Cady, you break your arm?" The attempt at humor went unnoticed by all but Daniel, whose maniacal laughter only pointed up its weakness, and the others looked at George in surprise.

"George made a joke," Sam explained, walking past all of them toward the path up to the house. George could tell from his voice that Sam, whose bid for martyrdom had been foiled by Cady's leniency, was very close to tears, but he took faint pleasure from the knowledge, peering away toward the surf for a sign of the unretrieved tennis ball.

"I'm going in, too," Celia said. "I'm bored with your silly game."

"Me, too," Daniel said. "You comin' home, Cady?" He started off in Celia's wake, squat and eager like a puppy.

Cady did not bother to answer him. He said to George, "What's Sammy trying to prove?" and George said, "That this morning didn't mean anything, I guess. I don't know."

"That was dirty, throwing the ball in the water like that," Eve said. She seemed to be waiting for them, watching Cady.

"I didn't mean to," George said to her. "I'm not that dumb." Angrily, he started off without them, conscious immediately of leaving them alone together. Remembering the bet he had made with Cady that he couldn't kiss Eve, he was jealous and ashamed, and kicked at the sand as he went up through the dunes. At the top of the slope, he could not resist turning and looking back.

They were nowhere to be seen.

I'll tell him the bet's off, he thought, I'll get him aside and tell him. And he ran back down the silent sand, stopping short when he saw them. Cady was kissing her. They would see him, think he was spying on them—panicked, he threw himself down behind a wind slope in the dune grass. In a moment he heard Eve say something, they were coming nearer, and he couldn't get up and run without being seen. They would never believe him if he said —and now they were abreast of him, Cady took her arm and stopped her. They were looking at him, looking right at him. Then they laughed and went away up the path.

He couldn't breathe. It was dark now, and the dune grass sawed mysteriously in evening breeze. Below him, the ocean came and went, he listened to the hollow cadence of it, the sharp hiss of the foam, and pressed his forehead against the cold dry running sand between the grasses

Was this the same sand they had known, still children then, or had the sand changed also, swept by the wind and buried and submerged—he let it flow away between his fingers, wandering across the terrace to the French doors gleaming coldly behind the skeletal rose trellises. In the morning light they mirrored him as younger than twenty-eight, a tall thin man with rodent gray-brown hair cropped around like a monk's cap and a face untried, not quite unwilling, which smiling obscured in a litter of lines the nervous wink of greenish eyes. He touched his forelock, "Good morrow, Mister George, you sorry bastard," and wincing, shambled through the door and then glanced back, as if to catch in the empty glass a sneering stranger. Indoor associations, careening forward like ancient odorous dogs, were banished unrecognized by a sudden bleak absorption in his face. He mounted the silent stairway to his room.

In the doorway he paused, then turned and braced himself in the door. He felt unthinking, here I'll be all right, here sure, here safe, as down the burnished banister the dust motes danced on a sunlit shaft of light, and formed against the darkness of the lower stair in images of past incident—there Eve, his mother, Sam, there Cady and the cat, Eve, Daniel, Eve. The periods of his past were like slow tickings of a cosmic clock, as once he had counted the endless time of childhood by moments of agony, the burns, cut fingers, scrapes, the pain, crying, here is Pain again, it has never left me, I have always been here waiting to be hurt, afraid. And as if, having outdistanced guilt, he had run hard upon an abyss, he turned to face his pursuers on the stairs and saw but one, the unforgiving stranger, who was

GEORGE MCCONVILLE. 1936. BOY'S POTATO RACE. THIRD PRIZE.

He held the diminutive cup in his hand. Its handles were twisted off, the silver paint was chipped. In it were two fishhooks, an old cartridge, a single die, three orange marbles, and his discharge emblem from the Army. He put it down again, standing in dull abstraction in this junk heap of his childhood. A ridiculous zoo of a room he had, with barnyard wallpaper, portraits of mastiffs and noble steeds, and a library of four-legged pranks and heroics which his mother insisted remain where it was, for *his* children, she said. He took up the ancient dog doll which—his mother again —had made *her* mother's infancy a joy, and delighted moths before the Civil War. For George, this shabby creature was the Cerberus of past unpleasantness, of rainy afternoons, no supper, measles, mumps, and tears. A smug squat hideosity, it had one foreshortened leg, no eyes, no ears, no tail, and a painted anus, courtesy of Samuel Rubicam. Once, in a rage, he had touched a match to it, but the dog withstood the holocaust as readily as it had a century of cuffs, kicks, slingshots, arrows, spears, and knives, acquiring only a certain brindle marking and a permanent stench, like old cigar butts.

George's tie had whiskey on it, and grease from the diner. On impulse, he strangled the Horrible Hairball (his sister Celia called it that) with the tie, then strung the carcass to the doorknob and gave it three uppercuts to the midsection, scraping his knuckles against the door panel on the last blow. He had so greeted it many times before.

He was astonished to find himself grinding his teeth and laughed, crossing the room again to the closet and taking out his

Army field shoes. He returned with these and sat for a moment on the bed—what was it he needed? Socks, heavy socks. In the top drawer of his bureau he found an old picture of Eve, aged eighteen, with the inscription, "To lovelorn George, from Eve's one-and-only, Sam." Sam's elbow was still in the picture, there was a highball glass and an ashtray reading "Emerald Club." Sam hadn't changed any, and perhaps that's just his trouble, George thought, he's still the same old—but that wasn't fair either. Eve had been in love with Sam, there was no doubt of it, she had married him, hadn't she? and as a little girl, she had liked Cady Shipman, too. This memory was more painful to George even than her marriage to Sam, perhaps because he was unable to extricate it from the hangdog ridiculousness of his own position at the time, the inadequacy which had culminated in his pursuit of Cady across the lawn

Running desperately, he called out in a loud hoarse series of croaks, "Cady, wait a minute! Cady, listen!"

Cady stopped when he heard George behind him. "What's up?" he said.

"Listen, I didn't mean to—I only meant to come back and tell you the bet was off, I was only kidding about you kissing Eve, and then—"

"What do you mean, the bet's off? You owe me a dollar. C'mon, fork it over."

"Okay, wait a minute, that's not what I mean. I mean I know the bet's still on and I owe you a dollar because I didn't tell you it was off—" George fidgeted violently, still panting from running, and he had to urinate—"but I wasn't spying on you just now, I was on my way down to tell you."

"You mean you saw us, then? You saw me kiss her?" Cady stared at George, confused.

"I guess I did. Not really, though, only kind of, and by mistake. And then I jumped behind this little dune so you wouldn't see me and be embarrassed or anything, only then you came along and saw me and laughed, and I just wanted you to know that I wasn't spying, I just came back to tell you—"

"No kidding, so you saw me kiss her. You don't have to take my word for it about the dollar, then." Cady grinned, shoving his hands into his pockets. "So you were spying on us, huh?"

"Listen, I *didn't* spy, honest. I just happened to see you, that's all, and I didn't want you to think I—you know, so I hid. And then when you came along and laughed like that, I knew you saw me and thought I—wait a minute." George shifted up and down getting his fly open, and when he relieved himself onto the night grass, Cady burst out laughing.

"I'm only kidding," he said. "I didn't see you at all."

"What do you mean? How come you were laughing?"

"We were just laughing at something, I don't know. You know how it is when you kiss a girl."

"Sure," George said doubtfully. He felt unhappier than ever. "And Eve—I guess she didn't see me either, then."

"Well I don't know about *her*." Cady's face wore a new expression. "Maybe she saw and didn't say anything. Anyway, you owe me a dollar."

"I know," George mumbled. "I'll pay you tomorrow." Vaguely he waved his hand in the air. "So you think she saw me?"

"How should I know?" Cady said. He eyed George carefully.

"I'd better go get Sam some dry clothes," George said. "I didn't mean him to fall in the water, either," he added, uneasy that Cady might still entertain some doubts on this other matter.

"He shouldn't play nigger-baby if he can't look where he's going," Cady said sourly.

"Yeah," George said. "I didn't want him to fall in, though.

Well, I guess I'd better go, I'll see you tomorrow." He backed away toward the house.

"All right." Cady turned and went on down the slope toward the cottage.

"So long," George called. His voice was high, a little desperate, floating through the darkness

He stubbed out his cigarette and started to dress. The rough clothes were tight and cold in the damp of the room as if they did not fit him, as if he had exchanged one suit of falsehoods for another, the city artifice for the country illusion of craggy health and woodmanship.

The doorknob resisted his turning, spinning crazily for a moment while the Horrible Hairball leaped and cavorted in woolen glee against his leg. He bullied the door open, cursing, and burst into the hallway in time to glimpse the cat-quick disappearance of Daniel's Rosa into the back stairway, then made his way down to the first landing, where he paused once more, at a loss.

Daniel Barleyfield and Rosa, he thought, they were on closer terms with life than he had ever been, and happy with it. The Indian boy adopted by Cady's father in 1926, the girl salvaged from the rum-runner *Menhaden*, shot to pieces off Further Island in 1929. Rosa Menhaden, the village called her, she had no other name, whom nobody in the New England village would accept as equal but the crippled Ferrari boy and now her fellow foundling, fellow outcast, Daniel Barleyfield. Here in this chronically empty house, away from the eyes and commentary of Shipman's Crossing, they managed to live together in peace, even to imagine in their innocence that they were fooling him. And he would let them think so, he had no reason not to.

George felt unbearably oppressed. Yet he knew there was

nothing unbearable in his life, he had but one immediate problem, and the guilty paradox of his existence angered him. He had money and friends and position, everything his father had wrenched so bodily from life, and he had love, at least until yesterday afternoon. Was it a surfeit of things, or simply a deepening inevitable boredom?

"Stop your moping and go to work!"—Cyrus McConville had knocked over a drink, George remembered, and his mother's eyes had widened with the spot on her Turkish rug and filled with tears. Yet how fatuous to work for more money, how fatuous to fill the shoes of the man who had crushed by his own example the incentive to do so. Taking George's arm down these very stairs, his mother once whispered to him, she whispered constantly, "We have so much, and others have so very little, George. Often I wonder in my deepest heart if God can have meant it that way," and put her bird hand over her deepest heart, then over her mouth in terror of her own daring, the speak-no-evil monkey, her wide eyes wider than ever. How different they had been, his parents, and yet they had loved each other, the vaguely ridiculous woman who now lived with other wealthy sufferers on Sutton Place, in New York, the deeply ridiculous man who wanted to die with his boots on and did, in a manner of speaking, like one of the kings of France, atop his whore.

He heard the car in the long October driveway and turned to the narrow casement as Daniel sprang grinning from the front seat and Sam appeared out of the back, his overcoat cloakwise over his shoulders. Why had he sat in the back, George wondered, why did he wear his coat that way? He moved on down the stairs out of the shaft of sunlight, his escape to annoyance temporarily dampening the thick slow fuse of anger curled round and round like a tapeworm in his rebellious gut.

CHAPTER 4

EVE ROLLED OVER AND, SQUINTING IN THE LIGHT FROM THE table lamp, stared at the clock. It was morning, a little after seven. Except for a trip to the bathroom she had lain there thirteen hours, ever since Sam had called. And Daddy, yes, Daddy had phoned last night, she had called him George. "Oh, listen, George," she had said. And she had agreed to come for the weekend, had even smiled at the phone and said, "Well, toodle-oo, old thing. Good-by, Daddy."

"Good-by, good-by."

Good-by. Good-by

Cady had done it. Celia McConville told her. Celia was seventeen then and very enlightened. She said Cady had killed the cat out of neurotic hatred for Percy Shipman, that Cady was a dangerous boy but rather cute in a way, didn't Evelyn think so? It was Easter vacation, and Eve, who was three years younger than Celia and, with her family, a weekend guest at the McConvilles', was very impressed. Celia was a senior at their boarding school, she had nearly been expelled and was considered beautiful, and Eve was in love with her. She was also in love with Cady Shipman, and when Celia remarked that he was cute, Eve blushed and undid her hair ribbon. Her heart was beating very fast, it was Celia's grisly account of the massacre, of course, that had upset her, for

64

Eve adored all cats and especially the big yellow one at Cady's cottage.

"I said, don't you think he's kind of cute?" They were sitting in Celia's bedroom, and Celia was filing her nails.

"I suppose so," Eve said. "I think it's awful about the cat, though, I'm going to tell him so."

"In fact, I think he's very sexy, don't you?" Celia eyed her.

"I don't know," Eve said truthfully. "It's hard to say."

"Of course you know. Listen, when I was your age, *I* knew. You can't be a child *all* your life. And besides, I heard you kissed him last night on the beach."

"I did not! He kissed me before I could stop him!"

"That's not the way *I* heard it," Celia said. "My, my."

"Who told you? Anyway, I didn't, you can ask him!"

"I already have. And he told me . . . well, it's really not *that* important, Evelyn, I don't see what you're so excited about."

"I'm *not* excited! And I didn't kiss him, he kissed me. He told me he wanted . . ."

"Of course he did." Celia inspected her nails, adding mysteriously, "They *all* do." She paused. "You've begun having the curse already, haven't you? I mean, you don't mind my asking?"

"No, I . . ." Eve yanked her hair ribbon between her hands. "Sure I have, two years ago, two and a half, even. What does that matter?" She felt hot and foolish, resentful.

"It doesn't matter, really, except after last night, I was simply thinking you might be careful, especially with a caretaker's son. I was simply thinking of something my father said to me when I was your age, but I don't suppose it would make sense to you, not yet."

"What? What did he say to you?"

"No, no, I really shouldn't tell you, Evelyn, I don't know what could have made me even think of it, darling."

"That's not fair," Eve said. "You can't begin and then not tell me."

"Well, you promise you won't take it seriously, I mean, go blabbering to your mother about it, or anything."

"Promise."

"Well, he said, 'Stay sober, and keep your knees together, and you'll never get in trouble!'" Celia laughed. "Of course, you would *hardly* . . ."

"Oh Celia, he *said* that? Did he? Did your mother *hear* him?"

"God, no! Poor old mother, she'd be horrified!"

"And you think . . .? Celia, you're nasty, you really are, I never heard such a horrible idea."

"Oh, relax," Celia McConville said. "You don't know how silly you look. Besides, it's normal, I'll bet you loved it. Was that your first little kiss?"

Eve burst into tears, she could not help herself, as Celia smirked and shrugged her shoulders. "I really didn't mean . . ." Celia started, and Eve gasped, "Shut up!" astonished at herself. "You've gotten pretty fresh," Celia said. Celia was a tall, thin-legged girl who carried her breasts and hips more prominently than they deserved. She had long blond hair worn loose on her thin face and eager blue eyes a little runny at the edges. These eyes watched Eve now, their cast in odd contrast with a mouth which seemed to be smiling. "Pretty damned fresh," Celia whispered. She had risen and was standing over Eve, who sat on the bed. "No," Eve said, "I mean yes, so what if I have?" "Why don't you get out of my room?" Celia said. She went to the door and held it open. "I forgot I was talking to a little girl." Eve rose and started out. "I forgot, too," she blurted, and the door slammed on the senselessness of her remark. She ran to the stairs.

Halfway down, on the landing, she stepped on the stomach of the dog doll, the Horrible Hairball, which had been hurled there by somebody else. She picked it up and set it in the casement, so that it looked out the narrow window, and then the door to George's room opened and Cady Shipman came out. She heard Sam's voice, "What in heck have I said to him *now*, that's what I want to know," and George said something as Cady called back, "I'm just sick of your lousy company." "Why don't you go hang around little Miss Murray, then?" said George's voice.

Eve went on down the stairs, and Cady followed her. "He's in love," said Sam's voice, and there was a whoop of laughter. Cady stopped on the landing a moment. Glancing back, she watched him toss the Horrible Hairball in his hands. He caught her eye, then expertly drop-kicked the doll up the stairs. It bounced through George's door, there was a curse and another peal of laughter. She crossed the hallway and went outside.

He followed her over the lawn as he had the evening before on the beach, quiet and noncommittal, incredibly handsome and mannish, she thought, in his tight dungarees, in the easy way he moved, cigarette in hand. "Listen," he had said in the darkness, "I want to kiss you," and he had done it, magically, before she said no, before she smelled the damp salt odor of his sweater, the tobacco of his breath, before she pulled away speechless and peered ahead to see if George had turned and witnessed the enormous act. "Oh," she breathed, "why did you . . . what do you think you're doing!" They had laughed together, but at the house, sensing he would kiss her again, she fled on the wings of his soft laughter. How dare he, she thought in bed, how dare he. She touched her lips with her finger tips. They are mine, she told herself, he had no right, he should have asked, and then I could have given of my own accord. If I had wanted to, that is. She giggled. The finger tips had come alive, they tingled with her lips, and feeling foolish, she kissed them swiftly in the dark, imagining. The resentment vanished, replaced by a sense of flesh, her body, his, and her heart had pounded all the night, I will die of this joy, it seemed to say, and she had imagined heroic scenes, in one of which he was washed in by a storm sea, she dragged him from the breakers and revived him in her arms.

In the morning, embarrassed, she avoided him, choosing to spend the gray April Sunday cooped up with Celia. But Celia had heard and ruined everything, Celia with her terrible lie about Cady and the cat, she must have lied, mean nasty thing, thinking she was so smart and everything. I hate her, I really do, Eve decided, moving faster down the hill, but she could not concentrate on Celia for Cady was following her still, and she thought, I must be a mess, all red-eyed from crying.

"Ev-e-lyn!" Her mother's voice resounded from an upper window. "Where are you going, dear?" The voice was high and disagreeable, it seemed to add of its own accord, "—with that young man?" and Cady heard this, too, for coming up to her as she turned, he said, "Tell her I'm taking you to show you the fishing down the beach," and passed her without looking back. "He's taking me to show me the fishing down the beach!" she called, and because this sounded odd to her, or perhaps in swift happiness, she laughed, turning to run after him. "Ev-e-lyn!"—but she did not answer. "Do be careful, dear, it's nearly time for lunch!" This was for Cady's benefit, he grinned back over his shoulder at Eve, who thought, do be careful, stay sober and keep your knees together. Mr. McConville had never said that to Celia, never in the world, and now her laughter died like bubbling water taken from the fire, and when Cady took her hand out of sight of the house, she took it back, answering his wary glance with sullen eyes.

"What's the matter?" he said. He stood there, feet braced apart, hands in his hip pockets. She could not focus on just what the matter was, and said unwillingly, "Celia told me about the cat." She watched the dune grass bend about his sneakers, listened to the ocean pounding, and he did not answer. "Of course I know she made it up." She looked to the water now, it was gray-green, lachrymose, and a single gull sat still in the air against the ocean breeze. "What did she say?" his voice said. "She said you murdered the cat on purpose because you were mad at Percy for something, and that George and Sam helped you. Of course I know she made—"

"I did it myself," he said. "They didn't help me. Celia's a liar." His face was gray as angry wind.

"You mean you did it, then?"

"I didn't 'murder' the cat," he said, after a moment.

She stared at him. Tell me you are telling the truth, tell me anything, I will believe it.

"I put the cat in to kill the rats. I didn't know that would happen," he said. His face was angrier now, set and strained, she could hear his breathing, and for one moment she knew he had lied before she went to him and took his hand.

"I believe you," she said, joyous.

"You're a sucker, then," he blurted, and wrenched his hand away.

"Why did you say that?" Eve said, and hurt, added ineffectually, "Maybe you're a sucker, too. Maybe I don't believe you at all. Maybe—"

"I lied to you," he said, his voice thick. "I never lied before." He took her upper arm.

"I have to go to lunch. You heard my mother, didn't you? Let me go."

"You made me lie. A girl, a little girl like you, I didn't want you to think I . . ." He stopped.

"Think what?" She sensed his confusion as a temporary advantage for herself, watching the flicker of self-analysis like sickness in his eyes. Then it was gone.

"Think I 'murdered' the cat," he said. "Well, I did. I put it in the barrel, and I knew those rats'd kill it. I lied to you."

"Why?" she said. "Why did you do it?"

"Percy took our guns."

"That's no reason to do a horrible thing like that."

"It seemed like a good reason yesterday morning. Percy's always giving me a hard time. I guess I wanted to show him he couldn't fool with me any more, I'm not a kid."

"Oh, Cady, that's horrible," Eve whispered. His hand was a vise on her arm, she tried not to strain against it, as around them the sun of noon appeared through the clouds and stroked the dune grass, and the sea behind them fell away into quiet. Despite herself, she suddenly wrenched free, and again a confusion almost childlike crossed his gaze. "You ought to be punished," she said. "You ought to be."

Without answering, he unbuttoned his shirt, the act made her blush but only for a moment, because he turned and threw his shirt down behind and she saw the still raw welts like long thin bloody mouths, "Oh, golly," she breathed, "oh Cady," and thought she would cry. "There's more here," he reached back without turning his head and patted his rump, "worse even." She could not imagine his welted buttocks even though, in bed the night before, she had imagined him naked in her arms on the beach, washed in from the shipwreck, imagined—she reached forward blindly and touched the cool skin between two welts, "Ow!" he flinched, and she drew back sickened at the touch of

his flesh, so cold it had seemed, so sallow and foreign. And she
backed away from him up the path, he stood and watched her,
buttoning his shirt, "Why did you kiss me last night?" she
whispered, and he looked confused again. "Because I . . . because . . ." then angry, as if recognizing the finality of her retreat,
"Because George bet me a dollar I couldn't."

"Oh! And George told Celia?"

"How should I know?" He shrugged his shoulders, winced. "All
I know is, I got my dollar."

"Your dollar! Your *dollar!*" She burst into tears and fled, glancing back only as she entered the French doors on the terrace and
seeing him staring after her, hands in pockets, alone against the
long beach to the south.

Sunday lunch that day was a terrible affair, she could not orient
it with the turmoil in her heart, with Cady, the cat, the treach-
erous Celia, the sea wind and the fishermen, the snarling welts like
carnivore's jaws across the sallow back, all the momentous things.
She told her mother she did not feel well, and her mother said,
how ridiculous, she had never heard of such a thing, and Eve was
seated between her host, Cyrus McConville, and her host's son,
George. Across the table, her mother smiled watchfully over her
and cocked a head no longer pretty to Samuel Rubicam, who re-
counted gravely the case against all boarding schools. At the same
time, Sam managed to pass signs across the table to George which,
from the comical leer of the latter, Eve adjudged to be a commentary on her own sexual behavior of the night before. Next to
Sam, Celia McConville sipped her tomato juice from a glass with
a frantic pheasant on it, the pheasant dipped its tail in a round
red pond whenever she tilted the glass, but Celia was unaware of
this, unaware of everything but the aloof elegance of her seventeen
years, and rewarded a remark addressed her by Eve's father,

Joshua Murray, with an arch, enigmatic smile which was rather beside the point. Joshua Murray was on Agnes McConville's left, on her right Philip Rubicam, a handsome cadaverous man who, encouraged by too many daiquiris in the noonday sun, was describing the eccentricities of his lately divorced third wife. Her tenure had been so brief that none of the company, his son Sam included, had ever made her acquaintance, and perhaps this fact, too, contributed to his abandon, for presently Philip Rubicam, who had passed most of his life in Europe, dismissed her case with a Gallic gesture of such violence as to empty George's tomato juice into its owner's lap. George sprang backward, sopping at his lap with Eve's napkin, there was a cacophony of replaced glasses, caught breaths, grunts, and chairs, and even Sam, who on similar occasions was always the first with a lighthearted remark, blushed furiously for his father and bent, frowning, over the billing cedar waxwings on his china.

"Damnit, I'm sorry, George!" Philip Rubicam apologized manfully. He glared at George, then at the door to the pantry, in agony at first and then in angry disapproval when no servant materialized immediately. Then, since there was nothing to be done, he turned once more to Agnes McConville and attempted to resume. "So you see, the wretched girl didn't even . . ."

But Agnes McConville, who disapproved of many things, interrupted him with her hand. She was a shy woman, even timid, but like many timid women she was intractable on the principles of things. Philip Rubicam was not to get off so easily. The hand, palm outward, suggested reproof, or horror, or pointed dismissal of the incident, but most probably all three, as her face assumed an almost characteristic and favorite "Dear, dear, dear, whatever will become of us!" expression which reminded Eve of ancient mice in Beatrix Potter's books for children. She was a small dark woman with a rosebud mouth, and she sat erect against the table, wide-eyed, as if she'd just popped from beneath it. Cyrus McConville said to Philip Rubicam, "Too many daiquiris, old man?" He boomed out a laugh alone, and this time George and Celia blushed and frowned, Celia whispering, diplomatic, "Oh really, Daddy, *must* you?" Philip Rubicam, in consternation, peered around again at George as if to perceive some serious aspect of the matter that he had missed the first time.

How ridiculous they all are, Eve thought, conscious of her own fourteen-year-old perspective, so much ado about nothing, until her mother said in her high affected voice, "Aren't we *all* being a *little* like the Mad Tea Party?" and giggled in a manner which brought heat to Eve's cheeks and sent perspective packing. Across the table she caught her father's eye, he winked minutely and squinched his nose as if sniffing the air, then raised his brows in mock response to a remark unmade by Mrs. McConville, whose prim palm jesuitical had lost control of the table. She had reached instead for a Queen Elizabeth bell, the golden shoes kicked peevishly against the royal bronze robe, and then Eve understood and laughed. "Eve-lyn?" her mother said, beaming nonetheless at this appreciation, from however lowly a source, of her own remark. Cyrus McConville rose gasping from the last of his tomato juice and, wiping his mouth, waved a huge freckled paw at his son and Philip Rubicam, "Now here's a little girl with a sense of humor!" and clapped the hand down on Eve's thin shoulder, his laughter clattering once more without response down the length of the table.

Stay sober, Eve remembered, and keep your knees together—she looked at him carefully for the first time as she wiped a fleck of his laughter from her cheek, the jowls and reddened eyes and thick coarse hair. She turned away in time to see Sam take advantage of the confusion by leaning across and whispering something about herself, she was sure of this, to George, in time to see Celia, who could not have heard a word of it, giggle, too. Despair returned to her. No, she thought, No, No, No, No, No.

"This really fixes my flannels," George observed, but nobody listened to him.

Agnes McConville found speech at last. Doughtily, she said, "It's nothing, Philip, really, it doesn't matter," and when Philip stared at her, added, "Really, I've rung and rung, I can't think what's keeping Nora."

"Tell me, Philip, will you be going back to France?" Joshua Murray said.

"The sooner the better." Rubicam's voice was haggard.

"Boy, you should have seen what happened to Cady on account of that cat," Sam said to Mrs. Murray. Mrs. Murray smiled inadvertently and peered across the table.

"Of course," Agnes McConville was saying, "with nine of us, I should have two servants at table. I asked Sarah, you know, the caretaker's, Percy's wife, but she wouldn't, oh no, not her, she's a Shipman. She said to me, 'Mrs. McConville, do you think I could be a common serving woman on an estate my family owned before the McConvilles came to America?' "

Here Agnes McConville simpered, this was as close as she ever came to sarcasm, and searched about the table for corroboratory astonishment. There was none, but Mrs. Murray shook a sympathetic head, she was a large sandy woman, a little mannish, who kept up a pretense of sunburn all year around. Her sympathy, as Eve was later to learn, was not with the ridiculousness of Sarah Shipman's airs so much as with the indirect slap at Cyrus McConville, against whom she was Agnes' strongest ally. Cyrus wasn't precisely nouveau riche, but he wasn't of the Old Guard, either, and

Agnes faced the fact with courage among her friends. Mrs. Murray, her dearest friend of all, knew the dirt from A to Z, and leaned now far out over the table, clucking for Agnes' eye, all set to wink.

Cyrus McConville stared from one to the other, crimson. Then he heaved about in his chair, the heavy tail-waving stomp of a horse removing a fly from its rump, and snarled, "Estate! The Shipmans be damned! They've gone to seed!"

The waitress Nora, entering, was terror-stricken by the damage, and red-faced ran for hot dish towels. George said he was fine, he refused to move his chair, and the poor thing could not squeeze enough, even on hands and knees, to reach the spot under the table. In the kitchen, the cook was spoiling for trouble over the impending conflagration of her roast, and Nora, who expected rebuke at both ends of her route, had beads of sweat, big pearls of her labor, on her upper lip.

"They haven't gone to seed exactly, they've lost their momentum," Joshua Murray said. "They've spread themselves too thin, made mistakes. But Barlow Shipman is still the man they look to on this coast."

"Daddy," Eve said, "I saw him on the beach yesterday morning, he wanted to send you . . ."

"Listen, it was Barlow who sold me this land, for nothing, I tell you, nothing! You call *that* smart? The fellow may have been here before the goddamn Mayflower, that doesn't make him any smarter in *my* books." Cyrus glared at his wife, then Mrs. Murray. "And what about his brother, that Abraham? A loony. Jumped right off that rock out there. And you tell me they haven't gone to seed! Why, they used to own . . ."

"Now Cyrus," Agnes demurred. "It's not important."

"What did he want to send me, Evelyn?" Murray's voice nudged her through the sound of Cyrus' spluttering.

"A striper. A little striped bass. Only there were only two, and Cady said . . ."

"Cady." Celia closed her eyes and giggled. "La-dee-da," she added.

"Not important! What the devil do you mean, not important?" Cyrus reddened, then dismissed his wife with a jerk of his head. He turned on Joshua Murray, who was watching the children, then switched his gaze to Philip Rubicam with an any-port-in-a-storm expression. "Listen," he said, "it's when the people with property sell out that the country gets in the mess it's in now, this Roosevelt, the socialism, all the bolsheviks in Washington, you give them an inch and they take a mile. Unions, WPA, free handouts, share-the-profits, all the rest of it. What the hell did our grandfathers fight for, the rugged individualists, the pioneers?"

"My grandfather died of drink, I believe," Philip Rubicam said. "During the Civil War, however, he pioneered a retreat into unexplored regions of the Great Dismal Swamp."

"Cyrus, I don't see why you can't control your language, in front of the children, at least." Agnes McConville did not dare face her husband, but her eyes shone with excitement. She caught and exchanged Mrs. Murray's wink.

"We aren't babies," George said.

"Not much," Celia sneered.

"What *did* our forefathers fight for, Cyrus, the rugged individualists and pioneers, I mean?" Philip Rubicam enunciated in the careful manner of a man who is amusing himself and, with any sort of luck, a few discriminating others.

"The free enterprise system," George said. He had started to raise his hand, but caught himself in time.

"There," Philip Rubicam said. "The advantages of a solid all-American education. Go to the head of the class, George."

Sam snickered. "George is a rugged individualist," he said.

"We aren't babies," Celia mimicked George, and smirked unnoticed at Philip Rubicam.

"Well?" Cyrus glowered. "Well, what's the matter with that? The American Way of Life . . ."

"I think what Cyrus means," Joshua Murray said to Philip, there was a warning insistence in his voice which held the table, "is that the Shipmans, once a wealthy and dominating family in New England, have parceled out their holdings and thereby weakened, as many other families have, the American form of aristocracy in favor of the community."

"What's that?" Cyrus said.

"What's that?" Philip Rubicam mimicked him, grinning. He was a little drunk, but aware of the tension he was creating, alleviated it by saying, "After all, Cyrus didn't *have* to buy the Shipman piece."

"Aren't we *all* being just a *little* like . . ."

"Like the Mad Tea Party?" Eve heard her voice finish her mother's question, the words had escaped her subconscious, she had had no definite reaction or sensation of speaking. But instead of paling and setting her lips, as Eve expected, her mother laughed fantastically, "We really are, you know," Mrs. Murray said, she seemed to preen herself, and again Eve sought her father's eyes for a solution, again he understood, for he shook his head reprovingly and looked away.

"I mean to say," Mrs. Murray went on, "we were talking originally about the caretaker's wife, Sarah or whatever, and I understand from Agnes that she isn't really *the* Shipman family at all, but a poor relation. A poor relation of poor people, imagine!"

So struck was she with this fancy that she sat back laughing, a little startled.

"Imagine," Joshua Murray said. His expression was dead, and in the silence that followed he did not return the gaze of the table but watched the pantry door, through which now appeared a vermilion Nora with the second course. The door swung to and fro on the subdued shoutings of the cook.

"If I hadn't bought it, some Jew would have grabbed it," Cyrus McConville said. His broad face was raw with dislike for everybody at the table, his daughter Celia excepted, and he glared at them one by one.

Look at them all, he thought, sitting around eating up my food and laughing at me, yes, goddamn them, they laugh at me, all friends of dear Agnes. I make the money, and what do I get out of it?

"Pass the Triscuits to your father, George," his wife said.

"I don't see what Jews have to do with it," George muttered darkly.

"Me either," Sam said.

"Keep a civil tongue in your head, Samuel," Philip Rubicam said, and after a pause, added, "Mr. McConville can prove to you that the Jew is the archenemy of the modern world, which, incidentally, they are hatching a plot to overthrow. They are led today by an international ring which includes Hitler, Mussolini, Stalin, Mr. Roosevelt, Mrs. Roosevelt, and Pope Pius XII."

"Philip . . ." Joshua Murray started, in his voice again an insistent note, not quite unpleasant.

"So, I say to you, Samuel, just eat your . . . ah . . . your— just what *is* that, Agnes?" He indicated a large casserole with a nod, both hands placed on the table edge as if he were about to spring into it head first.

"It's called pa-ayla," Mrs. McConville said. "It's a Spanish dish."

"Paella! Is it really?" He leaned far forward, peering at it. "*Sin vergüenza*," he muttered, and Joshua Murray winced. "It reminds me of Valencia," Philip Rubicam said, and laughed, delighted with himself.

"What does 'seen ber-guayn-tha' mean?" George McConville said. Eve watched his eyes, they were hurt and suspicious, as if he had taken it upon himself at sixteen to protect his family. She, too, had sensed that the phrase was insulting, and admired George for challenging it.

"It means, 'This smells delicious,'" Joshua Murray interrupted, and Philip Rubicam laughed again.

"That's it," he said. "It means 'Lo, a heavenly odor!'"

"At school they call it Spanish rice," Sam said. "We call it fisheyes-and-glue."

"That's tapioca," George said.

"Children, children," Agnes McConville warned, then smiled meaninglessly in the silence. "If anybody doesn't like it, they can wait for the roast beef." Her voice implied that the untutored tastes of the children, among others, might not appreciate her exotic dishes. Eve, although she disliked the look of the casserole, trembling in Nora's steamy hands, determined to help herself liberally. She watched her mother sift through it deftly for hidden goodies, there seemed to be a little of everything in it and Mrs. Murray hadn't missed a thing, the table sat spellbound by her skill. Then Cyrus McConville was sloshing through it, his mind was not on the casserole, a certain amount of which he dumped unceremoniously onto his plate. But when the dish had passed along to Eve, Cyrus stared at Mrs. Murray's plate, then at his own. His was almost entirely rice, a mass of discolored white by comparison to hers which, garnished with tomato, peppers, and gobbets of lobster, was gay and festooned with color. "What did you use," he said to her, "a magnet?" and was startled by the laughter around the table, he had not meant to amuse anybody. Mrs. Murray said, "Oh, this looks just wonderful, Agnes!" and once more he inspected both their plates in rueful disbelief. "She must have used a magnet!" he said loudly, and again was astonished to find himself laughing alone.

Eve watched Cady Shipman cross outside the window, which gave on the rocks overlooking the sea. He hurried past, staring straight ahead, and only at the last moment glanced in at her before he disappeared, leaving in his wake confusion, disillusion. Her heart was beating, a mouthful of the horrid food stuck in her throat, she could not swallow it. She wanted so badly to cry. And in contrast to her feelings, the behavior of the adults at the table, heretofore unquestioned, now struck her as paltry and absurd, she wanted to run from them, brush them off her consciousness like this wet, clinging rice and flee alone to some purity of thought through which she could analyze and understand what had happened to her. She did not yet see that her small sorrow had cast a first weak ray of judgment on her world, that the joyous acceptance of everything, which is childhood, had passed into shadow.

And she would think eight years afterward, in the marriage bed with Sam, it was to Cady, not Sam, that I lost the true virginity.

"There goes Cady," George said quietly, with an odd proud proprietary satisfaction. Sam turned, but Cady was gone. "Cady is the little tin god around here," Sam said. He looked from Eve to George and snickered.

"Jealous?" Celia said. She and Sam carried on a vague internecine warfare because Sam, alone of the children, would not submit to her years. He looked older than fifteen, he shaved irregularly and rather hopefully, but his self-confidence stemmed chiefly from the fact that in boarding school, at least, he was considered a comedian. So that now he perceived in Celia's mockery a faint flirtatiousness, a respect for the enemy based on the enemy's own confidence, and when, six months before, he would have said, "Sure I am," with defensive adolescent irony, he now grinned,

"Cady is my hero." This appeared to Celia as well as himself a huge step forward in sophistication, for she giggled a little and cast her eyes down upon her casserole. Elated, Sam said, "I'm studying to become a caretaker's son and be worshiped by George and Eve," and again, a little uneasily this time, he glanced at George and Eve across the table to see if he had struck home. He had.

"You wouldn't say that to his face," George flushed. "You weren't talking so big yesterday morning, down in the toolshed. You . . ."

"Sammy Sissypants," Eve said, unfairly, and was ashamed.

"How about last night on the beach?" Sam taunted her, his face gone pale. "You'd better forget about the toolhouse"—he was trying to threaten George through Eve—"or I'll tell about . . ." His voice subsided. Eve waited for George to betray her by betraying Sam. What possible reason would keep him from it? She thought she would run from the table.

"My son is an informer," Philip Rubicam said, poking at his rice with distaste.

"Are we to have some shocking exposé?" asked Joshua Murray. He winked at his daughter.

"Really, I do think we really are a little like the Mad Tea Party. . . ."

George glanced at Eve, a soft, sad, sideways glance. "What's the matter with liking Cady?" he said, in the same tone of earnest resentment in which he had said, "I don't see what Jews have to do with it." He himself was blushing fiercely now, and her heart went out to him in gratitude. And then she remembered, I do not love him, he bet Cady a dollar, he is only poor old George. She gazed at her plate, confused in her loss of the simple certain values.

"What the devil are they talking about?" Cyrus McConville demanded, like a spectator at an exhibition of aborigines.

"Children, children," Agnes McConville fretted, her fork all aquiver at her shining little mouth.

Children, children

But how odd that Daddy should have called, poor Daddy, rattling around the house down there in his comic-opera clothes, as he called them, saying and doing and thinking all the things Mother had never let him say or do or think in peace. How lucky it was, yes, how lucky, that Mother had left him, Mother who still phoned Eve from time to time and wanted to know if she wouldn't lunch and was always so disappointed when Eve said she couldn't, so proud of herself, Eve knew, because she had paid lip service to maternal affection and could go on her blowsy way with that species of good conscience which is nine-tenths appearances, one-tenth rationalization. Poor Daddy, who had not contested the divorce, who had never contested anything in his life, poor wise ineffectual Daddy, living out his days in a kindly limbo of his own construction, was grateful, *grateful*, when his daughter or a friend or anybody's friend went down to see him, and kept the big house, servants, an extra car, a tennis court, and the big bay horse Tenerife entirely for the use of others, as if, in recompense to the world for his failure to act in it, he welcomed the impositions of his fellow men.

Eve had never been quite persuaded of that fine distinction people made between using their benefactor and giving him pleasure. It was apparent to her that to visit her father would give him pleasure, and no less apparent that, although she adored him, she visited him only when it suited her mood to do so, when she would profit by it, in this particular instance through escape to his love. Cornered in the gloom of her apartment, she shortly persuaded herself of her own selfish motives. It was easier to reject all comfort, plunge deep into the abyss of depression, than to be driven there in painful skirmishes with the facts. The night before—it seemed an hour ago, how had she been able to sleep?—the night before she had said to herself, no, I will not go, I refuse to indulge myself at Daddy's expense, and make him miserable, too. She had found no comfort in the decision. On the contrary, its sophistry had increased the roiling sorrow in her, and she remembered thinking, this is no time to be a martyr, leave that to George, and repeating this to herself until it had lost its meaning.

How queer it was this morning, the anger and grief were gone, emotion itself was gone. How curious to lose emotion like an earring or a theater ticket, just like that, to have it replaced by a nothingness, like waiting for a hiccup, with the world outside the vacuum, and time at a stop. One could search everywhere for it, find only sterile vestiges, a sediment at the bottom of the mind, a tarnish on the heart, a taste of ashes. Emotion was a looking forward and a looking backward, one must have something to look forward to, to look backward on, and one must care.

I do not care, she thought, I will miss the train. I will call Daddy and tell him.

Tell him I am lying here without husband or lover, with a seed in my stomach for a keepsake, a tadpole rampant on a field of pink, to bind me to past anger, grief . . . how very past everything seemed!

She placed her palms upon her belly and pressed down with her fingers. There was nothing, yet she could feel its presence, would it have green eyes like George? How silly. Unexpected tears slid down her cheeks, idle they were as if indifferent. Why, I'm crying, she thought, why am I crying?

CHAPTER 5

ON SATURDAY, IN THE DINING CAR, SAM RUBICAM WONDERED if his breakfast wouldn't make him sick. He pressed his nose to the window glass like a pensive urchin, the glass was cool against his forehead, and drummed with a knife on the tines of his fork the weak tin rhythm of a rumba salvaged, like the beer-soaked paper matches in his pocket, from the night before. When the waiter came with a tray bearing color and smell, Sam sat upright and glared at his food, knife poised in doubt, a dark young man of poetic appearance, with full soft eyes a little bloodshot, thin black hair worn long, and a mercurial mouth pursed in chronic rejection.

Like George McConville, Sam fell prey in weaker moments to evaluation of his life, but unlike George, he was less disgusted with himself than with the knowledge of having somehow once again lost ground on the parchesi path his prospects had become. The end of the path, the victory, success, a reason for living, were no longer clearly in view, and his usual swift passage from remorse to rationalization was this morning slow, uncertain, and even disagreeable.

He took courage presently and drank his orange juice, feeling better immediately. The self-reproach fell from his shoulders like a wet cloak dropped in a hallway, and soon he was sufficiently strengthened to shut his mind entirely against thoughts of destiny, turning instead to contemplation of his bacon and eggs. He even felt a little giddy and, humming, stabbed an egg with his fork: How now, sirrah, for thy impertinence, my stainless steel shalt know thy yellow blood!—then glanced around at the other diners, fearing he had spoken aloud, and seeing he hadn't, giggled. The ravaged egg no longer appealed to him, however, it quivered pallidly with the train's vibration, and he pushed the plate away from him, taking up his coffee as the waiter came with toast.

How perfect, Sam Rubicam thought, to rush along like this forever, without responsibility toward self or neighbor. How perfect, and how very boring. One had to take responsibilities to avoid being bored, he had learned that long since, but as with so many things Sam Rubicam knew to be true, he did not act upon it. He constructed instead a certain delight in being bored, the sense of transcending the common ruck to observe and, wherever possible, to ridicule.

Beyond, by a siding, a tramp stood dark and damp, the bleak eye of penury and bare existence, his mask appearing and disappearing in the shroud of Diesel smoke like a symbol of lost identity. Behind him, the autumn woods passed adamant, exclusive, a regiment in color, then a ruined pond, dark hangout of rats, mosquitoes, of crows which rose and broke away with shouts of silence and were gone; a creek, a blackened bridge, a salt field trenched with oily ditches, from which a late great heron kicked aloft and flapped inland on wings as slow as the arms of a cold old man; a water tank, a dirtied orchard, ill-assorted slapstick houses of puce and brown and yellow behind a station slighted by the north express, where people paused on sour feet to watch as if in hopes that one day, miraculously, this train might deign to see their puny terminal and stop, and take them somewhere they had never been.

"Whatever became of Cady Shipman?" It was late last night when he had asked it.

"Cady? I'm not sure myself," George had said. George looked startled, half-turned on his bar stool. He had obviously been thinking of Eve again, Sam thought, noticing the tension in George's eyes, the restlessness of his hands.

"I mean, will we see him tomorrow at the Point?"

"I doubt it. He hasn't been around in several years, according to Daniel Barleyfield." George grinned. "Why? Do you miss him?"

"You're awfully clever tonight," Sam said.

"Awfully. Awfully clever every night, as a matter of fact." George reddened and looked away. He is ashamed of his joke, Sam thought, and he was about to tease George when the latter turned to him. He started to speak, then for a moment was silent. At last he said, "You're a strange guy, Rubicam, I sometimes think I hardly know you."

"You know me better than anybody else," Sam said.

"Maybe so. But there's something you hold back," George said, his brow furrowed in his effort to select his words with care. "There's too much of you uncommitted."

"Quite right," Sam said. "I'm civilized. I don't lose myself."

"You're too civilized, then," George said, and turned half away toward the tables.

"Sooner or later, George," Sam persisted, "a man gets sick of everything. Every idea from brothel to basilica has its share of meaninglessness, in any country, in any century, in any moment of time which has bred simultaneously rats, men, and mosquitoes. That is, ever since the inception of mankind . . ."

"You believe that, do you?"

"No," Sam said. "I'm a modern relativist, the culmination of civilized man. Sam Rubicam is my name. Nothing is true, and I believe nothing. What I've been saying is all very well, perhaps even valid, but it isn't true for me. My mind is never caught in the beginning, I simply play with ideas, and I stop finally when I get bored."

"Good God," George said.

Raising his eyes to George's face, Sam had been startled by the anger in it.

"I see what you mean," George said. "I'm bored to tears myself. Dear God Almighty, what crap!" Noisily, he sucked up the ice from the bottom of his highball glass, then shook his head in disgust, a little drunkenly.

"Exactly," Sam said. "That's just what I mean." He spoke triumphantly, swaying a little on his stool, but there occurred once more a note of desperation in his voice which embarrassed them both. Sam sat stunned by his failure, by the brutality with which his confidences had been received. I'm drunk, he thought, I haven't said what I meant to say at all.

In the hours past, he had tried to convey to George—what had it been, exactly? Not a way of life, but a pattern of behavior which had appealed to him in Europe. He had wanted to try everything, he said, experience life from every angle. Yet this hadn't sounded right, and the more he had tried to explain, the more the emphasis had been placed—was this his fault, or George's?—on the squalid aspects of the code, the perversions, the use of dope, until finally the over-all philosophy had been obscured entirely. Under the harsh light of George's scrutiny, intellectual curiosity became morbid, experimentation weakness, and even the candor of his revelations was no longer candor but pretentiousness. And worst of all, in George's contempt, he was forced to perceive a certain justice.

And he wanted to lash back at George, as if darting in and out of untried crannies in search of solace and finding none, he had been cornered in a bitter alley, pathetically snapping, like a renegade fox in a city.

"You can make of it whatever you please," he muttered finally, gazing around the bar in mute suggestion that George's observations were in tune with the vulgarity of the place, but he was stung far more deeply than he could admit. That George would disapprove he had counted to his own advantage, for if George would not knock at the gate to hell, he would still press his nose to its windowpane. But that George should see through him was something else again. He might regard Sam's past behavior in a new light, or even discredit it, and Sam did not want to be a casualty of this evolution in George's judgment. Sam placed little faith in friendship, and even his affection for George, the purest he knew, was especially valuable to him for reasons having little to do with George himself: Shipman's Crossing, the Point, was home to Sam, and had been even before he became the McConvilles' ward, and he regarded them as his family despite the fact that in retrospect the McConville parents seemed tiresome to him, despite the fact that he had taken her virginity from the McConville sister Celia. Like most rootless people, Sam had developed through need a sense of belonging somewhere. In his case, this sense was based on an optimistic view of the past, to which, by default of his ex-wife, the necessary link was George. Without George—Sam sensed this himself—he would be cast into a limbo of unreality, an alpinist swaying back and forth in space, and he was not sure he could or would want to make the long hard hand-over-hand haul back to a purchase on the world.

"Have a beer," George said.

"All right." Sam turned slowly and looked at George. "You were telling me about Cady."

"I tried to, but you kept handing me all that mess about yourself."

"I bared my soul to you, you mean."

"I hope not," George laughed, but his eyes were serious. "You think you shocked me, don't you?"

"I do, yes," Sam said. "Now let's hear about Cady."

"You did shock me, too, but not the way you think."

"I wasn't lying," Sam said. "It's just that you don't want to believe it."

"I'd have believed it willingly if you believed it yourself. And I'm also a little angry that you considered me simple enough to fall for it."

"You used to be just about that simple," Sam grinned, thinking, if only I can get him to laugh he'll forget the whole business. "You're not the same dull boy any more, more's the pity, as the man says."

George laughed unwillingly. "What do you want to know?" he said. "I told you he went to college for a year."

"What did he study, the Marquis de Sade?"

"Are you going to tell this or am I?"

"You are."

"Why do you want to hear about him, anyway?"

"I'm not quite sure. He fascinates me, rather like a half-picked scab. And then, what you were just telling me about Abraham . . ."

"Listen, forget that," George said impatiently. "I should have known better than to mention a silly rumor like that, especially when it was Daniel Barleyfield who started it."

"It intrigues me," Sam grinned. "Abraham, the Tarquin of the Tidewater, and Cady, a real old-fashioned natural son, like Edmund the Bastard. I never thought Shipman's Crossing could be so colorful."

"Stop it, for God's sake. What would happen if Cady ever got wind of that, how do you think *he'd* feel?"

"All right." Sam laughed delightedly. "Still, you've fascinated me, George, I never thought you had it in you. And so the bastard —I use the term in the figurative sense, George, merely to suggest my personal feelings—and so the bastard was packed off to a seat of learning, to return with the noble bearing which was his heritage."

"You're drunk," George said. "Drunk and verbose." But he smiled himself, and added, "Anyway, Cady was decorated in the war. Our old pal was a hero, a red-blooded American boy and all the rest of it."

"And after the war?" Sam signaled to the bartender.

"He stayed in the Marines for a while. Then he was caught in an incriminating posture, as they say, with an officer's sister and was given a bad conduct discharge."

"He got off lightly."

"I know, but remember, he was a hero," George said. "It made him a little bitter."

"Couldn't he seek comfort in his books?" Sam was very pleased with this remark and slapped George on the shoulder.

"You're a riot," George said. "I'm damned glad he *won't* be at the Point tomorrow."

"Me too," Sam said. "I wouldn't get a wink of sleep. Besides, what do you expect? Everything you tell me about Cady is so macabre, it's as if you liked him for the very things that I detest in him. You're *proud* of his cruelty, in a way."

"It's not that," George said, but he was obviously startled by Sam's observation, glancing momentarily toward his right as if something of interest were taking place there. "It's not that. But he has a certain force I wouldn't mind having, do you know what

I mean? He doesn't compromise every two seconds like the rest of us, he does what he pleases."

"So do animals," Sam said. "You surprise me, George." But George had not surprised him, George who had separated himself from Sam in the same way, before and since the April morning more than a decade before when Cady had killed the tomcat. "Do you remember the time when . . ." He stopped.

Do you remember the time

Sam Rubicam lay alone on the ground with George standing over him accusingly, George standing over him ashamed. Sam smelled the shame in him even then. And when Cady had gone, he whispered, unable to rise, "The skunk. The miserable skunk."

"Don't tell me," George had said. "Tell him." George standing there in his silly righteousness not knowing where to go or what to do, and rebuking Sam for a cowardice shared between them, as if he were saying, if you want to hang around with Cady and me, Sam, you have to take care of yourself, because we're a pretty tough pair, Cady and me, we don't fool around with sissies. He hated George in that moment, less for his betrayal than for the fact that George held the power of friendship over him—the Point was George's house, the family his family, Cady Shipman his friend, the beach his beach, the world his world, and for the fact, perhaps his first compromise with life, that he wanted George to think well of him again even though he himself thought badly of George.

And George had said, "Don't tell me, tell him," in a local accent like Cady's, standing over him the way Cady had stood over him, as if by identifying himself with the voice and posture of the caretaker's son he might escape the lostness which the incident had brought to Sam.

Sam remembered, too, that Cady was punished. The following day, it was Easter Sunday, they were calking a skiff at the edge of the inlet down below the house, he and George handing tools to Cady and Cady boasting indirectly, casually to George about a girl he was seeing now and again in a shed behind the high school, "Rosa's got 'em, all right, nice big ones," Cady was saying, when Percy Shipman appeared on the bank above them with a switch in his hand.

"Cady," he said.

Cady's Rosa slipped scantily clad into guilty corners of their minds.

"Cady," Percy Shipman repeated.

"Yessir," Cady said. He straightened, waiting.

"You know something about that yaller tom?"

Cady was silent. Sam and George fidgeted, poking at the seams of the boat, and then George bounced a pebble off its stern. Behind them, the tiny wind waves slapped in the saw grass.

"I asked you a question," Percy said.

"He's dead," Cady said, his voice low as water over small stones in a rivulet.

Percy Shipman rolled a denim sleeve.

"Dead?" The word snapped like a winter twig.

"Rats. Put him in a barrel to kill them rats I trapped."

"Come here to me."

Cady walked to him, already peeling off his khaki jacket and shirt. The sun was cold. When he turned again and faced the others, Percy Shipman struck him sharply twice across the back, and Cady grinned sharply twice at George and Sam.

Percy Shipman glanced from Cady's face to the stares of the other two, Sam was terrified he meant to beat all three of them, but Percy only said to Cady, "It ain't your back I want. Take down them pants and bend."

Cady stood unmoving, and the stick laced him like a curse. Sam thought Cady would turn and kill Percy then, there was an odd cast to his eye like forming ice in the corner of a pond, yet he seemed to enjoy the stoic role because George was there, refusing the pain only, as Percy had guessed, when it jeopardized his dignity.

"Take 'em down," Percy said, and struck him again.

Cady dropped his pants almost idly, as if to relieve himself, his eyes daring George and Sam to laugh. Sam did not feel like laughing, he felt sick with nervousness and a frightened hate of Cady which Cady's performance increased in him. Cady was watching him now. Percy waited, but Cady did not bend. Then the switch halved the air in hot whining strokes against the meager buttocks until, coming away red, it glinted in the sunlight.

Percy Shipman was out of breath. He looked a little startled.

"If you'da hollered, boy, you'da saved yourself a lot of misery after," he said. He dropped the switch and walked away.

Cady remained immobile, his pants forlorn about his boots. Although he was sighing with shock, his eyes were dry and frozen hard, and after a moment he reached back with his hand and brought it up red. The hand was shaking, and he had to hold his wrist

NEW FALMOUTH. NEW FALMOUTH STATION.

The city of New Falmouth sheathed the train in its own steam and smoke, a waterfront of black warehouses clicking past. The buildings blocked from view the confetti of closed yacht yards strewn out along the harbor to the east, and the high bridge crossing the river mouth toward the north from beneath which now

slipped a submarine outward bound, huge and fast in its shoreward confines like a shark in a tidal shallow, and gleaming in the
early sun. A swamp of tarred pilings jutted from the anchorage
edges where docks had been before the hurricane, and the sleazy
harbor gulls gapped and defecated on them while waiting for low
tide at the sewage outlet down the pier. A man with an expression
of going nowhere came along the platform and glared at Sam for
a moment before firing a jet of Bull Durham like melted aspic at
a rolling Dixie cup, then glanced at Sam again and erected for
him, in slow and solemn mystery, the middle finger of one hand.
Sam returned the greeting, and the stranger bowed shortly from
the waist, spat once more upon the platform, and shambled on.

He had to hurry to retrieve his bag and leave the train.

The local jerked backward, then drew forward, sliding in silence
from the station. Sam rose, moving rearward toward the smoking
car as if in defiance of this forward motion, yet losing ground so
rapidly that by the time he reached the vestibule between the
cars, the railway air was rushing up in raw gusts past the connect-
ing plates, which slid back and forth across one another with the
clumsy disharmony of mating turtles, and the jaundiced outskirts
were fleeing past the window. He glimpsed the buttocks of a bending mother, a black smoke of starlings curling down among
pinched rooftops and television aerials, a limping dog, a fruit
stand selling green apples or pears, a little boy running somewhere,
everywhere, nowhere perhaps.

Sam sat in dull contemplation of the red plush seats still dusty
with summer and the thin scarred door at the end of the car
which flew open upon a roar of air and metal to admit the ancient
redfaced man who called to his flock as he locked them out of
the latrine. He watched as passengers rose and reached for their
poor packages, there was something pathetic in the way they

would stand for minutes beside their empty seats simply because they had heard the magic word of home or tryst or sanctuary, something pathetic in the way the other passengers sat staring out of dirty windows upon the suburbs of a meaningless town, or at a newspaper left behind by somebody else—all faced straight forward being borne somewhere, as if the train had seized them up and they had no choice in the matter. Nor did they, he thought, they had to get off at one particular place, and when they had arrived, how many really knew where they were going, why they had come? How many would journey ever again if they knew what was truly in store for them this time, knew how poorly events would compare with expectations, love with the daydream of love, home with nostalgia for home?

He removed his chewing gum and stuck it under the seat.

Because there is nothing to us. Life was a wasteland between hope and dream, and where it overlapped them lay reality. Life was a series of moments not understood, for time understood was past and dead, and mystery living and present, even the mystery of other years, just as a woman known was romance lost, resuming her place in the endless anonymity of acquaintance, while a woman unknown or never fully known retained her place in the imagination. Eve, for example, though he had married her, was permanently with him. She had never given all of herself and could not be put behind him, whereas Celia McConville—a brief affair, and at the end of it, she had meant little more to him than a favorite suit of clothes outdated.

He was eighteen then and Celia nineteen, and at the time of their last pathetic assignation they had been sleeping together for one fall and winter, early in the war. Celia took a very romantic view of the affair. The steel spring in her New England morality had been a little tighter then, and to sleep with someone one did not love was simply not done, just as later, to her way of thinking, not to sleep with the particular loved one became the cardinal sin. Sam could remember wincing when, after the war, an acquaintance said of George's sister—it struck him at the time that this identity was more disturbing than his own past relations with her —what was said so often of so many in that period, that she slept only with her friends and didn't have an enemy in the world.

Sam, nevertheless, had been the first, and because Celia was older and complimented his vanity by making to him what he regarded at the time as a noble sacrifice, he imagined himself in love with her. On their final evening together, she was to be alone in the McConville apartment on Fifth Avenue. It was early May, and her parents were in the country. The tryst had been planned for several weeks, the circumstances seemed perfect, and he was astonished upon arrival before dinner to have her giggle to him at the door, "Eve Murray's here, she'll be our chaperone."

"Why?" he said. He hesitated in the hallway with the incriminating suitcase.

"Oh, here, darling—" she took it from him—"she won't make the slightest difference, I've told her about us and she thinks it's wonderful. And it looks better to the elevator man and all."

He followed her inside. Celia kissed him passionately, and over her shoulder he saw Eve Murray watching them from the living room, over the top of a magazine. He could only see her eyes and thought, why should she think it's wonderful, for God's sake.

He disengaged himself and said, "Hi, Eve."

"Hi, Sam." She did not lower the magazine.

He caught then—or imagined—a something shared between them, a mystery, a sadness which expressed itself to him in a swift longing to be alone with her. And he hardly noticed Celia, poised excited at his elbow as he removed his raincoat and laughing in her happiness, "Oh, I am so glad to see you!" even though they had had lunch together.

He made martinis, icing the glasses in a professional manner and pouring the vermouth into each glass, then pouring it out again before emptying the shaker of chilled gin, which contained no vermouth at all. He had heard of people doing this, and Celia made much of his daring, sipping with courage at her glass. But Eve tasted it thoughtfully and said, "I'm sorry, Sambo, I'd like a little vermouth in mine, if you don't mind," and held her glass out in a manner which appeared to him very provocative indeed.

When Celia disappeared to prepare their dinner—"My first culinary effort!" she called gaily from the kitchen, and Sam grinned obligingly, uncomfortably until he saw Eve watching him and stopped—they sat in silence, fingering the cold vapor on their glasses. Then he said, "You down from school?" and she answered, "Just for the weekend." He said, "This must be your last year, I guess," and she said, "Yes."

They looked at each other a moment before Sam dropped his eyes and reached for a cigarette.

Eve seemed subdued by the heavy rain at the windows, which closed off the lights in Central Park as if to isolate the self-conscious threesome from the city. At the poor little dinner, they sat in silence and listened to their cook. Celia was very effusive, smiling hugely from one to the other and chattering on every subject at once, and he knew she was trying to convey her own sophisticated attitude toward the night of illicit love ahead. The outcome of her efforts, far from placing the emphasis elsewhere, was to seat sex at the table with them like an unwelcome fourth. And although he fought it, his impatience with her was quelled not by his love but by his desire, and by the feeling that, with a pretty mistress beside him, he cut a more dashing figure in the eyes of Evelyn Murray. Sam did not affect Celia's insouciance but selected instead an air of weathered resignation toward the frailty of the flesh, toward the compromises with true love that man must make to satisfy the virile compulsions within himself. He permitted himself every now and then a penetrating and mysterious glance at Eve.

She gazed right back at him, her eyes inscrutable beneath the soft round hood of hair.

"God, but you're silent, you two," Celia said. She looked from one to the other, her mouth slightly open as if in surprise. "Do you hate my poor dinner?"

"Dinner's wonderful, it's that goddamned rain," he said, remorseful. "It's enough to make anyone gloomy."

"But *I'm* not gloomy, darling, why should you be? Tonight of all nights, especially—" Celia glanced at Eve and stopped. The color was bright on her long wan cheeks.

"I'm not gloomy, either," Eve said peacefully to Sam. He had risen like a crimson ghost from under the table where, at Celia's remark, he had dropped his napkin.

"That's fine," he said. "Nobody gloomy here but me, then." He tried unsuccessfully to laugh.

And later, in Celia's bedroom, he failed to laugh again. Celia had said, "But you *couldn't* love me," her voice wet and mournful from the darkness surrounding her bed. He was sitting in his pajamas on the windowsill, where he had gone without making love to her and waited for her to say just this. The music from the piano in the living room was muted by the rain, and by the walls and doors which held it out, and he knew Eve was playing in the dark because there had been no light in there when he had crossed the corridor to the guest room for his cigarettes.

He tried to laugh, and then he said to Celia, "Don't be silly,

Ciel, of course I love you, I just don't feel very well or something," and wondered if Eve was playing out of terror or tact, and why she had turned off all the lights in the room. The music came and fell away, he recognized a Chopin étude, watching the fire of his cigarette and the water which flew downwind across the window-pane.

"You don't. If you did, you'd at least come and kiss me. . . ."

And he thought, could I be in love with Eve, and Celia, too? Or is it just that I want them both in love with me? Sam always leaped to the basest possible motive so that in absolving himself of the extreme guilt, the lesser, more accurate one could be forgotten. And now he thought, I owe it to Celia to go and talk to Eve, find out. He would sit beside her on the piano bench as she played, and there in the darkness—his imagination had already outstripped his conscience—would take her in his arms when she had finished. He could feel the cool face next to his, so different from Celia's teary hot one, the freshness of her cheek and the slow, sleepy eyes regarding him, half-closed . . . God.

He said to Celia, "I will in a minute, just let me finish this cigarette," and listened clinically for the broken sigh.

The music stopped. In a moment, a creak in the hallway, a light switch, swift carpeted tiptoes down the corridor past their door. She must be using George's room, he thought, and the bathroom across the hall. He tried to picture her undressing, but could not. When George's door opened again and the bathroom door closed, he rose from the windowsill and went to the bed, standing over Celia in the white monogrammed pajamas which he had saved out especially from the ratty selection in his laundry.

"I'm sorry, Ciel," he said. "I don't know what's the matter with me."

"Lie down," she pleaded, feeling for him and taking his hand.

He sat for a moment on the edge of the bed, then bent and kissed her eyelids, tasting the salt of the tears. She clung to him harshly, and he felt her thigh slide over his for one wild instant before he stood. "We can't," he whispered. "It wouldn't be any good."

He stood there a moment, indecisive, listening to Eve brushing her teeth and deriving from the half-imagined sound a sense of intimacy with her, as if he were living with her instead of Celia. Then Celia spoke. Her voice was different, high and false yet somehow controlled, "Aren't you going to kiss me goodnight, then?" And kissing her, he felt her teeth bite hard on his lower lip and the tears start in his eyes before he choked, bent over and ridiculous, amazed, enraged, "Stop it—let go!" She bit harder. Then he struck her with a heavy downswipe of his open hand, and she fell back in tears and fragile laughter.

"What in hell do you think—" he began, tasting the blood in his mouth and panting.

The laughter stopped. "Go away," she said, in a small dark voice from the pillow.

Sam made his way from the room, stubbing his toe on her dressing table, and cursing. In the corridor, he closed the door softly and turned around.

Eve was standing there, a few feet away, with her hand on the door to her bedroom.

He did not know how long the moment was that they paused, each in pristine white like children, and regarded each other in the half light of the passageway. She glanced at Celia's door, then back at him—Sam remembered this afterward, years afterward, when it occurred to him that he might be responsibile in part for Celia's subsequent disillusioned behavior—and somehow he was frightened of Eve, the serenity of her, the dignity. He held his ground as his heart ran wild in him, and a feeling for her, for the music and night rain and loneliness in her expression, so filled his lungs that he nearly cried out across the vale of fear between them. He heard the turning of the doorknob and an ugly froggish voice which croaked, "Hi, Eve," and she whispered back, "Goodnight, Sam," and disappeared.

Perhaps it had only been a second. He stood a minute in the corridor, trying to collect himself. One moment he was tempted to knock on Eve's door, ask her to come talk to him in the living room. The next, a briefer instant, he considered returning to Celia, she would be grateful, he thought, and then we could— No, he gritted. And finally, angry and ashamed and restless, he went to the guest room alone

SHIP-MAN'S. SHIP-MAN'S CROSSING.

The platform slid into view, and Sam felt the nervous elation he always experienced upon arrival anywhere. He saw Daniel Barleyfield standing square and smiling, his cap faced backward on his head, but the train was several cars past Daniel before it yanked to a stop. Sam, descending, had time to cross the platform and enter the waiting room so as not to be seen by the small whitehaired man in the English riding jacket now greeting Daniel whom Sam had recognized as Eve's father, Joshua Murray, and whom Sam did not want to see or talk to any more than he had two years before when Eve had left him. Yet, standing by the window, he felt foolish and guilty, he wanted to go and face it out, but of course he could not now, he told himself, it was too late, what excuse could he possibly give for having gone skulking into the waiting room? And so he stayed fuming where he was until the old man went away, then waited a moment longer while the train jerked into motion again and Daniel was coming down the platform before he stepped through the door and looked studiously around for whoever had come to meet him.

"Hey there, Sam, I been looking all over for you!"

"Hello, Daniel." They shook hands, and Sam matched the other's smile with effort. "I had to go to the washroom," Sam said.

The sight of Mr. Murray coupled with his own behavior had drenched his already dampened spirits, which were assaulted again by Daniel's next words, "Goddamn, ol' Sammy Sissypants, well goddamn, it's been a long while," and a clap on the back which infuriated him. He was about to snap at Daniel, but the Indian was already leading him toward the car, saying, "Listen, you know who was just here, Mister Joshua Murray. He said give you his regards. Miss Eve was supposed to be on the train, but she wasn't."

"Don't tell George that," Sam said, not knowing quite what had prompted him.

"Why not? I gis George'd like to see her, why not tell him?" Daniel snickered craftily, opening the rear door of the car and hurling Sam's bag into the interior.

"Never mind why not. Just better not tell him, that's all." Sam's voice was more surly and stubborn than he had intended, especially since the matter was of no importance to him one way or the other. Or was it? He climbed into the back seat after his bag, thinking, Christ, things are really getting off to a flying start down here, as Daniel Barleyfield, face fallen, stood watching him, holding the car door open even after Sam had settled himself.

"Listen," Daniel said, "how come you . . . don't you wanna ride up front with me?"

"Oh yeah," Sam said. He sat forward, then slumped back again.

"Hell," he said, not meeting Daniel's gaze, "it doesn't matter, I'm in here now."

Still Daniel did not close the door, as if he hoped Sam might change his mind. Sam knew he was thinking about people in the village, that they might say Daniel wasn't the friend of George McConville, Sam, and others that he claimed to be, and laugh at him for giving himself airs. He did not stop to think that Daniel's feelings might be hurt.

"Let's go," Sam said.

They drove out under the yellow elms of the village and onto the coastal highway. The day was brilliant blue and warm, as if the air were fired by October's incendiary trees, too warm, Daniel remarked, there might be a storm later on. He turned off the highway before the roadhouse and raced down the hard sand road to the Point. The road avoided the salt marsh, running straight through the whitish woods like a new beam stretched in barren grass until it reached the headland, where it crossed the last length of Abraham's path and circled onto itself in a rush of gravel before the house.

Back from the driveway at the point where it crossed the path stood the toolshed where the cat had died, leaning rain-streaked and unused into the prevailing wind until the moment when it would sag in rotten silence into the waiting wet place by the woods.

CHAPTER 6

IT WAS NEARLY DAY WHEN THE HORSE SLOWED TO A SWIFT
pacing trot, then a walk, heaving cold sweat like frost from its
withers, and blowing. When it stopped altogether, the man started
into wakefulness, aware on the instant that the horse had out-
smarted him, had broken its gait when it lost the feel of his hand
as he had dozed, and was already turning on the highway shoulder
to start its long journey home.

"You son-of-a-bitch," the man said, matter-of-factly, and yanked
the horse to attention with calm violence, the head tossing in the
air, the heavy working hoofs picking out a dance in the dirt as
horse and rider circled together against the breaking sky.

The horse would go no farther. When the man drew its head
around to his knee, it circled again, slowly, feeling its way crab-
wise back in the direction it had come and snorting outraged
against his hand. They struggled for a moment before the man
knotted the reins and cracked the knot with a flick of his wrist between the crouching ears. The horse moved sideways in one stiff
shiver and snort, violently, and planted its hoofs in the wet brown
grass of the roadside.

"You son-of-a-bitch," the man repeated, and grinning, dis-
mounted. He stood against the horse for warmth in the dawn air,
kneading the soreness in his crotch with fingers cramped cold
from the reins. Nearby, a bent crow balanced on a treetop. In the

distance its mates were shouting, and when the horse stamped, it left to join them. The treetop shivered, stilled.

Maybe a half mile to the roadhouse, he thought, half an hour to the Point.

He felt in the corners of his field jacket for the tobaccoed sugar, tossing it a moment in his hand before he held it to the horse. The long head jerked backward, then pushed forward again, the great delicate lips picking over the lumps with the aid of the nostrils before passing them, one by one, among its yellow teeth. He watched the horse, breathing the sweet reek of it, the stink of sweated leather. The ears rose slowly, flicking in the remote tom-tom of a marine engine, the cry of distant gulls across the marsh, the body shifting single-step as the white foam congealed on the withers and around the saddle.

The man loosened the girth a notch, then removed the pack and the shotgun in the saddle holster, laying them across the toes of his boots before tying up the reins on the horse's neck. When he stepped away, the pack in one hand and the holster in the other, they watched each other a moment.

"Get the hell out of here," he whispered, "and much obliged for the ride. You nearly fractured my butt."

The horse stared at him pensive, then stretched tentatively toward the roadside grass. Putting the pack and holster down again, the man slipped his belt out with a practiced gesture, hesitated with the buckle end, then struck the horse with the flat across the rump. The blow cracked like a pistol shot among the dry autumn trees, catching up with the falling ice of its echo the shriek of a bluejay and the hollow ringing of the horse's hoofs moving around the bend of the highway and away inland.

They'll never catch *that* son-of-a-bitch, even if they see him, not if he goes the way we came, he thought, grinning ruefully as his fingers found a cigarette, bent and broken, and tossed it away.

Seizing up his belongings, he moved on an angle off the road and into the woods on the inland side, striking in a hundred yards before he shifted step and paralleled the highway toward the village. Where the low sun pierced the branches from the east, the gray dawn air was fused with gold. The woods floor was soggy with autumn rains, and as his nostrils warmed from the long cold ride, he scented the mildewed humus of the leaves, sharp and strong and seasoned with the odor of clean wood. He went swiftly but not hurriedly, a man of middle height in khaki pants and boots, with lank lion-colored hair over eyebrows much darker, and a wide thin mouth under flaring startled nostrils which lent his face an odd expression, humorous and angry at once. His steps were quick and tight, and although the pack and holster were slung across his narrow shoulders, his arms did not swing as he walked. The right arm was carried forward and slightly higher than the left, like the wing of a crippled hawk.

A half hundred yards from the roadhouse he crossed the highway to the shore side and Abraham's Path, pausing there a moment to study the square black country cars parked in sullen servility around a new convertible. He stepped back unconsciously when the roadhouse door swung open and several men stepped out, calling back to someone inside. They were dressed for hunting, and he recognized two of them, Bart Shipman and the Portagee, Joe Ferrari; he had fished with both of them on a Shipman trawler. Joe Ferrari belched loudly, a sound like tearing canvas, and the other man slapped him on the back.

The sound of their laughter disturbed him, he wanted to go up to them, go in and have a cup of coffee, maybe ham and eggs. Coffee and toast, and a chance to sit a minute where it was warm.

Thinking about the warmth, he shivered in the field jacket. Maybe when they were gone he would go in, because the Greek didn't know him from a hole in the ground, and he could leave the pack and gun behind a tree. The goddamned gun, he'd be all right but for that, he should have sent it back on the horse. Nobody'd catch that horse until they closed the door of his stall on him. Look at those guys, they think they're really comical, really big time. They were all right, though, he'd had fun with them, sort of, the poor rubes. Hell. It was funny the way a guy couldn't depend on anything to last, like the guys who were buddies in the foxholes and swore they'd live in the same town when they got home, and by the time the ship hit the Golden Gate, they couldn't even remember the other bastard's name. Finnegan, that was Charlie's name, though. Or was it Flannagan? Whatever his name was, Charlie got run over in a gutter the first night in the States, and he hadn't even gone to visit him in the hospital. And Charlie wouldn't even have helped *him* out of the gutter, for Christ's sake.

The door opened again and George McConville came out. He nodded to the other men, they spoke to him casually, and then he got into the convertible and drove away toward the village, bypassing the road out to the Point.

Well I'll be damned, the man thought. I'll be goddamned.

He turned abruptly and headed into Abraham's Path. It was indistinct in its outer reaches and he moved slowly at first, letting the wooded edges, the tree placement, the breaks of sky seep from his memory, moving faster as he caught the sense of the wood like an odor out of the past, in a long loping Indian stride, knees bent, feet pigeontoed and low to the ground, so that the dead sticks were turned like plowed earth rather than stepped on. He passed through the coppered woods and down the laurel slope to the marsh, where a pair of blue-wing teal jumped from the reeds

at his feet, scaring up a black duck farther out, and a bittern
which flapped in the wake of the ducks like an old brown nurse.
Farther along the dark edge of the water he came upon wide footprints and two red shells, and paused, tossing the shells in his
hand. From the sweet gunpowder smell of them, he knew they
had been fired the day before, and he also knew from the absence
of tracks leading into the shallow water that the hunter had
missed. He skirted the old blind at the heel of the marsh, it had
been rebuilt but badly camouflaged, and mounted the short slope
into the woods again. The path was now clearly defined, for somebody had used it from the Point.

From the edge of the field, he studied the caretaker's cottage.
Fifty yards away, no more, he could probably make it without
being seen, and the barren windows told of no inhabitants. Home,
he thought, switching his gaze immediately to the brown house
high on the headland. It was still, completely still, as houses rarely
are, and the smoke from its chimney hung warm and clean as
cotton against the bright ocean sky beyond.

He crossed the wet place, trotting rapidly to the rear of the cottage. The windows were locked, but there was an outside cellar
trap door slanted low against the planking. There was a padlock
on it. He wrenched this off, the lock hinge pulling easily from
the rotten nail holes, and stepped down the stairway slippery with
dead leaves, the weight of the door on his palm as it closed over
his head, the other hand already feeling for the wall. He made his
way through the darkness, boots sloshing in the cellar rainwater,
and up the steps more ladder than stair which led to the ground
floor. The door was open. Carefully he stepped into the kitchen,
catching his breath on the humid cold of the place, and crossed
to the window facing the McConville house. The smoke had not
stirred. He unshouldered the pack and the gun and placed them

in a corner, runting into the pack for the stale chunk of bread from the night before. On the backs of his fingers, the kiss of the service .38 was icy. He drew it out, turned it over in his hand, and put it back again, taking the bread and stepping toward the front room as he ate it.

The front door of the cottage was open.

He started back, then stopped. Nobody. The cottage had four rooms, no second story, he would have heard any footsteps on the bare warped floor. In the corner of the room, draped on a saw-horse, was a small-mesh gill net, the heavy anchoring lines at each end of it dark and raw with fresh sand and the net itself still tattered with kelp. Beside the sawhorse hung a fisherman's full-length overall, complete with cutting knife.

A distant door slammed, and Daniel Barleyfield appeared over the hill. He was carrying a suitcase, the net anchors, and a yellow sou'wester, and stumbling under the weight and his haste. The man stepped back into the kitchen, waiting until Daniel had plunged into the room, dropped his burden with the other gear, and puffing, started out again, before crossing under cover of the other's clatter and leaning with his feet on the sill as Daniel turned to close the door.

"You better hurry, Daniel," he said. "George is on his way out here."

Daniel's hand fell back to his side, but his face showed no surprise, showed nothing at all. They watched each other, and the man took a noisy bite from his bread.

"You forgotten me?" he said.

"No." Daniel stood motionless. "I thought you were workin' over at Mister Murray's."

"You don't look very glad to see me."

"I ain't," Daniel said. He seemed to be waiting for something.

"Nothin' personal, Cady," he added. "I just don't feel good when you're around."

"Nothing personal about *that*," Cady Shipman grinned. He wrenched another mouthful of bread and, chewing, said, "What a way to treat your long lost stepbrother on his homecoming." But Daniel's words had bothered him, and there returned the bitterness he had felt against the men at the roadhouse, against all people he had known. It was as if they judged him for something in himself he did not understand or even admit which made him prefer to live alone. And he hated them for making him prefer it, then holding him responsible.

Daniel said, "I'm just surprised, I gis." He smiled abruptly and held out his hand. "Shake," he said.

Cady took his time, still chewing, then glancing at Daniel, picked the hand out of the air as if it belonged to neither of them, studying the olive-brown flesh against his own for a moment before dropping it unshaken. He glanced at Daniel's eyes again, there was a lot there now, a blink, a flicker, a hard glow like the eye of a tomcat stalking. How different from another time, another year at Easter twilight, when Eve had gone, had left him alone with Daniel

His back was stiff and throbbing again from Percy Shipman's beating, and he stood impatient over the smaller boy who rose from the weeds, a gaudy tin can in his hand, rose very slowly, solemnly, and backed away.

"C'mon," Cady said. "I just want to see where you buried the cat, that's all. C'mon."

"I didn't tell, honest I didn't, Cady, you can ask—"

"I'm not going to hurt you. C'mon. I'll show you where the rookery's at, even, the herons'll be north any day now, you can show the kids at school. C'mon."

"I seen the rookery. Sam showed me. I buried him under that big tree down by the marsh. I don't wanna go. I—"

"C'mon," Cady said. He seized Daniel's hand and led him toward the woods. A robin gave its strident alarm, fleeing gray-backed before them into the twilight, and the April wind tossed the blackening treetops. "I'm scared." Daniel had to trot to keep up. He had one hand shoved in his pocket and moved very clumsily. "I gotta pee," he said. "Pee, then." They waited while he peed. Then he ran, and Cady caught him. "I'm scared," Daniel said. He was crying now. "You weren't scared this morning when you told Pa on me." "I didn't tell, I didn't. I told him I found it in the weeds, honest I did." Daniel was stumbling on purpose, and dragging his feet. "C'mon," Cady said.

They passed the great tree where the cat was buried. "That's where he is," Daniel said. "I wanna go home now." A barred owl mothed out over their heads, its round wings billowing the soft swamp air, and Daniel fell down sobbing. He would not get up.

"You want me to leave you here alone, or are you coming with me?"

The smaller boy rose and took Cady's hand, crying back over his shoulder as Cady led him past the place where the path turned uphill again into the woods toward the highway, making his way along the fringe of the marsh through tangles of dead underbrush and briars, Daniel wailing hopelessly into the gloom when the briars raked him, and Cady cursing. They came at last to a hollow wood, a grove of leaf-stripped spectres whose tentacles, guano white, clutched black shapes like monstrous insects in a web of night, and the white trunks rose from the rotten floor of foliage like spirits on a far forgotten battlefield. On the sea horizon, low to the dunes which ended the marsh, the black clouds hurried in late chastened streamers on the wind, but in the rookery no air moved, no life, no sound, nothing but white decay and the acid stench of carpeted offal beneath them, and the breathing of the other. "How do you like it?" Cady whispered. In the stillness, his voice transfixed itself in the vacuum above their heads. Daniel did not answer. He had sunk to his knees, eyes rabbit-wide and both hands clutched to the sleeve of Cady's sweater. "You were lying," Cady said. "Sammy Sissypants never brought you here. Get up outa that birdcrap, you'll get all white. You were lying, weren't you? You're always lying, and getting me in trouble, you little sneak. Aren't you? I said, aren't you?"

"Yes," Daniel breathed. "Please, Cady, please . . . home . . . please, oh please."

"You stay here and close your eyes," Cady whispered, already backing away, "and in a minute we'll go home again."

"Please oh please oh please oh please." But Daniel had closed his eyes, holding his hands out before him as in a dark corridor. From behind a near tree, Cady could see his silhouette, it had taken on the praying stillness of the grove. He waited, uneasy himself, looking over his shoulder every few moments, and at the creak of steps through the white wood his heart pounded loudly enough to be heard by whatever was coming after them.

In endless seconds it appeared, crossing in front of Daniel's statue on delicate hooves, a little buck which loomed enormous, its antlers etched on the pallid background. It's beautiful, Cady thought, and then, if only I had my .22, what an easy shot, and then, why doesn't Daniel see him, he must hear him. In the breath of the moment Cady forgot the punishment, he wanted Daniel to see the buck, tick, tick, tick, its hooves pierced the tinder leaves, and then it halted, turned its head. It would go in a moment. "Danny!" he whispered, "Quick! Take a look!" The air was raw with the whirling crash of the buck's escape, and Daniel's screams were neat white clips hewn from a birch tree, clean terror screams pure of thought, and then there was silence.

Cady peered after the buck, then softly rose and padded into the open.

Daniel was gone.

He listened, frightened now, alone in the skeletal wood and the night beyond it, until from the direction they had come he caught the high choked crying of the running boy, his course already a distance away toward Abraham's Path.

He'll lose the path, Cady thought, he'll fall into the marsh, plunging himself through the underbrush and onto the path, pursuing his quarry on winged night-time feet, stopping again to listen, going on.

Daniel had fallen on the path, the weakness of terror caving his legs, and lay run to earth like an animal, waiting. Cady approached him in silence, tasting the power like hot blood in his mouth, gritting his teeth in hatred of Daniel for making him feel ashamed. "Get up," he said, and the boy thrashed to his feet, his briar-striped legs already running from Cady, who caught him in a stride. "You see the buck?" he said. He took the little boy's hand and led him out of the woods. "Don't tell," he said. "Maybe you learned your lesson now." Daniel backed away from him, then turned and ran

He won't run any more, though, Cady Shipman thought, sensing an odd satisfaction in his brother's dislike, his *brother*, for God's sake, a stupid illegitimate Indian picked up out of charity, or maybe idiocy on the part of Percy.

"What kind of a handshake is that?" Daniel muttered. "I ain't your goddamn servant, Cady."

"I know it," Cady said. "You're George's goddamn servant."

"I'm his caretaker. I could throw you off this place for trespassing."

Cady looked him up and down. "I don't think you could," he said, "and even if you could, I wouldn't try it." He nodded in the direction of the fishing gear in the corner. "Who's George paying you to fish with, the Shipmans?"

Daniel looked at his gear as if he hadn't seen it before. "That's just stuff I keep down here out of the way. I ain't fishin' right now with nobody."

Cady took another bite on his bread. "You always were a liar," he chewed, "always. And I suppose you're going to tell me it wasn't you shooting down by the marsh yesterday, even though you've got that black mud all over your boots."

Daniel looked startled, glancing swiftly at his boots, then back at Cady. "George don't mind me shootin' there. What the hell are you after, anyway?"

Cady nodded at the gear again. "I'll tell you when I'm good and ready, okay, Daniel?" Daniel said nothing, his face expressionless again. "And in the meantime, don't go telling people I'm here, including George."

"Why?" Daniel said. He cocked his head a little, not quite smiling.

"Why? Because maybe I want to surprise him, that's why."

"That the only reason?"

"That's the only reason you're going to get."

Daniel's eyes winked sleepily, he was smiling at something over Cady's shoulder. "You ain't changed a bit, Cady," he said. "You're as full of it as ever, ain't you."

"Just about," Cady said. "Just about." He stepped abruptly into the yard, expecting Daniel to flinch. Daniel did not stir. His big hands hung loose, too loose, at his sides. Cady eyed him. "You think I was going to swing on you?" he whispered.

"I think you know better." Daniel's smile was broad. "Hokay.

You forget you seen the fishin' gear, I'll forget I seen you." He
turned and went away up the slope toward the house.

He's changed, Cady thought, he's changed a lot. But that crazy
smile, that hasn't changed any, it makes you mad to look at it, as
if the dumb slob is laughing at you when there's nothing to laugh
about, never read a book in his life and thinks he knows all the
answers. What in hell am I doing, he thought, what am I doing
standing here in a cold cottage when a lousy Indian has the run
of the Point, when by rights I should be up there as eldest son
and heir, for God's sake, instead of sneaking around down here—
what in hell am I doing?

Or was that all a lie, and how was he ever to know? He thought
of the odd tempestuous woman who was his mother, he was sure
of *that*, at least, Sarah Shipman, daughter of a poor relation to old
Barlow. He had been seventeen, and he believed her story because
he knew her tacky snobbishness by then, knew she would rather
sin with a rich man than marry a poor one and had probably
compromised by doing both. She had howled with laughter over
it, a big-boned impressive woman, drunk or sober, "Caleb, my lad,
your mother is a lady, and if your father hadn't drowned himself,
you'd be sitting at the table up there like Little Lord Fauntleroy,
what do you think of that?" and he had stood by the kitchen
table watching her. "You might as well know it now as never,
you're the Shipman heir and you're a gentleman, what do you
think of that, hey?" And he said, "Why did you marry Percy?"
And she said, "I've just told you, your father drowned himself, and
Barlow—he had to find *somebody* to make an honest woman of
me. Besides, he wanted to sell this piece of land, which is right-
fully ours."

God, how she'd laughed, the roof had nearly fallen in, he standing by the table feeling his gut go dead in him and wanting to

knock her out of her chair, but only muttering, "So Percy's my cousin, then?" and listening to her coughing. "Percy was the black sheep of the family, or maybe what you call the sacrificial lamb!" Another shout of laughter, and then Percy was there, sallow un-impressive Percy who struck her to the floor. Lying on her back, she had laughed as she cursed them, laughter like weak sunshine in the rain. "He lets a goddamn caretaker hit his sainted mother, what kind of a little gentleman is that!" She rose and staggered to the mirror and pointed at herself, "Well, what do you think of that, hey?" before she had turned in tempest and hurled the dirty dishes at them. He'd had strands of spaghetti on his shoulder from it.

Percy had told him not to listen to her. She was sloppy drunk, he said, and then she yelled all over again. Percy was getting paid, at least, what was she getting out of it, she wanted to know? And Percy said, "Why don't you *tell* him what you're gettin' out of it, you lousy slut, tell the poor kid *that*, too." And suddenly she subsided, crying, her big breasts swollen with her sighs, one of them came out of her dress, and Cady stood still by the table blushing, saying nothing, looking at the floor and wondering if Daniel asleep in the other room had heard.

What do you think of that, hey?

He had never known what to believe. Sarah Shipman denied the whole thing the day after, saying she had only said it to tease Percy, she had been a little tipsy, as she put it, a little tipsy, and then she had looked him squarely in the face and laughed.

What do you think of that, hey? Just a little tipsy.

A savanna sparrow flicked into view, hopping fluffed across the yard. Cady watched it, breaking off a corner of his bread. When he ticked the scrap into the yard with his finger tip, the sparrow vanished, returning again in a moment alert and trim, tacking sideways in slight flutters toward the bread.

For Cady Shipman, as for George and Sam, the big house was a beginning and an ending, home in all the childhood connotations of the word, a sanctuary, a source, although his memories were less of pleasant happenings than of the pleasant anticipations which passed for them. He shared their feeling despite the fact that he did not belong to the house nor to its family. But he had spent far more time there than the other two, they had gone away to school, and he knew better everything about it. Part of the place was his because it was part of him, and his sense of belonging, even proprietorship, was reinforced by his Shipman ancestry and by the whisper of his parentage.

He thought of this now, turning his back upon the house and watching as a raft of sea ducks tattered the ocean, breaking free into the air and speckling out against the last night streaks of the further sky, a man still young but weathered of illusions who thought, if I listened to the whisper, I would live here now as Abraham Shipman's son, but the first man who throws bastardy in my face will be the last.

Caleb Shipman, Esquire. He laughed and was startled by the loudness of the sound as it wandered across the thin grass swaying toward the water. Below, the seaweed shifted here and there where the waves came broken in split white tongues and the barnacles, limpets, periwinkles held a dull purchase on their world, and he sensed unthinking, that is how it has always been, will always be, a meaningless rise and fall of everything, walking rapidly past Abraham's gravestone toward the kitchen door.

The door was open, there were warmth and coffee smell and shuffling feet which stopped as he entered the service hall, and the sleepy voice, "Who's there? You forget somethin', you crazy darlin'?"

Cady Shipman did not answer, walking down the hall in prac-

"I'm not going to harm you," Cady whispered. "You hav
crapped on me yet." The sparrow flew from the whisper but set
nearer the scrap. "Go ahead, Buddy, eat your head off. Share a
share alike, that's Cady Shipman." He grinned as the sparr
seized the scrap and fled with it. "That's it. Don't ever take ar
thing for granted, just grab it and run or you won't get it at all
He stopped grinning suddenly and, glancing at his crust of breac
dropped it to the floor and stepped on it.

Now the day was warm with the wild brilliance of October, too
warm, even, the weather would change by evening. He regarded
the big dark shingled house on the headland, then stepped into
the sunlight and moved swiftly up the hill.

Before him, the house twisted around upon itself in a broken
forest of lines, sprawling over the white drive like a dark enormous
mongrel with a bone. The rear of the house, on the ocean side, was
wind-smoothed and bland, but the misplaced Georgian front was
cluttered with a protruding kitchen area at one end, a terrace at
the other, with elaborate empty dog kennels too close to the drive,
transplanted trees long since stunted by the salt mist, and a broken
Italian nude, once a tying post for horses. The interior was as
confused as its shell, he could see its dark chaos as he passed across
the terrace and around to the seaward side, the ground floor of
clumsy rooms, uncomfortable furniture, unplayed pianos, and un-
read libraries bought wholesale by an interior decorator. On the
upper floor were human stalls, each unlikelier than the last, as if
the decorator had attacked the house as a mighty experiment and
retreated with the job half, and very badly, done. Its prevailing
condition was darkness, yet in the sheer shining mass of the bric-
a-brac and trumpery, there existed that grandeur of monumental
falseness which, in some mysterious and impractical past, had not
been false at all.

ticed silence to the kitchen, where the girl in the Navy raincoat was already coming around the table, fork in hand. They stopped when they saw each other.

"Well I'll be damned," Cady said. He studied the full smooth face above the black coat turned bathrobe, and the big eyes widening out of sleep and hardening in wariness.

"Daniel know you're here?" she said.

"Yeah," he said. Rosa turned away to put the fork back into the skillet and wipe her hands, and he watched the play of her buttocks under the black cloth, the full hips and the high breasts as she turned back again.

"You want somethin'?" she said.

"Yeah," he said. He stepped into the room and pulled a chair up to the white enameled table. "I'm hungry."

"All I got is hominy. You want that?"

"No. Hasn't Daniel got anything better for George than that?"

"We didn't know he was comin' until he called. That was late last night. Daniel's gettin' stuff this mornin', down in the village."

"I can wait," Cady said. "I'll take some coffee, though." He watched her again as she turned, his legs restless beneath the table. "You the lady of the house these days, Rosa?" he said.

"I'm clearin' out before George comes," she said, not turning.

"Okay. Nobody's to know I'm here, either." She glanced at him but said nothing. "You have anything on under that coat?" Cady said.

"Maybe I have, maybe I haven't, but don't get any ideas, Cady."

"I already got 'em," Cady grinned. "You're a very pretty piece, as I see Daniel has learned."

"Don't talk like that," she whispered. "I have one man now, and that's plenty."

"You're not married, though."

"We will be, pretty soon."

"You think George is going to like you shacking up in his house?"

"I told you I was clearin' out right away, if Daniel don't persuade Mister George to have me come in and help over the weekend, that is." She grinned briefly, turning away to the stove as if the question were settled forever, but there was tension beneath the black coat. "Anyhow, I don't think he'd mind."

"Maybe not," Cady said. "Maybe he'd be more interested in how you came by that raincoat."

"I didn't steal it! It was just rottin' away in the hall closet."

"If I were George, I wouldn't like just anybody using my coat." Cady rose from his chair and moved around the table to her, and Rosa Menhaden backed away from him, holding out the fork.

"What do you want from me?" she breathed.

"We're very good friends, remember, Rosa? The shed behind the high school?"

"Listen," she whispered, "please, Cady, I don't wanna do that, please. I got a man now, and I'm happy this way. Please."

"Nobody'll know," Cady said, following her around the table. When she got to the chair, she held it between them. "Daniel warned me about you," she gasped. "Daniel warned me. I never done nothin' to hurt you."

"I'm not going to hurt you, either," Cady Shipman said.

CHAPTER 7

GEORGE AND SAM CAME AROUND THE CORNER OF THE HOUSE, oddly small and tentative against its shuttered bulk like two vagrants wandering from the wings onto an empty stage set, idling uneasily conscious of not belonging, and sticking close together in the unnatural quiet. They wore two sets of George's hunting clothes, uniforms of heavy khaki over black boots rolled down to the knee. George's khaki was faded but Sam's was creased and orange. Its newness was garish against the weathered shingle of the house, and even his boots, worn noisily duckfoot, had the silly shine of unused things— Here, they squeaked, is a man who loathes the out-of-doors. And this was true. Sam was bored in the country, he enjoyed it only in terms, George knew, of friends and parties. With nature itself he was uncomfortable, so much of it was functional and distasteful, compromising man's refinement, like a garbage can or a deodorant. Or, as Eve in bitterness had once told George, the animal aspects of sex.

George glanced at the outlandish figure of his friend. Eve should have kept that to herself, he thought. Yet his disapproval was less with Eve's indiscretion than with the unwelcome insight it afforded him into the character of Sam, the same Sam who once had seemed to George, then timid and jealous, the most successful of lovers, strolling always on the more verdant side of their path and calling back to his plodding friend about ever new

121

forays into experience, as if George were the mundane link with convention which heightened the particular adventure and was necessary to full enjoyment of it. He remembered how women would sit up when Sam Rubicam entered a room, like big doe rabbits—he supposed Eve had been the same, goddamn it.

Eve. Evelyn Murray Rubicam. Eve is having a baby.

Everything is changing, George thought, even the weather. They were standing in silence at the edge of the lawn, hands in pockets, as if waiting for something, an impulse, a decision. It was nearly noon, and the autumn Saturday lay windless under a weakening sun, half-born and already dying, like a faint March flower. The trees in the woods by Abraham's Path stood stiff as sentinels, livened now and again by a rummaging squirrel or a breath of silent southbound birds like a ghost of spring. November was coming, the season of transition, and even the ocean, so seemingly changeless, fretted softly along the shore. Beneath their feet, the crab grass had molted here and there to winter brown, spreading away down the slope to the inlet and the marsh, from which rose now three widgeon, mounting straight for one stretched moment before leveling out over the beach and down the coast.

"At last," Sam said. "I was beginning to think we'd wandered into a wasteland of some sort, inhabited by Daniel Barleyfield."

"I know it," George said. "I know what you mean. There's something queer about today."

"Daniel said we might get a storm."

"Maybe that's it," George said. He wandered away from the conversation, turning at a little distance to regard the house. The windows on the ocean side were blinded by shutters, but as he watched, one shutter creaked open, he glimpsed a man's hand and thought, it's Daniel, airing rooms. Then the window closed, staring blankly down upon him as on a stranger.

Even the house was changing for him. A whole feeling for the place was missing—something to do, he thought, with no longer being anxious to refind and explore the rooms, as he had each visit since early childhood—a bright thread slipped from a fine warm weave of dream and association, leaving it colder, less familiar.

"Remember the time we went rabbit shooting at night, from the car?" Sam called. "One sitting on the hood and blazing away, and the other driving and drinking simultaneously? And we made car tracks all over the lawn, and wound up with the car stuck in the wet place by the woods?"

"I thought I did that with Cady," George said.

"No, just you and me, remember? And your old man got wind of it, he was in New York, and told me I couldn't come down from school for Christmas vacation?"

"Are you sure? I could have sworn I did that with Cady." Stop it, George told himself, what does it matter, why are you being such a—

"Me," Sam said, as if he were trying to identify himself with a friendship and a home in which he had no confidence, and George glanced at him, ashamed. He tried to focus on his own reasons for denying this part of their past to Sam so stubbornly, abusively even. I am sorry for him, and I don't want to be, George sensed, I want to tell him how much he has, how much he could do, how I have emulated him, inadmissably and always. But he would only laugh, embarrassed, and say, cut it out, and I don't want him to say that, I want him enduring, standing for something, if only for the part of him in myself.

He shook his mind free of this progression, as Sam repeated, "Me. I've spent a little time down here, remember?"

"I know that. I just couldn't remember about the particular time, that's all. I did it another time with Eve."

Sam paused, then said with viciousness, "I even spent my honeymoon down here. In the master bedroom." He smiled.

They regarded each other full in the face, each recognizing the widening cleft between them, each rushing to close it, the door on a disclosure too personal to be discovered which the viewer persuades himself he has not seen. Sam blurted, "The place means a great deal to me, George, that's all," and George flushing, "It should, it's your home, isn't it?" Both were relieved. George watched him try to suppress the grin which swam for a moment out onto his face. In the deep dark eyes in the narrow forehead, the happiness was genuine.

George searched for another topic but was unable to find one. He was bothered at the same instant that he and Sam should suffer an awkward pause at all, and thought once more about the change in both of them.

"It was fun, though, that rabbit shoot," Sam's voice concluded.

Of course it was fun, George said to himself, you don't have a place like the Point and not have fun at it. That would be against the rules, it would kill free enterprise and advertising, the American dream or something. But they had all been moving forward then, the world was real before the war. And war had been the greatest reality of all, but when it was over, reality was gone.

Is nothing left to be done, he wondered, but go through the motions, follow others' footprints through the snow? Surely this was an era of shame, it floated in the atmosphere like heavy lint, we sit around like diseased monkeys and pick it off each other.

Cyrus McConville had never felt ashamed. He knew what he wanted of life, and he didn't need to know the reasons, or know himself, for that matter. He would damn us for a pack of good-for-nothings, and perhaps we are, yapping at the tires of other people's progress, choking up their dust before wandering whining

back down the road to the past, or outward into the bogs and by-
ways of the isms, but never forward—categorized, predictable, and
desperate only to eke out our days not as ourselves but as society
chooses to tolerate us.

Perhaps he wanted it that way, like all the others. He thought
of Eve, whose present dependence on him had reawakened a
doubt nearly vanquished. Given another year, he was sure, all his
misgivings, frustrations, depressions, and ideals could have safely
been assigned to a youthful phase. "Why, I thought like that
when I was a youngster, too!"—he could hear his father now. It
was appalling, the eager acceptance of relativism, of rationalization,
and yet how safe it was, after all, how very tempting.

"It really was fun," Sam's voice said. He was peering at George
in expectation of a corroboratory remark about what fun it all had
been.

"You look like hell in that outfit," he said to Sam, and forced a
laugh.

"You bought these duds, not me," Sam said. "There's no accounting for tastes." He glared at the orange khaki in alarm,
holding a fold of it between thumb and forefinger like the tail of
a dead mouse. "I feel like a character part in a musical comedy,
you've made a figure of fun out of me." He cocked his head then,
squinting. "You, on the other hand, cut a pretty salty figure. It's
too bad Cady isn't here to show you up, decked out in his leathern
buckskin or whatever it is these local types are supposed to wear."

"I wish he was here, at that," George said.

"Good God! Why?"

"I don't know, the place isn't the same without him, I suppose.
He's part of the atmosphere down here, whether you like him or
not. Take an attractive girl, for example, if you take away her
little faults, what have you left?"

"All right, take Eve, for example," Sam said.

"Let's not."

"Let's. I suppose you would be grieved if she lost her pig-headedness. Or the mole on her behind, say."

"Yes, I would. She wouldn't be Eve any more, without her temper."

"Or the mole—"

"Or the mole."

"Then you like the mole?"

"I love the mole, as it happens."

"You love the mole. I mean, it's a perfectly good mole, if you happen to love moles. You might write an ode, 'Ode to a Mole.' 'O, round, brown sculptured mole, Perched high upon the thigh of my be-loved . . .'" Sam strolled toward the rim of the slope, waving one hand against the sky, holding the other to his heart. When George said nothing, only watched him, Sam turned and stopped, and they regarded each other candidly at a little distance.

Why should everything happen at once, George wondered, the change in friendships, the change in the house, Eve having a baby—Eve having a baby, that was the main thing. God.

Sam Rubicam came toward him across the lawn.

"Or you might say," Sam started, "'O round brown mole, perched thither upon the withers of my Be-loved . . .'"

"I'm going down to the beach," George told him.

"Speaking of thighs," Sam said, "I saw a very pretty pair of them twinkle down the hall a little while ago. A little heavy for my liking, but one could make do, no doubt. Whose were they?"

"That's Daniel's girl, Rosa," George said, moving on.

His glance invited Sam to stay behind as he repeated, "I'm going down to the beach."

Sam Rubicam raised his eyebrows but did not comment. When

George turned away down the slope, he said, "I'm staying here," and laughed.

The path to the ocean paralleled the inlet, descending the low bluff to the flecked sand waste behind the dunes, where it disappeared. A number of ducks rose with his coming, taking the widgeon's path down the coast toward the south, where Cady had told him they would veer in again and light in the brackish ponds near the highway. The small duck, the wood duck and the teal, mounted sometimes against the trees and dropped back behind the horizon branches into black woodland potholes, but today they followed the others, in clumps of threes and fours, out over the beach against the sky.

George McConville descended to the water's edge, his black boots heavy in the sand, and stared at the sea which nuzzled the sand, apathetic, boneless, a sour silent sea like a populace in a city place, sullen and waiting for an event which it knows ahead of time will anger it, will turn the picking fidgeting quiet to a turmoil of noise and destruction, a storm. There will be a storm, he thought, he could feel its first soft breath at the neck of his shirt.

A small wave rose to surround his feet, plucking at him as it withdrew, tentatively, a beggar's hand, and his heels sank further into the sand. He stood immobile as the tide mounted, drew back and came again, in inches and minutes like the time of life, pushing pulling, sucking at his heels as he stood transfixed by the ocean nothingness, losing his thought in the passing time as he might before a fire, before a windfilled forest, before anything moving in a rhythm deeper than his own, the fish in a sea pool or the herring gulls sailing, losing his thought because he wanted, however briefly, to feel at peace, at one with simple existence. To be a part of things was not to be lonely. So long as he did not think, he was part of the sea world, standing on the edge of its fastnesses, if only because this small part of it must fold its tongue about him, and the sand must erode and fill in over his feet, and hold him.

When he thought again, the water was at his knees, pressing the cooled black boots to his calves and washing up the beach for several yards behind him. He turned to go back and his weight, caught at its base by the sand now above his ankles, pitched him down on his hands into the water. He wrenched free with violence and, gathering his legs beneath him, rose and floundered out onto the beach.

Sitting down and drawing off the boots, he regarded the sea, which had crept up on him in stealth. Its water poured from the boots and made its way over the hard sand to its source

There was a time when things had been uncomplicated. Sam was off on his affair with Celia, and George and Eve, more innocent, were taking long walks on this very beach, and dreaming, and touching cautiously when all alone. It had been beautiful, melancholy and beautiful. At eighteen melancholy and beauty were still enough. But then he had gone into the service, and while in training had made by mail a decision with Eve they had not quite wanted to make when together and happy. Perhaps, in the ugliness of his new environment, George had to prove himself a man, and perhaps Eve was afraid that otherwise she would lose him to an older woman. The reasons do not matter, but the decision lost them something they would never have again.

George could remember sensing this, riding north on furlough in the train. But he dismissed his misgivings as nervousness, which was justified in part, and never imagined that he would lose her. Five years later, finding her again, he remembered all too clearly what had happened.

Upon leaving the train, he had washed and shaved in the

terminal latrine, then made his way uptown. Despite the pictures in his billfold, he had lost the feeling of her appearance and was startled by the creature who met him in the hotel lobby, the beauty of that wonderfully virginal resolute face beneath the bamboo hood of hair but also—and perhaps it was this that frightened him a little—the confidence she radiated that they would spend that night together which would have been brazen could she have kept her hands still on her purse.

"George," she whispered. Her smile was their secret, and he fumbled for the key.

"Hi," George said, kissing her uncertainly.

She glanced at his suitcase, then quickly away. "How about a drink?" he said. They fled the suitcase, pushing it at the porter on the way into the bar. Eve chose a table in the corner, and they talked about the months since they had seen each other, laughing much more loudly and frequently than was necessary.

"Well," Eve said, at last.

"Well," George said. "How are you?"

"Fine. How are you?" She had a way of saying this which made it an important question.

"Fine," he said.

She held her cocktail glass like a shield between them, and there was a silence. "Your uniform is terribly becoming, George."

"Listen, Eve, we should think about where to go," he blurted, and reached immediately for a cigarette. "Do you still want to—?"

"I think we should go to some little place on the West Side," she said immediately, blushing with him. "Quieter and less crowded."

"Less chance of getting caught, you mean. How'd you find that out?"

"A friend."

"What friend?"

"Just a friend," Eve said, and smiled mysteriously.

"All right," he said. "It makes no difference to me." He reached under the table and scratched his ankle, restraining the annoyance so alien to the occasion.

"What's the matter, darling? Are you angry about something?"

"No," he said. The alarm in her tone lessened the sense of inadequacy the intrusion of her friend had encouraged in him, and now he fought her for control. "I think we should drink quite a lot," he told her. "It helps."

"Helps what?"

"Beginners," George said, and smiled as mysteriously as he knew how.

"Who says so?"

"A friend," George said.

"Don't be mean, George," she begged him, lowering her glass to the table. Repentant, he laughed and squeezed her hand.

But later, as the taxi rushed them through the park, leaning back in their seats like two children rowing against the wind, George wanted to cry out his desire to default. He sensed she was going through with this out of love for him, out of what she imagined to be her duty, and he suspected her of nursing the moral considerations in the sanctity of her corner. Because he could not run, he longed for the feeling that the whole affair was done with, and to his credit, realizing in a stab of uncynical perception that this feeling was what, originally, he had desired most of all.

The cab driver left them at Sixty-fifth Street and Central Park West, looking back over his shoulder as he drove away. George was sure that their mission had been discovered. This ill-lighted neighborhood awaited with bated breath the one false move which would wreak disaster upon them. He imagined the discreet innuendoes of the house detective, the search for the wedding license, and finally the faraway siren of the vice squad and the astounded voice of Joshua Murray over the telephone. Paused on the corner, George did his best to ridicule these thoughts, but he could not bring himself to laugh. Staring abstracted at the girl beside him, he was startled by the sudden wedding ring upon her finger.

"Come on," Eve said to him nervously, a little irritatedly, he thought. He led her into Sixty-fifth Street, where the hotels they came upon at last were full. The situation was contrary to the experience of Eve's friend, and George berated the friend and then Eve herself until she stopped and said she would go no further if this was the way he was going to behave. George said that she was only looking for an excuse to back out, but the charge was so true of both of them that they were startled by it and went on.

Eve would not walk with him but only behind him, a sign that the responsibility was now entirely his. He felt alone with the two guilty suitcases, and her presence in the rear was less a support than a reproach. Back somewhere along the dim brownstone steps the last glow of adventure had been extinguished, replaced by a nervous illicit feeling.

George listened to his shoes against the concrete. They went reluctantly, going nowhere. When he walked faster, they seemed to run away from him, and when he slowed, Eve would ask him a pointless question from behind or demand a cigarette. Then they were forced to stop and look at one another.

Eve said she was getting tired.

George, conscious of the weight of the two suitcases, asked her what she wanted him to do about it.

Eve said she just happened to mention she was getting tired, and why couldn't he be helpful instead of disagreeable?

George said he was tired, too. They journeyed on.

At the fifth hotel, the Hotel Clarence, Eve came in with him and stood by the two suitcases near the door. He lit a cigarette, sure now that she looked too young to be anybody's wife even though her nails were manicured. Her left shoe, casually perched on top of her suitcase, failed to draw attention from her panic.

The lobby was yellow and musty but brightly lit. Its odor was of crowded people although the sole inhabitant was a colored man who stood behind a desk-switchboard arrangement in one corner. He was reading a magazine and did not look at them.

George glanced at Eve, who looked away. He stepped forward. "We've just come in from the country," he started, "and can't find a room, and we were wondering . . ."

"How long you want it for?" the man said. He did not look up, but turned a page of the magazine.

"Oh, just one night," George said. "We're just here for one night."

"I'm full up, soldier," the man said, lifting his head, "but if you want to wait a little while, you can have a room for a couple of hours." The thin tan eyes appraised George over the desk. He was a tall Negro, very pale, dressed in a maroon shirt buttoned to the throat. On the breast pocket of the shirt was stitched, in vermilion thread, the name "Clarence." From beneath the desk rose Clarence's hand and ran its finger tips slowly and delicately over the lettering.

A full dark woman appeared from a back hallway, leading a mocha poodle which carried its head too close to the floor. She was swinging a patent leather purse from her free arm like a little girl, and smiled with genuine admiration at Eve Murray.

"George," Eve said.

"I don't get you," George told Clarence truthfully.

"All right," Clarence said, and now he was looking at the mocha poodle. "I told you I was full up, but if you want to wait a little while, they's a room will be free for a couple of hours. Maybe more, if you need it."

The woman's laugh was deep and friendly. "These kids ain't that type, Clarence," she said. "They're class. They even got bags."

"They don't belong in here, then," Clarence said to her. He paused. "I spoke to you already once about that dog."

George understood then, he cursed himself for his stupidity, but he did not move. He watched the woman, wondering if the Negro had insulted Eve and whether he should say anything. He decided against it, observing the woman's heavy coquetry as she said, "Take it easy, Clarence, Edith don't do no harm."

"I spoke to you already once," Clarence said, fingering the lettering. His voice was stubborn and very quiet, as if he were recounting an injustice.

"She's named after Edith Piaf, the French chan-teuse," the woman confided to Eve. Eve tried to smile without appearing tarnished.

"We wanted a room for the night," George said, to the woman this time.

"Sure, honey," the woman said, and winked. "They want a room for the night, Clarence."

"They all do," Clarence said, unsmiling. "I'm runnin' this hotel," he told the woman, "and I ain't goin' to fool no more with that dog."

"How about the room?" George said.

"Look," the woman said, "I'll just leave Edith here behind the door, Clarence, and get her later."

"No you won't," Clarence said, without raising his voice. "You leave it there, and you're gonna find it out in the street, along with all your trash. I spoke to you once already."

"Please, George," Eve said.

"I guess we'd better go someplace else," George said. He glanced at the suitcase, overcome with the inertia of failure.

"I don't have to take your lip," the woman said to Clarence. "You're forgettin' your goddamn place."

"I already forgot it. You don't have to stay here, neither."

"Don't hold ya breath until ya see me in here again!" the woman glared. She flounced out the door, dragging the mocha poodle. George watched her go.

"I already spoke to her," Clarence complained.

"I know," George said.

"You don't want that room, then."

"I guess we'd better look someplace else," George said. But he dreaded the street, and turned to Eve for support. Her shoe still propped on her suitcase, she stood like a foolish figurine, as if a touch would shatter her into a ruin of emotion. "I guess we'd better look someplace else," he repeated, at a loss to comfort her.

"That's the best I can do," Clarence said. He followed George's gaze to the girl, then added in a softer tone, "You come to the wrong place, soldier."

"Well," George said. "Thanks a lot anyway."

"Wait a minute," Clarence said. He moved slowly from behind the desk and went down the hallway. "Come in here," his voice came back.

Eve had retreated outside. She was watching George through the revolving door, as if he were in a cage. If only she were older, more adaptable, he thought, then she could see how colorful the situation was, and they could laugh about it.

"Come in here." Clarence's voice was peevish.

George glanced at Eve with a just-a-minute expression, then hurried back along the hallway. Clarence was standing inside a large room, contemplating it, his thin back to the door. The room, entirely furnished in the maroon color of his shirt, looked quiet and unused, as if it did not belong to the hotel at all but only to their imagination. Clarence said in a savage whisper, "I don't rent *this* room out to them whores, not even for a half hour," and fingered the lettered name on his breast pocket. "I wanted a nice place, a nice hotel," he added as if to himself.

"It's a nice room," George said. "Only I guess Eve wants to go." In the silence he watched the other with curiosity. This man's pathos, like the prostitute's pride, was a chink of light through a door he had never opened. He paused, his hand on the latch, forgetting Eve in the excitement of new experience.

"All right," Clarence said. George followed him back to the lobby, moved and somehow elated.

"I did the best I could," Clarence said, in the doorway.

"I know," George said absently. He saw Eve watching him but did not notice the cab in the street behind her. "There's a room . . ." he started, without enthusiasm. "Get my bag, George," Eve said. She was crying.

George went back inside, where the two suitcases crouched at angles to each other. He picked up Eve's and returned to the street. "Come on," her voice said, remote in the far dark corner of the cab. "Where's your bag?" But he knew she wanted him to close the cab door, and he did not want to suffer with her the retreat across the Park. He leaned inside and kissed her startled mouth with a confidence he had never known with her before. "I didn't know, George, I just didn't know," she whispered. "It shouldn't start like this, that's all."

He pressed her fisted hand. "I'm going to get another cab," he told her. "Maybe I'll have a drink somewhere or something. I'll call you tomorrow." She nodded, not caring, and he closed the door.

The driver's profile announced that an address had already been given. He stepped back onto the sidewalk. The cab, easing back into the night time, seemed to take part of him with it, as if he were watching, long ago, a childhood self driven off to school.

"Where's she going?" Clarence was leaning in the doorway.

"Home," George said. He got his bag and came outside again.

"Jesus," Clarence said. "I did the best I could."

"I know," George said. "Thanks a lot." He walked down the late lonely street toward Broadway.

On the corner the dark woman was swinging her purse. She was still muttering, but returned his nod when he paused. "What happened to Edith Piaf?" he said.

"Aw, I left her with my girl friend. An old one that ain't hustlin' no more. They get along good, her and Edith." She looked at him. "So what didja do with that little doll, push her into a manhole or somethin'?"

"She went home. Didn't feel well."

"Can ya beat that! Class, though, like I'm tellin' ya somethin' ya didn't know awready. That goddamn Clarence, he don't know who he's talkin' to. Park Avenue, I bet."

"Yes."

"Can you beat that!" The woman shook her head. "Poor little doll. So where you off to, soldier?"

"Nowhere. I mean, I haven't got any plans."

"Ya wanna go someplace together?" Her voice assumed a grotesque coyness. "I think you're kinda cute."

"All right." The very coarseness of the woman attracted him, the gross carnal carriage of her, and her friendliness, almost motherly, eased his nervousness. How much more frightened had he been with Eve, whom he had always known, and who loved him! He offered the woman a cigarette, and she put it into the patent leather purse. A taxi cruised past them, slowed, then went on. The woman said, "Ya got any dough, honey? I mean, let's don't kid ourselves."

"How much did you have in mind?"

"Fifteen. That's for all night, and you'll get ya money's worth, too. I got what ya might call a professional pride about it if ya know what I mean. Ya can ask anybody about Gloria, they'll tell ya." She took his arm, and they started off down Broadway under the naked street lights.

"Wadja say ya name was, honey?"

"George," he said. "My name is George

In the afternoon, George and Sam went hunting. They went in a bright green skiff belonging to Daniel Barleyfield, an old skiff, not in years, but because it had been built of old pieces of things. The interior was a scrapheap of odds and ends, but the outer hull looked clean and new, the brightest green they had ever seen. Daniel claimed it was luminous in the dark, "heaven green" he called it, laughing his odd high laugh as pure as another man's crying.

"It's called the 'Fishing Fool,'" he said, backing away and shaking more laughter out of his head like bright glass out of a bag, as if the business of living was too complicated to fathom but certainly amusing, not caring that their laughter was indulgent nor whether they laughed at all.

George pushed it out into the shallow inlet from the ocean, managing its crude scull from the stern, which rose precipitously

against the weight of Sam and the canvas sack of decoy ducks
lodged firmly in the bow. They made their way across the open
water, headed back inland from the house into the marsh, pushing into the reeds again on the far side of the inlet, where a water
path opened up like a corridor before them, and the ducks rose in
singles and pairs above the marsh grass ahead.

Sam Rubicam was thrashing furiously with his shotgun, twisting
around to get a shot at the ducks and aiming finally at a slow
short bird which fluttered up nearby.

"Let it go," George whispered. "You shoot the birds out, they
won't come back, not this afternoon, anyway."

"Okay, mate," Sam said, adding, "You've cheated me out of the
first easy shot I've ever had."

"It wasn't even a duck," George said. "It was a rail bird, a
clapper rail."

"It flies, doesn't it?" Sam demanded. "I'm no ornithologist, for
God's sake. If I hit something, I'll eat it. All it's got to do is fly."

They pushed ahead across the marsh, crossing sudden pools and
alleys, working back toward the damp woodland which made the
inland border. Daniel had rebuilt the blind, a crude jutting platform sided by reed-draped brush, beneath which the skiff could
disappear. Before it lay the broadest pool in the marsh, baited with
duck rice and bottom grass. George landed Sam on the platform
with the shotguns and shells, then sculled around to the front to
lay out the decoys. They were heavy wooden birds, each with a
line and lead anchor, and he set them in a lifelike pattern, grouped
as Cady once had shown him.

Sam Rubicam heckled him from the blind.

"Get the hell out of the way," he said. "I want to practice up
on the decoys."

"Stool," George said. "You call them stool when they're set out like that."

"*I* don't," Sam said. "Stool means something quite different to me, quite different, I don't care to talk about it, even."

"If you don't stop jumping around in the blind, there'll be nothing left of it."

"There wasn't much to start with. I've got claustrophobia in here."

"Talk in a whisper, at least. There won't be a duck for miles around." George pulled the last of the decoys from the sack and tossed it far out on one wing of the pattern, the splash ricocheting on the now silent marsh and sending centrifugal wrinkles whispering into the reeds, still golden in the sinking sun of the afternoon. He drew the skiff around behind the brushy platform and slid it beneath, then climbed into the blind.

"I'm trigger happy," Sam whispered. "I'm going to open up on something any moment."

The blind was warm in the sun, which stole upon the marsh like a weak creeping thing, pursued by the shadow of twilight. The night was already roused in the trees at their backs and readied itself to follow the twilight in the great circling hunt of the hours. The time passed softly and peacefully as they peered out over the water and the grassy waste, their faces two white patches not quite lost in the scene, like egrets frozen at the border of a slough.

Cramped in his hideout, the protecting trees behind and the un-navigable open before him, George experienced a sort of animal safety, the snug well-being, as he imagined it, that the fox must have when deep in its earth or the snake in its sunny wall. He pressed his face in unconscious ecstasy into the papered leaves of the dead branches, drawing from their faint dry odor a sense of permanence, and prayed that Sam, shifting uneasily beside him,

would not shatter the spell of the haven with his nonsense. He
had told him to be quiet, however, and Sam was quiet, searching
the sky as if his life depended on it.

Far away to their left, the roof of the house was screened by the
much nearer branches of the woods, but the slope to the dunes
was plainly visible, meeting the horizon of salt grass behind which
lay the ocean coast. The wild ducks came usually from the
brackish ponds to the south, but sometimes they came in from the
sea, trading over the horizon in black silhouette like winged mis-
siles, and sometimes they would come from back overhead, heard
long before they were seen, the high sibilant whee-wee-wee of
their wings across the stillness.

George heard them now, and his heart flew with the wings. He
nudged Sam Rubicam with his elbow softly, softly, Sam rearing
around like a bothered hog and saying, "What?" the high wings
already gone, fallen away over the marsh to the right and crossing
George's vision for one swift second as they rose again and swept
inland over the farthest treetops.

"You fathead," George said.

They waited again. The ducks were moving now, the evening
flight, stray pairs and bunches tracing the fading light of the
horizon and settling into the marsh far out toward the beach,
only a few coming in as far as their decoys and these circling wide
and settling in way off to the side.

"They don't like the smell of us," Sam whispered.

"Keep still."

"Mum's the word," Sam said.

More wings whispered overhead. George inched his neck
around, two black duck going away, arching, swinging back—they
were setting in, coming in low and fast from the right—Sam's gun
roared, once, twice, the heavy sound echoing over the marsh like

a fusillade, the blacks crashing on the mirror surface of the pool as the earlier comers, farther out, got up. The air was alive with sound and wings and broken suspense.

"I got them, I got them!" Sam shouted, standing.

"Nice going," George said. He had fired himself and missed and was astonished at Sam's double, for the birds had come from a difficult angle. He salvaged what he could by awarding his friend full credit, feeling vaguely proud of himself in doing so.

The birds were floating belly up in the water beyond the decoys, in still dark witness to the noise, the decoys bobbing unconcernedly in the wake of the deaths like litter from a sunken ship.

"Did you shoot?" Sam said. "It sounded like a battery of guns, to me."

"I missed," George said, still perplexed by the efficacy of Sam's shooting.

"You take the next ones," Sam said. He was too delighted to try to be funny, George noticed, observing the rare happy grin which dominated Sam's narrow face like a flush of health in a sick man.

They settled back in silence, waiting again. It was nearly dark now, way past the legal shooting hour, George knew, but he hadn't had a shot all afternoon. When the small teal flew up out of the darkness, George was startled. His gun resounded twice, too rapidly, and although he knew he had missed and was ashamed of his weakness even as he spoke, he said to Sam, "I don't know if I got him or not. If he fell in the reeds, it'll be too dark to find him, but I don't think I missed him."

And Sam, still excited, said, "I think you got him, he probably fell in the reeds." Sam's gaze traveled dutifully to the reeds, then returned to his two trophies drifting in slow circles into the darkness.

Then they went home.

"There's going to be a storm," Sam said. They paused a moment on the lawn and listened to the weather, the unquiet breath of the sea and trees and a swift flight of leaves around the corner of the house.

CHAPTER 8

INLAND, THE BIG BAY HORSE KNELT WILDEYED IN A GULLY, ITS nose forced into the embankment grass, its scream chaotic in the sunlight. The ascent of the steep field from the highway had exhausted the impetus of Cady Shipman's blow but still it had run, homing in a heavy rocking canter along the ridge and down a trail through the woods which ended on a plank thrown across a ditch onto the valley road. Too tired to jump or stop, the bay had plunged forward and down, and a foreleg had slipped between two conduits. The horse was hurled forward onto its chest. In this position, the girth made its breathing difficult, the bit was twisted on its tongue, and the knotted reins sat up high and decorative, a finishing touch, upon its neck. Its buttocks reared into the air as if it had been arrested in the process of lying down, which finally it did, rolling heavily and whinnying anew when the foreleg broke again between the pipes. Then the ants came, Lilliputian, traversing the twitching hide, avoiding the white lather and the huge wet eyelids.

Later, a farmer found the horse. He removed the saddle and bridle and took them home, returning after breakfast with a pistol. The horse screamed no longer, only waited, staring. The farmer was not used to the pistol, his hand shook, and because he leaned away from the noise, the job required several rounds. Then he went home again, leaving the carcass to the ants and flies, and inspected the saddle and bridle a little before calling the police. The police called Joshua Murray.

"What color horse? How many hands?"

"I don't know, Mister Murray. A big brown horse is all I know. We thought it maybe was yours."

"Wait a minute, please, officer, I'll go and see."

Joshua Murray laid down the receiver and went outside and down to the barn. The single stall was empty, and a saddle and bridle were missing. He sat down on the oat bin, a prematurely white-haired man with an open unwrinkled face, and smoked a cigarette and thought a little. It was early still and he was sleepy. Then he returned to the house. "Cady," he called. "Cady!" He had left the front door open, and the telephone murmured unheard, "Mister Murray? Hello? Hello? Mister Murray?"

He came back inside and passed the telephone without noticing it, picking up small objects off the living room tables and placing them elsewhere on a circuitous route toward his library, where he sat down at his desk. There was a newspaper spread on the desk, with a can of lubricating oil, some rags scarred with black discs of gunpowder, and an assembled cleaning rod for shotguns. After a moment, he spun in his chair, rose once more, and went to the gun rack. An English Purdy, the best gun in his collection, was gone.

At least he cleaned it, Joshua Murray thought, at least he did that.

The cook came to the door. "Are you on the telephone, Mister Murray?"

"Yes," Mr. Murray said. "Yes, I suppose I am." He followed his servant down the hall to the telephone.

"Hello? Hello?" the telephone said. "What do you know about that? The old guy has . . ."

"Yes, it's my horse, I think," Mr. Murray said. "A big bay named Tenerife, is that the one?"

"Listen, where in hell did . . . I dunno, Mister Murray, I guess so. You want to prefer charges against somebody?"

"Yes. There's a gun missing, too."

"A gun? Anything else taken there, Mister Murray?"

"I don't know." He paused. "No, I really don't think so."

"What's the name on that, Mister Murray?"

"The name?" Murray sat down on the chair by the telephone. "Tenerife," he said. "The full name is Evelyn's Tenerife."

"You said you wanted to *prosecute* somebody, Mister Murray."

"I suppose I did, yes. Well I think I won't, officer, thanks very much, though. No, I don't think I will. Good-by, officer."

"Listen, Mister Murray, ya sure about . . . will ya catch that, Fred, the old sap has hung up on me, he wants to . . ."

Joshua Murray had not hung up. Idly, he laid the receiver on the table, resting his hand on it a few moments before reaching for a cigarette.

"Yeah, for Christ's sake!" The hobgoblin voice of the police officer danced in the receiver. "First he wants to prefer charges, so I ask him the name on it, and he gives me the name of the nag, Eve-lyn's goddamn Tennessee, or something. . . ."

When Murray smiled, his cheeks protruded in the sympathetic manner of the squirrels, rabbits, moles, voles and gophers in drawings for children, and his eyes, very bright under thick white brows, unmistakably twinkled. "Rumpelstiltskin," he thought, smiling at the receiver which, when he wandered away into another room, he neglected to replace on the hook.

The time was a little after nine.

A little after twelve, returning from the station without Eve and wondering why she hadn't called, he said to himself, "I do

believe you've left the receiver off again," and getting out of the
car, hurried into the hallway.

"That's correct, Operator, Murray Hill 3—yes, now you have it.
Evelyn Murray. Of the Murray Hill Murrays," he added, and
frowned at himself in the hall mirror. Facetious old jackass, he
thought.

"How do you spell that, please?" The operator's voice was
suspicious.

"Rubicam. R-U-B-I-C-A-M. Mrs. Evelyn Rubicam."

"Do you wish to speak to Mrs. Murray or Mrs. Rubicam, sir?"

"Mrs. Rubicam, thank you."

"R, as in Rhubarb?"

"R, as in Rhubarb, precisely."

Through the window giving on the drive, he watched the black
car coming. It rocked to a violent halt before the door, and a
policeman got out.

Evelyn's Tenerife, he thought. He had always liked the name.
Some day he would have to go to Tenerife, the Cape Verde
Islands, wasn't it? Or was it the Canaries? Evelyn had chosen the
name, she was such a romantic, Evelyn, a delightful child—
"Hello, Evelyn? Tell me, is Tenerife in the Cape Verdes or the
Canaries?" he demanded.

"Daddy? Listen, did you leave the receiver off again?"

"Yes, I did. You weren't at the station, Evelyn."

"Oh Daddy, listen, I've been trying to reach you all morning."

"Of course you have, is something wrong? You don't sound
well. You didn't sound well last night. You'd better come right
down here and get some rest, I think. Hello?"

"Daddy, now listen carefully, I am coming down this afternoon.
Can you meet the seven-ten?"

"Delighted to. Well, good-by, then, my dear. So glad you're coming after all, the place just isn't the same without you."

"Good-by, Daddy."

Because she was too restless to read, too restless to do anything but wonder, she lay back again on the sofa in a calculatedly uncomfortable position which suited her mood. So Sam was back. Why on earth was she lunching with him on Tuesday? Would she ever even have married him if George had not virtually driven her to it, if he had not deserted her that way because of what happened at the Hotel Clarence—that was it, the Hotel Clarence.

This wasn't entirely fair to George, and she knew it. In the first place, he had not truly deserted her, for he had gone overseas with the Army, and in the second place she hadn't had to marry Rubicam. It had just seemed to happen to her, for want of anything better.

And this, on the other hand, was hardly fair to Sam. After all, he had held out certain attractions for her. His sophistication, on the heels of George's callow incertitude, had been one asset. Another was his intelligence, which seemed to her at the time better matched to her own, for she was a very good student in college, which George had never been. Like many confident girls in this position, Eve Murray had despaired in the realization that her education would almost certainly go for nought, that with marriage her cultivated mind must perish in the thick weeds of household and motherhood like a rusty scythe. Her resentment of this prospect was such that she was able to persuade herself of Sam's superiority to George, especially since George seemed lost to her. She fell back upon Sam's idea that he could rescue her from the bourgeois death so loathed by her political science professor. Sam was a painter, after all, and urbane and witty into the bargain.

My God, she thought, what a fatuous ass I was.

Things happened swiftly, casually, as was Sam's way. One day they seemed to be discussing George, the next they were discussing marriage—it was as sudden as that. The decision had been reached at Shipman's Point, on a houseparty weekend arranged for Sam by Celia.

Eve and Sam had stayed up later than the rest. She had been flirting with him, and he had risen eagerly to the bait. He gave an impressive discourse on the majesty of Bad Taste as represented by the McConville house and, as a veteran of her college debating team, she argued another viewpoint.

"But there's something so false about the house," she said. "It's a façade for something unreal and unpleasant." She was lying before the fire in a half curl, the rich slope of her hip and thigh not quite matter-of-fact in the firelight. "The spirit of the place is too small for the rooms, it's lost in here. There's just about enough for this room and a bedroom or two, and that's all. The rest might as well be some old stage set."

"That's precisely its charm," Sam said. "The size and the uselessness, even the artificiality of its being here to begin with. Impracticality is the great allure of the past."

He was standing at the mantel, his elbow on it, his ankle pressed against her side.

"I don't like the past," she said. "I mean, I like it, everybody likes it, but I wish I didn't. We spend so damned much time in it, as if we were walking backward all of our lives, and before we know it, we've tripped over the present and just get a glimpse of the future as we're going down for the last time. And if we're not gaping off into the past, we're gaping off into a future so remote that the life we are actually living has no meaning, and even then, this remote future is in terms of the past, a time of our lives which will make up for something gone, or impress somebody we have already known, or justify a failure, you see what I mean? We never actually *live* at all, we dream."

"Speak for yourself," Sam said. "I pride myself on living my life to the fullest."

"You're very lucky, then," Eve said, "except that I don't believe you. You're fonder of the almighty Past than anybody I know. If you weren't, you wouldn't like this terrible house."

"Of course I like the past," he said. "It gives me a basis for comparison, it's a part of the savoring. And I like this house because of its associations for me, to start with."

She was aware of her movements as they spoke. Her body seemed relaxed and separated from her, inert and waiting as if resigned to the thrashings of her brain, shifting easily from time to time in pursuit of thoughtless comfort, like a cat. How curious it seemed. There she was, considering as Samuel Rubicam the brain and the thin hand which drummed on the mantel, and not taking into consideration at all the assemblage of bones and flesh and complicated parts that constituted the creature known as Sam to others. Others, of course, would take his brain into consideration, but only as an inseparable factor of his smile, his face, his mannerisms—*Isn't Sam charming!* Sam's brain, as such, as a phenomenon of another's experience, did not exist. Perhaps a brain only existed by itself when transposed to paper. When one spoke of Kant, for example, one actually spoke of his brain.

Eve thought all this impatiently, in a series of mental doodlings. Her body was now off on a tangent of its own, vaguely seeking contact with his, and suddenly it was as if the two fleshes had seized command of the faltering mental atmosphere, for he sat down beside her and took her hand.

"Do you remember, Eve, the night at Celia's when you played the piano and we ran into each other in the hall?"

She nodded, her heart beating.

"I've loved you ever since," Sam muttered. "I want you to marry me." He seemed so vulnerable, even frightened, and she was so startled that she only kissed him on the cheek. Sam was subtle enough to sense her hesitation. He lay down beside her, the lines of his body aligned with hers before the fire, and after a time their hands controlled the silence like the flight of four pigeons in a quiet street

Everybody came to the engagement party in the country. "Isn't it lovely, everybody's come," Eve's mother said, and it was true. People Eve did not like and people who did not like her, accompanied by the vaguely known and the never heard of—everybody, in short, of Eve's mother's acquaintance. The women entered and took Eve's hand and held it too long between their own and said, "Isn't it wonderful, dear, aren't you simply thrilled?" and the men bestowed roguish kisses upon her cheek, saying, "Hope this young man knows how lucky he is," and laughing aloud to show this was all in fun. Then they stood uneasily waiting to be confronted with the young man, last seen by somebody in the neighborhood of the bar. "Eve-lyn," Mrs. Murray pouted, "you've got to make that bad Sam behave." The guests would chortle like poor relations and Eve would go once again and seek Sam out. It was a confusing party.

"Mummy wants you to meet everybody, Sam," she said.

"I want you to meet somebody," Sam said, indicating the barman. "This is good old Charlie O'Brien, the wandering barkeep. He's been the key figure at every one of these things since before you were born, right, Charlie?"

Charlie O'Brien grunted agreement. He was a round old man whose role in the summer was to keep people happy but not too

happy. "Now I want you to keep them happy, Charlie, but not
too happy—" each hostess would waggle a subtle finger under
Charlie's nose and be vaguely surprised that this unsubtle man
knew precisely what they meant. In the wintertime, when the
hostesses had migrated from Shipman's Crossing, Charlie O'Brien
hibernated with their leftover alcohol.

"Come on, Sam," Eve said. "I've got to keep her happy."

"She should keep you happy. It's your party, isn't it?"

"It's hers. These are her friends, not mine."

"Well, that's some consolation, I must say." Sam took a full
glass and followed her onto the terrace. There Charlie O'Brien,
Junior, was playing the accordion in a three-piece band which included a saxophonist and a drummer. The band had two bass
drums, a small discreet one presently in use and a large flamboyant
one for high-school dances and Saturday nights at the Crossing
Tavern, which bore the inscription CHARLIE'S STOMPERS.

On the terrace she lost Sam again to a knot of young men down
from New York. Aggressively suave, these conscripts were his
ushers-to-be. She had the feeling that Sam did not know them
very well and that most of them were really friends of George,
and this observation made a very special contribution to her misgivings.

Nearby her father was speaking with Captain Shipman, who
had backed himself, lobster fashion, into a protective corner and
was followed into it by Joshua Murray. Barlow Shipman, subdued
in a white shirt and Navy blue suit, regarded the proceedings with
obvious alarm, and her father wore a look of pain, as if suffering
from a cramp. Seeing Eve, however, he managed a smile.

"Come talk to us a minute," he said. "We're old and lonely."

"All right," Eve said. "Hello, Captain Shipman."

"I'm very happy for you, young lady," Barlow Shipman said.

"I'm sure you've found what you wanted, and that's just fine. That's just fine," he repeated, and stared in awe at a passing tray of hors d'oeuvres. She did not know whether she was pleased he had come or not.

Her father was carefully observing her face, and aware of this, Eve blurted stupidly, "If I was fourteen, Captain Shipman, I'd be getting engaged to Cady, probably."

Barlow Shipman was astonished by the remark. "You would?" he demanded. "Why?"

"Oh, I used to think he was quite something, I guess." She tried to laugh the lilting laugh of the young girl engaged but choked and had a fit of coughing. "And now I hear he's re-enlisted."

"Good thing, too," Barlow Shipman said.

"I thought it was George you liked," her father said. Glancing at him, she could not tell how he intended this, for despite his smile his face was quiet, not quite lighthearted, even a trifle cruel.

"Now George is more like it." Barlow, relieved, took a mighty swallow from his glass.

When Eve was silent, her father asked her, "Is George coming down today?"

"No. His discharge hasn't come through yet."

"I'll bet Sam's disappointed."

"Of course he is." Turning, she saw the disappointed Sam fish a maraschino cherry from Celia McConville's glass. Celia was wearing her Continental air and, Eve thought, not a hell of a lot else. She had in tow a man of shiny appearance who kissed Eve's hand.

"I think it's marvelous, darling," Celia was saying. "She's such a sweet unsophisticated little thing, I never imagined that you, of all people—"

"Essentially I'm the homespun type." Sam smirked at the shiny man, who smirked obligingly in return.

Eve made her way slowly through groups of people to the edge of the terrace. Her own friends had chosen this moment to accost Sam's ushers, forming an eager exclusive band in which she had no place. At the bottom of the lawn, in the pasture, the bay horse Tenerife leaned tranquil on the white rail fence, swishing his tail at horseflies and monotony.

"I like your dress," said Philip Rubicam, materializing, impeccably drunk, at her elbow. He had a knack of making others uncomfortable, even when he smiled. "Tell me," he continued, "how does my son plan to support you?"

"I don't know. I mean, I think he's going to paint. Don't you think he has talent?"

"I couldn't say. It's not a fair question, really. We'll ask somebody else, somebody without prejudice of any sort, like Cyrus McConville." And before she could dissuade him, he had called George's father over. "Listen, Cyrus, you have to give us an opinion on something—"

"It was so nice of you to come today, Mr. McConville," Eve interrupted.

"Glad to do it," Cyrus McConville said. "Wouldn't have missed it for anything, by God. It's not as if we got engaged every other day like old Rubicam, here, eh, Rubicam?" He threw his head back to roar but seemed to think better of it, and flushed instead. "I'm only kidding, you understand," he blurted, his color so alarming that she thought he might drop in his tracks.

"Cyrus is full of fun," Philip remarked. When Cyrus glared at him, he added, "But we wanted to get your opinion, Cyrus, on my son Sam, to whom this magnificent young woman has plighted her troth. Sam wants to paint for a living."

"Paint? Paint what?"

"Pretty pictures, I presume."

"He wants to express the confusion of the period," Eve said, wishing she hadn't.

"Ah-ha," Philip said. "That's his game, is it?"

"Why?" Cyrus demanded. "I mean, what good does he think that's going to do him? That's the kind of thing Frenchmen do, and look where they are today. Good God!"

"We knew you'd have an idea or two, Cyrus."

"Damn right. Why listen, there's a lot of young fellows like that son of yours, get sensitive ideas and all. Take my boy George. For a while there, if he'd said or done one more sensitive thing I'd have strangled him with my bare hands! But they get over that if there's any good in them. Maybe what-sis-name, Sam, will too."

"You make me feel much better," Philip said.

"You don't think George is sensitive any more, Mr. McConville?" Eve said.

"Of course not," Philip said. "George is now completely insensitive."

"What do you mean by that?" Cyrus shouted. "I didn't say that! You're not trying to be funny again, are you? All I said was that George isn't like that kid of yours, and I'm damned glad of it, too."

"I think, Cyrus, that if for no other reason than the fact that you are talking to my son's fiancée, you might speak a little more thoughtfully." Philip was smiling slightly, and Eve was aware that he was not in the least offended for his son.

"All right, I apologize, goddamn it all." Cyrus stalked away toward the liquor table.

"Charming," Philip murmured. "Perfectly charming."

"That's what you wanted, wasn't it?" Eve said.

"You're not being impertinent with your father-in-law, I hope."

"Perhaps I am. I don't think so, though."

"No, I suppose you don't. Forgive me, Eve." Philip rested his hand for a moment on her shoulder before picking his way with elegant distaste in the direction of an ashtray.

"Evelyn! Eve-lyn!"

Her mother was gesticulating from the doorway.

"Come say hello to Mrs. McConville, dear, and do find that naughty Sam!"

Eve made her way to Sam and tugged at his sleeve.

"We have to go inside a moment," she said.

"Secrets, secrets," Celia said. "Must you drag him away?"

"I'm afraid so, Celia, but if you'll just hang on a minute you can have him back."

"I do believe they're squabbling over me," Sam said to the shiny man. "It's very gratifying."

Celia vented her soprano laugh and after a moment her escort chimed in with the alto part. Eve watched them, wondering at her admiration for Celia the night she had stayed with Celia and Sam, the awe of their superior sophistication which had extended itself in Sam's attraction for her. The awe, at least, was long since gone. Perhaps I am jealous, she thought, regretting in a way that this was not the case.

"Isn't he nasty?" Celia sighed, but her gaze, pursuing Eve, was not amused at all.

Mrs. McConville had never seen Eve looking so well. Ravishing was the word she chose. And Eve, with mixed pity and impatience, had never seen Agnes McConville looking so badly. Her hair had gone gray in less than a year, and her face was sharp and frightened. Mrs. Murray, sandy and sunburned beside her, looked very much younger and knew it. "Isn't Agnes looking wonderful?" she said, and beamed upon her little friend, whose gaze had wandered in search of her sanguine Cyrus. Agnes turned to them and said, "I do wish poor George was here to see you two."

Sam said off-handedly, "He's coming after all. Just called from the station. He got a weekend furlough."

"Sam, why didn't you tell us?" Mrs. McConville, gasping, placed her hands in a praying position before her chest.

"He wants it to be a surprise." Anticipating Eve, Sam added, "I sent Daniel down to meet him." Daniel had driven the McConvilles over from Shipman's Point.

"Isn't it wonderful!" Mrs. Murray exclaimed. "The best man! Now there's nobody missing at all!" But her smile fell away when she saw Sam's expression, and Eve's. "Now you two run along and talk to people," she said, and drew Agnes McConville aside.

"Well, Eve," Sam said, watching her.

"Hello, Sam."

"Do you love me?"

"You don't have to ask me that."

"Yes, I do. Are you glad he's coming, Eve?"

"Of course. Aren't you?"

"I don't know. In a way I am. I hope it straightens something out."

"What is there to straighten out, Sam?"

"If you don't know, I certainly don't." He paused. "Would you like a drink?"

"Not just this moment. I'll be right down, though. Will you wait for me?" She went through the hall and up the stairs to her room and fixed her hair and lipstick all over again, aware that Sam knew she was doing just this, knew her reasons and her shame.

She came down again when the car drew up in front of the house. Sam had disappeared, whether angrily or tactfully she was not sure. The front door opened and George was standing in it, with Daniel Barleyfield peering in over his shoulder.

"Hello, Daniel," Eve said.

"Hello there, Eve, congratulations. I think it's great. Who woulda thought that you and Sammy Sissypants—"

"Thanks for the lift, Daniel, I'll see you later," George said.

"Don't you want to come in, Daniel, and have something?"

"I don't drink yet, thanks, Eve." He went away and George closed the door. George's uniform was big for him and rumpled, and George, though very tanned, seemed thin and uncomfortable in it, not the least bit brisk and military. Sam's uniform, she reflected, had been very well-tailored by an expensive custom tailor at college. He had been in the Reserve Officers' Training Corps, had not gone overseas, and had not had to wait until now for his discharge. It seemed somehow characteristic that George, with one year of college before he enlisted, should now find himself three years behind his friend.

He put down a small suitcase by the door, the identical suitcase he had had the year before at the Hotel Clarence. She had not seen him since. "How are you, Eve?" he said. "Congratulations."

"I'm so pleased you could come, George."

"I think I'm best man," he explained, rather vaguely. "How's Sambo?"

"He's fine." They could not look at each other. "Do give me a kiss, George, it's been such a long time." When he kissed her, she whispered, "Why didn't you ever call me?" and blushed at having said it. George was blushing, too.

"Well, you see, my furlough was over—"

"No. You had another week. You didn't even write."

"Well, something happened that night—anyway, I was ashamed. I didn't feel I should see you for a while, I don't know why."

"Another lady?"

"Yes. I don't know quite how—"

"Poor thing, I don't blame you. I've been so ashamed of my-self."

"Perhaps we should go in," George warned her.

"Yes, perhaps we should. I just wanted to tell you, George—"

"Listen, I haven't really congratulated you yet. Where's Sambo? Can't I drink a toast or something?" He slapped his pockets for his cigarettes as they went in.

Afterward she avoided him, alarmed and disheartened by her own confusion and grateful to George that he had not let her say as much as she would have liked.

She was standing with her parents and Philip Rubicam when Sam came, well-dressed and handsome and by now quite drunk, and said, "Here we are, bless us all, the happy family group!" He raised his glass to Eve and with a gentleness she had never seen in him murmured, "I simply want to say before all of you how honored I am, how happy I am, how happy I hope I will be able to make Eve, and how much I love her." She knew he was sincere and kissed him, deeply moved. Could George have said such a thing, even if he felt it? And look at Sam, she told herself, he's handsome and intelligent and charming, and he has talent, and of course I love him very much.

So relieved was she with this decision that later in the evening when George, no longer in control of himself, attempted to re-sume their conversation, she was able to close her mind to him and change the subject.

CHAPTER 9

AFTER DINNER, WHEN THE SHOTGUNS WERE CLEANED AND PUT away, they had a drink in the library. Although dark, this room was the only pleasant one in the house, with comfortable chairs, thick carpeting, and books to hold the warmth given off by the fire. Drinking in silence, they watched the flames dance with the mounting wind outside the chimney, the reflection filling their whiskey glasses with warm golden smoke. For Sam Rubicam at least, sliding deeper into his chair as into tranquil water below a current, the interlude was a pleasant one, and he was startled, then annoyed by Daniel Barleyfield's invasion, there was an urgency about it, a foreboding.

"Listen, George—" Daniel said. "Mister George."

"George," George said, as Sam glanced from one to the other.

"Hokay, George. There's somebody out here wants to know if you want to see him."

"Who is it?"

"A man out here. You want to see him, or shall I tell him you're busy or something?"

"Who is it?" George demanded, rearing irritably around in his chair. "How do I know if I want to see him?"

"It's him. He's back."

"Goddamn it—" George started.

"It's Cady Shipman. You want me to send him in here?"

"Cady? Of course I do. What's the matter with you?"

Daniel shrugged his shoulders in Sam's direction, and when Sam winked at him, he grinned and disappeared.

"Cady," George said, reflectively, as if he were trying to make up his mind whether he was glad or sorry. "What do you suppose he's doing here?" He passed one leg over the arm of his chair in a gesture Sam recognized as nervousness. When they reached simultaneously for cigarettes, George laughed.

Sam was disturbed, uneasy, as if he had been startled out of sleep. It was always like this with any moment perfect in itself, it lasted only so long as one did not realize it had occurred, and then it ended. Somebody or something posing a whole new set of problems would invariably appear. He remembered the few peaceful evenings at home with Eve—a fuse would burn out with no spare in the house, or an acquaintance welcome at any other time would appear unexpectedly, brandishing repellent qualities one had never noticed before.

He was arranging his legs so that he could rise more easily when he heard Cady's footstep in the corridor.

Cady did not come in at first but stood just behind the doorway, his face white against the darkness. George said, "Come on in, I've never known you to be shy before." He rose, laughing, and held out his hand. Cady regarded George detachedly, as if George were acting out a part, then moved forward, saying, "How's it going, George?"

"Fine," George said. "Fine thanks, Cady. You remember Sam, don't you?"

"How've you been, Cady," Sam said, rising himself and aligning his smile with George's. He watched Cady grin and say to George, "Yes, I remember," before turning to himself. "Fine," Cady said. He rubbed his hand over a stubble of blond beard, his eyes flicking swiftly over Sam's orange hunting outfit, and his nostrils flaring in quiet laughter.

"Sit down," George gestured uncertainly. Cady Shipman moved a little and perched himself half-sitting, half-leaning on a chair arm, one boot idling free in the air. He had a manner about him which suggested domination, both physical and psychological, of any company he happened to join, as if no word should be spoken, no action taken toward the future nor interpretation put upon the past, which was not in precise harmony with his will. When Cady had smiled at Sam's costume, however quietly, George McConville had also smiled, and even Sam, despite himself, had felt a faint painful deprecatory twinge at the corner of his mouth. He could not understand it, and there had returned to him immediately that need to defy this man which he had felt in childhood, as if, with Cady, he had to struggle for an individuality which heretofore had gone unquestioned.

"I was just in the neighborhood and thought I'd drop in," Cady said to George.

"Hell, yes," George said, and after a moment, "You ought to stick around and go shooting with us tomorrow."

"I don't mind. I have my gear right with me, as a matter of fact." Again, Cady glanced at Sam, his eyes slightly squinted beneath the lion-colored hair.

"Great," Sam said. "You came prepared, then."

George broke the ensuing silence. "Sam hasn't changed a bit," he said. "He has a bright remark for every occasion."

Now they both regarded him, and Sam sank backward over the arm of his chair and picked up his glass from the floor. "You ought to get Cady a drink," he said to George. "What kind of miserable host are you?"

"You want a drink, Cady?" George said.

"All right," Cady said. While George's back was turned they sat in silence, Cady staring at the uneasy fire, Sam sipping at his whiskey.

George and Cady were reminiscing almost immediately, and Sam soon left the conversation. They had not made him feel a part of their past, and he took a certain pallid revenge in the realization that Cady and George could only meet on this one conversational ground. For a while he listened to them, each was recalling incidents reflecting some obscure credit on himself, but after a time he slipped away in pursuit of his own past, trying to recapture the mood he had entered prior to Cady Shipman's arrival. But the pleasant images would not return to him, circling warily too fleet to glimpse around the outskirts of his memory, and whereas an hour before he had reveled in that happiest of exciting memories, the mutual declaration of love, he now could only conjure up its aftermath and initial defeat.

Everything had gone very well at first. He noticed, however, that Eve, though far less experienced than he, controlled the direction of their love. And she gave signs, even in the early weeks of their marriage, of a certain wistful dissatisfaction with him, as if he were cheating her of something she had bargained for.

In that year, 1947, they moved into an airy apartment-room over Sheridan Square. La Bohème with a view window, Eve had said, but Sam was delighted with it. He was painting then. At least painting was his passkey to the endless barroom conversations in which he passed his days. He was an artist and sat with other artists, writers, poets, with lesbians, homosexuals, hopheads, tourists, with woolly dogs and Communists, with rummies, checker-shirted students, dilettantes, with all the character parts in a great false fascinating vanity fair, a would-be world-within-a-world of misfits, throwbacks, and aficionados of life's underbelly

whose false despair was made ridiculous by every passage through
their ranks of beggar, prostitute, and child.

These were the artists Sam Rubicam knew—all of us here are
artists, one of them had told him, no matter what we do or do
not do—the ones who wore sandals, smoked marijuana, accepted
such sallow fornication as came to hand and, after brief effortless
failure to pierce the critical screen, lay about like broken flies on a
dirty windowsill and buzzed away their art in conversation.

Sam delighted in them, their bleary fatalism in the face of the
dying world seemed wise and heroic to him then, and he was
astounded when Eve did not agree. One evening—jokingly, he
assured her the next morning—he suggested that they pose as
man and mistress, it would be more fun, he said, it would break
down the barrier between their less circumscribed companions and
themselves. She regarded him a little while in silence, lying back
on the bed in the corner of the wall, and he never forgot how
beautiful she had been at that moment, dressed in a black turtle-
neck sweater with a heavy Russian necklace, her bamboo hair cut
very short and round and her dark eyes muted in the shadow cast
by the bookshelf on the wall. From below them somewhere
sounded the rhythm but not the music of a jazz record, it pounded
ominously against the silence like a throb of pain, and when she
stirred, he held his breath and waited.

"You want very much to be like them, don't you, Sam?"

"It's not that. It's just that . . . well, when in Rome . . . that
sort of thing."

"Why do you?"

"Why do I what?" He could tell from her tone that she was
building toward an argument, that he could not prevent it, but he
feinted nevertheless, stalling for time.

"Want to be like them?"

"I don't. I was just explaining to you—"

"I don't want to break down the barrier," she said. Her face came forward out of the shadows, alert, eyes glittering with tears. "I'm not like them. I don't want to be like them."

"Oh now, come on, Eve," he said, and made the mistake of laughing lightly. "How can you say that when you wear the same clothes, the black and all, and wear your hair like a boy's the way they do? And besides, you told me—"

"I'm letting it grow out again. And I've always worn black things and always will!"

"Listen, sweetie, don't get so excited. I simply said—"

"I'm not getting excited!" She rose from the bed and crossed the room to get a cigarette rather than ask him for one. "I'm just sick of watching you trail around after these bums and get drunk and pretend to be a painter when you haven't painted a damned thing in months—it's so false and pointless. And now you ask me to pose as your mistress just so all these fairies and God-knows-what kind of phonies will think you're something you're really not and shouldn't want to be. If you want a mistress that badly, go out and find one, and I'll go home!"

"Listen, Eve, I didn't say that. I love you, don't I? All I said was—"

"You love me! To hell with that. You love yourself." She pulled away when he tried to kiss her, and he sat down again, a little angry now. "God, you're original," he said. "How many wives do you suppose have said *that* to their husbands? You sound like a Mrs. Babbitt or something."

"Maybe that's what I am. Why not? If you don't like it, go find somebody else. I'm tired of listening to you tell me how gauche I am, how conventional and stupid, and pointing out other women as examples for me to follow. I'm beginning to think—" She

paused, and he sensed she was thinking something far more irrev-
ocable than what she was saying, but he rushed in heedlessly.

"You never thought a minute in your life, or you'd realize I
never said any of those things," he said. "Maybe you've got a bad
conscience, maybe you're ashamed of being . . . that you might
be the housewife type, no matter how many liberal arts courses
you took."

"Ashamed of being what?" She spoke more quietly now, standing just behind him at his shoulder.

"I don't see why you have to get so excited. I just said—"

"Ashamed of being what?" Her tone was very quiet, relentless
now, he knew she had her campaign carefully planned and could
afford the manner of the patient seeker after truth.

"For God's sake, relax! Can't we ever talk like mature human
beings instead of screeching at one another?"

"*I'm* not screeching," she said. "*You're* screeching." This was
true, and he was silent. She continued. "Of being conventional
and stupid and dowdy, is that what you mean?"

"If you like," he muttered, regretting it. "Listen, did I ever say
you were dowdy? I've never known anybody to argue so unfairly.
All I'm trying to do is stop this haggling, that's all."

"Well maybe I am dowdy. At any rate, I'm sick of pretending
to be something I'm not, just to indulge you. I refuse to sub-
merge myself in the personality of a man who has less guts than
even the intellectual tramps you call your friends. Why should I
sacrifice my life to a ridiculous set-up like this? Why on earth
should I?"

"I have no idea," Sam said. He considered making a comment
about the obligations of love and marriage but decided against it,
adopting instead a resigned approach. Putting his hands behind

his head, he stared at the door and constructed a yawn. "Maybe it's you who should go find a lover, if that's the way you feel."

"Maybe I will," she said after a moment. "I've been thinking about it."

There was a quiet menace in this remark which terrified him. She was lying on the bed again, regarding him, the smoke from her cigarette idling reflectively in the air. "We're behaving like children," he said. "Be reasonable. I didn't say I wanted to be like those guys, darling, and I didn't say you were conventional and stupid and dowdy. All I meant was that if you think you can apply the puritan New England standards here, you're being foolish."

"It's hard to put your finger on the fool," she said.

"What do you mean by that?"

"Nothing. I don't know what I mean. It's just something I say now and then for the hell of it." She lay back impatiently and closed her eyes. "Among conventional and stupid people, it's a very popular remark to make."

"Oh stop it," he said, rising and going to the door. "You're being sulky now."

"Don't slam the door," she said. "I have a headache."

After that, there were many similar scenes, more and more frequent and acrimonious. Although he knew they could not go on like this forever, that he would have to do something to placate her, he never imagined that one night, when they had made up and he had gone to her and taken her in his arms and told her he adored her, she would whisper in his ear, "I hope you're not telling the truth, poor man, because I don't love you any more."

He had kissed her for several seconds after that, refusing to think, refusing to believe she wasn't joking, and only lifting his face to hers when he felt at his waist the slight pressure of her hands which was always her gesture of impatience or refusal of his desire. Her tears told him she was serious, and he felt his heart fall away inside of him to some black painful region between thought and breath.

"I'm leaving you," she whispered.

She left the following morning. His entreaties in the interlude seemed only to embitter her and make her cruel, and when he announced that he would go uptown with her, she said, "Are you going to hang around forever? Why can't you look the situation in the face?" Her voice was sharp, almost hysterical, and so stunned and hurt was he that he could not answer, even in anger.

Nevertheless, he accompanied her on the subway. From the window of their car, he saw reflected in the sour city faces that latent outrage against life which he felt himself, he pictured a scene in which he did away with himself beneath the train. Beside him, Eve stared straight ahead, a closed book on her lap. He wanted to cry out to her, to seize at the few words left them in the ruin of love's language as a man in a burning house seeks out his last most precious properties, but he could not. The car was crowded, and they sat side-by-side in anonymity. Only at the last did she speak at all, answering a last choked plea with, "Please don't think I would have left you, Sam, no matter what your life had been, if I had loved you. You must forgive me, not for leaving you, but for marrying you in the beginning." She was crying.

"Good-by, old dear," she said. "God bless you."

"Good-by," he said. He wept a little then himself, standing on the corner, thinking at that final moment when he first was truly alive to what was happening, I can't go back to the flat alone, I can't.

But of course he had, and from there to the Monaco Bar. So, one of the artists had said, you are one of us now, one of the rejected. I congratulate you. This man affected a cynical smile, from

the wounded corner of which a wet brown cigarette stub dangled
onto his beard. The cigarette reminded Sam of filth caught in the
hair of a dog. She found out about Muriel then, another said. Too
bad.

No, Sam said. She didn't find out.

But he wondered now if Eve had guessed from something in his
manner. How could she have, though, hadn't he told her he
adored her? And he meant it, there was no dissimulating there.
Muriel was only the exercise of her challenge to him, a temporary
replacement for the wife who turned her back to him in bed. He
had warned Eve once, "Listen," he had addressed her back, "I'm
not an animal, but I'm human. You can't expect me to put up
with this forever."

"I'm not asking you to put up with anything," she had said,
from under the covers. "You can do as you please. When you become an animal, let me know."

You see, one of the artists said, Sammy is unhappy. Sammy prefers the bourgeois morality.

For almost a month he waited for a letter in answer to his own,
although the period was without time for him after the second
week, an uncertain passage back and forth across the street. He
stayed longer and longer in the bars, until all he could remember
about his room was the yellow wall of it in the morning and the
face of the dark silent girl who sat in the corner and watched him
come and go. He would sit by the hour pressing the cold glass of
his drink to his forehead or rapping it on the table until somebody
complained to a waiter, and after a time he wouldn't miss Eve any
more but think of the crazy passion of Muriel for a little while.
To bolster the grief which he recognized as his better nature, he
would signal for another drink. The waiters were avoiding him, he
thought, they would pass right next to him in that oblivious way

they had when they were busy. And one day when he had almost forgotten Eve, he stopped a waiter with a show of force and found himself screaming into the late afternoon as he was pitched out into the street. When the people turned their backs to him he shouted at them, but the shout didn't come. He was soaking wet and shaking with cold, seated on the sidewalk with a large dog walking slowly around him and a waiter tugging furiously at his armpit. Goddamn lush, the waiter cursed him, ya'll get yaself run in next time. . . .

And it came to him that he was drinking himself to death on Eve's account, she would have to see him, he would go to her. After that, there was only the yellow wall of his room to which he turned his face as he lay in bed, and the sensation of falling apart. And then he acted, there were subways and noise and lights and panic, and there was the yellow wall beside him again, but it was in her hallway, and it was brown.

Miss Eve, the butler at Joshua Murray's enunciated, had taken a trip to the Virgin Islands. A divorce? Sam said. The butler was not in a position to say. Would Mr. Rubicam like to speak with Mr. Murray? No, Sam said. The butler excused himself, but he was very busy, as no doubt Mr. Rubicam could tell from the fact that he was in his waistcoat.

The week after, knowing now that Eve was lost to him one way or another and it didn't really matter how, but one way or another she was lost—the week after, he took a plane to Paris. He did not intend to stay there but he did, he had nothing else to do. And after a time, his grief became nostalgia and struck at him only in rare night-time moments. There would be music from somewhere, particular music out of his past with Eve, and in a lull in the conversation he would feel himself drawn away to the sounds of the boulevard, realizing that he had been listening to the music for some time and wondering where it came from. The lull in the conversation was only the conversation slipping away, for the others were still talking and so was he. And then his brain would swim in a dark nostalgic pool, and he would think, why am I here, in this particular café, this city, in this year—why? Who are these people? I scarcely know them—look at them talking out there! Do they know I'm here, or who I am?

Do they know who I am

At the crack of the storm shutter against the wall of the house, Sam started in his chair. The fire guttered a moment, then flickered on. He listened as George and Cady stirred, and then George got up and went to the liquor table. The silence was over.

"There's going to be a storm," Cady said. "I can feel it."

"Yes," George said. "I'm afraid so."

Sam felt compelled to say something.

"You remember what a lousy shot I used to be, Cady?" The question was sudden and nervous in the room.

"Yeah," Cady said.

"Not any more," Sam said. "You'd have been proud of me this afternoon."

"Is that a fact?" Cady said. When he scratched himself, his fingernails made a tearing noise on his khaki pants.

"Yes," Sam said. He flushed and relapsed into silence.

"A nice double," George said. "Two black duck."

Cady took a long swallow of his drink, looked at his glass, emptied it, and set it on the floor. "You should've had that little teal, George," he said.

Sam stared from one to the other, feeling his stomach tighten. George McConville was glaring competitively at Cady, who was grinning now in earnest. Forgotten by both of them, Sam rose to his feet, knowing the truth was unpleasant even before it occurred to him.

"Why didn't you speak up?" George blurted angrily.

"I figured you two were making enough racket down there without my adding to it," Cady said.

"Where in hell were you?" Sam said, feeling foolish in the new hunting clothes when Cady glanced at him.

"Behind that big tree there, right back of the blind." Cady had taken a match from his jacket pocket and inserted it now between two front teeth. "You two picked a rotten place to shoot, on a bluebird day like today. The ducks got a look at you too far off, all except the blacks and that little teal. It was dark when he came in, anyway. It's lucky I wasn't the warden."

When neither spoke, he shrugged his shoulders very slightly. "Now tomorrow that blind'll be just right, there's a wind coming up, and rain from the looks of that yellow sky this afternoon, and the birds'll want to set in there back by the woods, and they won't see you either. It's just up to you guys to see *them*, and not shoot up a box of shells after they've gone by." Here he looked carefully at Sam and winked.

"You saw the two blacks come in, then," George said.

"Yeah," Cady said. "I would have seen them go out again, too." He looked from one to the other. "I'm surprised you didn't hear my shots." Again they said nothing. "If we're going to get out there early, we'd better hit the sack," Cady said. He seemed uneasy, scratching the stubble on his cheek.

"I'll show you where you're sleeping," George said.

Sam said nothing. Too confused and disappointed to be angry, he watched Cady Shipman leave the room before putting his own glass down and following. Behind them, George switched off the lights, and in the moment he waited with Cady in the darkness, the rain flicked down in a first light rush against the stairwell window,

CHAPTER 10

CADY OPENED THE DOOR INTO THE BACK HALLWAY AND MOVING swiftly toward the kitchen without turning on the light heard the voices which paused giggled whispered then stopped entirely in one of the servants' rooms. His pack and saddle holster were lying by the stove. From a glance at the strap he knew the gun had been taken out and inspected, and returning through the corridor he kicked their door to startle them, grinning when he heard Daniel curse, and went out into the front hall. George was waiting at the foot of the stair, but Sam had disappeared.

"You might as well use Celia's room," George said. He led Cady up the stairs and, pausing at the landing, asked, "What was the idea of all that mystery today?"

"No mystery. I was just amusing myself. I didn't bother you, did I?"

"No," George hesitated, seeming anxious to find fault. "But Rubicam was sort of disappointed about his ducks."

"Rubicam!" Cady said. "He should have known he couldn't hit anything."

" I don't see why you had to tell him."

"You're pretty conscientious all of a sudden," Cady said. "You're not the same old George." It irritated him when George did not answer, but nonetheless he was disturbed by the rebuke and changed the subject when they came to Celia's room. "God, it

172

feels empty," he said, looking around. "Doesn't Celia come down any more?"

"Hardly ever. Eve's been here a couple of times, but otherwise the room hasn't been used."

Cady glanced at George, feeling an urge to talk to someone, and said, "So this is where she comes, then. Nice going, George."

"What do you mean by that?"

"I don't know. Just that a couple of times lately Mister Murray couldn't locate her in New York when he wanted her down for the weekend."

"Listen," George flushed. "Don't go jumping to conclusions."

"You sure you don't want me to?"

"Hell no," George interrupted. "And besides, it's got nothing to do with you, Cady." He turned to go, very red in the face.

"Of course it does," Cady grinned. "After all, I'm an old friend of hers, aren't I? Wasn't I the first to kiss her, George?"

George McConville stared at him. "That was years ago," he said. "She was only a child."

"Well, it's not as if I hadn't seen her since," Cady began. He wondered if he should tell George how he felt about her but checked himself, knowing it was the whiskey which made him garrulous. Instead he took a cigarette, striking the match as George said, "I'll set the alarm for five. Goodnight," and the door shut in his face. He held the match, staring at the door, until it burned his fingers, then crossed the room and sat down hard on the bed.

"To hell with you, George," he said under his breath, and put the burnt fingers in his mouth. I *was* the first to kiss her, too, he thought, Cady Shipman the caretaker's son.

In the silence, the words of the song rose clearly from the darkness below.

Listen, child, listen to the east wind risin'
Down on the long black shore,
And nobody knows that somebody is dyin'
Way down the long black shore.

At the sound of Rosa Menhaden's voice, he sat upright on the
bed like a listening animal, still holding the straps of the pack and
saddle holster which lay at his feet on the floor. He was angry and
restless, he did not feel like sleeping. The whiskey was still strong
in him, and he cursed himself for having told George too much
in the library, for having told anybody anything. He hadn't been
drunk, he had simply succumbed to a desire to talk at length.
George would have been one thing, but that crazy Rubicam had
hung around listening and not saying anything and being the pain
in the butt he had always been, the same old phony Sam. But
Sam had really been surprised about those ducks, that was one
thing. Yet George had gotten surly about it, he couldn't understand that, it used to be George who was the first to laugh at
Sammy Sissypants, any excuse at all. Things had changed, all
right. George had changed, and Daniel and Rosa, everybody but
himself and Rubicam. Cyrus McConville dead and his wife gone
away, Percy and Sarah separated and gone, Eve Murray married
and divorced already and living alone in New York, and even Celia
gone, she had never liked the Point, it had always been too quiet
for her.

He removed his boots and, rising from the bed, moved quietly
across the floor. So this was Celia's room. The closet was empty,
and so was the bureau. She had gone for good, then, not even an
old pair of sneakers. It would have been nice if she had been down
this weekend, he could have gotten to her somehow, and Celia
McConville really knew her stuff

Celia had a houseparty over the weekend, three boys and three girls, and didn't even ask him up from the cottage for one drink. And that Sunday afternoon, lying bored to death on his bed, he heard the car back into the Italian statue and swerve off down the road for half a mile in first. He rose and went out through the room where Percy and Sarah were sitting opposite each other at the table and Daniel was reading a comic book on the doorstep. "Where you goin'?" Daniel said, and he answered, "Never mind," and Daniel said, "Can I take your medal and show it in high school if I shine your shoes?" and his mother had said to Daniel, "No you can't, you'll only lose it. Leave Cady alone now, just back from the war and all," and Daniel said, "Okay, only maybe he don't wanta be left alone."

Cady went up the driveway from the cottage and inspected the toppled statue and set it up again. It had a white gouge where the nose had been on the green stone face. He walked around the house onto the terrace and watched the ocean for a while, it was late September and the water was brittle blue in the afternoon breeze. When he turned to go, Celia was watching him from the French doors. She looked very pretty until he came closer, strolling forward as casually as he could, and saw how crumpled she was, the circles under her eyes and a sort of tired sensuality in the way she leaned against the door frame.

"You didn't go with them, then," he said, feeling uncomfortable.

"Good God, no, I'm sick to death of them. They're just a bunch of kids."

"And what are you, their grandmother?" This sounded very stupid to him, and his laughter did not carry it off.

"I'm twenty-two, at least. That's all you are yourself, remember?" She smiled at him, lifting one leg up across her other

knee and scratching her calf. He did not want to look under her
dress, but could not help himself. She smiled again. Then she
turned and went inside, watching him over her shoulder until he
followed her. "You want a drink, Cady?" she said.

"All right," he said, and added, "It was nice of you to ask me
up for one while your friends were here." Again his laugh was un-
successful, and when she stared at him, surprised, he turned from
her and glanced around the dark twilight room as if in the captive
fog of cigarette smoke it held the secret of his unpopularity.

"Well listen, you know they wouldn't have—well, you couldn't
have *beared* them, really. And besides, I thought you'd probably
want to see your family and all, Sarah told me you just got
home—"

"Sure," he said. "I have a great time with my family. She and
Percy sit and scream at each other, and all Daniel wants to talk
about is dead Japanese. It's great." But it occurred to him that he
would not mind talking about dead Japanese to Celia.

"Well honestly, baby, I didn't know." She stood before him
holding out his glass, then slipped down beside him on the sofa.
"Do you hate me?" she whispered. He could tell from her tone as
well as from his inability to embarrass her that she had been drinking. Her long fair hair had fallen forward along the sides of her
head, her lipstick was all but gone, and one of her shoes was
missing. She removed the other one and tossed it aside, drawing
her legs up beneath her with calculated grace, then reached and
took his glass from his hand and sipped at it, peering at him over
its rim. When she returned it to him, she touched the ribbons on
his tunic with a long slow finger before letting her hand fall back
on his forearm. "You going to wear that uniform forever?" she
said. He shifted around so that he faced her, trying to fathom her
expression. When he took her hand, she curled softly about and

laid her head on his shoulder as neatly as if he had pressed a button. Disconcerted, he mumbled, "Well, I haven't gotten civvies yet, I might join up again. I just don't know."

"Don't join anything," Celia whispered. "Don't leave me. I'm so damned lonely."

"Me too," he heard himself say, and blushed for having said it.

"Me too," she chanted, "oh God, me too!" He knew from her expression that she wasn't laughing at him, there was a wild yearning in it which made his heart pound, and she regarded him unblinkingly a moment before raising her head and kissing him damply on the mouth. He felt the soft searching heat of her tongue and the fingernails which dug savagely into his neck, and he thought, be careful, for God's Sweet Sake be careful, but it was too late already. He thought no longer, passing through the deep lost minutes as through a painful dream until he was lying still again and listening to her breathing. And he dared not think until she whispered, "Are you sorry?" and then he sat up and put his head into his hands. "We're crazy," he said. "I didn't have anything—"

"It's all right," she said. "I know what I'm doing, believe me." Her laugh was curiously forlorn, and seemingly directed at herself. "I'm wearing a little gadget, it just so happens. I find that I wear it a good deal of the time." She laughed again, and he had to look at her to be sure she was not crying. "Are you shocked?" she said. Celia's voice had risen to a trembling shout, she was holding one of his hands to her meager breasts, and when he kissed her, the flushed skin burned against his cheek.

"No," he said uneasily. "Of course not."

"You are, though, aren't you!" She hurled his hand at him and stood up, furiously straightening her dress. "You took advantage of me because I was drunk, didn't you, Cady!"

"No," Cady said. "You wanted me to."

"And I suppose you didn't want to or anything! In other words, I seduced you, the poor little innocent caretaker's son, is that it? And I suppose you'll tell everybody you meet about it, won't you?"

"Listen, Ciel—"

"Since when do you call me 'Ceil'? Sam is the only one who ever called me that. Well, will you or won't you tell?"

"No," Cady said, and got up himself. "I'm not that proud of it." He hadn't meant this the way she took it and was astonished when she slapped him. He struck back with a reflex action, opening his palm only at the last split second before his hand struck her face and she spun sideways and down onto the couch, already moaning.

"Listen," he blustered, in agony. "I didn't mean it, you took me by surprise. Please, I—" When he sat down next to her, she kicked at him. "The war hero!" she screamed. "Is that how you won your poor cheap little medals, is that how you—you're nothing but an animal, a dirty caretaker's son, and maybe not even that from what I hear!" When she sat up suddenly, he was so shocked by her appearance that he lost track for a moment of what she was saying. Her hair shot out at insane angles, her dead white mouth writhed grotesquely on her face, and her eyes swam red and incredibly wet, as if they had burst. "They say you're old Abraham's son, an honest-to-God village bastard, is that right, Caleb? Christ, what a crazy name! Caleb! And you smell, do you know that, Caleb, you need a bath!" She screeched with laughter.

He stood before her, transfixed with horror and rage, and terror, too—he realized this later—yes, terror of the creature before him. He wanted to strike out at her, beat her back and forth across the head until that face of hatred disappeared, and the memory of her. She seemed to sense this, for when he moved forward a little she crouched back, grinding her teeth. "And you'd better not tell," she breathed, a little frightened now herself, "you'd better not, or I'll holler Rape until I'm blue in the face, I promise I will!"

He stopped.

"Don't say that again, Celia," he said, controlling himself. "About Abraham, I mean. If you weren't a girl, I'd beat you to death."

Inexplicably she burst into tears, and the sobs were unlike anything he had ever heard before, deep and coarse and tearing, from the soul of some terrible pain. She lay curled on the corner of the couch, her hands clenched over her face, and he stood still a moment in the darkening room and watched her, frightened. Then he crossed the room to the door. "Don't leave me, Cady," she cried to him, "I didn't mean it! Oh please please please don't leave me alone!" The word "alone" was drawn out in a moan, penetrating as a damp cold air from the sea, it seemed to trail him across the terrace and die away in the evening wind as he went down the lawn to the lights of the cottage.

"Where've you been?" Percy Shipman said to him. "You look like the devil was after you."

"Aw, Cady ain't scairda nothin', huh, Cady?" Daniel demanded. "How could a guy get the medals he got," he complained rhetorically, "if he was scairda somethin'?"

"Nobody asked you, Daniel," Sarah said. "Go wash your hands." She stood at the stove, fork poised above a pot, and it occurred to Cady how swiftly old his mother had become, she hardly seemed to care about her appearance any more. She stood heavy-footed in slippers, and her staled auburn hair, so striking once, hung in weak exasperated curls above the steam from the simmering vegetables.

Up on the hill the garage door banged and the McConville

station wagon started stalled then came down toward them, its tires ripping on the gravel driveway as it passed the cottage and howled away down the road. "Who's that?" Sarah said suspiciously. "Didn't they all leave before?"

"Nobody's supposed to touch that car," Percy said, returning from the door. "Maybe I better call the police out after it."

"No," Cady said. "That's Celia. She didn't go with the others."

"She ain't supposed to drive it," Percy insisted. He sat down again with an air of permanent weariness. "The boss'll only chew me out for lettin' her drive it, the crazy little—" He didn't finish.

Sarah Shipman cocked her head a little, sneering. "So," she said to Cady. "Is that where you've been? Fooling with that little hussy, showing her your medals, I'll bet. You're keeping pretty stylish company, my lad."

"You ought to be proud of him," Percy muttered. "He's takin' after you." He flushed beneath his sallow skin, fooling angrily with a piece of bread.

Sarah Shipman glanced at the bathroom door, behind which Daniel was running water from the tap. Then she shook the fork at Percy. "Don't you dare talk to me like that in front of my son," she said. "Don't you dare!"

"Ain't he my son, too?" Percy said. "That's what he's supposed to be, the way I heard it." He laughed abruptly, then glanced at Cady, adding, "Leave him alone, then. He ain't a kid no more."

Sarah said, "You're no better than a—" as Daniel came in. Daniel belched very loudly, and Sarah smacked him.

The following day Cady went to New York and re-enlisted, leaving behind him the sour confines of the cottage, the permanent and degrading odor of food, the sharp strife and sharper silences between his mother and Percy—his mind rebelled now against the phrase "my father"—and the alliance against life formed by Percy and Daniel Barleyfield in their loneliness. Cady had never noticed before the class distinction maintained within the household by his mother, how careful she was that they two speak proper English while letting the oblivious Daniel slip into Percy's nasal twang. He remembered how his cousin Bart and the Ferrari boys had baited him for his accent, accused him of imitating George McConville, and saw for the first time why this had come about. In the train south to Camp Lejeune, he had ample time to think about the cottage and the Point and Celia—where had she heard about Abraham?—about what Percy had meant by "He's taking after you"; was that connected with "Ain't he my son, too?" or was there something else—about all the world which was slipping away from him out into the long lonely miles of whistles and smoke and spoiled scrub country of America

Through the open window Rosa's voice drifted and fell within the wind, a song of remote mountains, a blues. He stopped his silent pacing and listened to her, imagining her in the black raincoat as he had seen her that morning and cursing himself for not having taken her, for having had a conscience, for Christ's sake— he'd been sorry for her, actually sorry for her, the way he had been sorry for George that night George owed him the dollar.

You can't afford a conscience, he told himself, a conscience is a luxury of the rich. He'd read that somewhere, and maybe it was right. A poor man had to fight for what he got the way a dog fought for a scrap, and he had a right to everything. But he had never considered himself a poor man, that's what he had told that longhair at the college. Wasn't he a Shipman, and didn't the Shipmans have one of the oldest names on the coast, like the Winthrops and the Coffins? What good is your goddamn name, the fellow had said, if you haven't got anything? My father had one of the oldest names in the Warsaw ghetto, the fellow had said, what does that make me, the King of the Jews?

That was one thing he finally learned in the war, that names no longer meant a thing, but only brains and strength, and the stronger the man, the more people took his orders. War was the Great Leveler of Values, he had read that somewhere, too, he had read a lot in those days. To the men in his company he was educated. Why, even that colonel's sister in Raleigh knew less than he did, and a stupid slut like that could get him a bad conduct discharge just because he wouldn't fool with her any more.

He had come home again, he wasn't a hero any more in 1948 but a man without a job. By that time Cyrus McConville was dead, and Percy and Sarah had left the Point. He went fishing with his cousin Bart and Joe Ferrari on the trawler *Katharine S.*, but the boat was too small for them, and his Uncle Barlow had come aboard one day after there'd been a fight and said, "Look here, Caleb, I'm going to put you ashore for a while where you'll have more room," and he had said—and was sorry afterward, for he liked Old Barlow—"You're not going to put me any damned place, because I'm quitting." And a week later he had run into Joshua Murray in the village and asked him if he knew of a job for a half-educated man, and Murray had said, "Do you want to manage my place?" and he had said, "Why not?" and gone along with him that same day inland

Motionless, clutching his belongings again, he listened to the raindrops which ticked against the silence like dead leaves blowing across a grave. He scented the weather change in the air slipping through the window, trying to clear his head of lust and whiskey and resentment by shaking it viciously the way a dog shakes a rat and, catching himself in the gesture, scowled disgustedly. He knew his thinking was getting him nowhere, he could not concentrate on any one thing, especially with that little piece Rosa yelping her head off down below. He should get some sleep.

He broke the shotgun and removed the two spent shells, tossing them a moment in his palm as if calculating their weight and relishing all over again the sound of the voices from the blind. "I got them, I got them!" Sammy Sissypants had shouted.

They hadn't even turned to look behind them.

In the night it rained, and in the morning it was raining still, cold driven rain before a northeasterly wind, and Cady Shipman, sculling the other two across the marsh before the light, could sense in the blackness and wet misery of the skiff a reluctance to hunt, intellectual on the part of Rubicam, physical on the part of George, who seemed to have persuaded himself that he must take advantage of this perfect shooting weather. Cady knew that if he himself were not there, both of them would still be in bed, and that Sam would be in bed, one way or the other, if he were less afraid of missing out on something. Cady did not pursue the impression any further, because already it sufficed for the case he was building against Sam Rubicam in his mind, nor did he bother to explore his anger against the other, because the anger was for its own sake, and he was content to let it evolve itself in an outward direction rather than let it degenerate into dissatisfaction with his lot, as it did when he was alone.

At the blind, he set out the decoys in swift unsplashing silence, working against the wind on the drifting skiff, gauging the distances and the anchor lines so that the wooden birds would not bang lifelessly together, then pulling back behind the blind as George watched him, thinking how lucky it was that no sun would rise to expose the decoys in their sparkling wet falsehood, and deciding out of a sleepless sense of survival to insinuate himself

into the south corner of the blind, where he would have first shot
at the ducks landing into the wind.

Sam Rubicam had a cigarette in the front of his mouth, standing hands-in-pockets at the rear of the blind.

"You two shoot first," he said to Cady. "I'm not awake yet."

"We won't get to shoot at all if you don't put that cigarette
out," George whispered.

"It doesn't matter today," Cady said. "By the time they see
that cigarette, they'll be lying in the water. Anyway, he'll have
finished it before it's light enough to shoot." As he spoke, he drew
the shotgun from its holster, idling into the south corner of the
blind.

"I've never seen a gun case like that before," George said.

"Where did you get it?" Sam said, obviously uninterested.

"It came with the gun." He watched their faces turn to the
shotgun as he spoke. Sam Rubicam looked away again, shrugging
out the morning with his shoulders, and George McConville
looked away, too suddenly, Cady thought, when he saw the fine
tooling of the metal.

"Present from Mister Murray," Cady said. "He had no use for
it."

George looked relieved, and Cady handed the gun to George to
feel.

"He didn't even bother to take his initial plate off the stock,"
George said. "That's a damned nice present, he must think a lot
of you."

"I guess he does," Cady grinned and, taking the gun back,
shoved two shells into the broken barrels and snapped it to, soundlessly in the rain.

George and Sam were wearing heavy parkas, and the water
streamed across their faces, but it fell free from the rear of Cady's

old felt hat. He was wearing what he always wore, a short field jacket and khaki pants, almost invisible under the high rubber boots, and he was wet across his thin rump and down the backs of his legs. In a little while, the rain would penetrate with its cargo of cold, and he would be sodden all over.

The dawn stole softly through the rain, tentative as though it might not stay, and the three men crouched low in the blind, Sam in the rear with his gun unloaded. Even in this weather, they could feel the stir of morning, and Cady was restless, clicking the trigger safety on and off as he had so often on Pacific watch, peering carefully through the brush, yet not seeing the first birds, three black ducks, until they had skidded in on the edge of the decoys.

George had not seen them at all, but he had heard the delicate splash, and Cady, without turning, sensed the tension of his friend. He watched the birds for a moment, they were picking their way suspicious among the decoys, and then he rose, bringing George up with a jar of his elbow.

The blacks froze for a moment, then broke the surface. George, off-balance, fired too soon and missed as the first bird fell, but his second barrel caught another duck as it leveled off, and it hit the water in a staccato splash with the third duck as Sam rose shouting behind them.

"That's it," Cady said. "That's three."

"Nice double," Sam said. "Almost as nice as yesterday's. I don't suppose you ever miss, do you, Cady?"

Cady looked at him before he answered. Sam's expression was guileless. "Not if I can help it," Cady said. He moved backward, ejecting the shells from his gun as he did so, and Sam took his place.

Cady loaded again while he waited behind them. A big bunch of teal came in next, and again they were among the decoys before they appeared out of the rain. George breathed nervously over his shoulder to Cady, "How'll we handle this? I always miss these little ones."

"Take two each, on the water," Cady whispered. "I'll kill two more on the rise."

"You loaded, for Christ's sake?" George's face was ferocious in the rain.

"Hurry up," Sam whispered. "They're not going to stay forever."

"I'll be damned if I'll shoot them on the water," George said. The greenwings rose. There was a barrage of noise, and three of them fell.

"Did I get one?" Sam said. "I think I got one."

"Yeah," Cady said. "We should have had six."

"Look," George said, "what the hell did you shoot for? It was our turn, wasn't it? And anyway, I don't like a gun going off past my ear like that."

"All right," Cady said. "Only we're out here to shoot ducks, aren't we?"

"For the fun of it," George said. "Not to shoot them on the water!"

"All right," Cady said. "I won't load up next time."

"You've already shot your limit," George said. "Let us shoot ours."

"It's not my fault you missed those teal, George."

George laughed angrily. "No wonder," he said. "I was scared you'd blow my head off."

"Look out," Sam hissed, and they crouched again. His was the only loaded gun, and Cady studied George's angry face as Sam rose again and fired twice, the second time straight up over his head, missing and falling backward onto Cady, already laughing and saying, "This is the way to shoot. Just lie on your back and blaze away as they go over. Where did he fall?"

"He didn't, you poor sap, you were eight yards behind him both times," George said. He was laughing, too, and Cady watched him, feeling the rain which slid off the back of his jacket as he crouched and ran down the back of his pants. He watched two more ducks skirt before the blind before he interrupted their laughter.

"They're going by us a mile a minute," he said. "We're not out here for laughs."

"We are," Sam Rubicam said. He had stopped laughing, and looked at Cady with a triumph almost feminine. Cady studied him unblinking until he looked away again, and George said nothing.

"It's funny how you feel, George," Cady said, "about taking birds on the water, I mean." When George gazed at him expectantly, the green eyes watchful under the hair plastered down across his forehead, Cady continued slowly, licking now and then at the rain which slid down his cheeks and tickled the corners of his mouth, and looking past the other two to where the birds would come from. "I didn't tell you last night about Mister Murray's shoveler duck, did I? The reason I had to leave my job? Well, the other morning we were sitting in his blind, watching the ducks in the morning flight. You've seen that big pond of his, it's full of birds all the time because nobody shoots there. The only gun on the place was this one"—he patted the stock of the Purdy—"which he gave to me for shooting crows. Mister Murray doesn't shoot any more.

"Anyway, we were just sitting there, it was a pretty nice morning and we had a jug of coffee along. There were big bunches of duck trading up and down the pond, pitch black against that early light before the sun, and the old man was identifying them, the different species, by shape and flight, he was pretty good at it, too. Well, the sun was just breaking out over the trees when this single came over all alone—"

"H-sst!" George whispered. "Coming in on our right." He and Sam rose together, and the harsh crash of their guns flew open-mouthed into the swirling mist of wind and water. "Goddamn it," Sam said. "Foiled again."

When they had settled, Cady resumed his account, remembering himself exactly how the old man had jumped to his feet and put his fieldglasses on the single bird, by that time only a black blur low against the trees across the cove. Mister Murray stared after it and when it was gone sat down again shaking his head.

"You know what that was, Cady?" he had whispered.

Cady had assumed it was a teal, but he said, "Nosir, I don't," just for the hell of it.

"That was a shoveler," Mister Murray said. "The first one I've ever seen this far north."

Cady had never heard of a shoveler, nor was he sure that the old man had gotten that good a look at it. "Is that right?" he said.

"I don't think I could be mistaken. I got a good look at its bill, you see, although it went past very quickly. However, I'd never put it down on my list without a closer look at it. It is simply a very rare thrill for me and like most rare things, it was gone almost before I knew it was there, like a wonderful smell or taste or sound." For a moment he seemed lost in reflection. Then he said, "It seems to me that a man can find much of the meaning of life in one simple event like the passing of that duck. There"— and pointed at a black duck disappearing over the trees—"the meaning comes and goes just like that, a man sees it clearly but only for an instant, and only in silhouette, and then it is gone again, and sometimes he wonders if it was ever there at all, or if it was only his imagination or his hope."

"He's kind of a sad case, isn't he, this man of yours," Cady said.

"Yes, I suppose he is," Mister Murray said, standing up in the blind and staring out over the pond. "But in this 'sad case,' as you put it, there still exists a capacity for struggle. When a man gives over his identity, his importance to a dogma of any kind, and with it the identity and importance of humankind taken one by one, he is already dead in his soul. Our man is still alive and thrashing, you see, he is confused, he doubts. As long as he is confused, there is hope for him as a human being. . . ."

"And so on," Cady said, angrily aware that he was paraphrasing the old man's ideas very badly. "Anyway, I was going to tell you about the shoveler duck. . . ."

"Good night!" Sam Rubicam said. "So the old bird's still handing out that sort of thing, is he?"

George and Sam looked up at Cady, their faces somehow angry beneath their parkas. All three were soaked now, the rain falling even harder as he sculled the boat back across the marsh. The wind had come up again in crazy gusts and charges.

"How come you didn't stay there?" George said. "It must have been a nice job." George glanced again at the Purdy shotgun.

The fact of George's suspicion did not interest Cady. He was thinking for the first time of another factor of his departure, the existence of which it was hard to admit—its effect on Eve. She's not going to like it about the horse, Cady thought. I hope they had the sense to throw a blanket over him when he got back. If the horse got pneumonia, she would never come near him again. He remembered her standing by Tenerife's stall, how well she looked in jodhpurs and riding jacket, and how she would turn to find him watching her, the riding crop tapping soundlessly upon her thigh as they regarded each other.

"It was a nice job," he said at last. "He's a nice old man, Mister Murray." Cady wondered if he should tell them, knowing ahead of time that he would. "Did you just get tired of it?" Sam Rubicam was saying, and Cady answered, "Not exactly," and paused. "I don't know just how it happened," he continued slowly, "but one morning a little afterward I was down in his blind patching it up. I stood up a minute to catch my breath, and damned if this big-billed duck didn't jump up out in front. It went on down the pond, then came back over the trees. I suppose it was after the corn I had in there. Well, I had a shotgun along, and there were decoys in the blind for when Mister Murray wanted to take photographs. I tossed a couple out and sure enough, in a minute or two this shoveler duck came in again, and I shot it."

"What for?" George said. He looked angry again.

"I don't know, to tell the truth. It was something to do with how rare it was, I had never seen one close up before, and I just got an idea I wanted to hold the son-of-a-bitch in my hand."

"I hope it was worth it to you," Sam said, and Cady watched him glance to George for approval.

"I didn't even pick it up," Cady said. "I just looked at it laying there belly up in the water, and thinking what it would have meant to Mister Murray to photograph it, and the next thing I knew, I had my shell pouch out. The other ducks were moving around on account of my shot, and they came right into the decoys, they weren't leery like ducks that have been shot into, and in they came, and I dropped them as fast as I could reload. I had a full box in my pouch, and I don't believe I missed a bird. Isn't that the damnedest thing?"

"What did Mister Murray say to that?" George said quietly.

"I don't know," Cady said. "I never stuck around to find out."

"And here you are," Sam Rubicam said.

"Here I am," Cady said.

CHAPTER 11

On THE STATION PLATFORM AT SHIPMAN'S CROSSING, EVE looked for George and wondered dully why he was not there until she remembered again and stood still where she was until her father came, calling and waving until he had reached her, kissed her, seized her suitcase, and bustled away toward the car, bumping into people and apologizing.

She let him talk, he was chattering out his pent-up loneliness, and kept her eyes on the country road twisting inland under the headlights like a serpent pursued. *Dr. Lichenstein had come again, but . . .* Home again, she thought, that was a comfort at least, perhaps she would stay forever. She would take the bay horse Tenerife and ride and ride until she had outrun everything, scream worry away into the wind blowing past her face and ride until she was purified again, and free. *I refused the injection, didn't I?* How wonderful to be home, where everything was done for you, planned for you, a place of firesides and stables, wood smoke and autumn colors, quiet, of favorite furniture and soft old clothes and talismans of other years. *I threw away the quinine pills, I was ashamed.* The familiar things, all the familiar things, the narrow dark New England stairs, the creaky floors, the andirons, the old bubbled glass in the windows, the faces on the walls, the shining copper, silver, glassware, the littered books, the sounds, the smells entrenched in memory of childhood. *Herr Dok-tor Rudolf Lichen-*

stein, Abortionist—it's not I who should be ashamed, it's George, George, George.

". . . oh, none of you have changed very much since you were children. But this fellow Cady—"

"He hasn't changed much either," Eve said. "What's he done now?"

"Weren't you listening, Evelyn? I was just telling you. So this morning the telephone rang. . . ."

She thought about Cady and herself in 1948, just after her divorce, she thought of it always when she was depressed. That was the year he had come as caretaker, "estate manager," he had called himself, "I don't want to be an estate manager all my life." Cady was hard and not quite handsome, appraising her that first morning in the stable before he said, "Look, everybody's so goddamned tactful about your divorce, they treat you like an invalid or something, do you want to talk about it?" And grateful, she answered, "No, not yet. But thanks anyway, Cady. It's not that I'm sensitive about it, I just don't have anything to say." After that it was a comfort to be near him, she sought him out to talk to, walk with, and once she made him dance with her in the roadhouse near Shipman's Crossing. He had gotten drunk out of pure embarrassment. "There's nobody else I'd do this for," he muttered in her ear, holding her tightly but away from him. She was high herself and wanted to come closer to him, and when he relaxed at last and pressed her against him, she felt a pure lust she had never known before. Later she let him kiss her, let him say the things she had no right to hear, how he had loved her always and would educate himself, do anything she wanted. His words were fevered, somehow suicidal, and yet she stopped him only when he spoke about the Shipman name and how she had nothing there to be ashamed of—"Cady, listen to me, we have to stop, we're tight, we don't mean what we say." And he had released her then and stared at her, already sober. "Why did you—" He didn't finish, clutching her wrist until it hurt, until more frightened than ashamed she said, "I like you, but I didn't mean to lead you on, forgive me," knowing he would not forgive her, would never forgive anybody anything. "You've made a fool of me," he said at last, and left her.

". . . and then when I went down this afternoon and found those ducks, I decided he'd gone quite mad." They were home at last, and Eve climbed tiredly out of the car and preceded him into the house.

"I thought you didn't shoot your ducks any more," she said, sitting down in an armchair without taking off her coat. "Is supper early, I hope? I'm starved."

"I don't believe you've listened to a word I've said. Cady Shipman shot the ducks, not me. At least two dozen of them, floating around the pond like so much refuse, it took me half the afternoon to round them up. And one, you see, was the shoveler duck. A most curious thing, because the other day with Cady I was sure I'd seen a shoveler, and on the strength of it filled the poor boy with a lot of queer ideas, philosophy, you know the sort of thing I'm given to—" Joshua Murray was pacing back and forth before the fire, as he always did when he had words to choose, and she knew he was about to tell her something unpleasant.

"The poor boy," she laughed. "How can you say that? What did he do it for? Where is he now?"

"I don't have any idea. The police want me to prosecute, but I don't think I will."

"The police? My God, for shooting ducks?"

"No, no, you haven't listened, my dear, although I must say, if I prosecuted him for anything, that would be it. Disgraceful performance." Joshua Murray flushed in anger, then shrugged his shoulders. "The only shoveler I've ever seen here, too. We'll be having it for supper, I suppose."

"Daddy, listen, you said the police—"

"Well, yes, Evelyn, I'm sorry to say he took along my gun when he left, that fine Purdy .16 I had. And that brings me to the most disagreeable feature of the business." He stopped and peered at her, as if to ascertain her capacity for bad news. "Tenerife. He took Tenerife wherever he went and apparently sent him back, because the reins were tied up on the neck. At any rate the poor beast stumbled into a ditch back down the road and broke his leg and had to be put down." Joshua Murray sighed and stared into the fire. "There," he said, turning to her, "now you have it all. I just hope it won't spoil your weekend, my dear, for there's nothing to be done about it. Now tell me about yourself, and what you've been up to."

"Of course there's something to be done about it," Eve said. "You've got to prosecute him! How dare he be so ungrateful, how dare he!" She found now in herself the anger she had searched for all that day, rising from her chair and taking her father's arm beside the fireplace. "And I know where he is, too, I'll bet you anything he's at the Point. I'm going to call the police this minute." She started toward the phone, but her father held her.

"No," he said. "I've been thinking about it, and the thing to do is to call old Barlow and have him speak to Cady and tell him to return the gun. If I call Cady myself, it will only anger and shame him needlessly. The indirect way is better. Cady respects old Barlow, and he'll listen."

"Daddy, listen, never mind about respect, the point is that you mustn't make that old man do what you should do yourself. The best way is to let the police handle it, and teach him a lesson."

"No. Please, Evelyn, I like Cady despite all this, and I think he likes me in that odd way of his. It's not a matter of ingratitude. He'll probably turn up with the gun tomorrow."

"If he doesn't, I'll call the police, I promise you."

"No. I think in a way it's a Shipman affair." Joshua Murray frowned. "You can't apply standard judgments and punishments these days," he said, and Eve could tell by his intonation that he was about to present some sort of philosophical argument.

"Give me a drink, Daddy, will you?"

"Be delighted to," he said, looking disappointed. A moment later, forgetting her drink, he sat down. "I daresay," he began, "that this mid-century is a transition from an old life to a new, and its people, not knowing how to adjust, are bound to behave queerly. We are losing the faith in the individual self, the contempt for the social categories which reduce man to what he often is, a predictable vicious mammal," Joshua Murray orated.

"What did Cady think of your ideas?" Eve interrupted him. "Are you planning to fix me that drink?"

Joshua Murray laughed sheepishly and made his way out of the room. Returning with her glass, he said, "I don't know what Cady thought, I doubt if he absorbed anything. Sam—" he glanced at her—"Sam would understand it better, but has he the perseverance to act on something?" When Eve said nothing, he continued hurriedly, "George McConville, though—do you remember the time he said to his father, 'I don't see what Jews have to do with it'? That Easter weekend we were with them at the Point?"

"Yes." How odd, she thought, I remembered that just this afternoon.

"I've liked him ever since. And what's George like these days?"

"He's a little mixed-up, I think."

"Well, most thinking people are, I suppose. I'm not at all sure, speaking for myself, that I want to see the changes your generation is going to see. I'm afraid I'm rather cowardly, though. It just strikes me sometimes," he added after a moment, looking worried, "that this might be a wonderful year to die."

"Perhaps George is cowardly, too," Eve said.

Her father glanced at her.

"I don't think so," he said, and after a moment, "He may need responsibility, though, toward other people as well as toward himself. His father, for one, would never give the boy a chance at it."

A note in his voice made Eve look up at him. "No, no, Daddy," she said, "you couldn't possibly understand."

"I suppose I couldn't," said Joshua Murray.

She awoke in the morning to the ripping of the rain across the roof. Rising on her elbow, she could see the gray smoke of it in the narrow trees, which hurled their last leaves skyward in sacrifice to the wind, then fell into the slow sway of the penitent wet woods. She lay back into the warmth of the bed. How splendid bed was, after all, how reassuring, she could imagine herself safe there against everything.

As a child in bed she had looked on breathless as her father opened the winter window and the cold air slipped across the sill and searched through the bedroom for her, slinking into the closet and along the walls and rustling around among the curtains until finally it found her and struck her nose. She would squeal then and pull the covers over her head entirely, leaving one small hole to breathe through and feeling secure and warm against Jack Frost, giants, goblins, ghosts, witches, and creatures out of the bright yellow, red and blue books by Grimm and Andersen, much as she imagined then that a rabbit felt within its burrow.

The morning wandered on and still she lay there half-dreaming half-listening half-wondering if, when she went to the bathroom, she would find that she had lost the baby, and if she would be sorry. The baby. It wasn't a baby at all, but a seed. There was a little book they had given her once about the saga of the spermatozoon, a plucky little fellow with a wriggly tail who survived all manner of hardships before finding refuge in the egg. All its little brothers and sisters, the book said, came to grief en route, and only little Skippy or whatever its name was made the grade and began the marvelous life cycle for which the author gave full credit to God.

To hell with you, Skippy, she thought, and smiled.

It was the smile which woke her irrevocably, and confronted anew with her pregnancy she held her breath. Her heart was pounding so that the bed oppressed her, she had to move, and she got up and went to the window, shivering in the chill wet air, and closed it with a peremptory bang. From below in the hall and the kitchen rose the sounds of the house, she heard a car stop in the driveway and glimpsed her father scuttling toward the front door with a huge sheaf of Sunday papers, holding his hat to his head with his other hand.

She drew on her wrapper, a baggy old thing of childhood discovered in the closet, and stood for a moment before the bathroom door. How familiar it all was, the somnolent Sunday mornings, the Sunday papers before the fire, even the weekend rain. And yet something was gone, she had felt it the night before at dinner with her father, a certain security, a restfulness removed from the implicit warmth of this comfortable country existence. Did it mean that after childhood there was an accounting to be made with the uncomfortable in life? If this was true, she thought, I'm off to a spectacular start.

Inspecting, and finding nothing, she sat alone for a time in the cold impersonality of the bathroom, bereft of thought. She did dare to think for fear her courage would not support her through another day, remembering only how she had hurled the quinine pills from the apartment window. Then her heart slowed, she could breathe again, and she prepared to dress herself.

A pathetic gesture, the pills, and to whom, to what? Not a sop to her morality, certainly, she couldn't fool herself that badly. Am I, Eve wondered, watching herself in the mirror as she brushed out her hair, afraid to lose the baby as well as to keep it?

Or am I afraid no matter what I do?

It wasn't a question of morals, that was really too silly, or of wanting a hold on George, at least not entirely, or even of mother instinct, one couldn't mother a seed. Yet there was something in that, all the same, she had used the word to Doctor Lichenstein— unnatural. Weak. Cowardly. Life was too brief to compromise, it was better to have the courage of one's mistakes and suffer for them.

But I don't have that courage, you see, her reflection said. And I think I have more courage than most.

Joshua Murray joined her at the breakfast table, rattling his newspaper. "The storm will grow worse, apparently," he said, and read aloud, " 'Winds of near-hurricane velocity tonight, followed by clearing and colder.' Odd weather for October, I must say. Well, you slept well, did you, my dear?"

"Wonderfully, Daddy. There's something about that old bed that does it."

"Well, and being in the country, of course. However, you're quite right, I remember myself that whenever I came home, to my first home, that is, I slept better than anywhere else in the old bed I had as a child. I suppose it's associations of some sort, or—" He paused and peered at her. She was staring tragically at her grapefruit. "I don't suppose such subjects interest you just now, do they, Evelyn?" Joshua Murray smiled ruefully, sympathetically.

"Of course they do, Daddy. I simply—"

"Is there anything you would like to speak to me about, my dear?"

"No." She shook her head, not rudely, yet with a finality which admitted to something wrong, admitted, too, that she was past paternal help. This was the first time she had ever denied him— for in a sense she was denying Joshua Murray the father and not herself—and he waited patiently but not hopefully outside the en- closure of their comradeship for her to readmit him. She could not. "I'm sorry," she said. "It's nothing, really," and thought, how frightened he looks, less for me than for himself, poor lonely man.

"My God," Joshua Murray said, "it's a dreadful thing when a man can't even help his own daughter."

The remark was so unlike him in its petulance that she started from her brooding and stared at him. "I'm sorry, Daddy, I didn't mean—" she began.

"No, no, I'm talking nonsense," he was muttering, "I don't mean it the way it sounds."

"Of course you don't." She remembered later how she had said this, the first time she had ever spoken to him in the consoling tones one adopted with children and old people. There was a silence. When she could bear his gaze no longer, she blurted, "Are you going to call Barlow Shipman, Daddy?"

"Call him? Whatever for?"

"About Cady."

"Oh, yes, Cady. Did you know that Cady was called Caleb after his grandfather?"

"No, I didn't."

"Well, he was."

"I suppose he was. Daddy, I'll call Barlow for you if you want."

"You've gotten awfully vengeful, Evelyn," Joshua Murray complained. "I thought you were fond of Cady."

"I am. At least, I sympathize with him. However, there's no excuse for behavior like this, he's rotten spoiled like the others, like Sam—" She stopped.

"And George?" He regarded her at length. "It's all got something to do with George, hasn't it, old girl? And you won't let me help you." Dolefully he shook his head as if expecting comfort from her, as if by tacit agreement he had passed in the recent minutes from a position of counselor to one of dependent. She was frightened and a little horrified.

"Daddy, I told you there was nothing you could do." She rose to her feet and started out of the room.

"My dear Evelyn, there's no reason to become angry—"

"I'll be back in a minute," Eve said.

For it had happened, and her heart pounded so that she felt faint and had to lean and press her forehead against the lavatory wall. I'm all right, she told herself, I'm not having a baby at all, and wondered why she wanted so to cry. But she did not cry, and after a moment felt enraged instead. I'm going to go see him, he's gotten off too easily, I'm going to go see him, first thing tomorrow morning, I'm— When she came out again into the hall, she went directly to the telephone and said to the local operator, "Will you get me Captain Shipman, please? That's right. I'm calling from Mr. Murray's." Then she felt her father's hand tremble down upon her shoulder.

"You have no right," Joshua Murray whispered. "He's my old friend, I'll speak with him myself."

She went upstairs again and sat on the edge of the unmade bed, as if here alone the disorder in her mind could be in harmony with her environment. And she thought irrationally, I hate you, George, if only you could hear me, I hate you. She tried to imagine him standing before her, or kneeling before her begging forgiveness, and she sitting back and laughing at him, I hate you, George, you pitiful adolescent jerk. Or perhaps she would say, I can't bring myself to hate you, George, it's really not worth it, I only wonder how I could ever have been attracted to you in the first place.

Or perhaps she would say, I love you, George, I love you, love you.

What had it been about him? Not his looks, certainly, although he was nice-looking enough, and not his charm exactly, although he could be charming, too. A certain shyness, perhaps, a humility and willingness to learn, to feel, to change, qualities that Sam and Cady had never had. She remembered thinking once that she wanted to mother George, but how quickly this feeling had become love. She had known it again when, despite the fact that he was in love with her, he tried to persuade her to return to Sam. He had had a letter, he said, glaring at the speedometer—they were returning to the city after a football game—and he was convinced that Sam was devoted to her and deserved another chance. When she laughed at his expression, he had tried to laugh, too, but managed only a small weak smile like a shaft of sun against a rain, and she realized then that she was still, had always been, in love with him. And she had dared to accuse him,

"But you love me, don't you, George?" He was driving too fast in the jockeying traffic, and at these words winced and shifted his hands on the wheel but did not answer. "Will you take me to dinner?" she said, after a moment, lighting a cigarette for him.

"Yes," George said. The implication "of course, I'll do anything you ask" seemed to smother the word, make it barely audible. For the rest of the journey they talked of other things, the football game, his job with McConville and Company—"It's not a job at all," he said, "it's a goddamned disguise"—and his father's death. He referred indirectly to the awkward circumstances of it, which she had already heard rumored, the heart attack suffered at Shipman's Point, with only Cady's mother, Sarah Shipman, to attend to him. Then he spoke of leaving the firm and going into conservation work, the Fish and Wildlife Service, or something, which he had always wanted to do and seemed farther and farther away from doing—"If I don't decide pretty soon, I'll become mature and sensible and never do it." She remembered long afterward this first confession of doubt which had ended in his departure from the firm.

They had cocktails and dinner in an Italian place on Second Avenue, and there she had asked him again, "You love me, don't you, George?" She had no right to ask it, having made no such admission herself, and yet she felt she had to know.

"Yes," George answered disagreeably. "I always have. I don't see why you bother to ask."

"Then why do you think I should go back to Sam?" She kept her voice bright, noncommittal, quelling a surge of new excitement.

"I don't. I mean, I *think* you should, perhaps, but I don't feel it. I want you myself, Eve." He flushed, and reached for his red wine. "I'm a bastard to say that, too, after what Sambo wrote me." He lifted his eyes to hers in open hope.

And she wanted to cry out, but I love you, George! It did not seem the moment, however, and after a while she said, "To hell with Sam, he's happier this way. If I went back to him, he'd run like a rabbit, you know that." George said nothing, and she continued, "This way he can play the romantic sufferer. Nostalgia is much more romantic than love for somebody like that. Sam is just the weak sort of—"

"Never mind," George said. "But if you feel that way, you'd better not go back."

"The possibility never crossed my mind," she laughed. "You and Sam cooked it up between you, I had nothing to say about it. And I think it's very uncomplimentary to try and send me away, I may say. What kind of love do you call that?"

They regarded each other carefully, Eve conscious of the coyness in her own expression, ashamed of it, yet exalted when he understood. "What are you trying to say?" he whispered.

"I don't want to have to say it, not here," she said. "Don't make me."

They left the restaurant and walked back across the city toward Madison Avenue, saying nothing, hardly breathing. Before her building they stopped, and she put her hand under his coat and against his shirt, over the heart. It was beating violently, and she smiled.

"That's not fair," he said. "I'm trying to be the cool collected type."

"Take me somewhere, then."

"All right. We can't go to my place, there's always somebody pounding at the door—" He stopped.

"You want to come upstairs, then?"

"If that's all right."

She kissed him, pushing away the disappointment that the decision had not been his. And she noticed too that, following her meekly into the lobby, he avoided the gaze of the night doorman as well as her own. After all, she thought, it's my building, my reputation.

"Do you think I should give him something?" George whispered.

"What for?" she said, impatiently. The elevator door slid to behind them, and she handed George the key to the apartment. He could not work the lock. "I could never even open my mother's purses," he explained, and cursed. She took back the key and preceded him inside.

Perhaps because it was her one misgiving about George, his lack of affirmation bothered her even on this evening of fulfillment, since now especially, and above all else, she needed to feel dominated, secure. In the living room, holding both his hands in hers, she wondered even as she spoke her love for him if she was not betraying herself, betraying him, and a little later asked, "But you don't want to marry me, do you, George?"

"Of course I do, what are you talking about, I only said we shouldn't marry too quickly, I have to—" He paused.

"Have to what?"

"Well, you know, what I was talking about this afternoon—either settle down and make the best of McConville and Company or strike off into something new. Something new means going back to college, perhaps, and we don't know where we would live or anything. And besides, we have to be sure. I mean, you're sort of on the rebound from Sam, suppose you changed your mind or something."

"You don't trust me, then," Eve said, not trusting herself.

"Oh, Eve, you see what I mean, don't you? I'm in a sort of flux just now, so are you, and this is too important to make a mistake about. I think we should wait a little while—"

"Play it safe, you mean. Keep a level head on our shoulders."

He laughed uncomfortably. "All right, goddamn it, we'll be married next week," he said, and put his arm around her.

"No," she said. "Stick to your guns, for once. We'll wait." She turned a little and lay back with her head against his chest and

tried not to wonder about anything at all. In a little while she felt
him stir beneath her and then he bent and kissed her. Please tell
me you are staying with me tonight, she prayed, please don't ask
me, just tell me, George. If you told me to take my clothes off and
do an Arab dance for you, I'd do it, but if you *ask* me to take even
my earrings off, I'll—

"It's getting late," George said, after a while. She slid one hand
up under his shirt and dug her nails ever so slightly into his back.

"I'd like to stay, Eve," he murmured, she could feel the tension
in his legs and stomach as he spoke. She refused to help him. "I
mean, it's up to you," he added, "just say if you don't think—"

"Shut up," she whispered. "Of course you'll stay. We're not
children any more."

He picked her up then and set her on her feet. Swaying in his
embrace, she felt his hands upon her, brutal and incompetent and
exciting. She reached up and unbuttoned the top button of his
shirt.

When she came out of the bathroom, he was already under the
covers.

"Come out of there," she laughed. "You're not a virgin, are
you?"

"No," he said. "I'm shaking like a leaf."

"With cold?"

"No." He sat up in bed and stared at her, then got out slowly
as she watched him. He slid the straps of her negligee over her
shoulders and lifted it from below and knelt and pressed his cheek
against her belly, his hands hard on her thighs as if he were praying to her, holding on. "I love you," he whispered. "I think I may
roll over and die, I love you so."

"Please don't die," she breathed. "Not yet."

And as he slipped after her into the bed, and they clung together in the first trembling flush of their love, she thought once briefly before giving herself to him, how can this be wrong, I have never felt so innocent

She lay back on the rumpled sheets and listened to the rain. I'm back where I started, she thought, it is just another Sunday morning.

CHAPTER 12

THEY DID NOT GO HUNTING ON SUNDAY AFTERNOON. THE STORM had risen, twisting through the woods and over the marsh, setting the rain against the wind in scudding charges, and blackening the sea.

George McConville moved restlessly from window to window of the house, peering outward now and again as if expecting some strange visitor to come wandering in out of the elements. Each room held a memory for him, and he traced the memories from door to door as a man follows a line through an ill-remembered cavern, pausing every other moment, going on. The memories were depressingly stale and unflavorful, bringing back no tenderness of childhood nor even a sense of belonging. And he had known they would not, or sensed it, at least, from the moment he had come, keeping to the library fire and to his bedroom like a little boy scared of the dark, who knows by heart what lies around each corner but no longer places trust in it.

This afternoon, however, he had felt oppressed by Sam and Cady. The restorative value of their companionship was no longer there, they seemed virtual strangers to him. He did not want to believe it, the sadness and transience of it, the feeling it brought of being entirely alone and dependent on a self he had learned to mistrust, even at times abhor. He needed Cady and Sam as he needed Shipman's Point, and now all at once he was losing everything. So long as they had been active together as in the duck blind that morning the illusion of the old days had remained. Trapped with them in the library, however, he could not look into their faces, less out of dissatisfaction than because there was none of the former elation he had felt with them—or had he only imagined even that? Their faces were simply faces now, soured and unreal to him, and the impending laughter of the past broke rarely from its bonds, with none of the flesh of humor but only the sharp stark bone.

Have I changed or have they? he wondered. Would they be friends now if I had not known them previously? Would this house seem an ugly museum of somebody else's childhood?

They must be thinking the same, he thought. They never liked each other, and now they did not like him. And yet how strangely they behaved. They seemed to seek his favor, in open competition with one another, Cady and Sam who used to lead him by the nose.

It's so damned queer, he thought, the whole business, even our being together here this weekend. And now this storm, as if things weren't morbid enough already.

George had wandered to the attic, and crossed now to the shadows and spidered eaves by the mansard window, where he traced the letters E-V-E in the dust of the pane. On the final letter his finger paused, then continued violently in a scrawled A-N-D-G-E-O-R-G-E and circumscribed it roughly with a heart. He crossed the whole out with an X, then superimposed an 8 on the scrawl, over which he wrote S-A-M as his self-conscious smile faded away and he jammed his hands into his pockets.

"Grow up, for God's sake," he muttered aloud, and the words wandered free in the cluttered attic, trailing a murmur of sound like exploring children.

George stood a long time, his back to the window, rifling the trunks and boxes with his eyes for the whisperings of the past but retrieving only an afternoon much nearer in time and spirit to his mood, when he had shown the attic to Eve.

Even then he had been preoccupied with the senselessness of his life, its lack of direction. Hope itself seemed elusive to him, a deceptive biscuit withheld from an anxious dog, and that day he had sought refuge in Eve, attempting to impress her with his inner sensibilities so that she, at least, would not desert him, deprive him of the solace of their immediate present. Sitting here in the litter of the McConville past, he had spoken out against their expensive schooling, the Christmas dances and debutante parties in New York, the war whose wretched wake had gelded it of any sense it might have made to friends who were killed in it, the war whose importance became so swiftly secondary to the subsequent emphasis placed by other friends, in college and after, upon clubs and liquor and callow amorality.

"Are you going to say it's all our parents' fault, George?" Eve was thumbing through a volume called *Frank at Vicksburg*, which lay propped between her sneakers on the floor.

"That's the thing to do these days, isn't it?" George laughed uncomfortably, knowing that his outburst had been silly, not even particularly sincere. "Blame it all on the old folks?"

"Look, I'm not teasing you, I just asked a question. I don't see why you have to feel ashamed of yourself when you're being serious. Or aren't you being serious?" She closed the book and tossed it back onto the pile before looking up at him.

"Of course I am, I'm being serious and extremely pompous. Anyway, we're not *discussing* anything if you let me do all the talking."

"I simply wanted to know if you thought—"

"I don't know if I do or not," George said. "I *do* know I was damned badly prepared for life. This sanctuary we lived in as children, and all the phony build-up to a life that doesn't exist, not any more, at least. Cyrus McConville, the robber baron, and my mother who still thinks she's cultured for the simple reason of her ancestry—what could they teach their children of life? If it hadn't been for the war, I'd still be getting toys for Christmas."

"Do you think people like my mother and Sam's father were any better?"

"You know what I mean, Eve. Why be so disagreeable?"

"I do know what you mean, yes, and I'm not being disagreeable." Eve rose and went to the window. "I just don't see how we can blame everything on robber barons and illiterate dowagers."

"Look, you're picking me up on details, you're too damned analytical. All I was trying to say," said George, wishing he had never mentioned the subject, "was that the people who were handed over the nation's heritage or whatever on their graduation days, our generation, anyway, are probably the worst prepared for the responsibility of all time. And one good reason is that the parents refused to recognize or understand the changes taking place in the world, the socialization and all the rest of it which had to come, even in Columbia, the Gem of the Ocean."

"And all *I* was trying to say, George, was that it does no good to snivel about backward parents and finished wars and the shallow anachronisms of fraternities and deb parties and whether or not we're as lost a generation as our parents were supposed to be, and if not, why not, as if we were proud of our own weakness—it's the people like us, as you put it, who brood about these things, other people haven't got time!" She turned from the window and glared at him.

"Who's sniveling? I just got through saying—"

"I know it's corny when some old windbag gets religion and love-of-country on Commencement Day and tells us about our Godgiven heritage as if we were the Chosen People or something, but does that mean we're no longer responsible? When he says the future lies in our hands, he may not want to believe it himself, but it's true, isn't it? If you don't like the way Cyrus McConville did things, do something different, but *do* something. I'm so sick of this talking, I heard enough from Sam to last me a lifetime!"

George was embarrassed and slightly irritated. "Relax," he said. "I'm sorry I brought it up. It's just hard to know *what* to do in these mixed-up times, that's all."

"What right have you to be mixed-up?" she flared. "Most people can't afford the luxury. What makes you think it's so much harder to live these days than before? And if it is, it's our own fault, nobody else's. It's because we're afraid, all of us, we're just afraid, and with so much to be done, we have bad consciences for not doing it."

"Look, Eve, you've gotten entirely off the point. Cady's mother was just as bad—what's she got to do with clubs and deb parties, for God's sake?"

"What did Cady's mother do? I don't even know. Did she try to crash a party here or something?" Eve had a habit, when angry, of raising her eyebrows and sucking in her cheeks, which made her look more foolish than severe. George knew she felt she had been childish. He lit a cigarette before he spoke. "No," he said. "I thought you knew. Cady's mother got in trouble with old Abraham Shipman, the one whose gravestone is down there by the terrace. Percy was called in by the family to do the honors when Uncle Abraham drowned himself, to keep Sarah and Cady out of the inheritance, they say—this land, for instance."

"Who's *they*?" She stared at him. "Are you sure of this, George, or are you just repeating village gossip? Barlow Shipman would never do a thing like that."

"It's more than gossip. Everybody believes it. Besides, they had to get her married, didn't they? And apparently they thought that Sarah had gotten in trouble on purpose, taking advantage of the old man's foolishness or something—"

"But you're not sure of it? I think it's pretty small of you—"

"Look, Eve," he said, flushing himself, "nobody's asking you to believe it. And whether you do or not," he went on earnestly, trying to persuade her of his concern, "for God's sake, don't mention it to Cady, he'd cut your throat."

"I doubt it. Cady and I get along very well, I'm astonished he hasn't told me. Which makes me believe it isn't true."

"*How* well do you and Cady get along?"

"Very well. Why?"

In the poor light of the attic, he could not tell if she was teasing him. He said suggestively, sourly, "You get along with him as well as you get along with me?" and was immediately ashamed.

"You're awfully clever, George."

"I get by," George said, and after a moment, "Look, Eve, there's no sense sniping at each other. I don't like it about Cady any better than you do, but what am *I* supposed to do about it? We've gotten off the point."

"Oh, no we haven't. You say 'What am I supposed to do about it?' about everything, about all the things we've been talking about, as if it were enough that you sit around and point out wrongs to other people like yourself who have time to listen. And that's fine for somebody like Sam, but you could do so much more, George, if you'd just grow up a little. I won't *let* you waste yourself, do you hear!"

She came toward him a little and stopped, and he was startled to see her on the point of tears. Moved, he nevertheless rejected her, saying, "You seem awfully sure of yourself, Eve." He could not for the life of him tell why he had said this, and stood there stupidly when she slapped him. Then she was going away toward the door. "Come back," he said. "Sit down here a moment."

"You can go to hell," she told him, yet she came with him when he went to her and took her arm, as if he were no longer the source of her grief but only the instrument, as if she had been defeated in a far more significant contest with which George was only indirectly involved. And so he talked to her, petted her, letting an apology worm its way out of his dying anger, and after a while she shifted in his arms and clung to him, facing toward the darkening attic window. She spoke only once, saying, "You'll have to find out what you're supposed to do about things, George, sooner or later," and since this was out of the context of what he had been saying, he realized she had not been listening to him

On the window the raindrops were visible through the lines of his scrawled emblem, making it shiver and jump like a thing alive. And he longed for Eve, deeply to the point of pain. He would telephone her and say, Eve, listen, Eve, I understand now, I have things straightened out in my mind—but would she believe him?

"You'll have to find out what you're going to do about things, George, sooner or later." And what was he going to do? What was there to do anything about, when one got right down to it?

Yet if this was true, then what was he looking for? And for the thousandth time he thought about how simple it would be to settle for the tangible values, the nice job, nice wife, nice house, nice children—and he wanted all of these things, it was true, yet not at the expense of something else, something he could not quite put his finger on, but which was missing in the future he saw before him now, whether he married Eve or not.

The house was alive with apprehension, a tramp ship in a port of storm, stirring fitfully in painful creaks as the wind on the windows resounded in dull echoes of alarm along its corridors. The suspense between gusts was painful as the wait between two dying breaths. Peering through the attic window, he could barely make out the dunes and beach which, drawn up in bleak indifference against the crazed encroaching sea, turned a shaggy coat to the wind and water.

Beyond his sight, where the wall of rain kited up and down the marsh, the wild duck banded in uneasy clumps among the grass roots, working their way in sallies toward the shelter of the inland edges. There, by the great tree on Abraham's Path, the earth eroded from the rotted saline banks and poured away, as other fresher soil descended from the woods above and took its place. Early in the afternoon, between two roots of the tree, there began to appear and disappear in the uneven wash a yellow surface, protruding slowly, tentatively at first like the slow face of a tooth, then quickly as twilight came and went and its grave fell away around it. The eye sockets of Percy Shipman's cat, appearing, ran with mud, and faced in cold blurred sightlessness out across the shifting marsh toward the house on the Point.

CHAPTER 13

SAM AND CADY HAD NOT SPOKEN TO ONE ANOTHER FOR AN HOUR, but sat as close and as far apart as strangers in a waiting room, staring at the fire.

I do not belong here any more, Sam thought, the dread searching through him like a fever, that he, Sam Rubicam, had become irrelevant to the world and that, laugh as he might, the world had not became irrelevant to him.

I am sick of laughing, he thought. I am deathly sick of laughing. Slouched in his chair, he shuddered with disgust, composing himself immediately under the watchful eye of Cady Shipman, whose glance flicked at him, alert and disinterested, then flicked away again.

If I could say, look, boys, forget everything you've ever thought of me or heard me say, I am a stranger, Samuel Rubicam—then things would be different, they would like me for myself, my real self, and not for entertaining them now and again, not for playing the fool.

Twelve years before he had sat in this very chair, directly facing George's father, who had sat in the chair now occupied by Cady. They had been alone in the room.

"I sent my wife and George out of the room just now," Cyrus McConville said, "because I wanted to have a talk with you, boy."

"Yessir," Sam said, uneasy.

Both of them stared about the room for a few seconds, clearing their throats, before Cyrus McConville said, "Now you have to have courage about this. You're a good boy, and I'm sure you'll have courage."

"Yessir," Sam said.

"Your mother . . . yesterday your mother was killed in a motor accident, and we want you to come and live with us," Cyrus blurted, his face reddening as if in anger. He rubbed the arm of his chair with his knuckles.

"Yessir," Sam said, because he hadn't understood yet, he simply felt a little breathless, knowing something extraordinary was expected of him, and trying to imagine the woman who happened to be his mother dead in a motor accident, the sound and the tearing metal and rubber smell, and the following quiet like a shroud.

"That's it, take it like a man, you're sixteen now, and you must be philosophical," Cyrus McConville told him, his eyes suspicious in the jutting face, as if he were trying to stare Sam down.

"Where?" Sam said. The shock was stirring in his lungs, and nausea in the pit of his stomach.

"On the Riviera, I believe. It doesn't matter, though. I'm afraid it must be a terrible shock to you."

"Mm-hm," Sam said. His voice was doubtful.

They sat in silence until George's father said, leaning across the gap between to pat him angrily on the knee, "Of course you will have a home with us. The Point has always been your home, for four years anyway, and now more than ever, of course."

They sat in silence for a while, the older man brooding and impatiently shifting his feet. It was nearly lunchtime.

The shock had disappeared as suddenly as it had come, and

Sam felt it go with alarm, missing the grief, so mandatory for the occasion. He felt cheated of it, he was being stoic with no grief to be stoic about, and he glanced at Cyrus McConville to see if his subterfuge had been pierced. It hadn't. They eyed each other uncomfortably for a moment before Sam was struck by the non-sense of their appearance, the brave sad youth and the gruff but kind old man, planted face to face in belligerent hypocrisy until a show of emotion, the unfailing purge, would free them of further responsibility to the dead and they could go to lunch.

The emotion arrived at that instant. Sam Rubicam hurled what passed for a cry of lament as a sop to Cyrus McConville, and ran off-stage and up the stairs in a breathless spasm of laughter which passed, to Mrs. McConville, wringing her hands in the hallway, as honest and uncontrollable grief.

She had come to his door a little later, tapping gently, and say-ing, "Sam dear? Can you hear me? Do you feel like coming down just now, or shall I have a tray brought up? Sam dear?"

He had put his face in the pillow and howled again, and then he had sat up, wiping his eyes, a little shocked at his behavior, yet marveling in the reaction, and his voice said, thick and muted, "Thanks, Mrs. McConville, I'm fine now, I'll be right down," because he knew he wouldn't laugh any more.

Poor thin suffering Mrs. McConville, he would have cried at her death, he supposed, or at least he preferred to think so, she had been a sort of mother to him.

Anyway, he had gone down to lunch. The stairs were heavily carpeted, they did not hear him coming, and he heard the old lady say, "Poor dear, I *do* hope he'll be all right."

And her husband, impatiently, "He took it very well at first, I thought he was going to snap out of it, but he sort of went to pieces there at the end. An emotional sort of boy, I suppose, highstrung like his father."

And George, embarrassed for Sam, said, "He'll be all right."

And he had been, that day at lunch, he had impressed them all with his good cheer. Mrs. McConville had beamed at him. He had never seen her beam at anything, before or since. He said he would be proud to consider the Point his home, he always had, anyway—relieved laughter, for the purpose of banishing any remaining tension—and thanked them in a simple and winning way—it was then that Mrs. McConville beamed—for their continued kindness to him, a sentiment which, although spoken self-consciously and for effect, he now realized had been genuine

"George has changed," Cady Shipman said, punctuating his interruption by flicking a cigarette butt onto the hearth and rising, undecided about going or staying in the room.

"In what way?" Sam said, after a moment.

"The place isn't the same to him any more. I don't think he can get his mind off Eve."

"What do you know about Eve?" Sam said. He looked at Cady now, suspicious, and lit a cigarette.

"Not a hell of a lot," Cady said. He moved to the fireplace, and stood there, both elbows on the mantelpiece behind him. "You know her pretty well?"

"I was married to her."

"Is that a fact? She run out on you?"

"You knew I was married to her," Sam said.

"I guess I did, at that," Cady said. "I just wanted to find out if you thought she was the right girl for George."

Sam Rubicam glared at him angrily, his glass tilted at a precarious angle in his hand.

"Do you like George that much," he said, "or are you simply baiting me?"

"Maybe both. I grew up with George, though, I know him much better than you do."

"What does that matter?"

"Nothing, except that George grew up with this place, he belongs here."

"So do I. Old Man McConville was my guardian," Sam said.

"The hell you do. You don't belong. You never liked it, even, you just wanted to hang around George." Cady noisily cleared his throat and spat elaborately into the fireplace.

"What makes you think you know all about it?" Sam said. "Your college education?" He cleared his own throat in a harsh imitation of Cady and, grinning, rose to his feet and stepped to the fireplace, where he let the spittle fall from his mouth onto the hearth.

Cady waited for his eyes, stalking the movements of the other while the anger came, wanting badly to hit him now, immediately, but knowing that to savor the anger for a moment would make it more pleasurable when it burst later on, overpowering and satiating.

"You haven't got much use for me, have you?" he started.

Sam glanced at him then, gauging him, Cady knew, gauging his chances of insulting Cady without being hurt in the process, a little less cautious than usual because a little more drunk.

"No," Sam said at last. He seemed to sense that, for a time at least, he could speak with impunity, the highball cocked in his hand like a dangled weapon, arrogant and a little threatening.

"Why not?"

"You know perfectly well why not."

"Why not?"

"You're a sadist. Uncivilized."

"You called me that once before, remember?"

"Yes," Sam said. "And you proved it again, with Mr. Murray's shoveler duck, or whatever it was."

"You know I could beat your head off right now, don't you?"

"You could, yes."

"But you don't think I will."

"No. You'll do it when you want to do it, one way or the other. It won't make any difference whether or not I call you what you are. I've seen your kind before, you're all the same."

Cady finished his glass and put his hands up behind his head as he leaned back in his chair, saying conversationally, "You still in love with Eve?"

Sam Rubicam flushed, a birthmark color on his thin pale face, his fingers twitching around the glass in his hand. They faced each other in silence, the heaving of the storm crowding at the window, and the sudden laugh of Rosa Menhaden in the kitchen wandered between them. He searched for words.

"I didn't hear you," Cady grinned.

"You think I'm scared of you, don't you?" Sam muttered. His eyes were very bright.

"Yeah. I know you are, Sammy boy."

"I understand you're in love with Eve yourself," Sam hazarded, after a moment. He took a sip from his glass to wet his mouth, and came up grinning, leaning forward from the mantelpiece.

Maybe I'll hit him now, Cady thought. He thinks he got me with that one. Maybe he did. He studied the face of the other, undecided. "Did George tell you that?"

"It's all over town. This hick town, I mean. All the yokels are saying it."

"You like to smile, don't you?" Cady said.

"Just call me Laughing Boy," Sam said, and laughed. Cady watched him until the laughter stopped, then blurted ineffectually, "I've seen hogs I had more respect for than you, Rubicam, you know that?"

"I've known some damn fine hogs myself," Sam said, and laughed again.

"In fact, if I was in your shoes," Cady said, infuriated by the childishness he could not control, "I'd have cut my throat long ago."

"You're smart, aren't you?" Sam said. "A logician. You must have gone to college."

"That's right," Cady said. "I have what they call an animal cunning, I believe in the survival of the fittest. You're not fit to survive. You're a pimple on the ass of society."

"Did you figure that one out all by yourself, or did you pick it up at home?" Sam shook his head. "God, what an adolescent."

"Picked it up. I'm too ignorant to figure it out by myself."

"We're beginning to agree on a number of things," Sam said. He was still leaning forward, intent, and Cady guessed that Sam had forgotten caution in his eagerness to vindicate himself, like a man lured into an alley by an armed adversary.

"Is that a fact?" Cady said. "For instance?"

"Your ignorance. Your opinion of mankind."

"What's my opinion of mankind?"

"The same as your opinion of everybody in this house. They have to live your way or not at all, which is precisely the difference between you and me," Sam said. He had filled his glass again and stood now at the mantel, waving his finger at Cady, his anger seemingly misted over by the alcohol, as if he thought he was someplace else. "Now *I* think people should live and do as they please," he said.

"That's what I'm doing. Just as I please."

"No you're not. Not at all. You," he said, pointing at Cady as at an exhibit, "you live according to the force in power. Power is right. That's why you're an animal, you're still in the forest. And there's a million more where you came from, that's the bloody hell of it. Stamped out like tin soldiers, with just enough brain to take orders. The modern robot race."

Sam was waving at the walls, orating, unseeing, and Cady did not move forward but waited. A little longer, he thought, a little longer. I have to have a good excuse for George.

"You take orders from society," Sam was shouting, "from popular opinion, from the advertisements, from the goddamned bullet-headed Marines. Who was the first to hit the beaches? Cady Shipman! Who kissed the colonel's ass? Cady Shipman! Who had the shiniest goddamned belt in the whole goddamned outfit—?"

Sam paused a moment and stared craftily at Cady.

"Do you know who?" he said.

"Yeah," Cady said. He stood immobile in front of his chair, calm again and sure in his hatred, which ticked into his lungs like cold water drops.

"Cady Goddamned Shipman, that's who!" Sam crowed, pitching back against the mantel in a spasm of delight, then falling away into his chair, his glass balanced with the impossible skill of the practiced drinker.

"You think I respect authority, then," Cady said. He was curious despite himself, he had never thought of this possibility before, and eyed Sam suspiciously as he sat down again himself.

Sam dismissed the question with a wave of his hand.

"Obviously," he said.

"How come I was kicked out of the Marines, then? Why do you

think I shot up Mister Murray's sanctuary? How do you figure that out as respect for authority?"

"I'm casting pearls before swine, I can see that," Sam said. He was staring at the surface of his whiskey in moody inspection, and waved his hand at Cady as if to banish him from the room.

Cady went to him and knocked the glass from his hand. Sam looked up slowly, not in the least startled because nothing could startle him at this moment, and gazed at Cady with interest.

"You spilled my whiskey," he said.

"Answer me, you crazy bastard."

"All right," Sam said. "I will." He rose again, and filled the empty glass, then stood there a moment in indecision. "What were we talking about?"

"Respect for authority."

"Hell, man," Sam said. "You don't respect it, you're a god-damned slave to it. Your kind always is. As for the Marines, you just made a mistake, and the other phenomena you mention, more or less proudly as I understand it, are simply manifestations of frustration, an attempt to prove to yourself that you're not the mechanical ape that everybody knows you are, you see what I mean?"

"Just as simple as that, huh?"

"Just about, as a matter of fact."

"You've got me all figured out for a moron."

"I wouldn't go so far as that," Sam said. He was inspecting the surface of the whiskey again. "There's a certain kind of animal cunning, as you put it. If there wasn't, you wouldn't be so dangerous to civilized men like myself."

"If it wasn't for my kind, your kind would be all right, then?" Cady listened to his own voice in amazement. Why don't I kill him, he thought, why don't I beat him to death right here and now? It was because things weren't clear yet, there was something confusing in the atmosphere of the room, with the wind howling through the window and Rosa Menhaden singing down the hallway, and George skulking around the house somewhere, and here he was, trapped in a room with a man he could never understand, a crazy drunk pointing at him and saying things he wasn't sure he understood, except that they were against him, and had probably been said behind his back a dozen times to George. That night in San Diego, the big man in the bar, he would have finished him. The man had been proclaiming the gratitude of the nation toward its servicemen, and illustrating his remarks with free beer. "Our boys over there," he called them, an uneasy drunken man whom Cady recognized as cultured, demeaning himself in a fleatrap for a bunch of bums. I'm not his goddamn nursemaid, Cady told himself, scraping his brain for the reason he cared at all, and knowing only that the man stood for Cyrus McConville's kind of authority, and that authority was necessary, and that it was being badly compromised by the drunk at the bar.

He had risen and gone to him, drunk himself and filled with inexplicable anger toward his own companions, toward people in general. "Get the hell out of here," he said to the man. "You're making a sap of yourself." "Ah," the man said, "a Marine. Welcome, leatherneck, welcome." Cady slapped him with backhand knuckles across the mouth. The man was still smiling, stupidly now, and the soldiers backed around into a circle.

"What did you do that for, my boy?" the man said, his voice gone suddenly high.

"For nothing," Cady said. "For being goddamn foolish, maybe. I thought it would do you good."

"You're right," the man said. "You're perfectly right. Do it again." He was crying now.

"Get the hell out," Cady said, and struck him again. "You've got no business here, a man like you," and struck him again, back and forth, harder, again and again and again before the bartender pushed the brass knobs over his knuckles with neat pushes of his fingers, like kid gloves, and belted Cady across the side of the head. The soldiers had stood and watched it all, sipping their free beer.

He rubbed his face unconsciously at the memory, wondering what had possessed him. He would have killed the man if the slaps could have killed him, and he realized now that he never thought about that before or during a fight, never thought about anything at all, just the blind mounting rhythm of striking something down, the ecstasy of power, intensified by the pain in his hands, which shivered back and forth orgastic across his shoulders and through his arms.

"No," Sam said. "My kind wouldn't be all right whether your kind existed or not. Mankind will always find something to hamstring itself with. If it conquers one thing, it erects another."

"Is that a fact?"

"That's a fact. That's a genu-ine all-American fact. That," Sam said, searching the ceiling for inspiration, "is the truest little ol' son-of-a-bitch of a fact that you ever heard in your life."

Sam was obviously enjoying himself, pronouncing his words one by one and deriving inordinate pleasure from each, as if he had come upon them for the first time. He raised his eyes to Cady's and grinned, and this time the grin did not fall away when Cady remained unsmiling. Instead, it seemed to judge Cady, to savor a victory of an unspoken kind which Cady could not possibly understand. Cady felt cheated, the initiative had been stolen from him and turned against him by the drunken man in the other chair.

Feeling his way now, Cady said, "How about George? Is he your kind or my kind?"

"He certainly isn't your kind, as you put it. He'll be my kind, or he'll go on being fatuous all his life, or get religion: 'Gimme dat ole time re-ligion, gimme dat ole time re—' "

"Who's being fatuous?" Cady interrupted. "If something's wrong, people better do something about it."

"I'd rather see the world blown up than let it become the way you want it," Sam intoned. "Better it die physically of decadence than morally of suppression." He peered gloomily in the direction of the window. "It sounds like the end of the world right now. If I didn't know better, I'd say everybody was dead except us, from the sound of that wind. I imagine that's what hell would sound like."

"You're a rotten kind of a man, you know that," Cady said. "You're like a vulture or something, you live on dead meat."

"It's a funny thing about that," Sam said, grinning again, "but I never could eat animals alive, now that you mention it."

"I didn't mention anything."

"I know you didn't. I'm just keeping up both ends of our charming conversation."

Sam Rubicam turned halfway around in his chair and offered Cady a smile intended to be patronizing, saying, "Doesn't this discussion strike you as a little unusual? A bit uncivilized, perhaps? Or at least rather childish?"

"I like it all right. I like to know where we stand. And anyway, you're forgetting something, I'm an animal, remember?"

"It slipped my mind for a moment," Sam said. "I almost forgot."

"I wouldn't forget, if I were you."

"Okay. You want me to lick your boots now, or later? I'll get Daniel in here to help me out, and maybe George. We'll all lick the boots of the Bastard. I mean, you are a bastard, aren't you?"

Sam paled even before Cady rose from his chair, and added hastily, "I take that back. I apologize, even. How's that?"

"That's just dandy," Cady said. "Stand up."

"Why should I stand up?" Sam said. "You'd just knock me down again. It's a waste of effort."

His voice was thin, however, and Cady sensed, not caring, that the other's drunkenness had been assumed, as of the past few seconds, as a last-ditch defense.

"Admit the logic of my remarks," Sam was saying, his hands pressed down on the arms of his chair, staring at Cady out from under his eyebrows as if to turn his face up would be an invitation to disaster. "Besides, we were having a gentleman's discussion, we are not in a saloon."

"Shut up," Cady whispered. "I've been listening to your crap all afternoon, and I hope you got a kick out of it because now it's my turn. Stand up."

"Don't be stupid," Sam said. "You sound like a radio criminal."

"Stand up."

Sam said, "I think it's about time we quit, don't you? We're like a couple of song-and-dance men, prancing around insulting each other. And pretty soon you'll have stretched your college education, you'll forget your lines."

"Stand up," Cady said, "or I'll hit you where you are."

"That's it, that's the spirit," Sam shouted, his voice high and parched. "If there's anything you don't understand, just start swinging. In case of confusion, close your eyes and swing, right, Cady?"

Sam rose suddenly and backed away toward the door.

"That's right," Cady said. He was following Sam when George came into the room.

George said nothing for a moment, looking from one to the other until Cady broke the silence.

"Your little buddy here is looking for trouble," he said.

"A slight difference of opinion," Sam said, and his laugh rang false, a strangled bell.

"S-sh-it," said Cady Shipman to the world. He stepped past George and Sam into the darkness of the hallway, his footsteps marking the time of the storm on the naked wood.

"What's the trouble?" George said.

"Nothing. It was silly." Sam made his way back to his chair and took a heavy swallow from his glass.

"What did you do, bait him? Cady's the wrong man to be sarcastic with."

"He certainly is," Sam said. "You saved me from the thrashing of my life just now."

"I'm sorry to hear it," George said. "I'm sure you deserved it, you silly jackass."

"The hell I did. He started it, not me." Sam's face was suddenly afraid, his mouth working on his face like a thin black nerve against the paleness. "Took a few sideswipes at me about Eve. What did you tell him, anyway?"

"Take it easy," George repeated. "I didn't tell him anything." But saying this, he remembered the picture of Eve he had shown to Cady earlier in the day. Cady had asked if Eve had left Sam because of George, and although this was not the case he had not denied it, only laughed, nor had he remonstrated when Cady had remarked that any woman would leave a half a man, sooner or later. Because I am jealous of Sam, he thought. I have always been jealous of him, in everything, it's a habit I can't grow out of. And looking at Sam, he was ashamed.

"He considers himself your keeper," Sam was saying. "He thinks you should come and live here, probably so he could be caretaker and you and he could be buddies forevermore, for Christ's sake."

Sam was staring into his glass again, crying in a terror and grief which George knew to be sincere, although he did not understand it.

"Take it easy," he whispered. "We're all acting the way we did at sixteen." He put his hand for a clumsy moment on Sam's shoulder, but Sam shrugged it off as a sulky child throws an offering to the floor.

"Oh my Lord," George sighed. He went to the liquor table in the corner.

Sam did not answer him. He was not crying any longer, only staring, the tear lines untended on his face, nodding soddenly with whiskey bitterness at the floor.

"What did he say about Eve?" George demanded, over his shoulder, and heard Sam mumbling, shuffling his feet, "He wanted to know if she'd left me."

"She did, didn't she?"

"As a matter of fact, she did, yes. You've gotten smug as hell, did you know that?"

"And you've gotten childish. I was only kidding."

"Like hell you were. You've never kidded about Eve in your life," Sam shouted, and George was forced to turn and face him.

"Take it easy, Sam," he stalled.

"Listen, if you tell me to take it easy again, I'm going to brain you with that poker, I swear I am." Sam's face was desperate, staring and wild like a possum's face, the eyes jet black against the white like holes.

"All right," George said. "Okay. Jump out of your skin if you like." He slumped into the other chair. "I've never known such a crazy night."

"Listen, remember what you said to me once? You said that no woman existed important enough to come between two friends."

"I was a pubert then. Anyway, she hasn't come between us."

"Not much. We're like a couple of snapping mongrels hanging around a bitch in heat, and Cady, too, except that I've already had a bellyful, and you two are still horny."

"Is that a fact?" George said.

"*Is that a fact*," Sam mimicked him. "Cady McConville, the Breath of the Swamp. Why don't you stop sucking around Cady Shipman, and be yourself for a change?"

"Oh, stop it." Defensively, George imitated Sam's bulging expression. "Sober up, or grow up, or something."

"A-a-ah," Sam breathed, sitting back in his chair again and shaking his head. "I used to think you were good enough for Eve, but I've changed my mind."

"Look," George said, "when are you going to forget about her? Every time I even think about her, I can feel your hot breath on my neck. You're one hell of a poor loser."

"You feel my hot breath because you're frightened of my competition, that's all. You're scared you're not as handy between the sheets as you might be, isn't that it, George, as a result of your sheltered childhood or something?"

"Whereas you're the handiest thing around, I imagine."

"I do all right," Sam said. His smile was grotesque in the tear-streaked face.

"Not with Eve, you don't. That's whom we're talking about, isn't it? Maybe she prefers my boyish charms to your seamy bag of tricks."

"I doubt it. I doubt it very much, in fact. Not a girl like that. All signs would point to a pretty lean year for old Eve."

"Look," George said, "I'd rather not talk about it, if you don't mind. She's not a whore, to be talked about this way."

"Are you afraid? Or just ashamed?"

"Neither. I just don't like to hear her name dragged through your sophisticated mud. And especially when you're drunk. You seem to acquire an especially rotten turn of mind at times like this."

"You don't have to be pious with me, George. This is your old pal Sam, remember? So let's thrash things out. I'm just in the mood to thrash things out." Sam peered at him, head cocked like a bird, his expression enigmatic like a sly old man. "When," he said, "do you plan to marry Eve?"

"Who's being pious now?" George snapped. He rose from his chair and went again to the liquor table. "You sound like her guardian."

"I'm just curious, George. An interested bystander."

"Why don't you run home and forget her?"

Sam was silent until George turned uneasily around, drink in hand, then he said, "I *am* home, remember?" with a smile that was patently false and self-pitying, yet sincerely bitter. "I am *chez moi*," he said, waving a grandiose hand at the walls, "and I must say it's peachy to be home."

Sam pronounced the word *peachy* with the emphasis of the parlor buffoon, but to George, standing still at the liquor table, there was an unpleasant ease in Sam's use of the word, there had been a vague back-and-forth twitching of the shoulders, a lilt of the eyebrows, which had come a little too naturally to be pure caricature. He's drunk, though, George decided, I'm getting there myself.

"When do you plan to marry her, George?"

"When I feel like it," George said slowly, coming back to his chair. "When I feel it's best for both of us, how's that?"

"You're afraid of my competition, though, aren't you?"

"Maybe I was, until a little while ago."

"What happened then?"

"Well, your behavior has shown me I wasn't up against very much, after all."

"It has, has it? What behavior, please?"

"Do you want to know?"

"I'm all ears," Sam said. He looked startled.

"Well, your childishness, then. And your vindictiveness, or maybe 'bitchiness' is a better word, a sort of feminine bitchiness."

George spoke slowly, cruelly, as if he were peeling away at last a plaster stuck painfully to his body, and although he knew he should not have spoken that way, he sensed it was necessary to their relationship to get it out of his system. For that reason, when Sam stared at him aghast, he did not have to flinch but stared right back.

"Maybe you picked it up from me, old pal," Sam was whispering. "You're doing pretty well yourself."

"All right," George said, "I'm sorry. But maybe I did pick it up from you, it wouldn't be the first thing. I'm also getting drunk, if that's of any interest to you."

Sam did not answer, only stared, as if he were trying to penetrate George's eyes in order to locate the answer to everything behind them. Then he rose unsteadily and groped to the window and pressed his forehead on the cool glass pane, which separated him by half a centimeter from the black wet night encompassing the outline of his head. He groaned a little, and then the whiskey glass dropped from his hand and sprinkled the floor in miniature, sterile mime of the downpour outside.

The noise of it seemed to startle him, for he turned again and peered at George, his brow furrowed, and then he made his way back and leaned against the mantelpiece. Against the fire, his

usually impeccable trousers seemed curved and wrinkled, at odds
with the creature within, like the fur of a sick animal.

"It's not," he said softly, as if the conversation had never been
interrupted. "It's not. In fact, I think I can safely remark that
nothing concerned with you is of any interest to me whatsoever.
I might also submit that nothing in the world is of interest to me,
because nothing in the world is interesting, but you are too stupid,
too pathetically human, to ever believe that, and so I will retract
it."

Sam Rubicam made a grasping motion in the air and grinned,
briefly, unaccountably, to himself.

"How about Eve?" George said, as gently as he could.

"Eve? Are you re-ferring to Missus Sam-u-el Roo-bicam? Because if you are—" Sam waved his entire arm in a vague gesture of
warning—"if you are, I should like to say that she is only a flaw
in my character. To HELL with her!"

Wildly, he swung his arm in a half circle, pointing in the direction of hell, and nearly fell into the fireplace.

"I don't think you mean that," George said. "You're stone
drunk in the first place, Sam, you'd better sit down."

Sam did not sit down. Absently, he brushed his sleeves, although
they had not been soiled, braced firmly against the wall by the
mantelpiece and studying George with one eye at a time as if to
get him in focus. Then he said, in slow pontification,

"You will find, dear George, as you stumble through life, that a
number of things exist which you do not understand. That is because your set of values is inherited, and because you live in a land
where everything is categorized. If Eve has divorced me, for example, I can no longer love her, and if I am potted, I can no
longer mean what I say. And one of the phenomenons—excuse
me, I should say phenomena—" at this point, Sam bowed—"one of
the phenomena which you do not understand is Samuel Rubicam

the First, and, I hope, the Last. As it happens, when I say to hell with Eve, I mean precisely that. If I had said it an hour ago, or even ten minutes ago, you would have been entirely right. But as of this moment, you are entirely wrong."

"All right," George said uncomfortably. "I think we've grown apart, then, because I used to know you."

"Wrong again. We have neither grown apart nor did you used to know me. What you knew was a set of values which happened to coincide with your own. Yours haven't changed, mine have. Another phenomenon you don't understand, you see, is yourself."

"You, on the other hand, know me very well."

"I think I do."

Under the gaze of the raffish, swaying man before him, George shifted irritably. He felt exposed, as he had once in a doctor's office with the trim nurse viewing him over the doctor's shoulder, unnecessarily undignified because she had no right to see him as he was, any more than the drunken man before him had the right to arrive at a certain truth. He knew that if Sam had not known him well, he would not have been under the latter's control in other years, as he now perceived he most certainly had been. And grudgingly, glaring at Sam's shoes, he said, "I think you do, too."

"Good for you," Sam said. "That's the first honest remark that's been made in this room for two hours."

"And I suppose you know Cady, too."

"I know Cady." He reddened, angry. "Cady is simple. Cady is that product of the industrial age, the age of power politics, known as the Fascist. Cady is . . ."

"All right, all right. I don't happen to agree with you."

"Of course you don't agree with me," Sam mumbled. "On a certain plane, your values and his have remained the same. You both say, is that a fact? for example. And that is why he is still your friend, and I am not."

Sam glared at George, made miserable by the truth of his own remark, his eyes wide and vulnerable in his face.

"Cut it out," George said. "You're going into the messy stage, the last stage. You'd better leave it alone for a while."

Sam stared at the bar in the corner, then made his way there as if he had forgotten its presence. "You know where you can go, George old kid," he muttered, but he did not pour himself very much, only a golden puddle in the bottom of his glass. "What's the last stage, may I ask? I feel as if I'd been in it for years, whatever it is."

George watched him coming back again.

"Anyway, my boy, marry Eve with my blessing, if you need it. I'm through with thinking about her, she is a snare and a delusion, you might say, but she doesn't interest me any more."

"Nothing is interesting," George reminded him, rising and taking the glass from Sam's hand and shepherding him into his chair. Sam sat there like a very old man, arms flat on the arms of the chair, an expression of such hopelessness on his face that George McConville winced with a stab of remorse.

"Nothing is interesting. Nothing in the whole goddamned lousy world is interesting," Sam muttered.

Down the hall in the kitchen, the voices sang to each other.

When Cady Shipman entered the room, the open door brought in the crash of slamming shutters, answering one another throughout the house like organized looters, a low one, a high one far away, a third so close that the walls shivered in the ebbing electric light, and as he stood there, the wind retched rain in huge bucketfuls against the house.

Cady had his shotgun in one hand and the pistol from his knapsack in the other. His face was angry, confused, a little drunk, yet concentrated, as if, the result of some metamorphosis, he was more the essential Cady Shipman than ever, refined and hardened to the narrowest limits. Despite the whiskey, his sallow fine-featured face was neat and set. Only his eyes, moving too fast across the mask, seemed indecisive, waiting for an impulse.

"I figured I'd clean these now," he said to George. "You have a rag and some oil?"

From deep in his chair, which was faced toward the fire away from Cady, Sam's voice said, "Enter Edmund the Bastard."

Cady came farther into the room and took a third chair by the wall, where he sat down carefully before he said, to George again, "What does he mean by that?"

"Not a damn thing," George said. "He's plastered."

"There you go again, George, the very thing I spoke to you about," Sam said. His eyes were closed, yet he spoke with a sureness a man has when he knows his listeners are watching and waiting for him, his voice cold and calm and poisonously bitter, a voice which had nothing to lose and sought only to hurt, more masochistic than abusive, more hopeless than angry, the voice of a man who can no longer bear to be despised and seeks relief in the more final, dignified condition of being purposely hated. There was a smile, a horrid Machiavellian twisting of his lips, it seemed to George, and his finger tips were touched together, parted every few moments, and touched again, in the slow excruciating rhythm of his purpose. His voice continued, "What I mean is, Cady my lad, is Edmund the Bastard. You're a college boy, you ought to know what 'bastard' means."

"Cut it out, Sam," George said. "You're making a jackass of yourself." And Cady said, tentatively, "I've been called worse than that."

"Yes," Sam said, "except that this time it means something, it expresses more than the opinion of your acquaintances. Edmund the Bastard is the illegitimate son. That's you. In the play, you are very busy screwing life up for other people."

Cady laid the pistol and the shotgun on the floor, two heavy metal sounds like distant hammers. He said to George, off-handedly, as if passing time before an important task, "What have you been telling him?"

"Nothing. He heard that stupid rumor. I told him there was nothing in it."

"You shouldn't have told him," Cady said. He stood up.

"Damn right," Sam said, and laughed. "Next to old George there, I have the loosest tongue in town."

"You shut the hell up," Cady told him. He was moving toward Sam's chair when Daniel came into the room.

"I'm sorry, Cady," George said. "I never thought . . ."

"Listen," Daniel Barleyfield said. He looked at once surprised and angry, there was a flush on his sallow face, and a lock of black hair lay plastered against the sweat on his forehead.

"Come on out here," he said to Cady. His voice was guttural, harsh.

"Out where?" Cady said, sitting down again.

"I wanta talk to you. Let's go."

"Talk to me, then," Cady said. "We're among friends." He glared unplacatingly at Daniel but did not rise from his chair.

George moved a little so that now he stood between Daniel and Cady, who was grinning. "Listen, Daniel, how about letting it wait until tomorrow?" George's tone was earnest, a little pompous and patronizing, Sam thought. He watched the green eyes under the cap of brown hair, they blinked uncomfortably, then deserted Daniel's sweating face and gazed at the floor. "I should think it could wait," George said.

"I think the best idea," Sam said, "is to give old Daniel a drink." He rose and tottered to the liquor table. "What'll it be, Daniel?"

"Give him some firewater," Cady said. "Indians drink firewater."

"Let's go, Cady," Daniel said. He shifted uneasily.

"But listen," George said. "If this is some old grudge—"

"It ain't no old grudge. It's brand new. He's pulled another one of his dirty tricks."

"You're a liar," Cady said. "In case there's anybody here who didn't know that already."

"Cut it out, Cady," George said. "I'm not going to try and stop anything if you're going to talk like that."

"Nobody asked you to stop anything, George," Sam said, and Daniel looked at him gratefully. Sam felt embarrassed for George, yet anxious at the same time to embarrass him, he could not tell why. He had sobered a little, but his mind was still unclear.

"That's right," Cady said. "And just so we can get this comedy over with, I may as well tell you what's eating Sitting Bull here. His girl friend back in the kitchen must have told him I molested her yesterday morning. If she did, she's a liar, too."

"Goddamn you—" Daniel started forward, and Cady rose from the chair, but again George was between them. "You really ask for it, Cady, don't you?" George said. His voice was flat as a tightened string.

Sam Rubicam, angry himself and nerved by George's resistance to Cady, said, "If she's a liar, how did you know what he's so sore about?"

Cady did not answer him. He said to George, "I tell the truth, if you want to call that 'asking for it.' I didn't touch her."

"Don't listen to him," Daniel pleaded. He seemed to sense himself close to tears, for he drank off his whiskey at a swallow and shivered. "Maybe he didn't touch her because he couldn't catch her. All I know is, he asked her if she had anything on under the coat, and then he said—"

"I changed my mind," Cady said to Daniel. "Take it or leave it."

"Sure you changed your mind. Sure you did, you dirty skunk."

"You seem to know a lot about her, Daniel," George said, "considering what you told me on the lawn yesterday. I thought you said there was nobody here, that you were going into town for somebody?"

Daniel backed away a little toward the door. "Hokay," he said. "Hokay then, I was lyin' to you. Rosa's been out here all along, and we're gonna get married," he added defensively. "Only I wasn't lyin' just now about Cady, and she wasn't either, and you guys can laugh all you want, that doesn't mean a dirty skunk like that can come out here and treat her like a whore. . . ."

"There's that insulting term again," Sam said to Cady, and laughed.

"Which one?" Cady said. "Whore?"

"No," Sam said, flushing. "Dirty skunk." He hated Cady for purposely misinterpreting him and, aware that Daniel Barleyfield was watching him, tried to recover by saying, " 'Whore' isn't a dirty word for you, Cady, it's part of your language." The remark was sententious, stilted, and he leaned away from all of them and pounded his cigarette into the ashtray.

"You hear that, Daniel?" Cady said. "Sammy here's on your team, he just threw you a fish."

"Stop it," George said, glaring at Cady and Sam. Behind him Daniel muttered, "She ain't a whore, and even if she was—" but nobody heard him except Sam, and Daniel wandered to the side table and poured himself another whiskey. Then he made his way back into the uncomfortable silence, his glass submerged in the big fisted hand. "Called her a whore and a liar, the dirty skunk," he said. He squeezed the tears from his heavy eyelids like melted drops of fat, wiping them away with a rough motion of his forearm.

"Good old Injun firewater," Cady said. "It's coming out of his eyeballs."

Sam and George laughed uncomfortably.

"That's right, laugh!" Daniel shouted suddenly. "To hell with all of you!" He paced around in a small circle in front of the door, glaring wildly at the walls. "You guys can sit around here gettin' drunk and makin' smart remarks and laughin' at me, but I got my rights as well as you, we got a life to live, too, like Rosa says, and just as important as yours, for us anyways, more important maybe because there's two of us and only one of each of you, you son-ovabitches—"

"Shut the hell up!" Cady shouted. "You better remember who you're talking to."

"Listen, Daniel," George started.

"Don't wanna listen! Listened enough. You guys are phonies, like Rosa says, you wouldn't know what it was to be happy like us—"

"You *look* happy," Sam said.

"—and when a skunk like Cady comes back here, what do you do, do you stick up for my rights, Rosa's rights, or do you kiss his ass?"

Cady grinned. "They kiss my ass, of course," he said.

"I'll take Rosa's, thanks just the same," Sam said.

"Stop it, Sam, you jackass, can't you see—" George stopped, clearing his throat disgustedly.

"And look at you, you're worse'n them!" Daniel yelled, trying to keep his finger pointed at George as his arm waved up and down like the arm of a prophet. "Worse'n them because you know I got my rights and you're runnin' away from standin' up for me with the excuse that I was lyin' to you this mornin', you're tryin' to put me in the wrong instead of Cady, and at the same time pretendin' to be everybody's little pal!" His voice had risen to a scream, and when the girl appeared in the door, he hurled his glass at George and Sam and Cady. The glass struck the mantel and tinkled aimlessly onto the hearth.

"Daniel," the girl said, terrified. "Come on outa here. Come on, now." She shook him, but he only sobbed and leaned against the wall. George went forward. Except for her eyes, the girl's face was flat and noncommittal. "He got too excited," she said to George. "He don't know what he's sayin'."

"Nothing would've happened if you hadn't lied to him about yesterday," Cady said.

"I didn't lie to nobody, Mister." She answered him without turning. "He didn't believe me just now when I told him maybe you was only foolin'."

"I wasn't fooling," Cady grinned. "Not in the beginning."

"I know it," Rosa said. She put her hand under Daniel's chin. "C'mon, darlin'," she whispered. "Come on outa here." Sam and George took him under the arms and walked him out of the room.

"Me and Rosa," Daniel mumbled, wincing. "Don't matter to us, we got each other. Just me and Rosa."

"Be quiet, now," she said, going forward to open the door into the back hallway. Daniel was walking by himself and sat down carefully on the edge of the bed in the servant's room. There were signs of Rosa's residence everywhere, and she seemed a little frightened in these surroundings, without her loyalty to Daniel to stay her nerve. "He didn't mean nothin'," she whispered. "There ain't a thing he wouldn't do for neither of you, you know that. It's just that Cady Shipman . . ."

"We should have let him go ahead," George said to her, then turned to Daniel, who was staring down into his lap. "I'm sorry, Daniel," he said. Daniel did not answer.

"All right," the girl said, for no particular reason. She stood patiently until they left the room, and then the bed creaked as she sat down beside Daniel. They heard him mumble, heartbroken, "I called them sonovabitches, George and Sam, two of the best friends I ever had. . . ."

And the girl's voice saying softly, "Be quiet now, darlin', just lay your head back now. . . ."

In the library Cady was pouring himself a drink. "Me and Rosa," he mimicked Daniel when they came into the room, "just me and Rosa. Do you suppose he really thinks she's not a tart?"

"Why don't you shut up?" George said. He sat down heavily in a chair and glared at the fire.

"This is turning into a very pleasant weekend," Cady said, rolling the ice in his glass. He winked at Sam, and Sam felt his heart beat as he pointedly disregarded the wink, he was delighted at the opportunity but could not bring himself to look Cady Shipman in the eye.

They drank in silence. Covertly Sam watched the anger cross and recross George's face like nausea, and thought, he's really changed when he will talk that way to Cady. Glancing at Cady, he knew that the latter was thinking the very same thing.

It had been unfair of us, he thought unwillingly, to laugh at Daniel when Cady deserved unpleasantness, when Cady only despised us for intervening. Daniel's revolt was innocent, almost passive, "He don't know what he's sayin'," Rosa had said, and this was true. And yet he had made a fool of himself while we, relentlessly drunk, had not. Or had we? It was hard to put one's finger on the fool. And fools or not, we cheated Daniel of his dignity. We cheated him.

Sam Rubicam dozed a little and awaking some minutes later felt dizzier than ever. Vaguely, in the background, he heard the mention of Daniel's name, and after a moment, waved his finger in the air as if summoning a waiter, and called, "Daniel! There you are, Cady, there's the man with all the dope on your ancestry, Daniel Barleyfield!"

"Goddamn you, Rubicam, you ought to know better," George said, standing up. Cady Shipman, coming forward, seized Sam's hair and yanked his head up over the back of the chair so that his body stretched stiff and trembling like a felled animal toward the fire.

"I'm done for," Sam said. "Put me out of my misery."

Cady pushed Sam's head away in violent rejection, visibly controlling the white clenched stone that was his other hand, and George was alarmed to see that Sam Rubicam was barely startled, only twisted his smile a little and coughed, before he said to Cady, although he was looking at the fire again and could just see the other's jacket at the side of his chair, "You make out to be Cady Shipman, when actually your name is Abraham Shipman, Junior. There's nothing honest about *that*, Abe. Dishonest Abe," Sam giggled.

George waited breathless, watching Cady's face, but the latter appeared to have spent his first impulse toward violence and seemed to await a second, better chance to attack Sam Rubicam systematically. He was watching George.

"I'm gonna slap him around, you understand," Cady said, as if he were warning George against interference. George went over to him and cupped his hand around Cady's shoulder, pushing him tentatively toward his chair. He had never made such a gesture before, and Cady, confused, allowed himself to be guided, as George said, "We're all pretty drunk, it's just not worth it."

"It is to me," Cady said. "I never let anybody speak to me that way."

"Take it easy, for Christ's sake," George snapped. The nervousness came over him now. "Haven't you ever been insulted by a drunk before?"

"You're forgetting that I'm not too sober myself."

"I know it. Me either. The whole business is crazy, it's being cooped up by the storm like this," George insisted, and was shocked a moment later by the sound of Sam's voice, insistent, unforgiving,

> Full fathom five thy father lies;
> Of his bones are coral made;
> Those are pearls that were his eyes;
> Nothing of him that doth fade—

The voice was in singsong, followed by a low harsh laugh of quiet rage, the eyes still staring into the fire.

"Shut up," George breathed. "Just for a few minutes, anyway. Just shut up, or I'll murder you myself."

Sam hooted in loud delight. "Okay. Mum's the word. You just talk to Old Natural Son there."

"You say that again, Buddy," Cady said, "and you'll never be sorrier."

"Okay, Buddy," Sam said. "Discretion is the watchword." He nodded his head regretfully, then raised a casual finger without turning and added, "Go to hell, by the way. I never let anybody speak to me that way," and hooted again.

Cady said to George, "What in hell did you tell him for? I don't like it out of your mouth, much less out of his."

"I told you I didn't tell him. It came up in a conversation, that's all. I told him there was nothing in it."

Cady said, "You think it's true?"

They could not look each other in the face.

"Don't be stupid," George said.

"I'm not being stupid. I've never been really sure, you see," he continued more quietly, "sure enough to forget about it. And it's too easy for you to tell me it doesn't matter. Maybe that's your trouble. Things have been too goddamn easy for you."

"My trouble?"

"Yeah. You've changed a lot, you know that, George? Things aren't the same any more."

"Things never are," George said. He could feel himself infected now with the tinder anger of the other two. "If you have something to say, why don't you say it?"

"You giving me orders, George? Times have changed, you know, we're all being born free and equal these days, as it says in the Constitution."

Cady was grinning at him, leaning forward, and the grin was humorless, a thin curved threat like a kris blade. George tasted the old awe and fear of Cady, an animal fear which expanded the pit of his stomach, and this time it was accompanied, for the first time in his life, with real dislike, dislike he knew could be hatred at a given instant.

"Sea nymphs hourly ring his knell: Ding-dong," Sam said, and raising his finger into the air, cried, "Hark!"—and smiled when they stared at him—"now I hear them—Ding-dong bell."

"It gets me, you know that?" Cady said. "The whole atmosphere in here. It gets me mad."

Cady rose from his chair, bending in the same motion to return the shotgun to the floor, and walked on stiff legs to Sam. Sam's eyes were closed again, and Cady stood over him, licking his lower lip.

"If you lay a hand on him," George said terrified, "when he's drunk and passed out like that, I'm going to do what I can to stop you, Cady. That won't be much, I'll admit."

Cady came back slowly, as if he had not heard.

"Wait a minute," he said. "Wait a minute."

He sat down on the edge of the chair and picked up the revolver, turning it over and over in his hand. For the moment, he seemed to have forgotten George and Sam entirely.

George McConville restlessly paced the room. At the window he paused, drawn to the invisible storm. He could hear it and feel it, there was a phantom force which shivered just inside the windowpane, and pressing forward, he tried to penetrate the darkness, but there was nothing, only a chaotic wail and mutter and the sound of water. Wandering in the air around him, above the fury of the storm, he caught the song that Rosa was singing, clutching her Daniel in the kitchen. They were drinking, too, George knew, a moaning terrified carouse, whatever Daniel had been able to secure from George's supply. The words did not disturb the harmony of song and wind but formed on the surface of the sound like water drops;

> Listen, child, listen to the east wind risin'
> Down on the long black shore,
> And nobody knows that somebody is dyin'
> Way down the long black shore.

Then the song disappeared into the distance of hearing, replaced by hectic laughter, a high shrill sadness like the call of a forest bird, as Sam and Cady stirred uneasily where they sat, the one head a narrow white mask of disintegration, the other sitting high on its weathered neck, angular and taut. Another blues began, "The Death of Dupree," accompanied by a rhythm of wooden spoons on the kitchen table, but the words were erased from the electric storm air in the room by a gust of wind which resounded throughout the house like a mighty cymbal, creating in its wake a backwater of silence which made all three men glance at each other. Then Cady said, his voice low,

"You guys ever see this done?" commanding their attention with his inflection. He broke his revolver and shook five of the six cartridges into his palm, then snapped the gun to again, spun the chamber with his finger, and putting the muzzle to his temple, pulled the trigger. The click snapped in the silence like the jaws of a trap.

George felt himself walking forward, but he could not speak, and Sam sat upright staring in his chair. Cady grinned.

"It's called Dead Man's Poker," he said. "It was a game of chance, for money, in the war."

"Russian Roulette," George said. "Why you crazy bastard, what did you do that for?"

"Give him a prize, George." Sam did not look at George, only stared at Cady Shipman, his face gone pale in a single instant, as if at an afterthought.

"Let's have that gun," George said, going to him. "I don't want any drunken horsing around like that in here."

"I'm not going to shoot anybody," Cady said. He held the pistol in both hands until George drew back, looking from one to the other intently. "I just want to separate the men from the boys in this room. We've all been talking pretty big, isn't that a fact, there, Sammy? And if I understood you right, you haven't got much use for life, isn't that right? And George, here—" looking at George now, and grinning again—"he's had things too easy for him, he needs a little experience of living before he decides anything, in my opinion."

While he spoke, he turned the revolver over and over in his hands, like a lure, the nose of the single cartridge protruding like the tip of a spoiled child's tongue, small but unmistakable in its meaning.

"Go to hell," George said. "You're out of your head, Cady."

"Let's see you do it again," Sam said. He managed to smile as he said it, but his body was rigid in his chair, and George was startled by the expression in his eyes, a fanatic tightening of purpose, an exaltation. "I didn't see it very well the last time. You may have cheated."

"You think I cheated, George?"

"No," George said. "Cut it out, Cady, he's too drunk to know what he's doing."

"I'm challenging *both* of you guys," Cady grinned. "I believe old Sam here is more of a man than you are, George, I do believe he wants to try it."

"Why not?" Sam said. He was leaning way forward now, as if straining at a leash, his hands fidgeting with impatience, and George sensed that Sam had no confidence in the durability of his resolution but had to plunge immediately or never. "Why the hell not?" Sam breathed. "Give it to me."

"Goddamn you, Sam, don't be an idiot, you're not kidding anybody. You're just talking this way because you know I won't let you do it."

Sam Rubicam turned to face him, smiling in wild triumphant hatred of the world. "Wrong again, George, I'm going to do it, and I challenge you to do it with me."

"I'm not going to do it," George said. "The whole thing is insane. And you're not either."

George felt Cady's eyes on him as he turned and moved toward the door, and heard the voice meant for him, but addressed to Sam, "All right, Sammy, just spin her once and don't look at her. Five to one's not bad odds, not for a philosopher like yourself. There aren't many things in life which give a man odds like that."

And Sam's voice, "It's not worth it to me unless George does

it." Cady answering, "Then that was so much crap you were tossing me this evening, you haven't even got the . . ." George inter-
rupting, turning back again, "Well George isn't going to do it,"
". . . guts of your own convictions," Cady finished.

George came back to them, shouting, "Cut it out, Cady, do you
hear me, cut it out!"

"You're yellow, George," Cady whispered. "I always suspected
it, and now I know it for a fact. If you haven't got any guts, let
a man alone who has, it's none of your business."

And then, mysteriously, Cady winked at him, and, as if the
wink justified the entire action, handed the revolver carefully to
Sam.

"Listen, Sam, he's making a fool of you, can't you see that, he's
getting back at you for what you said!"

"I know it," Sam said, turning the revolver over in his hand and
studying its lines as if it were a delicate bronze. "The fact is,
George, I don't give a damn."

Sam's voice was curiously still and sad, and the elation was gone
from his eyes, replaced by a purpose as final as the purpose of the
gun itself. "In any case," he added to Cady, with drunken self-
consciousness, "the odds are five to one *against* me."

George stepped forward and seized the gun from his hand, in-
tending to throw it through the window but holding it instead,
although Cady made no move, only sat and watched him, dark
eyebrows raised in savage judgment beneath the damp blond hair.

Then, maddeningly, Cady winked again.

George could not remember later how it happened. He was
standing in front of them, off-balance and out of context with
reality, the revolver firm and cold in his hand, the one sure thing
in the obsessed atmosphere, unconscious of the fury of frustration
possessing him, thinking only of the moment and the gun. He

found himself spinning the chamber with sharp painful blows of his fingers, around and around and around, longing to fire on them both, the two madmen crouched before him, their faces hungry, coaxing him to Do it, Do it with their eyes, thinking, too, I am drunk, I am dreaming, wanting to banish them forever with a single shot, a shout, a blow, yet afraid of that, afraid of losing them, the past and present, afraid and unbearably angry and afraid, and then it was over.

He had put it to his temple and fired, crying out as he pulled the trigger, not hearing the click, not even bringing down his hand again, but tottering back and forth on his heels, I am going to be sick, I am going to be sick, I am going to be sick, vomiting the other sickness centered in his heart, a sickness of weakness and betrayal and self-abomination which flew from his mouth in choking gasps.

He stood there fighting down all the emotion of his life, welling up in him as the past wells up in a drowning man, his eyes watching but not seeing Sam Rubicam rise and retrieve the gun, his ears hearing but not understanding as Sam said,

"In case I die, George, I should like to say that our friendship is the one thing that has made this trashy life worth while for me." Sam's face pleading, melodramatic, his body trembling and a wet patch growing on his trousers, George nodding, not understanding, and trying to focus on Cady Shipman's grin, while through the wall the blues song drifted again and another shutter slammed on the second floor.

The third click was as loud as the others, but Sam had fallen, and in a moment the room shook with his sobbing. George studied him, disbelieving, and then he was trembling himself, so violently that he breathed with difficulty, until Cady came over to him and slapped him very hard across the face, back and forth. "Forget it," Cady said. "Forget it," and then he stopped.

Cady took the pistol from Sam Rubicam's hand and went back to his chair. Sam Rubicam lay on the floor, twisted, grotesque, and George and Cady sat in their chairs and watched him.

When Sam stopped crying, there was a silence, modulated in its power by the peevish monotone of the fire, and after a moment there was another sound. Sam's head rose slowly from his arms, and he and George stared at Cady slouched easily in his chair, tossing the single cartridge in his palm, and laughing, a quiet fast vindictive laugh like the steady pant of a dog.

"Don't laugh at me," Sam whispered. "Don't laugh at me."

Cady replaced the cartridge in the chamber and turned the chamber carefully before their eyes, George understanding now and stunned, until the dummy was in automatic firing position, then slowly raised the revolver and, pointing it at the glass of the window, pulled the trigger.

The fourth click was the loudest of all, the impotent final sound of the world, and the water of the storm beat furiously on the window, oblivious to the unreality in the room, the flickering destruction of the fire, the steady dog-panting of the laugh.

"You son-of-a-bitch," George said dully, watching Sam's frenzied scrabbling charge in Cady's direction, Cady rising swiftly and moving outward into the center of the room, then inward again, closing Sam in the corner. His fists moved forward and back in the slow starting rhythm of machine gears, then faster and faster and faster as Sam's eyes caught George from the white blotching face already softened and losing consciousness in the angle of the walls, the irretrievable stare which read, "You were in on his trick, you knew, you knew!" before the eyes closed. Still he did not fall, supported by the whipping fists which drove him, nailed

him into the corner. Cady's feet were spread wide in an open
stance, weight on the balls of his feet, his face a mask but his eyes
straining from his forehead with the effort of the killing.

George sat in his chair and watched, unable to focus his resolve,
his decision, even his attention. He thought of the cat, of a small
dog he had once seen killed by a larger one, how impossibly dangerous it would have been to try to intercede in a blood lust, even
though he had known the big dog, ordinarily gentle and controlled.
But this, of course, was different, two human beings, it made his
heart pound and his palms run with sweat. He got up and went
toward Cady, saying, "Stop it, Cady, stop it, he's not even conscious any more."

Cady did not break his rhythm. His voice came to George over
a half-turned shoulder.

"Screw," the voice said, a voice which did not know him any
longer.

George stood there a second thinking, there it is, the cards are
on the table, we all know where we stand at last. He wondered
quite calmly what he should do. Then, as if he had been struck,
his mind snapped into place. The wet sound was deafening now,
punctuated by the rasp of Cady's breathing. He knew he could not
stop the slaughter with his fists. George observed himself, felt
every action of his body as if suddenly come alive, reaching to the
floor for the discarded revolver and picking it up. He hesitated one
second longer, then brought the butt down on Cady Shipman's
head.

In the silent wake of the nightmare, he listened trembling to
the singing from the kitchen and thought, now I am all alone, but
at least I am no longer afraid.

CHAPTER 14

UNDER ABRAHAM'S NAME, THE PATH IS AS OLD AS THE DAYS OF his death, but it was used by the red man in lost decades without history, and by the deer before the red man. The deer still travel it, singly or in pairs in the wake of perished herds, and rarely, in winter, one will pick its way onto the high lawn where the wind has cleared the thin coast snow, its coarse hide darkened in blown patches like the surface of a cove before a storm, to crop beneath the shuttered eyes of the McConville house. But the Indians, the Pequots and Algonquins, are decimated and dispersed, all but the few who eke out an identity and a living as professional savages on a reservation down the shore. These own special rights to the fished-out clam beds and migratory waterfowl of their bay, and have learned through a mail order house to weave Indian baskets. The reservation is dying now, its shacks, tin cans, and heritage forsaken by its young in favor of store clothes and progress. One of the earliest of these young departed was Ukulele Barleyfield, the daughter of the chief, who carried away with her a souvenir of her people.

His name was Daniel, and in 1926 he was dropped in the Common Pasture of Shipman's Crossing with the help of the McConville caretaker, Percy Shipman. Shipman came upon the woman in her labor and, as he often pointed out after she had vanished, spared not only by his aid but by his presence the last of the long line of chiefs.

Daniel Barleyfield rediscovered the path which, clearly outlined in the year of Abraham's death by the Sunday feet of the village, had returned to near oblivion behind the NO TRESPASSING signs erected by Cyrus McConville. He happened into it on a daily investigation of the world, a leathery child of six or seven, round and strong, with a face as bland as a tulip petal and a smile which was even then a feature of his expression, feeling his way into the wood and led without fear along the waking course by the same fine sense of nature and displacement that had guided the older white man of another year. He walked in wonder, drawing his hand like a sensory wand along the passing boles of birch, black walnut, elm as if to touch were to know, and made his way down to the heel of the marsh where the dead trees lay in underwater wait to frighten him. He halted, staring out as the deer stare, and finally sat himself straight up on a sunny patch of leaves, cheeks bulging, like a chipmunk in corduroy shorts, on one of the endless dateless breathless childhood mornings when it never rained, when all unpleasant aftermath was unimaginable.

Daniel!

And he trotted back toward the voice, pausing at the border of the woods to play his game of Hiding Rabbit as he watched their search. He had not imagined that the woman would slap him, there was no reason for her to do so. When it happened, he wept inwardly, uncomprehending, holding the tears until Percy Shipman released them with kindness, patting him roughly on the head and saying, "All right, there, Daniel, we was just scared you was lost somewheres, you hadn't ought to go runnin' off like that." The woman Sarah had gone back into the cottage, and Cady watching, fiddling with a stick and grinning idly in the way of ten-year-olds, was neither friendly nor hostile, simply curious.

He watched Cady open-eyed, not hating him, not yet, but seeking to understand this silent enemy as he had ever since Cady first scowled and pinched him under the table, and slapped away the smaller boy's goodnight embrace as if in prelude to their permanent alienation. Cady played with George McConville and the children who came when the big cars came, a boy named Sam and a little girl named Evelyn Murray. Daniel loved her because she smiled at him, but Cady never let him near enough to smile at her properly in return. Later he liked the boy named Sam, who sought out Daniel whenever he was banished by the others. They called him Sammy Sissypants, and his exile was so regular that Daniel learned to wait for him, squatting by the impassive hour in the dune grass, or under the big oak where the treehouse sat, and on rainy afternoons in the pantry of the Big House. It was Sam who embraced him once and was slapped for his tenderness by Celia McConville, and it was to Sam that he opened the secret path.

Sam betrayed the secret to reinstate himself, and Daniel watched as the three older boys and Evelyn went off together without him and watched again when Cady was beaten for losing "the city kids" down by the swamp. Daniel himself was beaten later for showing them the way to mischief, and like a puppy thrashed in the afternoon for a mess made in the morning, he did not understand. It seemed to Daniel that the members of his family attacked him at will, and he learned that an action infuriating one might pass unscolded by another, and that he was often assaulted for no reason whatsoever. In self-defense, he learned to lie.

So it was that he grew alone. He was used to loneliness and preferred it to the people of his world, retreating down Abraham's Path in quest of meanings.

For the moment, Daniel Barleyfield has survived. He has found a life, and a love in Rosa Menhaden. But has he forgotten the loveless days so recently his lot, forgotten perhaps one particular morning of Easter, 1940, when he was struck for the poorness of his lie by Percy Shipman, forgotten the dead cat and the voice which overtook him with the swiftness of a falcon stooping on a squirrel, "You there, goddamn you, Daniel!"

He turned in terror, holding the carcass behind him.

"Where'd you get that cat?"

"In the weeds," he said.

"How'd it get there? You kill it?"

Then he lied.

"It must have crawled in there or something. I didn't do nothing to it. Got killed or maybe died or something."

Percy Shipman seized him by the lank black hair and cuffed him. Percy was red in the face for a sallow man and sweating. "Don't lie to me, boy. What'd you kill it with, a meat chopper? Holy God!"

"I didn't do *nothin'* to it, I *found* . . ."

"Where's Cady and them other two?"

"Down by the beach gut. I *didn't* . . ."

Percy Shipman wasn't listening to him. He was cutting a switch from a clump of birch and Daniel fled. The yellow cat dragged in the air behind him, the battered head lolloping loosely when he slowed and spitting red droplets on his calf. He flew past the tool-shed where the cat had died, across Percy's truck garden, down through the wet place in the field and into the path, running exhausted from sobbing and his burden and the wear of his own silent screaming at his temples, Cady will kill me, Cady will kill me, until he fell among the roots of the big tree by the marsh, the cat belly-up face twisted red-whiskered snarling up at him from the bitter earth. Daniel knelt immobile, and the birds flicked back into the undergrowth around him, it was spring and the season of passage. They scratched light lines on the stone of his sightless stare, in colors of chestnut, flame, night blue, and he heard the insistence of their singing, as wistful as early flowers and reedy as scraping cattails and sad as the humming of a child who plays alone, before he saw them. His breath came easily now, and he whispered to the death obscene before him, "They know you're dead, poor Tom," and then, in explanation before the world, "I only wanted to give you a fun'ril like in church, I didn't harm you never," and bent his head after the burial in the sour earth as he had seen Percy do, for the Lord and old Mrs. Barlow Shipman, in the village church the previous winter.

In the ground beneath him, the insects stirred their feelers, then pushed mechanically groping toward the cat, the worms and purple beetles, the life in death.

George McConville sat across the kitchen table from Daniel Barleyfield and Rosa. Daniel and Rosa were as far apart as they could be and still be on the same side of the table. They sat and drank a little and listened to the wind go down, Rosa smiling from time to time, still humming a little, and both of them watching George.

"You think they're all right?" George said.

"They're okay. Neither of 'em's gonna feel too sharp in the mornin'. Sam has a broken nose for sure, along with them eyes and mouth—he ain't pretty, though—and Cady just has a lump, but that's some lump, all right."

"Maybe I fractured his skull," George muttered. "My God. And the whole thing was so stupid." He lifted his eyes to Daniel's. "I don't know why you bothered with them, after last night. I appreciate it, Daniel."

"That's what I'm paid for, ain't it? Cleanin' up after a party? And I like Sam, I don't like to see him lyin' in there all bloody."

"Party," George said. "My God."

They were silent for a while. The kitchen clock was loud above the irresolute wind picking against the window, the darkness outside somehow deepening, as if it had been blown from the earth by the storm and only now was sliding back into place.

"How long have you been living out here, Rosa?" George said. He felt swiftly sober, uneasy, feeling his uncertain way toward action again, reality, and watched carefully as Daniel and Rosa, who had been dozing like the dormouse, sat up and glanced at each other. Daniel Barleyfield, eyes wide, put his glass down on the table.

"Don't be nervous, Daniel, I'm not criticizing you necessarily." George watched Rosa nudge her lover, who was blinking at him. The kitchen clock toiled toward the dawn, dragging its steps a little, tick-t-tock, tick-t-tock, and Daniel whispered finally,

"Listen, George, I'm sorry about what I said in there earlier about you being phonies and all. I was kinda drunk there for a minute, you know what I mean? It's just that me'n Rosa were so happy before Cady come along, before all this mess had to happen, and for a minute I thought we were gonna lose everything we had just because—you understand?"

"Just because what, Daniel?"

"Well, because you guys were sore at each other and sittin' in there gettin' drunk and feelin' mean on accounta the storm, and I got the idea that Rosa and me was gonna take a beatin' for somethin' we had nothin' to do with."

"You think that would have happened?"

"Look, George, I ain't complainin' at all. You been damn good to us—to me, I mean. Okay, I know I shoulda told you Rosa was here, but I figured I'd wait until we got married and everything was all set." Daniel coughed importantly. "I wanted to ask you to be best man, George, like you was for Sam."

"You don't have to do that, Daniel."

"I know I don't. I want to, though. You're the best friend we have."

George, shifting in his chair, had difficulty composing his expression. Touched at first, and elated, he suffered an ensuing shame in the face of Daniel's vulnerable smile. "I'd be honored, Daniel," he said. "I really would."

"Oh, I've told Rosa all about you," Daniel chattered, taking the girl's hand. "We been friends a long time now, and we don't see nobody but each other."

"We don't need to," Rosa said. Both stared at George as if expecting a sanction of this phenomenon, perhaps a denial, but certainly a comment, and George, more and more uncomfortable, mumbled, "That's wonderful. You're very lucky."

He did not listen to Daniel any more. Here I am, he thought, sitting in a kitchen chair opposite two servants, who are bearing witness to my inadequacy and drinking my stolen whiskey because I, George McConville, of my own volition, invited them to do so, sitting in a kitchen chair in my father's house, in my house, in hiding from a girl now suffering from my own weakness, separated from two unconscious friends who are not friends.

He rose from his chair and saluted them with his glass, saluted Daniel who was terrified at having gone too far, saluted Rosa who was terrified because she was one with Daniel and his penalty would also be hers.

"Never mind," George said, and because that made no sense to

him, decided against speaking further. He replaced the empty glass
on the table and went down the servant's corridor, through the
doorway to the front of the house and up the stairs to his room.

Through the window, the night was lifting, there was a glimmer
of coming dawn. He undressed, staring outward over the lawn,
his hands meditating over every button, his feet unsteady, and
when he heard the front door crash to, he stumbled forward and
leaned palms down on the sill, and watched Sam Rubicam's
erratic flight across the lawn.

Why, he's running away, he thought. Where in hell does he
think he's going? "Sam!" his voice sailed through the window,
"Sam!" but the other did not turn, overtaking the departing night
in one swift instant, as if he had fallen through the surface of the
earth.

Although it was the very last thing he wanted to do, George
made himself dress again, feeling he must act but not yet knowing
how to go about it. He went downstairs and outside, and getting
into the car, drove toward the highway, for surely that was where
Sam had gone, toward the village.

In the library, Sam Rubicam had gained slow piecemeal consciousness as the night lengthened and the storm grew hoarse, then
weakened. As if he had been borne through oblivion on the wings
of chaos, sailing before the wind like a long dark scream, only to
be stranded on reality again, exhausted, the agonied parts of him
like tattered jigsaw bits drifting in together, one by one, each with
its special content of pain, to form once more a creature, shattered
but recognizable, which had to be accepted as Sam Rubicam. The
process was a long one, for the greater number of the parts had
dallied in the nightmare, and at first only those in direct distress
had burst from the turmoil into wakefulness, the face, the upper

chest, the wrist twisted under him when he had fallen, yet all of these less painful than his shame.

To a grotesque degree, the process of his waking was like others he had known, the half-drunk dry-mouthed fits of waking which caught up other shames of the hours preceding and struck them vengefully upon his chest, upon his lungs, until he had breathed with difficulty, groping in the hostile dawn for a consolation.

But the night past gathered in a wave of mighty nausea, and he lay swallowing in the dry suspension of his pain. Then he turned to face himself as a rat turns finally to gnaw its own leg from the trap, and he saw that this was the worst waking of all, not because he was ashamed of what he could remember, but because he had been caught in the final ridiculousness of his helplessness by the one person, George, whose friendship was left him after Eve had gone. And now this last sanctuary had vanished, too. There was only George's face in the mist of the room, enjoying the trick with the pistol the two, George and his right-hand man, had played on Sammy Sissypants and watching as he had years before over the massacred cat as Sam went down, irrevocably beaten, the words of his last summation as foolish as the smashed lips of his mouth.

No, he screamed, no, no, no, I don't have to bear this, I won't, I've been cheated, tricked, but the scream never came.

Then he was awake, stretched on the sofa like a corpse left alone in an operating room under a single light bulb burning, burning, life gone away without him, and lying there, he stiffened as the agony of his being surged to a final spasm, then dissipated to cold nothingness, his eyes opening almost peacefully under the single light, knowing he did not want to catch life again, how much easier to die, thinking longingly, without fear, of the cool pistol weight his hand had known and turning through the morass of pain to find it.

He did not see it, it was gone. Never mind, he thought, never mind, you will think of a way in a minute, his eyes voyaging the room and falling at last on the corner where he had been put to death, down the angle of the corner to the seated form of Cady Shipman, upright, unforgiving, his blind lids faced in the direction of the sofa.

Sam rose and pitched toward the doorway. On the table in the hall he found a message pad, a pencil, and scribbled his resolve, staring at what he had written for a moment as if, despite life's final retraction of its hope, he could be surprised once more, and then he went on, slamming the front door on the past, the present, the future, and ran down the lawn toward the inlet.

He did not think any more, running possessed through the black twisted tree litter of the storm, hearing the calling voice as faint as the weakening wind, running past caring for George's voice, the vague "Sam . . . Samm-m!" whirled from his ear before he could think about it as he ran past thinking itself, past everything but the sharp dawn cold moving in from the east on the heels of the storm, displacing the wind as authority displaces outrage, as finality displaces change, and the hard crisp grass which struck him like a fist of iron wool when he fell against the earth, recharging the driving pain in him and sending him on with one last souvenir of the implacable reality faced at last by every man before he dies.

Except that he didn't die, through no fault of his own, but simply because he did not really want to. His plan had centered on the heaven-green skiff of Daniel Barleyfield, which would take him to sea and from which he would plunge into the fast storm water racing the coast, to be borne without trace, swiftly and clean, to the last dignity of utter loneliness in death. There would be no trashy obsequies, no resentment of the trouble his death had caused—he would simply be gone, they would come and stand a moment on the autumn beach, and that would be all.

But the heaven-green skiff, hauled out upon the inlet bank the previous morning, was heavy washed with mud. The ancient wood had swallowed the rain, and the gunwales, upside down, had dug into the roil of the earth, so that he found not a skiff but the blunt back of all the contrariness and vast mule force which had always frightened him in nature. He clawed at it, under it until, his muscles trembling, he felt one side of the skiff rising at last like an enormous saurian jaw, the earth falling away in slime. He braced it at forty-five degrees and, sobbing, bullied it slowly over and upright, and fell into it exhausted.

He lay discarded in the wooden welter of the skiff for several minutes, thinking of nothing, and then the fear came again. The energy of his self-destruction was running away into the trampled mud. He had the skiff in the water then, moving slowly at first on the outrunning tide, then faster as he neared the ocean gut, poling at the amorphous bottom as the skiff, compliant, rushed him through the channel toward the tumult of the storm sea and breasted beam-on the rough feint of the backing waves before capsizing in the shallows. He gained the beach in one instinctive leap and rush.

The skiff slid oblivious through the surf, a dark sea monster, disappearing again in a shroud of white, as it made its way down the shore. He stumbled after it, stopping after a time to stare at the huge sea threat, the black dawn waves crashing down on the panic of running whiteness, the skiff sliding and turning and searching for sanctuary ashore or far away in the darkness beyond the surf.

The energy of death was gone. He was nothing now, shambling back in the direction he had come, unconscious of his legs across the dragging sand, moving gradually faster as he fled back into the nightmare of sound and pain. He skirted the house, forgetting the note, and fled down the long drive toward the highway. It was here that George, returning from his search, caught him for one moment in the headlights of the car.

The light had still not come a half hour later. George talked to Daniel in the hall, Sam Rubicam's note limp in his hand.

"He says you're to have his things in exchange for the skiff, and that this was the cleanest way for everybody," George said. He was not looking at Daniel as he spoke, and Daniel only shook his head in misery, not wanting to speak because the fright and confusion had run away with his voice, standing there in the cold of the hallway in his underwear. "For everybody," George repeated. "Holy mackerel." George McConville showed a face of anger, and Daniel could not understand that, either, this was a time for grieving, not anger, this was a time for people to pray a little, maybe, and thank the Lord they were still alive. He wanted badly to run back through the corridors to Rosa and just hold onto her under the covers until the light came again, the good daylight that would clear everything up, and maybe show it was all a dream. Men didn't act that way, except maybe that crazy Cady with his drunken games, but not two fellows like George and Sam, Sam who had always been pretty nice to him and now was gone to the bottom of the sea.

And then he thought, standing there waiting for George to decide something, maybe we better go see, maybe he's lying down that beach somewhere, we can tend to the body if we can't do nothing else, and when George McConville just stood there in the hallway saying nothing, Daniel asked him if he could go have a look.

George looked startled. "It won't do any good," he said, "I've already been down to the inlet, and the skiff was gone. I even went across to the beach. No sign of anything. If I were you, I'd go back and get some sleep."

"What are you gonna do, then, George?"

"I'm going to see if I can bring Cady around. I'm sober now, I might as well do that. I can't sleep, that's sure."

"Me neither."

"You go on back to bed. You're not going to find him, he must be off Race Rock by now, from the looks of that sea. And you don't owe him anything. You don't owe any of us anything after last night."

Daniel retreated, and when George said nothing, turned and ran back to his room and dressed.

Rosa Menhaden came with him. It was like so often when they had run from the house in the springtime and the summer, laughing and holding hands into the warmth of the nights, down among the dunes to sing and love each other the way the narrow bed would not permit, a wild rolling love against the earth, and afterward lying, asking nothing, only to breathe, to hold to each other, and on the way home sometimes they would sing because love was sad, love was lonely, and love was all they would ever have.

Now they were not laughing, they had never run like this before, and they held hands to protect one another from the dark unfamiliar coast stirring out of the darkness. And they continued to run because running left less energy to be afraid, to dread, and they were afraid of this dead wandering man, a victim of the storm, who even in final stillness could shock them sick with terror, a form, a thing already nameless and hollow-eyed, unrecognizable as the thin pale friend of the house, Sam Rubicam.

They stopped at the edge of the beach and peered out across the gray sand to the scene of the noise, the dune grass knifing their ankles, then shifted their eyes with the wind toward the south, where the beach flew on, a dirty trail beneath the tumbling water wall, and lost itself in the roar of the dawn horizon. They ran again, southward, carried fast by the northerly wind, like two fleet spirits of the passing storm in flight after the darkness.

The heaven-green skiff was black in the new light, a quarter mile ahead of them and surging in and out of the water like a sea rock. Rosa, seeing it, cried out her alarm and loosed his hand, falling spent upon the sand, but he did not wait for her nor heed her calling, running ahead on the last energy of exhaustion as if the wind would not release him. She rose again to follow, hand to her side and cold air carving out her lungs, and crying because she could not catch him, they were separated and he was lost to her. Then he was running and stopping, running and stopping again, the skiff sliding parallel to him. She gained as he shed his clothes and hurled them article by article onto the sand as if leaving her a trail to follow, she herself seeing everything in the light breaking cruel over the ocean, and kicking off her own shoes, barely slowing, so that they lay far apart in her wake like flotsam separated by the waves, pathetic and empty on the burning cold sand which seared her feet as she ran. She cried out again without hope of turning the silhouette of a man named Daniel Barleyfield, already moving into the water as she flew abreast of him and fell again, calling. He turned to look at her as the skiff angled outward into the main strength of the surf. His back was to the sea which surged beneath his loins and spat against his shoulders, calling to her through the megaphone of his hands against the uproar, a few words reaching her, tattered scraps like storm strays, Might be . . . skiff . . . body . . . the body . . . body . . . body . . . body . . . his face a mask of shock as the dark loins of him disappeared in turning and moved irrevocably into the sea. He could not swim and thought

he would not need to, did not expect the storm-hollowed sea
trench fifteen yards from safety, five yards from his heaven-green
skiff, which seized his footing and gave him back to the current
prostrate, already lost, although he reached the skiff and clung to
the turtle back of it until the ocean stretched its mighty mouth
above him for one long second of silence before a final explosion
of chaos, and then he was gone.

Rosa waited on the beach until the sun came up. She did not
stir because her body knew that to stir would bring an unsupport-
able reality, and her body was too tired still to bear this. But after
a time she opened her eyes and stared across the arm crooked
about her face, its hairs moving softly in the wind like summer
dune grass. Southward in the direction he had gone, she saw him,
not him at first but the angled carapace of the skiff, thinking, no,
no, no, please I want just to lie here and never breathe again, re-
jecting the dark jetsammed log at angles to the skiff just as the sea
had rejected it, until the ragged fish crow came and waddled onto
its back.

CHAPTER 15

CADY'S EYES FELL OPEN AND WATCHED THE MOVEMENTS OF
George's hand with the cloth of ice long before he was able
to think, long before George seemed to notice the eyes were
watching him and sat back abruptly on his haunches.

It was like coming out of anesthesia, Cady remembered later, a
feeling of calm detachment, receptive to certain stimuli and
sounds, yet entirely unthinking. He found himself propped upright in the corner, his eyes straight ahead, his hands flat on the
floor by his side, all feeling in him concentrated with the blood in
his head, so that the eyes throbbed under the pressure. He was
forced to close them for a moment in order to stay conscious. He
did not want to speak, he was not ready yet. Instead he watched,
listening carefully to George's questions and saying nothing, as his
body came alive again, his stomach first in soft sick waves, and
then his hands, but still he did not move.

"How do you feel?" George said, and then George said, "You
look a little green, you'd better just sit there a minute," and a
little later, George said, "I might as well tell you now while you're
too logy to do anything about it that I hit you over the head with
your revolver," and George grinned, in a very queer way, Cady
thought, very queer, but then George had changed so much, a man
couldn't count on him to act right. Then George put the cloth of

269

ice into his hand, or rather, turned the hand palm up and laid the cloth on it, because the hand wasn't working yet, he could just barely feel it under the ice, and then George rose to his feet and said, "Let me know when you feel better, and I'll get you something to eat," Cady feeling his own mouth fall into a grin, he couldn't tell why, as George disappeared from his vision and the door closed softly on him, sitting there unmoving still in the angle of the walls.

Later, he did not remember getting up and going out into the hall and down it to the front door and outside into the growing light for a breath of air, the ice cloth still in the hand which had closed on it unconsciously. He stood there on the flagstones of the front steps staring off toward the water, still not thinking really, only feeling the cooling sweat where his belly skin had folded in sitting and hearing the unnatural silence of the dead storm, swaying a little on his heels, his knees locked, and the stupor as tangible as soot on his face, as if only the stupor were alive and the skin beneath it dead, a sort of transient mask which for the moment he was helpless to remove.

In the clear air, he began to remember, opening and closing his sore knuckles and running his tongue over the backs of his teeth, but still he did not think, his eyes absorbing the wild progress of Rosa Menhaden down the beach, a minute speck in the beginning like a spot before his eyes but taking shape as the moments passed, until finally she was mounting the lawn toward him, with a crazy jerking of female arms and legs.

She's running barefoot, he noticed. His eyes had not once blinked.

"Mister George!" she gasped. "Mister George!"

And then she fell, half stretched on the ground, her feet bloody on the brown November grass, and the sound she made infuriated him, except that he hadn't the strength to be infuriated but only restless, his eyes moving listless over the sex of her out of habit and fastening finally on the heaving hip, his ear fretting under the sound of her breathing, cracked and immoderate with sorrow. Cady Shipman watched her, totem straight, unthinking, before he moved in one stiff motion to a lower step and seated himself, this action waking him and forcing him to listen to her.

And finally he said, "What's got into you, you stub your toe, running around barefoot like that?"

And she saying, "It's Daniel, it's Daniel, that didn't deserve nothin'!" the words coming in a series of separate cries.

"What happened to Daniel?" Cady said, thinking, my God, this stupid night isn't over yet, remembering Sam Rubicam at that moment and looking at his knuckles again.

"Dead!" she cried, raising her twisted face from the ground and staring at him with such horror that he was stirred despite himself, sitting forward on the step, "Dead! Dead! Dead!" she cried. "And Mister Sam wasn't even in the skiff!" and then she seemed to laugh, he couldn't tell for sure, he had never heard such a sound before, and again he felt an irritation with all sound, his head ached terribly, he wanted to slap her until she stopped. He was irritated, too, at being sorry for her.

"Get up now," he said, "this is no morning to lie on the ground, you're not a goddamn animal. Get up."

"Don't you speak to me! Don't you dare! You and your craziness, you went crazy in there, an' it ain't you that's lyin' down on the sand and never comin' home again! Never comin' home again—" her voice broke, as if she had thought of this for the first time.

"I'm sorry there, Rosa, I can't understand what you're saying, but I'm sorry all the same," Cady said, listening with astonishment and impatience to his own words as if his voice had betrayed him, and adding, "Get up now, it's no use lying around on the ground, and we'll see if we can't help out some way, you hear me?"

But she didn't hear him, only lay there shaking until George came running out, Cady sitting on the top step glaring down at her. When George knelt to her and asked her questions, Cady rose.

"I'm going inside," he said, and when George glanced up at him in wonder, added, "Get her up off that ground, she's not a god-damn animal. Daniel's dead."

He went inside and slowly up the turning stair, to his room, where he placed his military toilet kit and hairbrush back into the knapsack. Then he went downstairs again, as slowly as he had mounted them, the pack bumping at his ankles from the extended strap. In the library, he paused to absorb the scene, then moved to where the shotgun lay and retrieved it, glancing around for the revolver. Then he shrugged his shoulders, went out the door and slowly down the hallway and out into the naked morning.

George had gotten her inside somewhere.

Cady walked down the steps onto the lawn and stared at the ocean, listening, then turned and surveyed the house, his face impassive, before turning away again and heading down toward the driveway. A window slid loudly open.

"Cady," the voice said. "Cady."

He stopped and glanced toward the upper floor, where George's head protruded, white face in his direction. "Come back here a moment," George said.

He walked back to a point under the window, slinging the shotgun holster up over his shoulder.

"You taking off?" George said.

"Yeah," he said, "I guess I am."

"Nice of you to say good-by," George said.

"I'm not a very nice guy, George, you ought to know that by now. Anyway, I never liked good-bys, and I figured I must have outworn my welcome last night, you know what I mean?"

"Yes," George said. "I'm not asking you to stay. Only since you've decided to run out on all this, I just want to ask you not to come back again."

"What do you mean, run out? I've never run out yet. Only I guess the police will be around pretty soon about the body, and where the police are, I can't afford to be right now." Cady tapped the shotgun holster and grinned, but George did not grin back. To Cady, the face in the upper window looked tight and foolish, and impatiently he said, "Just one thing, George. Where's Rubicam?"

George paused a moment before he answered, "Rubicam's dead. He drowned himself last night."

Cady stared at him. "Holy Christ," he said, "what next? What did he do a crazy thing like that for?"

"I don't know," George said, and now he looked impatient himself, standing up inside the windowpane and lighting a cigarette before he leaned out again on the sill. "I don't think he really did it. He left a note, but I don't think he really did it. I went out to look for him, and I think I saw him, running toward the highway. I know I saw him," he added tightly.

"Didn't you yell at him?"

"No. He jumped out of the way, and I thought if he was that ashamed of himself, I'd better let him come back or telephone of his own accord."

"My God. And did Daniel know about this?"

Watching George's face, Cady knew that George wanted to think, wanted to say, that Daniel Barleyfield had drowned in trying to save his skiff, and guessed from George's expression that this was not the case.

"No," George said, after a moment. "I didn't tell him."

George's voice was calm, and its calmness, its finality, stirred Cady's admiration. This way, the death was something queer and terrible. Daniel was dead. And maybe if he hadn't played that trick with the revolver . . .

"Listen, George, I'm sorry about everything, I really am. And I'm sorry to leave with the mess to clean up, only I guess you can see that I have to get out, or else."

George flipped his cigarette down, fluttering it so close to Cady's shoulder that it might have been aimed at him.

"All right," he said. His face still wore the funny tight look, and his eyes were looking away over Cady's head toward the water. "Listen," he said, "never mind what I said about not coming back, Cady. I don't know *what* the hell I mean any more."

"That's all right," Cady said. "I'm not coming back again," thinking, *I* don't know what the hell I mean, either.

"No, listen to me," George said, still not looking down at him. "I'm not saying what I'm saying out of kindness. The thing is, I was thinking about last night, and in a way you have as much right . . ."

"Cut it out," Cady snapped.

". . . you have as much right here as I do. More, in fact, because you can have the goddamned house if you want it. I'm not coming back again."

"Shut up," Cady said. "What in hell would *I* do with it, even if I had a right to it, which I don't." He picked up the pack and holster again and started away.

"You could sell it," George said, and Cady stopped.

"It's not mine. It's not my house. That's the McConville house.

My name's Shipman." Cady laid the holster on the ground again. "I'd appreciate it if you got this gun back to Mister Murray some way. I took it in place of back wages, but I guess I can get by without it."

"All right," George said.

Cady kept on going this time, down across the lawn toward Abraham's Path, passing the cottage, the toolshed, the swollen wet place without looking back. But at the edge of the woods he stopped, and turned to regard the house again. The sun was higher now, there was a metallic sheen on the eastern cornices which blurred his vision of the place, left only the high bulk of it on the headland, shuttered and bolstered against the winter. It wasn't the same any more, it had changed for him as George had changed, it was only another house as George was only another man. And yet the sun stirred something else in him, a remembrance of years of bright new mornings, of projects, plans, and expeditions, of unceasing warfare against the challenges of that lost uncircumscribed world, the creeks and foxes, the surf and striped bass, the trees and the crows, the salt marsh and the hawks—all that had been something important and all that was gone, and he would never be as good at anything again, perhaps, nor ever again be the leader.

He went into Abraham's Path. Because the early air was cold, and because he was restless with the urgency departure brings when it has no destination, he moved very rapidly. In the woods, the signs of the storm were everywhere, the fallen branches and naked dripping bushes and gaunt black sticks, and there was the savage cleanness, sharp and painful to the nostrils, which hangs in a wood in the wake of October rain. Despite the ache in his head and whiskey in his mouth, he felt invigorated by the cleanness, a sense of adventure, and did his best to stifle his sour conscience.

Monday morning, he thought. And I'm right back where I

started from on Saturday, except I haven't got the horse any more, and I haven't got the gun. I'm still in trouble if they want to make it for me, and I've lost whatever hold I had on George, and Shipman's Point. All in all, he grinned—he shifted the pack a little higher on his shoulders—a very successful weekend.

He skated on the wet leaves of the bank down toward the salt marsh and slid to one knee at the bottom. Look at that, he thought, laying the pack on a stump and scraping at the black daub of mud with a twig, I can't even take care of myself any more. He felt in his jacket for a cigarette. There were none, and he cursed aloud. It was at this moment, standing there indecisive, that his eye was caught by an odd yellow spot farther down the path. It lay near the foot of the great tree behind the duck blind, and without really thinking about it, he kept it in his sight as he stooped once more for his pack.

The skull of the cat was still underground, but a surface of it had been unearthed, washed clean by the rain. He kicked it free with the toe of his boot and picked it up. It was curiously thick and heavy, and large, the size of his fist, with enormous eye sockets and lines like tiny crow's feet across the cranium. He tossed it a moment in his hand, like a baseball, then returned it to its ravaged grave and went on, faster.

He traveled up the slope again and through the wet woods toward the highway. Get a coffee at the roadhouse, he thought, and keep on going. Where am I going, though? Maybe I'll join up again, there'll be no trouble if I volunteer for combat. Or maybe go to sea, join the Merchant Marine and see the goddamned world. Or go back fishing.

Not here, though, not in Shipman's Crossing.

He hurried forward. You've got to make up your mind, he thought, and not just go wandering around, like that night in the

war you fell into a ditch in San Diego. Those poor dumb South-
erners, yelling down the street like that, "Wheah in hell you
headed fo', Yankee, the ol' who' house is thisaway!"

And he had yelled back, "I don't know where I'm goin'," just
before he fell, "but I'm gonna get there if I gotta kill you and me
both to do it."

The scrub trees near the highway were scrawny with winter's
coming, crowding beggarly, thin arms outstretched, upon the path,
and everywhere, twisted down upon the waste of leaves, their
fallen branches.

George remained in the window until Cady had disappeared.
He watched him pause at the edge of the woods and turn to look
back, and after a moment George waved to him, not knowing
that in the glare of the sun on the windows Cady could not see
him, knowing only that Cady did not wave back and that, a moment later, he was gone for good.

And still he did not leave the window, for the same reason
Rosa had lain so long on the beach, because even the nightmare
was preferable to reality, the reality of death, the reality of the
desertion by the two men who, until this morning, had represented
to him the virtues of friendship, the reality of being alone with the
responsibility for Rosa Menhaden, and the dark mound on the
bright Monday morning beach.

He left the window, moving slowly out into the corridor and
down the stairs and back into the servant's room. She lay on her
back, eyes to the ceiling, her hands folded on her stomach. He
stood over her for a moment before seating himself on the edge
of the bed and taking one of the stiff hands into his own, as if this
way they could share. But she removed the hand, not uneasily but

because her stillness undisturbed was the least painful state for her.

And she said no when he asked if she would like some coffee, and no, that there was nothing she wanted, not for a while, at least. He told her he would go and see to Daniel before the tide came in again, and then she rolled over onto her stomach and moaned into the pillow, and the other pillow with the empty imprint lay beside her.

He was in the doorway again when he heard her rise.

"I'm goin'," she said. "I don't wanta see him again, not like that. I'll go on to the village, and somebody'll come out after him in the mornin'."

"It's morning now," George said, his voice vague, thinking, Rosa, too, she's leaving, too. "I thought I'd wait until eight before I called the police, though."

They stared at each other as if there was some meaning to be found in his words which would register on one of their faces, but there was nothing, and they glanced away again. Rosa spoke to him, sitting on the edge of the bed: "Don't you feel bad about it, Mister George, it ain't your fault, not like them other two."

"It was the fault of all of us," George told her. He had not analyzed the feeling yet because he had not wanted to, but he knew it was true, and that perhaps it was always true. "Only it doesn't matter now, the fault, I mean, because all the fault-finding in the world won't bring him back." He paused. "I wish that made me feel any better, or you, but it doesn't."

She shook her head slowly.

"No it doesn't. And I have to have a reason if I don't wanta go crazy, and the reason is the same as the fault—to me, anyway."

"I guess that's right," George muttered, "even if you can't find the fault with anybody but yourself."

"It ain't my fault," she said, and began to cry.

"No," he told her, "it's mine. Sam didn't die, and I knew it, and I didn't tell Daniel because he saw the note. I thought Sam should let us know of his own accord. I thought—"

But she had forgotten his presence again, retreating into the sanctuary of her tears, and although he had been on the point of insisting on the agony of his conscience, he now decided against it. His confession would be less self-punishment than relief, it would serve only to increase her misery because the truth was meaningless, a terrible joke which a devil alone would laugh at. And so he only came to her, on an impulse, and leaning, kissed her on the forehead, catching a glimpse of her terror as he left the room.

He went outside again, knowing she would flee before he returned, and that now he was utterly alone.

Could I have been mistaken, he wondered, could I conceivably have been mistaken? No, there was no mistake, and he didn't know whether to be angry or relieved about it, the fact that Rubicam was living, because it was only abstractly significant and not in terms of Rubicam but of Daniel Barleyfield.

He made his way down the slope toward the beach, trying so hard to remember that he sloshed unheeding through the shallow channel of the gut. He had seen Sam's face, the blood on it, and those crazy eyes—it was the eyes which had begged him not to stop, not to ask—the man stumbling in the roadside ditch on the way to the cover of the trees, a failure even in flight. George had slowed the car momentarily but had not stopped, as if something intimate and obscene had caught his attention and forced him to go on, thinking in the seconds following, he did not want me to see him running away, nor to stop him when I saw him, and he will persuade himself because he has to that I never saw him at all. By similar reasoning, he knew that Sam would have retrieved the note if he had not still wanted it believed, that Sam, whether or not he had sincerely attempted suicide, had drowned himself in the ultimate falsehood of denying responsibility for his own existence.

On the heels of the storm, the world ran hungry, and he with it now, hurrying downwind toward something he could not imagine because the dead form of someone known is unimaginable until it is seen, following the three sets of footprints, then the two, and finally, in the last two hundred yards, the small pair of female feet alone. When he came to the shoes, he stooped to retrieve them without stopping, pausing at last and lifting his eyes to the waiting corpse as to an enemy, standing still for a time before walking slowly forward.

The dawn wind had fled before the clear sun of autumn, and the ransacked land gathered its silence about him, unmoving, mysterious beneath his steps, while over its back its creatures scurried, like ants upon a melon, biting at the vulnerable places. He could hear them, the gulls, but he could not hear the five small fish crows rising from the skiff nor the eagle erect on the woolen shoulders. It waited until its timorous cohorts had fled before spreading great wings like fingered warnings and rising in a floundering forward motion into the wind toward George, turning ten feet from the ground to flap and sail back over the skiff, curving upward and inland. Then he was there.

The eagle had come late. Daniel's eyes had been open, and now they were gone from their sockets, carried into the shadows of the woods in the bellies of the crows.

George saw and kept on walking, moving down to the sea, where the spent surf washed over his hands and knees as he vomited, one swift violent regurgitation of everything, which racked his lungs with pain and left him exhausted. He rose again and made his way back to the skiff, where he sat down, facing southward away from the body and listening to the pound and rush and suck of the sea, and when his strength came back he moaned aloud, not with horror but with impotence and rejection, not with pity but with anger toward himself and toward what he represented of the world. The moan was all he had, circling in the air about his ears because it had nobody to hear it, no place to go, as if it would stay there forever, a guardian angel against his past indifference. From now on, he would have to move ahead, the glass house had fallen, and without it he didn't even know who he was, nor where he was going, not thinking this but feeling it, a sensation as real as the gull scream and the ocean din and the presence of death stretched out behind him like the first obstacle in the gauntlet path back toward a meaning.

He went to the body and pushed the eyelids down with his finger tips, then hauled it up and propped it over the skiff, wincing as the water ran from the mouth and nose and tentacled swiftly over the wood down onto the beach, where it ran across the hard sand back to the sea. Then he turned and knelt, back to the skiff, and reaching behind him, pulled the drowned man onto his shoulders, hooking his arm under and over the legs on one side, under and across the shoulders on the other, so that the corpse belly was pressed against his neck, its arms hanging loose. He rose painfully under his burden, his thighs straining to force him upright, and pitched forward, almost falling, in the direction he had come.

He carried the corpse the full mile back to the house, stopping but not ever letting it down, and driving his wooden legs with anger when they would go no farther.

At the house, he telephoned the Coast Guard, who came immediately. They upbraided him for moving the body, there might be trouble with the police, they said. "I don't care if there is," George said. "The tide was coming in, I had to move him anyway."

When the body was gone, he went down to the beach again and along the coast to the heaven-green skiff, appeased in his anger by the ache of his back but not yet satisfied.

The morning was beautiful now, fresh and clean after the wind, its sun warm and bright on the foam of the tide coming in again perpendicular to the beach, with only a slight southward set in remembrance of the storm. When he crossed the gut, wetting his boots on the jump, a congregation of gulls lifted and poised at his coming, then slid in a tight glide out over the surf, where they passed in heavy lilt up the shore behind him. He saw the fish crows on the skiff again, waddling disconsolate, like black-robed functionaries at a funeral, and then they too were gone, their weak caws audible in the morning quiet like faint foolish laughter, and he was alone with the heaven-green skiff in a world entirely empty.

He shifted the oars carried down from the house to his other shoulder and looked from the skiff to the surf and back again, measuring. The tide coming in was licking the angled prow, washing away the sand beneath it, and although the gunwales were buried, he knew the skiff could be freed when the tide came a little higher. The sea was moving now in regular breaths, long and full as if catching its second wind after the storm, the waves mounting high in their last moments to fall hard on the storm-deepened slope of the beach, an angle, he judged, of forty degrees at least. It was possible, if he chose his moment, and if he did not mind getting wet, and it did not occur to him to wait for help because nobody else had anything to do with the heaven-green skiff, it was his problem, and the solution of it had a significance for him which he did not trouble to figure out because he knew it for a truth, not intellectually, but with the corporate knowledge of his being.

And so he sat himself for the second time that morning on the skiff and waited, the oars still over his shoulder, and thought of Eve. In the past, his thoughts of her had not been thoughts but daydreams, vague hypotheses flirting high over the realities like butterflies over the water. But now, as he knew it was up to him to return the skiff whose owner was dead, he knew, too, that not only was he responsible to Eve but that he wanted her, needed her, and that she was now beyond his reach. He did not feel sorry for himself. After the night before, he could not, nor did he want to.

There was a handhold under the gunwale now. He seized it, straining as a thin wave slipped forward and banged its hollow cacophony in the wooden interior of the hull, the skiff giving way to his labor and rising away from the sand and water, rolling around out of his grasp and settling upright. It rocked for a moment shedding sand as a fallen man totters erect, already brushing himself. On each succeeding wave, he edged the boat a little toward the sea, reaching in the interims of ocean rhythm to hurl the oars inboard, and after them his shoes and socks, stooping twice more to roll his pants. He waited again, the skiff turning sharply in the eddies and bruising painfully against him, he waited for a heavy backwash, a longer pause between the blows of the surf. Then he was in the water, soaked in the first second beyond the roll of the trousers, and suddenly past the waist as he plunged into Daniel's sea trench, the skiff prow rearing in that moment against the incoming wave, balancing for a lost second as he clung to the side soaring up on the water wall, and then the wave was past. He shoved the stern forward with his hand, hearing the tick-tick-tick

of water against wood as it cleared the swell without him, his feet
already touching as he plunged through the wave and up again beyond the breakers, stroking to and clambering into the skiff and
placing the oars and pulling out of the thunder's reach even before
he had found his balance, even before the shock of the cold swept
over him like a blow, he half standing, half squatting over the seat.

Sinking onto it, he rowed a little, straight outward, then stopped
and caught his breath as best he could with the shaking of his
body. The skiff swayed restfully on the silent swell, and standing,
he drew off the gloved heavy garments one by one, until he was
white and naked under the sun. His skin was alive with a clean
glory he had not known since a child, a sense of beginnings, of
infinite possibilities.

Beneath him the skiff was southward bound again, sliding in
slow circles with a current too mild to have been noticed from the
shore. He took up the oars and pulled against the cold taking its
sure possession of his body, against the ground lost by Daniel and
Sam which, changing by the slow ocean second, passed beneath
and away with mute insistence. The skiff was tractable, easing
around and onto a northerly course up the beach, holding its own
at first then slipping forward, its progress broken by the rise and
fall of the long waves voyaging beneath its beam in the direction of
the land. He felt at peace, his effort displacing thought, the strokes
of the oars building a harmony with the ocean rhythm, the vast
invisible world where man had come from and which Daniel
Barleyfield had gone back to, he crawling naked across its sun-
warmed surface, so cold and still beneath, like a fly across a great
dark carcass parching on a strand.

He rowed a mile which was more than a mile, losing a foot between every stroke, and it was nearly noon when he found himself
parallel to the gut. He slowed, profoundly tired, and blinked across

the water glare to the high house on the headland. It was dark and oppressive, a solitary cloud against the sky. Moving the skiff inshore, he rode uneasily on the mounting shoulders of the waves, the crash of the water very loud again, sliding in a little only to check and pull back, until the skiff seemed to teeter on an edge between security and oblivion, waiting again for the smaller wave which never came because he capitulated to the suspense and cursed aloud as the frail craft no longer obdurate and heavy hurled itself forward on a crest, mounting interminably before a wild careening descent across the face of the breaker, a blow of impact, and a jarring passage into the mouth of the gut, where the prow spun sideways and caught on an elbow of sand as he flew out of the skiff and landed on his back in the shallow sea stream, the pain unlocated as he rose again and struggled with the angled skiff until it was free, washing ahead of him on the extension of the following wave into the gut. He pounded beside it through the shallows and out of the ocean reach, and jumped in as the sand changed to silt beneath his feet and the water deepened again in the salt marsh, poling it up the inlet, still not breathing, with the remaining oar.

At the edge of the bank where the skiff had been originally, he sat back exhausted in the stern, eyes averted from the house, and did not see the girl who came slowly down the lawn in his direction.

CHAPTER 16

HE DID NOT KNOW HOW LONG SHE HAD BEEN STANDING THERE before she spoke to him, the voice as gentle as the odd warmth of the day, before he whirled on her, thrashing upright in the skiff and staring even before she had finished saying, "You're bleeding, my poor George."

And when he had turned she laughed in whispering mirth, adding, "Why, how do you do?"

"God," he said. "I'm naked!"

"Don't be foolish. You've got to come and do something about your poor old lacerated behind."

He stared stupidly at himself over his shoulder, craning like a preening goose in the swaying skiff. "Yeah," he said, "maybe I'd better," then turned on her, furious, "Listen, Eve," but she did not turn, looking him up and down and smiling.

"With all that blood, and that purple color, you look like a baboon or something, you know, with those leathery patches."

But he was already reaching for the sodden trousers. "Listen, Eve," he said again, but she interrupted him, "Never mind putting those things on, come on up to the house before you get pneumonia. I'll walk ahead if you like."

She got up then and started up the lawn.

"Goddamn it," George said without knowing exactly why except that everything was back in a state of confusion, she had caught him unaware, and there was so much to tell her, to ask her, which could not wait until they got to the house, and he stood there glaring after her calm departure before jumping clumsily from the skiff and hauling it hard on the bank. He picked the wet clothes from the bilge and followed her, running and trotting, the ridiculousness of his nakedness crowding everything else to one corner of his mind. "Goddamn it!" he shouted after her, "at least let me kiss you hello or something." But she neither turned nor answered him, and he realized that she did not know about the night before, that she did not know about the change in his attitude, of course not, how could she, it had only just come to him, and that she must still be hurt and angry about Friday afternoon. He realized, too, that she had changed. He could feel it. He did not know how she had changed except that she was in control of things just from the way she led him, naked and foolish, up the lawn to his own house. And when, in the doorway, he caught her and pressed her to him so that she could see nothing but his head and shoulders and kissed her, he knew what he had never really believed until that moment, that she was no longer his. She did not resist him, but only tolerated him, relaxed and enigmatic, as if waiting until he should release her to turn and continue her relentless march into the house. When their eyes met, he permitted his face to adopt an expression of boyish wistfulness, intended to suggest the sincere sadness he felt. When she recognized his expression as false and twitched her lips, more wry than pained, he released her in silence and watched her disappear into the hallway.

"Go up and put something on," her voice came back, "I'll fix you some coffee." The voice was amused no longer. To George, it sounded resolute, hard, and he came in out of the noon sunlight and climbed the slow stairway to his room, not feeling ridiculous any more, not feeling anything. And later over the kitchen table, before she had spoken again, because now each knew every word would count toward something final, he said to her, "Why did you come then?"

"I wanted you to hear the good news in person."

"That you don't love me?"

He said it as if it didn't matter because under her gaze there was no other way to say it, and she waited a moment before she answered, "That I'm not having a baby." And when he stared at her, not caring, she lied, not caring either, "The doctor said that some women are late when they are under a nervous strain. I was almost two weeks late."

"I didn't know you were under a nervous strain," he said, not caring about this either.

"I'm not," she said. "Not any more."

Then they looked at one another again, for as long as he could bear it, and when he looked away, they remained in silence, listening to the coffee percolator on the stove and the big tin clock, George thinking about how it had been out in the boat and wanting to believe that he deserved her now and knowing this wasn't true.

"Do tell me what you were doing out naked in that boat," Eve said, "and why Sam isn't here, and where the servants are, and how relieved you are because you are not going to be a father, and why you look so much like a little boy lost, not that you always . . ."

"I'm not relieved," he said. "I'm rather sorry."

"I'm rather sorry, too, if you can believe that, which I can't, at least I can't understand being sorry, I should count myself damn lucky."

And when he looked at her, she studied him, cruelly, adding, "I suppose I thought the baby would be a hold on you, but I was mistaken, apparently, and now I can't imagine having wanted a hold on you in the first place, isn't that funny?"

"Do you think it's funny?"

"No. And I can't understand that either. The whole thing makes me so sad I could weep. In fact, I think I will."

And he watched in astonishment as she burst into tears, turning away from him, and laughing, too, in anger.

"Why?" he whispered. "What makes you sad, Eve? That I failed you?"

"No. That I don't seem to love you any more," she blurted, and went on crying. When she stopped at last, he said nothing.

"And do you know the terrible thing, George?"

He shook his head, vaguely because he could not listen to her, he wanted to cry himself for the first time since he could remember, and his mind was given over to the dramatic things he could say to save the situation, to render it all untrue. There was nothing. He didn't feel dramatic but fixed to his chair by his sadness, a sadness so tangible and true that anything he could say would be false beside it. . . .

". . . is that I don't feel I can ever love anybody else, love anything at all. I simply feel nothing, an emotional vacuum, sitting here like a dunce on a stool, wondering whether or not I want to bite my nails or something. . . ."

And if I am to believe that this is the result of my dirty work, he thought, what am I supposed to do now? He knew very well what he was supposed to do, supposed to do, only that if he did it, if he got to his knees and prayed out his sorrow for having destroyed her soul as she believed or wanted him to believe, the whole thing would be more false than ever, and he said before he thought, "All right, Eve, I'm sorry, only what's the use of saying anything, what do you want me to do about it?"

She stood up violently. In the instant before she spoke, he knew he had been mistaken again, that she had not wanted sympathy, was only sharing the sadness with him because it belonged to both of them.

"I didn't ask you to do anything but be the poor sap you are, George. I didn't ask for your sympathy, and I wouldn't have asked for it if I needed it, which I don't. I simply stated a fact, do you understand, a fact which is true today and I hope will be false tomorrow, and if you tell me you are sorry again, I'll spit in your face."

"All right," he said. He wasn't angry, and when Eve sat down abruptly, he knew she wasn't either. "All right," he repeated. "I'd like to say something to you, though, but nothing quite covers the way I feel." He looked up at her then. "I wish I had another chance, Eve."

"Don't, George, please . . ." She wrinkled her nose in distaste, then attempted to smile. "Let's go for a walk, would you like to?"

And as he paused a moment watching her and trying to piece together one last final argument, the telephone rang. The sudden sound of it, breaking the spell of the silent house, confirmed his feeling that the two days past were lost to the world, perhaps had never been at all, and as he picked up the receiver, he felt oddly relieved. But the voice from the outside world was that of Sam. "That you, Sport?" the voice said. Sam was sour, apologetic, he tried very hard to laugh. "I'm risen from my watery grave," he said. George said, "Daniel was drowned this morning, Sam. What? No, it's not your fault, I told him not to—yes, I showed him the note even though I knew—yes, I saw you on the road. . . . I don't know, Sam. Are you coming back, there's quite a mess about Rosa

and all. . . . All right . . . All right. That's all right, Sambo, I
know how you feel, I guess. . . . Yes, I'll tell her. . . . All right,
Sam." He did not say good-by.

"Daniel's dead?" Eve said, from behind him. "Oh my God,
George."

"Yes." George frowned as if he had forgotten something. "He
said if I saw you to tell you not to forget your lunch date tomorrow. Let's go for that walk, Eve."

"God," she repeated, getting up. "Me and my little troubles."
They looked at each other. "You were very patient with him,
George. Was it his fault?"

"I don't know." He opened the front door and followed her out
onto the lawn. "I don't know whose fault it was."

They did not walk on the beach but back along the Path the
way Cady had gone, stooping to pick up twigs and leaves and
fiddling them in their fingers without saying anything, until they
stopped in a clearing and sat far apart on a lichened rock and
shared the one limp cigarette which tasted of perfume from her
jacket pocket. He was startled by the touch of her fingers in the
exchange as he hadn't been since sleeping with her first, as if this
were the first time he had been in love with her and even proxim-
ity could stimulate him, and longed to kiss her now far more than
he had ever longed to sleep with her in the past. Covertly he
studied her profile and the knees embraced by the folded arms,
the embryonic pose sequestering him from any relation to it, past
or present. His heart went out to her then unselfishly, and he loved
her more purely than he had ever believed he could love anything,
longing and desperate to discover something he could do for her,
some sacrifice he could offer, not because he wanted her back—at
least, he didn't think of this—but entirely for her benefit. But a

moment later the majesty of his sentiment was spoiled by the dis-
covery of his own elation with it.

"You haven't told me yet what happened, George," she said,
and he was startled to find her gazing at him over the elbow of her
sleeve. And then he told her, whispering because the woods were
quiet, telling her quickly in an impassive monotone exactly what
had happened, and failing to dramatize it as he would have ordinarily because he was living it all over himself and before he was
through had almost forgotten that anybody was listening at all.

When he was finished, her eyes closed above the jacket sleeve
and the wood resumed its hush once more, and it was several
moments before George, still lost in the aftermath of the account,
realized she was speaking to him, had even repeated the question,
"George? George, will you see Sam again?"

"Yes, I suppose so."

"I'm glad," she whispered. "Poor Sam."

"Poor Sam?" he glared. "Good God! What about Daniel?"

"I know," she said. "But I think it's even sadder about Sam,
somehow. Daniel's dead, he's safe in a way. Sam is the one to be
sorry for, George, he's got to live with an unreal life or run from
it, and neither will be very pleasant."

George was thinking of the face in the headlights again, and he
nodded now, less in answer to her reflection than in affirmation of
his own emotions, the wake of spent chaotic feeling through the
surface of which, as through a rolling surf, it was so difficult to
peer, so difficult to discover the solid ground below. He listened to
the girl beside him, whispering in the stillness, "And who were
you making it up to when you rowed the skiff back through that
sea, George? Was it Daniel or Sam?"

"I don't know," he said. "Perhaps I just felt like it. Perhaps it
was to all of us, Cady and Rosa, too, maybe even you." They

looked at each other again. "I don't understand, George," she said at last.

"I don't either, I only feel something," George said. "As if I owed something to everybody, not only the people concerned, but to you, to everybody, do you see? Or perhaps it was only because Daniel would be alive if I hadn't played along with Rubicam's hysteria, or fallen for Shipman's crazy trick—I don't know which of us to pin the blame on, but if it isn't all of us, I guess I'm as good a candidate as any."

"It was an accident," Eve said.

"Maybe it was. But the thing is, the way the three of us were acting, the way the three of us were living, even, or not living, if you like—anyway, the way things were, we don't deserve to call something an accident which was the result of an untruth, a ridiculous game, do you see what I mean, Eve?"

"Yes," she said. "I see, but I don't agree with it. Responsibilities are more complicated than that."

But he wasn't listening to her, hunched over himself on the corner of the rock like a great sick bird. "Do you remember the Easter weekend before the war, when all the parents were here, and Cady killed Percy Shipman's cat? and all of us were in love with you? Things haven't changed much really. But we weren't so much to blame for the cruelties then, we were children still. Now we aren't children any longer, and the game should be over. And that's why we're responsible for Daniel's death.

"That's what I mean," he whispered aloud to himself, because in speaking to her, he had faced the seed of his distress "That is the terrible thing to me."

She leaned across to him and stroked his hair too quickly with her fingers, then rose and started off in the direction of the house, he trailing her absently as she said, "Poor George. And so you went to sea in the heaven-green skiff."

He laughed uneasily, and after a moment, staring at the ground, she smiled, and her hand touched his thigh until he took it in his own, and they went back toward the house together.

At the edge of the field where Cady Shipman had stopped to look back at the house, they paused, and pausing released each other's hands, as children do in the moments of silence between dances, unable to face out the intimacy. George laughed, and so did she, but they did not take each other's hands again, George telling himself immediately that his hope of the minutes before of a reconciliation were groundless. And then he told her of Cady's departure, standing at her side as they gazed up the hill at the house.

"And Sam won't come back again, either," he finished.

She watched him, waiting, and he shrugged his shoulders, turning to her. "Nor me, either," he said.

"Oh, George, why? That's so foolish."

"No it isn't. What would I be coming back to? The place represents a lie, two lies, in fact, a pleasant and an unpleasant one. The first was the idea that childhood would go on forever, the second was the past two days. Cady and Sam shared in both of them, and they are gone for good. I have the feeling—I had it in the boat—that I have to start all over again."

"Perhaps you're running away again," Eve said, abrupt and a little sour. He knew she was thinking of all the words which Rubicam had used to rationalize his perpetual retreat, and of the words he had inherited from Sam and used with her himself.

"No," he said to her, "I don't think so. I'm not trying to dismiss anything. I don't think I have any choice but to take it with me, the past, I mean. If I don't, I'll make the same mistakes all over again."

"Well, ta, ta," she said to him, turning, and there was a tense tight rage in her face which he had never seen before. "Bon voyage. Happy journey on the road of life, or whatever I'm supposed to say."

"I didn't ask you to say anything, Eve. I was simply thinking aloud."

"Well think aloud with someone else, then. I'm sick and tired of it. And I have to hurry if I'm to get back to New York tonight."

Her words were as tight and quick as her steps, and when they reached the house, she was crying. He did not know this when he put his hand on her shoulder and turned her around, and then she slapped him, the tears following hard on the blow as she ran down the corridor into the library. Standing shocked in the hallway, he could hear her, she had never cried like that before, and after a while he followed her. When she had quieted a little, he said to her, "Why are you crying, darling? I'm the one to be sad, not you. Who's leaving whom?"

And she glared up at him, her eyes infected with her near hysteria, and said, "And where does that leave me, what did I mean in your rotten past, that you've eliminated so nicely with your cheap philosophy, that isn't even your own philosophy, probably. What . . ."

"I'm not eliminating anything," he interrupted her. "I want to marry you, Eve."

George knew she believed him this time, she couldn't help but believe, because it was written like shame on his face, and for a moment she said nothing, only blinked at him wetly.

"You do, do you," she breathed at last. "That's too bad, George, because I don't want to marry you, now or ever, do you understand?"

She faced away from him in the chair and started crying again. But after a while, she suddenly said, quite calmly, "And what did Rosa say when you told her it was your fault?"

"She didn't say anything," George muttered. "Nothing at all. I wish she had, I wish she'd screamed her guts out," he added passionately. He went outside onto the terrace by Abraham's grave and hands in pockets stared out over the ocean.

Three torn white herring gulls made their way toward him across the water. Nearing, one poised, stooped, fell upon a floating object in the tidal rocks, as its mates wheeled crying and converged, driving the first gull from the surface and pursuing it seaward. It dropped its prize and another seized the bit of food as it struck the water, flopping away to windward with the third gull yawping after it. Their victim settled upon the water, blinked, gapped, shook its head and peered at George, then rose and followed in the direction taken by the others.

She thought, perhaps if I sit quietly in this chair and stare at him, and dream, I will pass through the window to his world again, a little girl enchanted, like Alice through the looking glass. We will stand together by the sea as lovers are supposed to do, beyond all questioning and common sense. Eternity in the water and emotion in the wind, and purity, and finally peace.

But perhaps, she thought, I do not love him any more, as I have told him. How easy that would be, how very sensible. No, George, I would say, No, No, No, No, you're just a little boy like all the rest, like Sam and Cady, and I'm tired, I need a man, George, do you understand, a man who will think of me in terms of me, not of himself, and love me for myself and not himself.

Then sacrifice, offered and not exacted, will be no longer sacrifice. A man will be my keeper, and I will love him as you will not let me love you, George, in a way which would embarrass you.

She watched him turn his head from the gray sea and gaze at her. Can you hear me, George? Do you know that I have called to you for the last time, that I have sorted out, rejected all our chances, one by one by one, until there is nothing left us but remorse?

Outside, he turned abruptly and moved toward her, rapidly across the terrace toward the door, and she felt the tears of rage and the hands which tightened down on the arms of the chair and the traitorous heart which leaped like an ill-trained idiotic dog.

The telephone was ringing. She went to it herself.

"Hello? No, he's not here. No. Is that you, Captain Shipman? No, I don't know where he went. Listen, Captain Shipman, if you'd called last night as Daddy asked you, you would have reached him. What? No, this is Evelyn Rubicam, Evelyn Murray, that is. Yes. Yes, he took the gun with him, it's outrageous. I'm going to call the police this minute, do you hear? Yes, I know you are. . . . What?"

Then George took the phone away from her.

"Hello, Captain Shipman? George McConville speaking. . . . That's right. Listen, sir, Cady left the gun with me, it was all a misunderstanding, I'll get it back to Mister Murray this afternoon. . . . No, there's no reason for you to bother about it at all. . . . Yes, I know he is . . . you mustn't mind her, she's upset right now, she didn't mean to be rude. . . . I'm sorry, I didn't hear you, Captain. . . . Oh, yes, we had pretty good shooting, thanks . . . that number .5 shot was much better, you were right . . . yes . . . well, very sorry for the trouble, it was all a mistake

. . . a mistake, I said, everything was a mistake. . . . Good. Good-by, Captain."

"I guess he hasn't heard about Daniel," he said to Eve.

"All a mistake!" Eve was whispering. " 'She didn't mean to be rude.' "

"Cady left the gun with me," George said, and after a moment, "You didn't have to talk to the old man that way."

"You've gotten awfully conscientious all of a sudden, George. Do you think you should talk to me about right and wrong?"

For a second George considered making amends to her by backing down. Then he said, heavily, "Yes, I do. What's happened between us has nothing to do with it."

He went upstairs to change his clothes, sure now that he had sacrificed his last chance, yet at peace with himself for the first time since he could remember. I've lost her anyway, he thought, and there's no use losing what I've learned from this as well. When he came downstairs again, Eve, too, seemed curiously calm.

"Are you driving to New York?" she said.

"Yes. I want to get some money for Rosa. I'm coming back down for the funeral."

"That's very sweet of you, I'm sure. But I'd like a ride, if you don't mind."

"How about your car?" He was too astonished at her request to co-operate with it.

"I'll drop it back at Daddy's now and you can pick me up."

"All right. Will you take the gun?"

"Yes."

When she had gone, he went about quietly closing down the house, retracing each still empty room as he locked the windows. It was already twilight, the days were growing shorter, and the gray air slipped in like a deathbed attendant, gray air, he thought, which would be shut in here for good when he had locked the final door and gone away. In his own room he came once more upon the dog doll, the Horrible Hairball, and this time on impulse did what it had never occurred to him to do before. He opened the window and, standing back a little, hurled the odd shape out over Abraham's grave. It bounced soundlessly and rolled down through the rocks into the outgoing tide.

The front door bolted, he went out through the kitchen to where the car was, leaving somehow clandestinely the house which had been his past, and not looking back at it even through the mirror of the car although behind him he could feel its sullen bulk on the autumn headland, like some vast grotesque monument at the end of Abraham's Path.

Eve awaited him at her front door. Joshua Murray stood silhouetted against the light, he seemed more stooped than usual and gave no answer when George called out to him. There was something in this nameless mute defeat of the older man that made George feel most deeply that a period was over.

Then they were driving again, the silence between them long past discomfort, permanent as the cold air against the windshield, the highway thinning out as the evening went on until they were traveling very fast through the New England silence, a four-wheeled cosmos with no relation to the world about it but the hum of tires and the hurdy-gurdy vulgarity of radioed sounds and voices, oppressively cheerful, which called out to them as "friends," and the cigarette smoke which curled peacefully out of its glow as smoke curls out of a windless ruin.

They were still far out of the city when they thought to stop for dinner, getting out several times before they found a kitchen still serving. And at the last inn, the kitchen was closed, too, but the people could not afford to turn them away, not at this time of

year, not in their old age, because even in the summer, "in the
season," they said, they lost ground each year to younger establish-
ments.

They sat opposite one another in the unpopular room as if
banished forever to empty places, and not even in company of one
another. The world had left them behind to fret over their mutual
solitude and all their furious driving would not be swift enough to
catch up ever again. They waited for an ancient supper served by
ancient hands in ancient ware, until Eve said to him, like a voice
in the darkness in its suddenness, "I can't bear to go out again,
George, we'll have to drive too far, and they have rooms here."

He did not answer at first, leaning forward elbows on the table
prodding the red checked squares with the tines of his fork, thinking less about what she had said than about what he had been
thinking before she spoke. But he could imagine the stark iron
beds native to these old inn chambers, the warped floors and
skimpy rugs and antique artifacts which went with the antique
name of the inn, giving it atmosphere and taking away its clientele,
all but the solitary old ladies who hibernated at this time of the
year. To drive all night would be far easier for him.

"Yes," he said. "All right."

"You don't have to stay, you know," she told him. "It's all the
same to me. I don't suppose I have to tell you we'll want separate
rooms."

"I don't suppose you do, no." He licked his lips, not looking at
her but at the tines of his fork scraping parallel to the red checks.
Then he picked up his bad brown martini and swallowed it at a
gulp.

"And I don't know if this is quite the place for a drunken party,
either. Maybe you'd better go on to New York."

"No party," he said. He knew he couldn't go but would have

to wait until she could leave him in complete confidence that it was she herself who had made the choice, and against his will because he loved her still, or maybe for the first time, it didn't matter. He owed her that much.

Yet he wanted to be angry with her, he had never seen her cruel before nor known that she was capable of cruelty, and he tried to persuade himself that she was no longer the same girl and that therefore he was no longer in love with her. It didn't work. The abnormality of her mood was too evident, her eyes had a dull metallic glint and her mouth was clenched, as if only by the greatest effort she was keeping herself from crying out, as if, holding on a little longer, she would arrive at a state of emotional torpor of the sort she had described to him at the Point but obviously had not yet consolidated within herself. And he knew this best when she said, apropos of nothing at all, as she might have remarked on the drear of the dining room,

"You've changed, George, did you know that? In three days you've changed."

"I know it," he said, looking up at her. "But what makes you think so?"

"I don't know." She smiled very faintly. "You're older or something."

"Is that bad or good?"

"I think it's good, at least in your case. Only it makes it much harder for me. My mind was made up completely, I wasn't even particularly unhappy."

"Why did you come, then?"

"I wanted to tell you in person. And I wanted to be absolutely sure, I thought I would be." She glared at him. "In most ways, I am. It's just harder, that's all."

He paused before he said, as quietly as he could because the old man came now with the first course, "How do you think *I* feel about it?"

And she did not wait until they were alone to answer,

"I don't give a good goddamn *how* you feel about it, George. That's the terrible thing. I don't care about anything now except myself. I can tell by your silly expression that you think I am being unkind to you, and to have you think that would have killed me before, but it doesn't now. It simply *doesn't*," she insisted, as if pleading with him to believe her. "And something even stranger is the fact that when I arrived I felt serene, not the least bit cruel, only decided, and it's the change in you, the change in you *for the better* that makes me cruel. You don't deserve to upset me again, George, you just don't deserve it, do you hear!"

She was on the verge of breaking down. He sat stunned saying nothing, and when her voice came again it was choked and whispered. "I want to hurt you," she said. "I want to hurt you so damned badly."

They did not talk again during supper, and the old man brought them wine, and George praised the wine in a voice not his own, as if Eve were not there. He did not think any more, his mind moving through a series of dead impressions, dead reactions, until over the coffee she leaned forward again and said in the same choked whisper, "Why do you hang around? Why don't you go off to New York and leave me alone?" and he knew then that he must make a decision. He could be angry or hurt, and depart without a backward glance, closing the door behind him very gently. Or he could assert his triumphant manhood, defy her cruelty and disdain it, fight as a trapped rat fights. But he had not done either, and later he did not know whether his judgment had sustained him for once, or whether his feeling for her overruled his feeling for himself, for he said, combining all of his reactions into one remark yet conveying concern for her, even kindness,

"I'd like to stay, Eve, if you'll let me. I'll try to get in your way as little as possible." A moment afterward, he regretted what he had said, ashamed of the martyred quality, alarmed at the defensive sarcasm, embarrassed by the sincerity of the feeling behind the words themselves, and yet she took it as he felt he had meant it, there was gratitude in her glance.

As they left the table, she said to him, a little tipsily, "I want so badly to love you again, my darling. I would give anything to love you, but I can't resurrect anything, I feel as if I were dead in some way."

And he fought down an impulse to seize her by the shoulders, to shake her angrily and shout, "But you've *got* to love me, you've got to, do you hear!"

"We'd like two rooms, if you have them," he told the old man, and the old man nodded, violently alarmed, and croaked for his wife, who came and peered at them for a moment before bustling away upstairs. George went outside and got her bag and came back in again. Eve had already gone up to the rooms, which were out behind away from the highway. Although they were alone in the inn, the rooms were not adjoining. The fact hardly mattered, yet he cursed the old woman under his breath for her scruples, and pointedly stared at her with disapproval when she, equally pointedly, feigned confusion as to where to direct the solitary suitcase. Her husband stood behind her, looking worried, and George sensed that while each of the couple had considered refusing them as overnight guests on the strength of the one bag, the man would not act because he was shy, the woman because she could manifest her disapproval and get her money, too. And standing in his room awaiting their departure, he reflected that a request for a double

room would have caused no suspicion at all, and laughed in anger
at the old woman when she inserted a warning face into the doorway and demanded to know whether he had everything he needed.
He asked her then where the bathroom was, and she pointed, saying that he would have to share it with Miss . . . ? Her bleak face
was gouged in warning again, and he said to her, "If it will make
you feel any better, Mrs. . . . ? we have just broken our engagement."

She said she was sure it was none of her business, and he nodded
angrily, feeling more foolish than he had before as she slammed
the door in a manner which suggested that she always slammed
doors wherever she went, out of pure efficiency. He opened the
door again and went down the corridor to Eve's door and knocked
and asked for her toothpaste. Eve looked over his shoulder at the
old woman silhouetted at the top of the stair and laughed, and he
laughed, too, then, not because he was amused but because Eve
had laughed and he knew her pent-up resentment of him had
eased. Eve was standing in her slip, although the mistress of the
inn could not see this from her vantage point on the stair, and
George watched her as they waited for the old woman to go away,
which she finally did. He felt choked with things he must say to
Eve but none of them would come to his tongue, only the final
fact of his wanting her so badly that he trembled, wanted not to
make love to her but to hold her to him, to lie somewhere quiet
with her and forget that the past few days had ever taken place,
to forget, to forget, to forget. . . .

He was startled to discover that she was no longer smiling but
crying, not aloud but in silence, her bedlamp glinting upon the
tears which fell in slow abandon across her cheeks. She did not
turn from him, she seemed unaware of her tears, and for a moment he could only think that she had cried more in the past

twelve hours than in all the years he had known her, and then he whispered, "Don't cry any more, darling, you don't deserve to cry," and leaning, kissed her on the forehead and turned and fled down the corridor to his room.

The room was very much as he had imagined it. He turned off the light and stood in the middle of it, his heart pounding so violently that to lie down in the bed would have been impossible, but after a while he undressed to his shorts, leaving his clothes in the middle of the floor, and without washing crossed to the bed and stared down at it, then went to the window, taking the cigarettes from his coat as he passed, and sat in the chair there, smoking and looking out at the windless nothing.

The night was clear in the new cold, there was a low moon strung like a lamp in the gnarled treetop silhouettes. He listened to the frantic clatter made by the woman downstairs somewhere and from time to time her voice as if she were talking with herself, but after a time he did not hear her any more, only the hiss of the skinny radiator behind him. He could think of nothing but the past shared with Eve, all the little things, his lungs sewn tight by the agony of nostalgia.

In his mind he followed her on a long and silent sand, and tried to explain, to explain, gesticulating wildly with his hands as his voice mounted higher and higher in the stillness. But she went on too swiftly for him, her profile hard and changeless as a profile on a coin, along the flat steel sea. He was running now, but still, without effort, she outdistanced him, and he cried out, but listen, this was the end of youth, don't you understand, I saw it happening, isn't maturity what you wanted of me? What am I to do with it if you don't want it? And slowly she turned her head and seemed to smile before she disappeared, and left him stumbling along in utter loneliness.

He did not know how long he had been asleep or if he had been asleep at all when he started to find her standing at his side in her nightgown, and then remembering, not daring to breathe because she might go but sitting immobile, his arms tight on the arms of the chair as she reached and touched his lips with the tip of her finger, whispering, "George, oh George," then came around and sank to her knees before him. He heard her again, then, she was saying so softly that he could barely hear her, "It's all right, darling, everything's all right now," and then, "Just don't ask me any questions, not for a while, just please don't ask me any questions." He could see her face, every detail of it, in the light through the window. It was childlike, incredibly childlike and pure as it bent slowly to him and lay upon his lap. When the face rose again, serene as before but with the smooth eyes closed, his arms stirred finally and his hands moved slowly across the closing space between them and cupped her head and drew it forward to his own. He lifted her across him. She was lighter than he remembered her, as if returned to girlhood, and her body was limp and quiet. They drifted into the blissful unthinking of relief. When he rose at last and carried her across the room, he clutched her to him, frightened that she might go once more, clutching her so tightly that he knew he must be hurting her. She did not cry out. He laid her down and pulled the covers up over both of them against the past and the coming winter, and they slept with their arms around each other until morning.

Peter Matthiessen was born in New York City in 1927 and had already begun his writing career by the time he graduated from Yale University in 1950. The following year, he was a founder of The Paris Review. *Besides* At Play in the Fields of the Lord, *which was nominated for the National Book Award, he has published four other novels, including* Far Tortuga. *Mr. Matthiessen's unique career as a naturalist and explorer has resulted in numerous and widely acclaimed books of nonfiction, among them* The Tree Where Man Was Born *(with Eliot Porter), which was nominated for the National Book Award, and* The Snow Leopard, *which won it. His other works of nonfiction include* The Cloud Forest *and* Under the Mountain Wall *(which together received an Award of Merit from the National Institute of Arts and Letters),* The Wind Birds, Blue Meridian, Sand Rivers, In the Spirit of Crazy Horse, Indian Country, *and, most recently,* Men's Lives. *His novel-in-progress and a collection of his short stories will be published by Random House.*